THE ACQUISITION

An Angela McCormack
Adventure

Rachel Ford

A NineStar Press Publication

www.ninestarpress.com

The Acquisition

© 2021 Rachel Ford
Cover Art © 2021 Natasha Snow
Edited by Elizabetta McKay

Printed in the USA

ISBN: 978-1-64890-376-2

First Edition, September, 2021

Also available in eBook, ISBN: 978-1-64890-375-5

CONTENT WARNING:
This book contains sexually explicit content, which may only be suitable for mature readers. Depictions of kidnapping/abduction, graphic violence, gun violence, death caused by a POV character, workplace harassment, use of ethnic slurs and misogyny by a POV character, power imbalance/harassment, and unprotected sex.

When Sutherland Bio buys up the little bio research firm Human Resources specialist Angela McCormack works for, she tries to adapt. Even though her shady new boss's smarminess and sexism makes her stomach turn. She sticks it out through the verbal abuse, and through the benefit cuts and layoffs.

But when her boss, George Sutherland Jr., tasks her to recruit replacements for the people he laid off—and lets it slip that the layoffs were just part of a regime change strategy—she's ready to throw in the towel. As much as she hates the idea of shoveling manure again, she'd rather return to her family's farm and petting zoo than stay with Sutherland Bio.

Then George Jr. takes a particularly bad day out on her. And Angela decides she's tired of the humiliation. She's going to fight fire with fire. She makes it her mission to fill George Jr.'s team with the worst possible candidates she can find.

But she didn't take into account falling for one of the new hires. All of a sudden, she's not sure she wants to leave. Not yet.

And that's just the first chicken to come home to roost. Little does she know, George has plenty of secrets of his own. And when one of them turns deadly, Angela will have to rely on her handpicked sabotage crew for survival. She might just wish she was back home shoveling manure after all.

To my mom, for always believing I had what it took to be a writer. To my sister, for reading every word I've written. And to Patty, my Imzadi, for believing in me even when I didn't.

Chapter One

You don't piss off the person making your food. You don't piss off the woman who gave birth to you. And you don't piss off the HR lady. Everyone knows that.

Everyone, it seemed, except George Maxwell Sutherland, Jr. As with most memos, George Maxwell Sutherland, Jr. had missed that one. Along with the one about manners. And treating employees with respect. And showering every day instead of wearing a bucket of cologne to work.

Angela McCormack wrinkled her nose and stared at her boss's feet. They were at eye level since he had them propped up on his desk. The sight made her stomach turn a little. It wasn't so much the untrimmed talons on the ends of his toes, or the hobbit-like growth of untamed hair. It was the fact that she could see them at all. *And the no-feet-on-the-furniture and don't wear flipflops into work when you're the CEO memos.*

Yes, there were quite a few memos George Maxwell Sutherland, Jr. had missed. But at the moment, it was the one about not *downsizing* people out of their jobs just to recreate the same position two months later that weighed the heaviest on her mind. Because, unless she'd misunderstood everything he had just said, that's what he was doing here. And despite George's propensity to torture a simple sentence into a longwinded monologue for the sole pleasure of hearing himself talk, she was pretty sure she hadn't got it wrong.

"Excuse me, Mr. Sutherland," she said, "just to clarify, we're refilling the positions we just downsized?"

He cocked an eyebrow up at her. "No, not at all. These are *different* positions, Angie."

God, she hated when he called her Angie. "Yes sir, I heard you say that. But if I'm understanding you, the titles will be different, but the positions will fill the same basic function as before. We're looking for an IT team lead to replace Dawn. You need a Director of Business Services to pick up where Mark left off, and so on?"

He flashed her a toothy grin that, she supposed, he assumed was charming. It wasn't. It was the kind of smile she'd expect from someone selling a car that probably wouldn't make it out of the lot. "Now you're getting it. You know how it goes. New era, new regime. If I'm going to do this right, well, I need people I can trust."

He studied her for a long moment with keen blue eyes. "That's why I kept you on. I had a good feeling about you. And you know what I say—I'm a man who goes with his gut."

Angela McCormack forced a smile and lied through her teeth. "Of course, sir. You can always trust me."

"Don't call me sir. Call me George." He smiled again. He smiled too much for her liking. Grinning CEO's, smiling politicians, and gas station sushi: she reserved the same measure of trust for each of them. "Now, I'd like these listings up by Friday. Is that something we can do?"

We. As if he'd lift a finger to help.

"I'll get the drafts to you by the end of the day tomorrow. If the revision process goes smoothly, I don't see why not."

He nodded. "Excellent. Excellent. Well, that was all I had, then. Oh, my dry cleaning's not back yet, is it?"

"No sir. I mean, no, George."

He winked and clicked his tongue as a kind of sound effect to match the finger guns he aimed her way. "That's better. I don't like a formal workplace. I'm all about casual. I think it builds better morale. Don't you?"

Angela smiled and lied again. "Oh, absolutely."

She had nothing against casual, as long as it wasn't the kind of casual that involved dirty hobbit feet on the desk. But George had come into Fenwood Bio like a whirlwind, laying off staff, axing benefits, and implementing draconian cost reduction programs within his first two weeks. The turnover rate was already higher than the layoffs. Which was one of several reasons why she was currently filling the role of the entire HR department, as well as admin, IT department, and supply requisitions. All for the same salary as before, of course, but with a much slimmer retirement package, and no life insurance benefits.

No, Angela McCormack didn't want to hear the word "morale" pass his lips. He'd personally shredded every last bit of it and flushed it down the toilet.

"Me too. You might say, it's one of my core philosophies." He nodded, to himself it seemed, then added, "Well, I'll let you get to work, then."

She didn't mind the dismissal. Hell, it couldn't come soon enough as far as she was concerned. "Right."

Retreating to her office and closing the door after her, Angela breathed out a long sigh of relief. She hadn't been afraid he'd called her in to lay her off. He'd gotten that out of his system within the first few weeks. Still, she'd seen so many come and go, she would have been lying if she said the thought hadn't occurred to her.

Mostly, she detested him. And she had the kind of face that didn't know how to use its inside voice. When someone tripped her BS trigger, well, her face broadcast it loud and clear before she even realized it.

George Maxwell Sutherland, Jr. lived in the BS zone. And Angela McCormack needed her job. She had a mortgage and a house she loved. Sure, she could have found a job elsewhere that would have paid as well, or maybe a little better. But she didn't want to give up her house. Not after all the years she'd spent restoring it, a room at a time.

Nor did she want to leave Fenwood. She'd grown up here, and she planned to grow old here. *Older*, she thought with a sour glance at the calendar. She'd be thirty-five in two days. She didn't want to have to start over at thirty-five.

And that's exactly what finding a new job in human resources would be. Fenwood Bio—now Sutherland Bio Research—was the biggest employer in the area, and those companies that did have HR departments weren't hiring.

She knew because she'd checked. So, if she was going to find another job, it would mean leaving the area. It would mean moving a hundred miles south, or seventy-five miles north, or even farther east and west.

Fenwood was one of those smack-in-the-middle-of-nowhere towns, with more cows and horses than people. You either loved it or hated it.

Angela loved it, and she didn't want to leave.

So, she pulled open her archaic software suite and started filling in the job listings they'd talked about. Did it make her a modern-day Judas Iscariot, helping this son of a bitch after he'd fired so many of her friends on the pretense that their jobs were redundant, now that Sutherland Bio Research had acquired them?

Maybe. Then again, Judas didn't have a mortgage. Angela stared at the screen, trying to focus on the work. But the work didn't—couldn't—make up for the feeling in the pit of her stomach. The feeling of betrayal that left her a little sick. *God, I hate this job.*

She started as her messenger application *ding*ed. Glancing at the clock on her desktop, she frowned. Somehow, half an hour had already passed.

Angela brought up the messenger window and groaned. It was George, and he'd flagged the chat as a high priority.

Can you come to my office?

Grimacing, she typed, *On my way.*

Angela practiced her fake smile on the way. It probably wouldn't have convinced anyone who wasn't as obtuse as George, but at least it wouldn't be scary. Or, so she hoped anyway.

She knocked on his closed door and immediately heard, "Come in." She did, and Sutherland smiled at her. "Ah, Angie. Thank goodness. We've got a situation."

Oh no. "Oh?"

"I forgot I had an appointment this morning."

"Really? I didn't see anything in your schedule."

"Oh, I forgot to tell you about it. I would have had you add it to the calendar. But that's not the issue. Point is, we don't have anything for them to eat."

Now, she did grimace. So far this month, he'd sent her on eighty-some dollars' worth of coffee runs, lunch pickups, and pastry runs. For a millionaire, Mr. Sutherland was chronically short of cash. It had all gone on "the tab."

The tab didn't exist, except as a figment of his imagination. Angela had her doubts that it would ever be settled. He'd pay off ten or twenty bucks here and there. But it always seemed larger than whatever cash he happened to have on hand.

"What did you have in mind?"

"Oh, I don't know. Whatever you can find."

"When are they going to be here?"

"Nine-thirtyish. Maybe ten. I'm not really sure. They were going to be here when they could. They're flying in from Philly. Shit." He shook his head. "I need to have something here for them. They probably haven't eaten yet."

Despite herself, Angela felt his tension get to work on her mind. "Well, I can put a call into Tealeaves & Coffeecake. I'm sure we can get a breakfast tray."

He nodded. "Good. Good, their stuff is good. For Fenwood food anyway. See if you can get one of those breakfast quiches, and pastries."

"Will do."

"Nothing with mushrooms though. I can't stand them."

"Got it."

"Oh, and what are we going to do about coffee?"

"I'll make sure we have a pot freshly brewed by nine-thirty." It wasn't her job, but if it quelled a panic? Well, Angela would do it.

But George wrinkled his nose. "I'm not going to force them to drink that crap."

She blinked. "You mean, the office coffee?"

He nodded as if she was agreeing with him somehow. "You'll have to get one of those jugs of coffee. French roast. You know how I like it."

"All right," she said, then added, "I'll let you know how much it costs."

He nodded absently. "Sounds good. Thanks, Angie, you're a lifesaver."

"Anytime," she said, leaving his office before the scowl set in.

★

Tealeaves & Coffeecake promised to have a tray waiting for her, and a mushroom-free quiche too.

Angela poked her head into her boss's office to inform him. "It'll be fifty-eight fourteen."

He nodded in the same absent way he always did when she mentioned money. His eyes glazed over, and he said, "Right. Just add it to the tab, will you? Thanks again, Angie. You're the best."

She scowled all the way across town, and only an extra-shot lavender latte wiped the expression off her features. Tealeaves & Coffeecake was the rare local coffee shop, and not part of a chain. They made their own food onsite and even prepared their own syrups. The lavender latte was her favorite: a strange, earthy, floral flavor. It shouldn't have been good.

But it was divine. Or so Angela McCormack thought anyway. And, sipping it as the barista brought her order from the back, she felt the anxiety of the morning melt away. Still, it might have eased the tightness in her chest. But it couldn't resolve the source of it. It was just coffee, after all. Not magic. Even if the two were easy to confuse sometimes.

What the hell am I going to do about this job? I can't stay there. I just can't.

"Angela," a chipper voice called. She glanced up to see the coffee shop's owner, Lauren Grant-Ellis, come out of the back. Lauren was a year older than Angela, and insanely cute. Not Angela's-type-cute—even if Lauren hadn't been happily married—but just-stepped-out-of-the-salon cute. All the time.

Angela didn't quite know how Lauren did it, but she certainly appreciated the other woman's efforts. Even if she did feel like a schlep by comparison sometimes.

"Let me guess," Lauren said, blue eyes twinkling. "Lavender latte."

Angela smiled. "Am I that predictable?"

"Oh, honey. Do you have to ask?" Lauren wrapped her in a hug. They'd been best friends growing up—back when she'd been Lauren Ellis, the gangly kid from the farm next door. That was decades ago. Now she was all grown, even though she didn't seem to age.

Angela laughed. "I guess not. But how was Italy?"

"Italy was great. But that'll wait. How are you doing?"

She sighed, more dramatically than she'd meant to. "You know how it goes. Another day in paradise."

"Oh no. That bad?" Lauren glanced at the tables. There were plenty open now. "You want to grab a seat? I'm due for a break now anyway."

Angela snorted. "Due for a break? You're the manager. You're due for a break whenever you say you are."

Her friend laughed. "Maybe. Still, you want to pull up a seat? I can grab us a slice of quiche."

"I'd love to. But I can't. I'm here to pick up an order."

"Oh, that was you? The breakfast platter?"

Angela nodded. "Yup. Another important meeting he didn't plan for."

"And now it's your responsibility?"

She nodded again. "Yup."

Lauren shook her head. "You got to get out of that place, Angela."

"I know. But let's not talk about that idiot. Tell me about Italy. Tell me about Rae."

Rae was Lauren's wife—Rae being the Grant in Grant-Ellis. The mention of her name put a smile on Lauren's face. It was one of those soft, unconscious smiles that painted themselves on the faces of lovers and fools. Angela smiled too. Not that she had couple goals anymore, but if she hadn't given up on romance for good?

Well, Lauren and Rae would have been her couple goals. They'd been together for twelve years and married for ten. That was the reason for their trip to Italy: a long-postponed honeymoon.

They seemed more in love each time Angela saw them. *Maybe that's the reason she looks like she hasn't aged past twenty. True love, or some shit.*

"Italy was divine. The villas and vineyards we saw, Angela. But Rae is happy to be back. She—you're going to laugh—she missed her horses."

She did laugh. "That somehow seems very on-brand."

"Doesn't it?"

Rae was a walking country butch lesbian stereotype: flannel and horses and farm living.

"Yes, it does. But she had fun too?"

"Oh, yes. Got quite drunk a few times."

The barista appeared now with the tote of coffee and boxes of food. "Here you are, miss."

Angela wouldn't have minded the excuse to stay, chatting with her friend on company time. But she thanked the girl and took her food. "Sorry, Lauren. I got to get back."

The other woman nodded. "Hey, let's meet tonight for drinks. You, me, and Rae. I'll tell you about the trip, you tell me about the asshole."

Angela laughed. "You got it. Text me with details, okay?"

Chapter Two

George Maxwell Sutherland, Jr. was at his desk when Angela returned. The food looked good, and he dug in right away. The truth was, he'd missed breakfast, and the tray was as much for him as it was his friends.

"Mmm, thank God for good coffee."

One of the office curmudgeons, an old guy named Steve-something, scowled over. George didn't know what Steve did, exactly. Finances, he thought. Or maybe legal. Anyway, Steve was sore about the coffee.

The office coffee fund had been one of the first things George had slashed in cost reductions. That and the water bubbler refills. These people drank an exorbitant amount of coffee and water. And they were welcome to keep doing so. Just, not on the company dime.

If they really needed the caffeine like they claimed, they could get it as easily from the hotel-supplier coffee they'd switched to—at a third of the price. And as for water, well, they could drink city water. They didn't need filtered. Or they could buy bottled water from the vending machine, like he did.

Still, the dinosaurs harbored some resentment over the fact. George didn't mind.

Hell, he thought it was kind of funny. Sutherland Bio Research was pretty selective in its acquisitions. If anyone had asked him, acquisitions were a giant pain in the ass. Not that they did ask. George Sr. did as George Sr. thought fit.

But rocking the boat and tightening the reins? That was one of George Jr.'s favorite parts of acquisitions. Nothing quite like a cold dose of reality to the dinosaurs who had gotten too comfortable and set in their ways.

So let Steve-something stew and scowl. George Jr. didn't mind one bit. He breathed out a long sigh of contentment.

"Good stuff. Thanks, Angela."

"You're welcome," she said.

Angela was attractive, in the way older women were sometimes. She was probably in her midthirties somewhere. Unmarried, and a little bit of a sad sack in her personal life, or so he gathered. She had an old house, no boyfriend, and no kids. He wasn't sure if she was chronically depressed or if the aura of sadness related to the home situation. Still, she hadn't let herself go, and that was something.

She was thin and tall, with dark hair and curls that were pretty, but a little too wild, and blue eyes that sparkled sometimes, but were a little too quick to judgement. He kind of liked her disapproval though. It was cute.

The rest of her features weren't the kind that made it onto magazines, but they weren't bad either: a straight nose, full eyebrows, nice teeth. For a woman her age, she didn't look bad at all. And in a place like Fenwood? She might have been a Philly five or six. But even at thirty-something, she was a Fenwood ten.

While he was engaged in his own thoughts, she'd put the receipt on his desk very deliberately. And, knowing him well enough to know he'd ignore it, she added, "I made sure they printed a receipt for you."

He smiled. "Great. Thanks."

He could see the annoyance in her face when he deliberately missed her hint. He didn't know why she got bent out of shape about it. He'd pay her back, sooner or later. He always had, hadn't he? Maybe he still owed a little something. He lost track of the amounts. But it wasn't much anyway. He was sure of that.

Still, he didn't resent her feelings. They were her problem, not his. *Not my circus, not my monkeys.* "Let me know when my visitors get here, yes?"

"Will do."

She left, and he watched her go. That was another thing about Angela. She had a nice ass. She wore those middle-class chain store business casual slacks that people in places like Fenwood thought looked professional. For all their failings, well, they sat nicely on that ass.

He wondered if she was a runner, or if she just hit the gym a lot.

Still, he didn't spend too much time on the topic. That way, trouble lay. He knew that from prior experience. He wouldn't have minded sampling the local goods, so to speak. He didn't doubt he'd be able to score if he tried. But the world had changed with the Me Too movement. It wasn't a safe place to be a man anymore.

As it was, Sutherland Research had already had to settle one lawsuit over a little harmless flirting. Not that he'd meant anything by it. His assistant hadn't even been that hot. Mostly, he'd just been complimenting her. And the uppity— Well, he had words for her. But she'd walked away with a good settlement, and he'd been on the receiving end of George Sr.'s wrath ever since. That had been a few years ago. But right now, George Jr. couldn't afford to piss off his dad.

No, change was in the air. George Jr. loved change, for the most part. As the scion of a billion-dollar research company, change usually meant opportunity.

This change certainly did. It had been coming ever since the elder Sutherland's medical scare late last year. George Sr. had been hospitalized with palpitations of the heart. And though it had been nothing more than stress, it seemed to have shifted his father's perspective.

Unless Junior was very much mistaken, pretty soon there'd be a different George Sutherland at the helm of Sutherland Bio. At least, as long as nothing interfered. He wasn't going to risk his shot on a little ass.

Nope, Angela McCormack was out of luck.

George tried to focus on his food. Nothing in Fenwood was gourmet, but for what it offered, Tealeaves wasn't bad. They used organic, locally sourced ingredients too. And though he didn't really care where they came from, he did like knowing he wasn't scarfing down pesticides.

George Jr. wasn't a fitness freak or a health nut. But he took care of himself, and he took care with what he put into his body. He hit the gym five times a week and avoided pesticide-laden garbage. He didn't want to die at fifty of something preventable, like heart disease or cancer.

And he was quite certain they were preventable—if you actually took the time to care for yourself. No, George Jr. had too much to offer the world, and too much left to do, to let himself die like that.

The morning passed slowly. He'd kept his schedule clear in anticipation of his friends' arrival, but their plane had hit a delay. Now, he didn't have much to occupy his time.

There were emails and voicemails, sure. But what he couldn't delegate to Angela or Trevor, his assistant back at the main branch, he'd deal with later. He returned to his online poker game.

He was on a winning streak when Angela poked her head into the doorway of his office.

"Sir?"

"George," he reminded her patiently.

"There are people here for you. A Tommy Carter, Ralph Pearson, and Kendall Hale. To go golfing, they said?" She hesitated. "I…well, I did mention you had a business meeting. But they said you wouldn't mind."

George couldn't help grinning. "Oh, it's not a business meeting. They're friends from school. They're down to do some golfing."

Angela blinked as if the revelation stunned her. He laughed. Had he given the impression that this was a business meeting? Maybe. Maybe he hadn't wanted her to be difficult about breakfast, or payment.

"Thanks, Angie," he said. "Send them in, will you? And make sure they get coffee and food. You haven't seen hangry until you've seen Kendall miss a meal."

★

The morning passed in a very enjoyable fashion after that. Fenwood didn't have much in the way of entertainment or dining, but it did have a very nice golf course. It could have been bigger, but that was George's only fault to find with it.

His friends agreed. "Challenging course, but not too challenging. You were right—it's a good one," Kendall said.

They were waiting for their lunch on the veranda of Tres Amigos, a Mexican place that he didn't hate. He'd explained his scale for restaurants in the area. "There are no good restaurants around here. You have to find the ones that suck the least. This is one of my least hated places, which—for Fenwood—is a glowing recommendation."

"Still haven't learned how to cook for yourself, eh?" Tommy teased.

"I don't have time."

"Fair enough. But I don't know. If it's as bad as you describe, you might need to make time. Or hire someone from back home to fly out here."

George shook his head. "I still have no idea why anyone would build a bioresearch facility here." He spread his arms out, gesturing at the town as if the dilemma was obvious. "There is nothing here. Nothing but cows and hillbillies."

They laughed, though Kendall threw a glance at the patrons at the other end of the veranda, who seemed oblivious to their conversation.

"We saw some horses, too, on the way up," Ralph offered.

"That's true," Tommy agreed. "And lots of corn."

George shook his head darkly. "If I didn't know better, I'd think Dad was exiling me, sending me out here."

"But it's only for a little while, right? Just until you finish the transition?"

George nodded. "Yes. Only a few months now, I think. I'm surprised it's taking this long, honestly. I don't know if dad's second-guessing the acquisition or what."

"Why, is it a money pit?"

"No, it's a good firm. They're a little spoiled. The 'family business' vibe inflated their egos a bit, I think. But I'm working on that."

His friends nodded.

"From what I've read, they've got some good scientists," Ralph said.

"They do. We acquired all their ongoing projects, and they're currently under review. But chances are, we're going to greenlight most of them."

Now, a waiter appeared with plates full of colorful dishes. They'd ordered chimichangas and fajitas and two chicken dishes George couldn't quite pronounce. They made their own salsa and guacamole here, and also promised to use organic ingredients. It was something of a thing in the area, or so he'd gathered. They had some real back-to-nature, in-touch-with-the-land kind of hippy vibes going on. *Ah, small towns.* Well, at least he didn't have to worry about ingesting pesticides.

They dug in with gusto. They'd spent awhile on the links, and for his own part, George was starving.

Kendall and Tommy started grilling Ralph about his upcoming nuptials. Of their party, he was the second to get married. Kendall had been the first, but that ended inside half a year, and no one mentioned it anymore except to give him shit. Usually, when alcohol was involved.

George wasn't particularly interested. He'd met the future Mrs. Pearson, Kelly Wu, and he felt sure Ralph was making a mistake. Then again, the Pearsons always married poorly. Ralph's mother was a writer and a feminist, with an obsession for social causes and justice that drove him to distraction. Ralph's grandmother had been some kind of military intelligence operative during WWII, and the entire family was ridiculously proud of her.

And Ralph, in turn, was the kind of guy who would proudly announce that he came from a family of "strong women." He was a good guy, sure. But, also, kind of a pain in the ass. And as humorless as his mother.

George would have been content to leave their friendship a thing of the past, and not have to censor his language, or worry that any little comment might be called out. But Ralph and his other university buddies remained close, and so, by extension, they remained close too. Not close enough that George cared about his wedding though. He'd attend because he had to. He'd get him a gift that would do the Sutherland name justice. But he barely cared about Ralph. He certainly didn't care enough to listen to him drone on about Kelly and her plans.

Instead, he focused on his food, wondering if he'd be able to arrange things next time so that he could forget Ralph.

"Hey," Kendall's voice broke in, "that's that guy from the plane, isn't it?"

The three friends followed his gaze to a dark-haired stranger, wearing an expensive suit, Italian leather shoes, and enough hair gel to meet a small nation's needs.

Tommy laughed. "Jesus, it is. Check him out, George. This dude cosplaying a mafioso, or what?"

George didn't laugh though. George almost spit out the mouthful of chimichanga he was eating. He didn't hear Tommy's joke except as background noise, but he might have been more discomposed if he had. Because Tommy Carter had hit the nail on the head.

The stranger was no stranger to George. It was Joey Caruso, or "The Italian," as his bosses called him. And whether Joey worked for the actual Mafia, or his outfit was corporate owned, George didn't know. He didn't want to know. He had more pressing questions at the moment anyway. *What the fuck is he doing here?*

Joey glanced around the veranda, letting his eyes linger on George a moment longer than his companions. Then he walked back inside.

George's friends had still been talking, laughing about the comic appearance of the man.

"New money. Am I right?" Kendall said. It was a joke of his, since his father was first generation new money. It usually made his friends—all from long-established families—laugh.

But he wasn't wrong in the instance. Joey was one of those upstarts who thought the price tag and fit of his suit conveyed class. Never mind that he looked like he'd stepped out of a cheesy mobster movie.

Fucking hell. George's mind was racing between disdain for Caruso and fear for himself. *What the hell is he doing here? Gilmore knows we're on schedule. Fuck, fuck, fuck.*

He cleared his throat. "Damn. I think something went down the wrong way there. I'm going to the bathroom. I'll be right back."

Ralph glanced up at him, and George realized some of his anxiety must have reflected in his features because Ralph's eyes widened. "You okay, man?"

"Yeah, fine. Just give me a second."

He headed inside as fast as he could without running. He didn't want to raise suspicion, but he also didn't want to provoke too much worry. It wouldn't do to get caught confronting Joey because Ralph took it into his simple head to check on him.

Joey Caruso had settled at the bar and was giving his order to a man in the white-and-black standard of Tres Amigos. The bartender nodded and headed off to make whatever Caruso had ordered by the time George crossed the restaurant.

Caruso looked up at his approach and plastered a stupid grin across his face. "George. Long time, no see. What are the odds of bumping into you here?" He clapped him on the back and pulled him onto a stool.

That might have been for the benefit of their fellow diners, but George wasn't playing along. "Pretty high, I'd think. Since something tells me you came looking for me."

Caruso cracked another grin: bleached white teeth against a tanned olive face. "You're getting paranoid in your old age, my friend. I'm just here for the scenery."

"The scenery? In Fenwood?"

The bartender returned, some kind of fruity drink in his hand.

Caruso tapped George. "That'll be six-fifty. You want him to just put it on your tab?"

George scowled but slapped a ten on the bar.

"Keep the change," Caruso said.

George scowled that much deeper. "You're not here for the scenery," he hissed once the bartender had gone.

"'Course I am. This place—it's paradise. Like *Little House on the Prairie*. But with cows. Lots of cows. I've never seen so many cattle in one place. Holsteins and Angus and I don't even know what else. You ever seen so many cattle anywhere?"

George glanced back at the veranda where his friends were. He didn't have long, he knew, before someone came looking for him, worried he'd choked to death in a bathroom stall. He sure as hell wasn't going to waste it bullshitting about...well, bulls. "Don't give me shit, Caruso. You're not here for cows any more than I am."

Caruso shrugged. "Maybe. But it's definitely bullshit that brings me here." He cracked another one of those smarmy grins.

George wished he could introduce his fist to the other man's perfect teeth. "What the hell do you want?"

"You know what I want. You've been awfully quiet lately. Mr. Gilmore is getting worried. He sent me to make sure you were okay."

George was surprised the building's alarms hadn't gone off already with the smoke that must be rising from his ears. "I told you, everything's fine. I told Gilmore everything's fine."

Caruso nodded. "Good. Because we've been hearing things. Rumors."

"Rumors are shit. Your boss should know better than to listen to rumors."

"Maybe." Caruso shrugged, then gestured widely.

God, what is it with Italians and the hands? Was this guy just a walking stereotype, or were they all like that?

"But you know how it is. Sometimes, there's a grain of truth under all the bullshit. And sometimes...well, sometimes, there's smoke where there's fire."

George grimaced at the haphazard mixing of metaphors. "I don't care what you've been hearing. Nothing's changed. We're on schedule. And..." He glanced back at the veranda. He could see someone's form rising through the windows. "I got to get back to my table. You tell Gilmore everything's all right."

"I will." Caruso tapped him on the chest with the back of his hand, in a kind of affirmation. "I will, George. But I think I'll stick around all the same for a bit. You know, you might not know this about me. But I'm a bit of a bovine enthusiast."

Chapter Three

It just so happened that it was margarita night at Marty's. So when Lauren, Rae, and Angela met, of course it was at Marty's.

It was one of those bars that was somewhere solidly in between "dive" and "respectable." You didn't have to worry about walking in on an impromptu lovemaking session in the bathrooms, but now and then, you might catch sight of members of the oldest profession on the lookout for clients.

But on margarita night, when cocktails were two for the price of one—or twenty dollars for all the margaritas you could drink between six and nine—the atmosphere changed. It looked like the local PTA meeting had just gotten out. Middle-aged women, and women like Angela, who were getting too close for comfort to middle age, lined the bar and occupied the tables. Women who counted calories every minute of every other day crowded Marty's on Wednesday nights to completely sabotage their diets.

Angela was moaning about that very fact. "I shouldn't be doing this. I'm going to regret it tomorrow. Plus, I'll have to work it all off anyway."

"Oh, give yourself a break," Lauren said, sipping her peach daquiri. "God, this is good."

Angela sipped her margarita and sighed. "Yes, it is."

Rae grinned at them, tipping a brown bottle their way in a mock toast. "Give me a stout, ice cold, over that fruity crap any day of the week, ladies."

Lauren waved her away. "Philistine."

Angela laughed.

Rae's dark hair was shorn close to her head in a styled but short fashion. She didn't usually wear makeup, but tonight, she'd added a little lip color. It was a nice shade of red that matched the flannel shirt she was wearing. Angela had mentioned it earlier, and she'd called it her "date night flannel."

Rae was a walking stereotype, and she knew it. It was something of a joke between the three friends. The beer just added to the picture.

"Well," Angela said, "you can have your beer. I'll still take my margarita."

"And my daiquiri," Lauren added.

"I see I'm outnumbered. And a wise woman knows when to pick her battles. Let's call it a truce, shall we? And by way of a peace offering, why don't I order us a basket of wings?"

The two toasted their victory—for a victory they declared it—with gusto, and Rae laughed. "Jesus. How many of those things have you two had already?"

"This is my second," Angela said.

"Mine too."

"Looks like I'll be driving home."

"True." Lauren grinned. "But don't pretend you mind me after a few drinks."

Rae's cheeks pinked, and they all laughed. It was one of the things Angela loved about them. Rae was supremely confident in just about every aspect of her life. But when it came to Lauren? Well, she still blushed like a teenager on a first date.

Angela shook her head. She didn't want to spend too long thinking about romance. She already felt like crap after the day she'd had. "All right, lovebirds, don't start that this early. You've still got to tell me about Venice." So far, she'd heard about their tour of the countryside and the coasts. But they hadn't gotten to their time in the floating city.

But Lauren shook her head. "No. Enough about our honeymoon. I want to hear about that piece of shit."

"Oh, yes. Mr. George." Rae nodded. "I've heard a lot about him."

Angela scowled at the mere mention of his name. "That son of a bitch. You know how he had me go rushing out to buy breakfast for his 'big meeting'?"

Lauren nodded. "Yeah."

"There was no meeting. He had buddies from school coming down."

"So...not work related at all?" Rae asked.

"Exactly."

The other woman shook her head. "Jesus. What a prick. Now you know why I prefer working with animals. The bullshit I have to deal with scrapes up with a shovel and washes away with a hose."

Lauren ignored her significant other's input. "Did he pay you this time?"

Angela shook her head. "No, of course not. He said he didn't have cash. But that was a lie, too, because he grabbed a bottle of water from the vending machine. Paid with a twenty and had a wad of bills in his pocket."

Rae laughed. "The man is clearly a psychopath. Who pays a vending machine with a twenty? That's like paying for your meal in pennies."

Lauren shivered. "Like Missus Matterson."

Mrs. Matterson was the closest thing the owner of Tealeaves had to a nemesis. She was an older lady, but not old, who came in on Sunday mornings after church, at precisely fifteen minutes after ten o'clock. Like her arrival, her order never varied. She'd ask for a slice of the quiche of the day, a cup of coffee, and a scone. And inevitably, something would be wrong with her order. Her coffee was always too warm, or too bitter, or too dark, or not dark enough. The scone had been overbaked, or underbaked. Her quiche was never quite right either. Some days, it had too much of one ingredient, or not enough of another. She couldn't taste the feta, or she could taste nothing but spinach. She didn't care for tomato with eggs, and she was sure she'd read something about that being bad for digestion. But the bacon quiche was her favorite target for wrath. "If you advertise bacon in your breakfast, my dear, there's supposed to be bacon in it. Otherwise, that's false advertising. Which I'm sure you're aware is against the law."

And she always, always, paid with spare change, counting out her pennies first, then her nickels, then her dimes, and finally quarters. The nearest thing Mrs.

Matterson ever did to varying this routine was occasionally bringing in a half-dollar coin.

"I'm surprised you know what that is," she'd tell the poor young soul stuck behind the register. "I've read that your generation doesn't anymore." If she felt particularly cantankerous, she'd explain the coin. "It's a fifty-cent piece, my dear. I know they don't teach you about that anymore. But it's real money. Look it up on your phone if you have to. Or call your manager. But hurry. I want to get off my feet."

Angela had come into Tealeaves once on a Sunday morning expressly to glimpse the infamous Mrs. Matterson. And she'd not been disappointed. That particular morning's tantrum involved a piece of golden-brown toast that was "burned to a crisp." Mrs. Matterson was certain she'd chipped a tooth on it.

Now, she laughed at the memory. "Oh God. Good old Mrs. Matterson."

Lauren seemed unwilling to linger on the thought. "You've got to start 'forgetting' cash yourself, Angela."

"He'll tell me to put it on a card."

"Get ahead of that. Tell him you don't have any cash on hand. 'But I can run your card, if you want.'"

"He'll have forgotten his wallet," Angela predicted.

"Then you forget your purse." Rae shrugged. "And keep forgetting it until he starts paying upfront."

Angela considered the plan for a long moment. "It might work. But if I piss him off…"

"What's the worst that'll happen? He'll downsize your position like he did the rest of HR, and you'll be out of a job you hate?"

"It's not that simple. I've still got a mortgage."

Her friends nodded now. They all knew Angela's love of her historic home. It had been a fixer-upper, and she'd gotten a good deal on it. But it needed work—a lot of work—and she'd sunk a good chunk of change into it over the years. She loved that place in the way that gearheads loved their cars.

"Yeah, but your dad would always hire you. You know that," Lauren offered. "He might not be able to pay you as much as Sutherland Bio, but at least you wouldn't lose your house."

Angela groaned. "I'm not a farmer. I never have been."

Rae shook her head. "You don't know what you're missing."

"I do," she protested. "I grew up on the farm. I hated it. It's not even the animals. It's—well, strawberry season, and pumpkin rides, and corn mazes... It's people every day, all day. It's customer service, all the time. Screaming kids and angry parents and people trying to haggle and..." She shook her head. "I worked there through high school. And I hated it."

"Yeah, but it's different when you're a teen versus an adult. Adults think they can push you around when you're a kid."

Angela snorted, her mind going back to George. "Believe me, they still think they can push me around as an adult."

Rae laughed. "My point is, you've got a backup plan."

Angela considered for a long moment and then nodded. It wasn't a backup plan she wanted, but it was a backup plan. Her dad had been trying to get her back into the family business for years. He'd mention it every time she complained about work. "That's true. At least I'd have a job."

"Exactly. And you could look for something else, but you have a paycheck in the meantime."

She nodded again. "But it's bullshit that I have to worry about it."

"Yes, it is."

"He treats me like I'm his personal secretary. And expects me to run a whole damned human resources department all by myself at the same time."

"He's everything that's wrong with corporate America," Rae said. "Guys like him? They're one of the reasons I couldn't wait to get out."

For a long while, the friends talked about George Maxwell Sutherland, Jr. And the longer they talked, the angrier—and drunker—Angela got. And the more she ruminated on all the slights she'd suffered, and all the wrongs he'd inflicted on her co-workers and former co-workers. And the more she felt she couldn't stand working there any longer.

"I don't know. Maybe I should just talk to my dad. They always need more help. And I could quit then. I don't want to hire new people—not after he let so many of our team go. No warning, no severance."

"He's a son of a bitch," Lauren agreed.

Rae nodded. "I tell you—men like him? They're ruining this country." Rae had limited herself to beer, but she'd had more than a few. And the more *she* drank, the more political she got. "If I see one more goddamned billionaire on my TV, blaming the middle class for the problems his class created..."

"I just...it pisses me off to see what he's done with the company. I used to like working there, you know? We did good work." Angela shook her head. "We were helping people. And now? We've lost so many employees. He doesn't even give a damn."

"People are commodities to them," Rae agreed. "Not human beings. If someone expects to be treated like a human, they'll replace her with someone a little more desperate for the job, someone who has no choice but to put up with their bullshit."

"It's how revolutions start." Lauren nodded darkly and a bit drunkenly. "Nothing ever starts with guillotines. It starts with greed."

Angela laughed at that. The corporate world didn't quite work like that, but maybe, she thought, it should. Maybe instead of golden parachutes to ease them out of workplaces they'd destroyed, CEOs like Sutherland should be run out of town on a rail. "It's too bad we can't revolt."

They all nodded, contemplating this workplace revolution in silence.

"It'll never happen," Angela sighed after a space. "Everyone needs the job too much. We don't all have dads who can hire us."

"It's how they get away with what they get away with. Pay just enough to keep people around, but not enough so you can be independent. And then use the threat of losing that pay to keep the employees docile."

Angela thought about that for a long moment. "But you know who doesn't need the job?"

"Who?"

"Me." She tapped her chest for emphasis. "Yes, I may hate hayrides and apple cider and pumpkin patches. But I've got a job that'll pay my bills. What the hell am I still doing there?"

Rae tapped her beer bottle on the table. "There you go. Tell him to take his job and shove it. And to pay you back, or you'll be pressing charges."

Angela, though, shook her head. "No. I mean, I will. But I can do better than that."

"What do you mean?"

"I mean, I'm the head of HR. Hell, I'm *all* of HR now. He treats me like a personal servant.

"Well, you know what? I'm not his servant. I'm a dedicated professional, and I deserve respect." She slapped the table for emphasis.

"You're damned right you do." Lauren nodded.

"You earned it."

"Yes, I have. But if he doesn't want to treat me like a professional..." Angela grinned broadly, ear to ear. "Well, then, I won't be. I'm going to make him pay."

Rae and Lauren exchanged glances, cracking grins of their own. "What's the plan?"

"He wants me filling those positions? Okay, I'm going to fill them. With the worst goddamned candidates I can find. I'm going to find people that will make his life a living hell, just like he's made ours."

Her friends were cackling now, and Lauren started to applaud. A few patrons glanced their way.

Their enthusiasm only heightened her own. "You want to piss off HR, George? Okay, well let's see just how far that gets you."

★

Angela sat at her desk, head in hands, and groaned. What in the hell had she been thinking? She must have downed half a dozen margaritas the night before. Her head felt like a punching bag, in use at the moment. *Oh God. This day is going to be torture.*

She'd managed to drag herself into work, and she'd been on time at that. But the prospect of spending the next eight and a half hours here?

She groaned again. No, margarita night had definitely not been the right call. It had seemed like it at the time. She'd enjoyed hearing about her friends' travels. It was good to vent too. Sure, in the clear light of day, she wasn't sure she'd go through with her plan to leave. And, of course, she knew she'd never follow through on her revenge scheme.

For a minute, she smiled at the thought of that. She wished on some level she could. But she was a professional, and that would be deeply unprofessional. And, anyway, she probably didn't have the guts to see it through.

No, it was all well and good to dream. It made a good revenge fantasy, to think of her boss surrounded by clueless bunglers in lieu of the competent staff he'd fired as a corporate show of force. She liked to think of what a fitting parting gift that would be.

But no. She was a professional. She couldn't do something like that. It'd be wrong. *Very wrong. No, I can't do that.*

She could leave though. She'd talk to her dad today. No, it would not be ideal. Yes, she'd be giving up her dream job, leaving the place she'd loved working at and so many people she'd loved working with. *But it's not the same place you started at. Not since Sutherland took over. Cut your losses and move on.*

She'd had to do a lot of that these last few years. She'd had to say goodbye to the woman she'd planned to spend the rest of her life with. And here she was, alive and well. If she could survive losing Carrie? Well, she could survive anything. A job was just a job, after all.

She heard the office front door buzz open. Someone had badged in fashionably late. Heck, at this point, it was too late to be considered fashionable. Which meant only one thing: Sutherland was in the office.

She grimaced and closed her office door softly. Until she actually handed in her resignation, she was going to stay on schedule. And she'd never be able to do that if she kept getting sent on food runs or interrupted for small talk when he was tired of sitting at his computer.

Her aspirin was starting to kick in, too, so her head felt a little better, and she could concentrate a little more. Angela focused on her tasks.

She'd been making good headway on her backlog. If everything kept on schedule, she'd be able to get the job listings to Sutherland for review by midafternoon.

She was lost deep in her work when a series of heavy, urgent knocks sounded at her door. She yelped and pushed to her feet to admit whoever it was. But before she'd taken two steps, the door opened anyway.

George Jr. stormed in, a box in hand. She froze in place and stared in stupefaction, as much at the scowl on his features as the redness in his cheeks. "Mr. Sutherland?"

He tossed the box onto her desk with a force that sent its contents scattering this way and that, and she retreated a step at the sheer violence of the gesture. He didn't bother with a greeting. Instead, he snapped, "I know I said I run a casual office, but this is a little too casual. Even by this place's standards."

She blinked. "What?"

He gestured at the box and its contents, some of which littered her desk and keyboard.

She'd been too focused on him to take in the sight. Now, she saw that it was food rolling around on her papers and settling into her keys. "Uh...what is that? And why is it...here?" She was trying to keep her tone even, but the sight of a cream cheese Danish flipped onto her number pad really didn't help.

George Jr.'s expression darkened. "Exactly what I want to know. We don't leave garbage around the office, McCormack. Is it really too much to clean up after yourself?"

Angela was at a loss. She had no idea where this food had come from, or why in God's name he'd just chucked it all over her desk. She tried to fit that thought into a sentence that wouldn't get her fired. "I'm not following, sir. Where did this come from?"

"What the hell, McCormack? You know damned well what it is. You brought it here."

She glanced back at the food, and specifically at the box. Then she blinked. It was a to-go box from Tealeaves. She couldn't see the name, but she recognized the familiar teacup and leaves logo of her friend's shop.

She quickly understood. She'd refrigerated the leftover quiche and left the pastries in their box in Sutherland's office after he'd left. She'd expected him to return in the afternoon, but that never happened.

"Are those...the breakfast pastries?"

"From yesterday?" he snapped. "Yes. They are. And they were still in my office. Garbage. You left garbage in my office, Angie. That's disgusting. I expect better from you."

It seemed an exaggeration of epic proportions to call day-old donuts and muffins "garbage." Ideal? No. But hardly inedible. Hell, if he'd put them out in the break-room instead of decorating her keyboard with them, they would have been gone in minutes.

But something told her this was no time to argue. "I didn't think I should throw your food away, Mr. Sutherland," she said instead. "I didn't know when you'd be returning."

"It's George. How many times do I have to tell you that? And I don't want to hear excuses. We may have a casual atmosphere, but we're not pigs. We have to have some kind of professional standards." Now, he raised a finger, jabbing it in her direction. "Don't ever let me find something like that again. Do you understand?"

It was everything she could do to respond civilly, but Angela murmured a yes.

Sutherland's color deepened. "What? If you're talking, I need to be able to hear you. That's kind of a basic rule of communication."

Motherfucker. "Yes," she said, forcing a smile that, if looks could kill, might have felled dragons. "Of course, George. I'll keep that in mind."

"Good." He retracted his finger from her personal space. It hadn't touched her, and in the moment, her own cheeks blazing with fury, Angela felt that that was a good thing. For his sake. He turned now but paused at her door to gesture at the food all over her desk. "And for God's sake, clean this mess. I don't want vermin in the building."

Angela did clean it after he'd gone. She scraped sweet cheese filling out of her keyboard and scrubbed glaze out of the carpet. She swept crumbs into the waste bin and sorted which of the sticky papers on her desk she needed to hold on to, and which she could reprint.

And then she sat back down to work. The heat of fury had passed. Now, an icy cold certainty had settled in her chest. To hell with being a professional. To hell with taking the higher road. To hell with the company.

George Maxwell Sutherland, Jr. had gone too far. And he was going to find out the hard way.

She ignored the rest of her work and brought up the candidate recruitment software. Then, a grim smile on her face, she got to work.

Chapter Four

Angie McCormack poked her head into his office. "George?"

George Jr. glanced up and smiled at what he saw. Angie somehow looked a little brighter lately, a little livelier. She was also smiling more, which was a good look for her. It seemed that ever since he'd put his foot down the other week, she'd straightened up her act. No more "Mr. Sutherland." No more grimaces, or harping about his tab either.

She'd put in work over that weekend—unpaid, of course, since she was salaried—to kickstart the recruitment process. She'd even been spending her off hours looking through LinkedIn. And résumés were already coming in.

Maybe a little kick in the backside, a little reminder of the pecking order, was all she'd needed to start really taking her job seriously.

It hadn't worked quite so well with all the other employees. Steve—curmudgeon Steve—had quit on the spot after George chewed him out for taking too many coffee breaks. Well, that was no loss. He always seemed to find the other man by the coffeepot. And, anyway, Steve was old. Not that he could say it out loud—not without risking a lawsuit—but he hated seeing old people on the payroll. They cost more to insure as they had more health problems. And that meant more time off and less productivity. They were a drain on a company, from every angle.

No, if George had had his way, the Steves of the workplace would have been quietly shown the door a long time ago and downsized into oblivion. But he might have had to explain that decision to George Sr. He was pretty sure that wouldn't have escaped his father's notice.

And the senior Sutherland might not have seen it his way. He was another old guy, and old age had made him risk adverse. Even if solidarity hadn't stayed him, the fear of that trend being picked up on by an enterprising lawyer and leading to discrimination lawsuits probably would have.

George didn't have much good to say about his father lately. It had been George Sr.'s decision to exile him to this damned cow-filled, hillbilly town. And, worse than that, he figured his father was the reason he was in a pickle with Gilmore. His father's indecision and waffling had slowed everything down. He was the reason that bastard Caruso was still hanging around Fenwood, like a great, fake-tanned sore thumb. He was the reason Caruso shadowed him, showing up at the same restaurants, or even at the golf course, with that goddamned smarmy grin, just letting him know he was there, watching.

And George Sr., consequently, was the reason for his short temper lately. George Sr. had been responsible for Steve's resignation and all the whining that had caused in the lab. He'd been responsible for the ensuing shortage of staff and the scramble to find a new senior analyst.

No, George Jr. had nothing good to say about his progenitor. Nothing good at all.

But Angie McCormack, on the other hand, as she stood there wearing that pencil skirt and that blouse? Well, there was a lot he could say about that.

It could have been a little tighter. He wouldn't have minded that at all. She could have left one more button unbuttoned. He wouldn't have minded that either.

But still, with her attitude adjustment had come a wardrobe upgrade. She wore more skirts these days, and fewer trousers. She had nice legs, and he liked seeing them. And her ass looked even better than usual in a skirt.

He knew better than to be thinking like that. Hell, he didn't mean to be so damned thirsty, but, for God's sake, he was stuck in Fenwood. The pickings were slim—or, *not* slim. That was part of the problem. He had no use for hefty housewives and stocky farmhands.

"George?" she said.

He blinked, realizing he must have missed something between *George*'s. "Sorry, what was that?"

She smiled sweetly. "I asked if you had time for interviews later this week?"

"Oh." *Interviews. Right.* "Sure. The sooner I get this team together, the better." *The sooner I can wrap this merger up and get the hell out of Fenwood.*

"Great. I'll add them to your schedule, then, as I get them set up."

"Good. And Angie?"

"Yes?"

He flashed her a grin, one of his most charming. There was something, in his experience, the ladies found irresistible about a lopsided smile and a mouth full of pearly whites. "Good work. You're doing a great job lately. I really appreciate it. I want you to know that."

She thanked him, smiling again, and took her leave.

Yes, he decided, biology was definitely on his side. She probably didn't even realize what had happened. And yet, here she was—a lot less frigid and a lot more compliant.

He laughed. Biology was a bitch. *No matter how much we try to resist, at our cores, we are who we are.* It's what made men like him leaders, and set the whole world on a silver platter, ripe for his picking.

It's what made men like Steve—followers—bitter, when they reached their old age and realized they'd spent their whole lives following.

And it's what made women like Angie predictable to a fault.

Not that he was complaining. Biology had been kind to him. He'd evolved to be the lion among the lambs, the king of the jungle.

And, sure, things might have hit a rough patch lately. But he just needed to be patient. It'd work itself out soon enough, especially once George Sr. did finally retire.

Patience, George. The lion bides his time.

★

Operation Payback—which was what she was calling it—was going swimmingly. Angela had been conducting pre-interviews for the last half a week. She'd been very selective in which résumés she answered.

Chock-full of spelling mistakes was a good sign. Paragraphs of fluff was a better one. And comic sans? Well, a résumé written in comic sans was an automatic interview, guaranteed.

Some part of her felt terrible for wasting people's time. But she'd done everything she could to filter out the good candidates. She'd sent out those rejections right away, so nobody wasted their time on a callback.

There were plenty of crappy candidates left though. Not least of all because she'd gone through the job application archives and pulled all the résumés that had been flagged as absolute no-gos.

Those were some of the most promising. Her old team had already put in the work isolating awful candidates. Now, she only had to figure out which ones among them were still looking for jobs. And she had high hopes.

Thus far, Angela had interviewed a few prospects for the admin position. That was most important to her since a new admin would mean she'd be able to focus on her other work. Consequently, it had been her priority.

It was a tricky business. She needed someone competent enough to lighten her load but wretched enough to make Sutherland's job miserable. She'd conducted half a dozen interviews already.

There'd been Blake, whose résumé had been a delightful mess of spelling errors, run-on sentences, dangling participles, and other treasures. He'd been a strong contender until he readily conceded he didn't know how to use basic word processing and scheduling tools, and chewed his fingernails throughout the interview.

She decided he'd been a little too on the nose. So had the next interviewee, Frances. It wasn't even that her body odor preceded her into the room. That was a problem that could be fixed. But her insistence that she would never touch a computer, and could perform her job without one? Well, that just wasn't going to work.

Nate, the third interviewee, was a better bet. He was youngish, good-looking—but not good-looking enough to make George insecure—and had outstanding manners. It also took him five minutes to transcribe a simple email. Yes, Nate was a very good prospect.

The next three interviews had been less spectacular. They were all reasonably competent candidates. She'd certainly seen résumés from more proficient applicants. But they seemed sufficiently adept and personable.

Angela did feel bad about wasting their time. But she treated them to lunch and left them with no false hope as kindly as possible. And, she consoled herself, in a way she was doing them a favor. Sutherland Bio was a terrible place to work. She'd be doing them a bad turn if she actually hired them.

It didn't *quite* assuage her guilt, but it went a little way to easing her conscience. She had another interview this morning for the admin position. She glanced at the clock. Two minutes before he was due.

She frowned at that. Most applicants were early. Even the most confident prospects timed it so that they got in well before the specified hour.

Angela waited. Another minute passed. *Hmm.* She glanced at the file.

Conrad Walters. He'd graduated from engineering school thirty-five years earlier. *Sixties-somewhere. At least.*

He'd worked for three decades in engineering. The five-year gap in his résumé was, she assumed, due to retirement. Well, retirement wasn't for everyone. Some people needed to be active again. Some people needed that clock, the nine-to-five.

The expected *ding* sounded on her desktop, indicating that a visitor had checked in for her. *Finally*. Technically, Conrad was right on time, to the minute. But he almost seemed late. She got to her feet, pausing to check her appearance in the mirror.

The whole thing might be a farce, but she had been making sure she looked the part. It was almost kind of a private joke. The less professional her behavior, the more carefully and professionally she presented herself.

Angela plastered a welcoming smile onto her features as she stepped into the lobby. An older man was waiting for her.

"Mr. Walters?" she greeted, extending a hand.

"You must be Miss McCormack?" He cocked an eyebrow, then glanced down at his watch. "You did say ten o'clock, didn't you?"

Angela glanced down at the face of her phone. *One minute after ten*. She smiled. "Indeed. I'm sorry, I just had to grab my pen."

"Hm." He reached out, now, and took her hand. "Well, a pleasure, I'm sure."

She broadened her smile. "The pleasure's all mine, Mr. Walters." She meant it. Rude, abrasive, and obsessive and unforgiving over minor details? Well now, that sounded perfect. She just had to make sure it wasn't gender based. It wouldn't do her any good to hire a misogynist. "You can come with me. We'll head back to one of the conference rooms."

He nodded, and they began to head back.

"So," she said, "tell me about yourself, Mr. Walters. Or do you prefer Conrad?"

"Either's fine."

"Do you live in the area?"

"Yup."

"I see you worked in Madison, Wisconsin before this?"

"Yup."

"You must have moved, then?"

"Yup."

"Recently?"

He considered for a moment. "I suppose you could say that."

Delightful. They'd reached the conference room, and she ushered him inside. "Have a seat, please."

He glanced around the room, one skeptical eyebrow raised. Then he chose a seat at the far end of the room, with his back to the wall. "You don't mind if I take this seat?"

"Uh...no, not at all."

He nodded, offering the cryptic explanation, "I don't like to leave my six open."

She smiled, not entirely sure what that meant. "Right. Well, umm, tell me more about you. Why Sutherland Research?"

He shrugged. "You're hiring."

She laughed out loud. That was a good one, and she started to tell him so. But he stared at her, and she realized he'd actually meant it.

"I mean," she said, "it's a good reason to apply."

"Oh." He nodded, seeming to accept this at face value. "I thought so."

"So, looking at your résumé, you've been an engineer for about thirty years."

"That's right."

"This is quite a career shift."

"That's right."

"Want to tell me about that?"

He sighed but spread his hands. "Sure. I retired five years ago. I don't want to go back to that rat race. I want to try something else. Something—between me and you— that doesn't require a lot of brains. I need to be active, but I spent the last thirty years thinking every day on the job. I'm tired of that."

She smiled. "So, if I'm hearing you, you're excited to bring your analytical skillset and attention to detail to a new career path?"

He blinked. "Right. That."

"Awesome. That's a great answer. Mr. Sutherland will be happy to hear that. He loves when candidates embrace challenge with a can-do attitude."

Conrad grimaced at the words. "Really?"

"Oh, yes."

He grunted. "So, this Mr. Sutherland...would I be working closely with him?"

"You would."

He grunted again, and she took the opportunity to test him.

"Will you excuse me just a minute, Conrad? I need to check on one of my colleagues. He was supposed to be here for our interview."

Conrad nodded. "Do what you have to. I'm not going anywhere."

She left the room quickly, heading to her desk phone. *Be there, Richard*, she thought as she dialed the lab.

"Richard Kaplan, research department."

"Richard, can you come up to conference room *C*? I'm conducting an interview, and I'd like you to meet our candidate."

Richard sighed into the phone. "Sure. But you know we're way behind here, Angela. Ever since Steve left—"

"I know. It'll just take two minutes."

"Fine, fine. I'll be right there."

She hung up the phone and headed back to the conference room. Conrad was exactly where she'd left him, in exactly the same position: hands folded neatly in front of him on the table. He glanced behind her. "He's not coming, then?"

"What?"

"Your colleague."

"Oh, no. He'll be right here."

"Ah."

The pair waited in awkward silence. Angela did nothing to break it, curious to see how Conrad would respond.

His response was to not respond. He sat there, still as a statue, until the door opened and Richard Kaplan stepped in.

Richard was a bespectacled man of middle age and high nervous energy. He glanced between Angela and Conrad. She beckoned him in.

"Conrad, this is our head of research, Richard Kaplan. Richard, this is Conrad Walters."

"Nice to meet you, Conrad."

The old man raised an eyebrow at the department manager and his proffered hand in exactly the same way he'd done to her. "I hope I didn't take you from anything too pressing."

Angela had to fight the urge to smile at the acridness in his tone.

Richard shook his head, seemingly oblivious. "Don't worry. It's all chaos, interruptions or not." The answer didn't seem to impress Conrad. His eyebrow arched a little higher. "So, what are you interviewing for?"

"Administrative secretary. Which, I believe, should have been on my application."

"It was," Angela assured him, pretending not to pick up on the pointedness in his words.

"Admin, huh? Well, I suppose we'll talk frequently, then."

"I look forward to it," Conrad said, in a fashion that made it clear he certainly did not.

Richard nodded. "Likewise. Well, if that's all, I really should get back."

"By all means, don't let me keep you."

Angela thanked her colleague and returned to the interview with her mind much at ease. Conrad had been at least as rude to Richard as he had to her. And she'd introduced Richard as a department head; not even the title had checked Conrad's incivility.

That boded very well, and she delved into the rest of the interview with a newfound confidence.

Conrad Walters was the perfect candidate. He was technically proficient, knew the software he'd be using, so would be more than up to easing her workload. But he'd be a monster to work with on a day-to-day basis.

Perfect. Still, Angela didn't want to miss anything. So she continued the interview as if she hadn't already made up her mind.

Getting information out of Conrad wasn't easy. But she did pry out that he'd been in the military and served in Beirut in the eighties.

She'd hinted, very casually, that he should mention the fact to Mr. Sutherland. "It's a Sutherland initiative to hire veterans."

"Yes, it makes great PR," Conrad said, not even bothering to hide the resentment in his tone.

Angela smiled and made a point of not disagreeing. "Mr. Sutherland's father has set an informal quota for each site. It would definitely help our branch reach our goals. Not that that would be a factor in your hiring, of course."

Conrad grimaced. "Of course."

"But I'm sure Mr. Sutherland would appreciate that as—well, an added bonus."

Conrad surveyed her for a long moment, then nodded. "Thank you, Miss McCormack. I appreciate the advice."

"Advice? Oh, I wasn't giving advice, Conrad. If I was giving advice, I would have said something like, 'Make sure you smile. Have a few lines and laugh at all George's jokes. Call him George if he asks you to, and Mr. Sutherland otherwise. He likes a firm handshake, but not too firm. And make sure you tell him it was a pleasure to meet him.'" She smiled. "But that wouldn't be appropriate."

He nodded slowly. "Of course."

"Well, Mr. Walters, I have a few more interviews. But, would you be available to come back for a second-level interview with Mr. Sutherland, either sometime this week or next?"

He nodded briskly. "Absolutely."

"Good. And when we'd emailed, you mentioned you could start as soon as we needed you. Is that still accurate?"

He let loose a snort. "Truer now than before."

She glanced at him questioningly, and he shrugged.

"My grandkids will be out of school soon. My wife babysits them during the summer, and, well, I'd rather be anywhere else than home.

"I retired to retire. I put in my time, Miss McCormack, if you get me. Don't misunderstand me. I love my grandkids. They're wonderful children. But an hour or two every other weekend is more than sufficient to appreciate them."

She smiled. "I understand. And, if we offer you a position, that will work out well for us too. We're very eager to fill that one, as soon as possible."

Chapter Five

Angela dropped hints later that day to her boss that she'd spoken with an impressive candidate. "Veteran too. Served in Beirut."

George wrinkled his nose at that. "Ex-military? You sure she'll be a good fit? You know, with the atmosphere of the place and all that?"

She fought the urge to grimace. "Oh, I'm sure he'll be fine."

"He?" George's face relaxed. "Oh. But...a male admin?" He considered for a moment and then shrugged. "Well, ex-military? I suppose he'll be efficient."

"Oh, yes. He was quite punctual and precise during our pre-interview."

George nodded. "That's good. Punctual is good. And I suppose hiring another veteran will be good. We're a little below quota."

"Yes." Angela surveyed him and his noncommittal expression. She'd thought selling this might be easier. *Well, time to sweeten the deal. Time to lie.* "And he was very excited about working for Sutherland. He told me he'd thought of applying the other year, before the buyout. But he didn't have confidence in the old leadership. Now that it's a Sutherland Research facility, he wants to be a part of it."

"Oh?" George's interest seemed piqued. "Really? Why?"

"Uh, well, after his time in the service, he was an engineer for several decades."

"Really? Decades?" His brow creased. "He must be awfully old."

Dammit. They seemed to be taking two steps backward for every step forward. "Yes. But, you know, he's *military* old. They don't age like we do. They keep that energy. He had been retired, but he couldn't stay still. That's why he's looking for work now."

"Oh. And...well, I suppose we don't have to worry about healthcare coverage. Not that that's a factor, of course. But, you know, always a perk when the best candidate for the job saves us some money."

She smiled, and it wasn't even a forced smile. *There we go.* "You have to appreciate that when it happens, don't you?"

He grinned now too. "Good. Good work, Angie. But how does being an engineer relate to Sutherland?"

"Oh." She tried to bring her mind back to that particular lie. "Well, um, he'd been researching the company. He was very impressed with the efficiency. And results."

George smiled. "Good. Excellent. He sounds like a good candidate. Sound judgment and all that. By all means, set up the interview. Let's scoop him up before anyone else does."

Bingo. She left the admin problem alone. As long as Conrad passed the final interview—and she hoped her hints would push him over the finish line—she didn't need to worry about finding anyone. He'd be the perfect fit.

She turned her attention to the other positions. George had tasked her with filling four more spots: Information Technology Team Lead, Acquisitions and Supplies Specialist, Strategic and Business Development Leader, and Personal Assistant.

The IT team lead was something of a misnomer. At this point, that person would be the entire team, responsible for the branch's networking, voice, video, and development needs. It would be an almost impossible spot to fill for the salary George wanted to pay.

At least, it would have been if Angela was really trying to fill it with a qualified candidate. She wasn't though.

To locate the perfect fit, she'd scoured the HR archives of rejected IT candidates. There was one name that really stuck out: Casper Caspersen. And not for the obvious reason—that it was a ridiculous name. No, Casper was flagged with a great, big red mark, and a note that warmed Angela's heart.

Terminated from prior employer for streaming pornographic images on work device during work hours, and after internal review following several missed deadlines.

If God had been testing her these last few months, like some kind of modern-day Job, it seemed her days of tribulation were over. Because Casper Caspersen picked up the phone when she cold-called, and informed her excitedly that, no, he hadn't found a position in the eight months since he'd applied; and yes, he'd be delighted to set up an interview. No, God was done testing her. He'd gone back to blessing her.

Casper Caspersen was everything she hoped he'd be, and then some. He was a walking stereotype: a lanky ginger with bad posture, pale skin, and spectacles. For most positions, that'd count against him.

But in IT? Well, when they'd talked about hiring a new IT team lead, George had told her to find a new "chief nerd—someone who knows what he's doing but isn't senior enough to ask for more than our range." Well, Casper Caspersen *looked* like a nerd. And looking the part was all the creds he'd need for George.

And it only got better as soon as he opened his mouth. He spoke in nasally tones, and as the conversation turned toward technical topics, his voice took on a touch of condescension. The fact that he liberally seasoned his speech with industry jargon and technobabble was just the cherry on top of it all.

Oh, yes. George wouldn't question his technical expertise. Casper was the right combination of awkward and arrogant to convince her boss that he must know what he was talking about.

"So, I do see a gap in your résumé," she observed after a while of his prattling. He'd been explaining how he'd configured firewalls and set up routers and built voice servers at his last company. "About a year."

"Well," he said, "eleven months, actually."

God, he's insufferable. He's going to be perfect. If he can answer these kinds of questions to George's satisfaction.

"Eleven months and two and a half weeks," she said through a tight-lipped smile. "But who is counting?"

Casper laughed nervously. "Right?"

"Would you like to explain?"

"Well..." The young man shifted in his seat. "I, uh, took some time off."

"Really?" That wasn't going to fly with Sutherland. "Just to take time off? Or did you mention on the phone that you'd been working on some kind of startup?" He hadn't, of course. But he needed something better than taking time off—or getting fired for watching porn on the job—if he was going to get past George.

"Yes. Right." He laughed, a high laugh, and wiped his palms on his pants. "I'm surprised you remembered that, actually."

She smiled. "But you didn't give me many details."

"Oh. Well, uh, I can't say too much about it."

"Why?" she asked, and when he blinked blankly at the question, she prompted, "Did you sign an NDA?"

"Oh, yes. That's it. Exactly. NDA."

"Ah. I think you mentioned it was something to do with social media, though? An up-and-coming platform?"

He shifted nervously. "Well, uh..."

"That's the kind of experience Mr. Sutherland will appreciate having on his team."

"Oh. Well, you know, I can't say much about it. But, yeah. It's—it's going to be huge."

Angela was pretty happy with Casper Caspersen by time the interview wrapped up. He'd grown more confident in his lying, until he was really owning it. Yes, George would buy it hook, line, and sinker. She'd drop a few hints that they might have the next Steve Jobs in their office, and Casper's stereotyped look and ego would do the rest.

So, she checked IT lead off her list too.

Her next pick was Kathryn Myers. She'd been let go from her last job for kleptomania. The official story was that she'd left. But her previous employer's HR mentioned that "Nothing had ever been proved...but there were a lot of thefts when Kathryn worked for us. And they all stopped when she left."

Now, Angela had never considered herself a poet. But sometimes, when the stars aligned and the universe smiled on her, magic happened. And hiring someone to Acquisitions and Supplies who had been fired for acquiring other people's property? *Pure poetry.*

Outwardly, Kathryn presented as a consummate professional. From her sharp suit to her impeccable shoes and the hair that didn't shift a centimeter when she moved, she was the picture of a respectable businesswoman.

But under the veneer lay someone with an insatiable appetite for anything that didn't belong to her. She'd never been charged, probably because she'd never targeted anything of significant value. But she was the bane of staplers, the doom of pens, the end of hole punches. Key chains and magnets, trinkets, and even potted plants: they'd all gone missing at her last place of employment.

Yes, Kathryn Myers was definitely a keeper. Angela didn't even have to coach her about what to say. She'd obviously prepared for the inevitable questions about her last job and the gap in her résumé.

"My grandfather had broken his hip, and he needed around-the-clock care. Unfortunately, no one in our family was equipped to handle it. I was the only one in a position to take an absence from my work. So, I did."

"How is your grandfather now?"

"Much better. I live in the condo across from him and Grams, so I can keep an eye on them, and do the little things—you know, shoveling the driveway, mowing the lawn, all that kind of stuff."

It was a perfect cover story. Rather than leaving under threat of termination, she'd sacrificed for her elderly grandparents. Angela was quite sure that was the kind of story George would eat right up.

Once again, her intuition proved more or less accurate. She mentioned Kathryn's impressive résumé. "There is a little gap in her work history, but I don't think it's a problem."

"Oh?"

"Her grandfather had broken bones and needed care. Ms. Myers didn't want to send him to an assisted living facility. She wasn't sure her grandmother would have survived that separation."

Sutherland nodded. "Well, that's as good a reason as any, I suppose. It won't be a problem moving forward, will it?"

"What?"

"The grandfather—she won't be quitting out of the blue to take care of him again, will she? I mean, he's not going to be getting *younger*."

"Oh...no, I don't think so. I don't think, uh, her situation would make that feasible."

"Good. Character is everything. I always say that. It's the most important quality in an employee. It's what builds your workplace. Skills can be trained into someone, but character? That's out-of-the-box. It's either there, or not.

"But, still, you don't want to lose a good employee six months down the road. Part of character is respecting all your commitments, and your work family."

"Absolutely. That sounded like a matter of life and death. And—well, if I can be blunt, George?"

He flashed her a smile. "Always, Angie."

"Well, she wasn't working for Sutherland. She didn't say anything, of course, but you know how it is. Good leadership fosters that sense of family."

He considered her words, then nodded. "True. Well, her résumé sounds perfect. Set up the interview."

★

George Maxwell Sutherland, Jr. tapped his fingers on his desk nervously. It was three past seven. Andy Gilmore should have called already. They'd said seven, hadn't they?

What was the delay, then? He'd sent the plans this morning. That should have been plenty of time to review them.

So where the hell is he?

It had been three and a half weeks since Caruso showed up in Fenwood, and George was feeling the strain of every minute. He didn't quite know what Joey Caruso did. He was an enforcer. That was clear.

But did he confine himself to being vaguely menacing, as he had so far with George? Probably not. Did he go as far as kneecapping and bodies in the river?

Well, he was Italian. George didn't consider himself bigoted, exactly. He had an off-color sense of humor, that was all. He'd describe himself as "not very PC." It had gotten him in trouble now and then—oddly enough, with his dad more than anyone else.

The elder Sutherland didn't have a sense of humor, and he spent way too much time trying not to offend people. George's philosophy was different.

Offense wasn't given, it was taken. If someone got bent out of shape over a few words, or a simple joke, that was their problem. He couldn't censor himself for other people's volatile emotions.

At least, he would not censor himself where the threat of a lawsuit didn't come into play. George tended to be a bit more circumspect in the workplace, if only to save Sutherland Research problems.

All at once, his video chat application rang. Despite expecting the call—indeed, waiting impatiently for it—George started.

He'd been thinking of Caruso, and lawsuits, and cement shoes—all of which rather put him on edge.

He tapped the incoming call icon. A bland face with bland features and a head full of bland, sandy-brown hair appeared on his screen. The bland man was Andy Gilmore, of Gilmore and Sons Pharmaceuticals. Andy was one of the sons originally referenced in the company name, but by now, the titular Gilmore had long retired. And, despite being only two years older than George, Andy Gilmore had assumed the reins of his father's company a good decade ago and remained at its helm since.

The unjustness of that particular ordering of the universe was not lost on the younger Sutherland. But he managed a thin-lipped smile all the same. "Andrew."

"George, how are you?"

But George wasn't in the mood to play at civilities. "I take it the research was what you needed?"

Andy smiled too. "Top notch, as always. Your people do such good work. It's always a pleasure doing business with you."

George grimaced. A pleasure that didn't exactly cut both ways, these days. Not when Caruso was stationed nearby, bringing with him all the threat that that implied. "Yeah. Just remember—no immunizations. You can use it for whatever you want outside of that. But my dad's going to get suspicious if you keep beating him to the market on the same projects."

Andy raised his palms in a placating manner. Even through a screen, George could feel his smarminess. "I told you. Your assets are safe. Gilmores keep their word. Always."

George snorted, not loud enough to actively challenge the assertion, but just enough to leave Andy wondering if he'd actually heard something. "And you can call your pit bull back now?"

"Joey?" Andy's eyes widened in faux surprise. "He mentioned you'd been acting a little off. You didn't think...? Well, you know we sent him to help you, right? Make sure no one got in your way. I hope it didn't come across as anything else?"

George stared daggers into his camera. "Yeah, he was a big help. Stalking around bumfuck nowhere looking like an extra on a bad mobster set. That didn't draw unneces-sary attention."

Andy smiled. "It's a free country, George. People can go where they like. Anyway, he tells me you have quite the farm country out there. He's a bovine enthusiast. Did you know that? I didn't even know that was a thing. But to each their own, right?"

George wasn't amused, and he said nothing. In an-other circumstance, his answer would have been a lot more forceful than silence. But Andy Gilmore, prick though he was, had bailed him out of tight spots more than once. And Andy Gilmore had enough dirt to bury him for a hundred lifetimes.

Not that that was a one-way street. George was no fool. He'd collected enough to put Gilmore away for dec-ades, just in case. *Call it an insurance plan.* But you didn't sit down with the devil without some kind of exit strategy.

And Andy Gilmore was the devil. George knew how to bend the rules, and when. He'd figured out how to look after himself when George Sr. seemed to forget his son was no longer a boy. Andy had been invaluable there. He'd thrown him a lifeline when George had overextended his credit. He'd helped him get back on his feet and made him rich again.

All without George Sr. being the wiser.

And Andy had made out just fine in the process. Gil-more Pharmaceuticals had been able to forego years of re-search. They'd beat companies all across the globe to mar-ket with some of the decades' most cutting-edge drugs. So far, they'd maintained a good balance: stealing some of the revenue from Sutherland Research's work but avoid-ing their primary projects.

George had had to go toe-to-toe with Andy once or twice on that score. But they both benefited from the gravy train. Dry that up, and, well, no more gravy for anyone. A strong, healthy Sutherland Research was mutually beneficial.

But now, change was in the wind. George Sr. was looking to retire. He hadn't said anything directly, but he'd been dropping hints.

And the younger Sutherland had a pretty good idea those hints had made their way back to Andy. And that was the reason Andy had sent Joey Caruso, in turn. It was the reason he was being so damned jumpy lately.

Andy knew how these things worked. It had been in George's best interests when he was but a cog in his father's machine to siphon off some of the company wealth since he was getting such a big cut of the stolen intel. But when he ran the machine?

Well, things changed. And his interests would shift with it. Which brought George back to the point about Andy being the devil. How did you walk away from the devil?

Gilmore Pharmaceuticals was infamous for its brutal acquisitions and corporate dominance, most of which could be attributed to Andy's particular brand of cunning and ruthlessness. Andy knew business, and he knew people. He knew how to persuade people, how to play them, and when to crush them.

Which, in turn, was where George's insurance policy came into play. That would protect him, when the time came, from the other man's wrath. That would convince Andy Gilmore that, though their partnership had been mutually beneficial, it would be in both of their interests to walk away on friendly terms.

But in the meantime, it wouldn't do to piss him off. So George smiled through Gilmore's lies and nodded when it seemed right.

No, he wasn't mad about Caruso.

Sure, he understood Andy needed to protect his investment.

No, he hadn't realized he could call on Joey at any time if he needed anything. That was thoughtful.

And he'd try to have a good day. "You too, Andy."

"Great. Talk to you soon."

And with that, the conversation ended. George Jr. let out a breath of relief. No, he had no intention of pissing Andy off. Until he wasn't, he'd be behind him all the way.

After all, that was the best position to be in when you intended to put a knife in someone's back.

Chapter Six

Angela and her friends had met up at Marty's again. And, it was margarita night again. This time, though, she vowed to drink sensibly. No more hangovers.

Rae applauded her decision. "Good. You're bad enough on your own, but you two drunk together? I'm surprised we didn't get thrown out last time."

It was a bit of an exaggeration, but they'd certainly had fun too. Now, though, Angela had no intention of slipping. She was a woman on a mission, and she couldn't allow herself to slip up. She had to be on top of her game and two steps ahead of George Sutherland at all times.

"Well?" Lauren prodded. "How's Operation Payback going?"

Rae laughed as Angela grinned ear-to-ear. "Oh, no. You mean, you really are going through with it?"

"I told you she would," Lauren said. "And I'm glad. Someone needs to knock that son of a bitch down a peg or two."

"Well," Angela said with a smile that was just a touch smug, "I am assembling a crack team that will, I think, do exactly that."

Her friends exchanged glances.

Lauren laughed maliciously. "Well? You know we need the deets."

Angela took a long sip from her margarita, letting them stew in their curiosity for a bit. Was she savoring the moment? Yes, definitely. She'd been planning and quietly executing her diabolical scheme for so many days she had to allow herself a little bit of suspense before the reveal. That's how it went in the movies, anyway, whether it was the villain or the hero making the dramatic announcement. She hoped, in this case, she was on the side of the heroes, albeit probably one of the masked vigilante crusaders—a Zorro or Batman. Or, in her case, probably a Darkwing Duck: on the side of right, but a little ridiculous all the same.

Hmm. Maybe I should slow down on the margaritas. Angela had gotten here half an hour earlier than her friends and had already worked her way through one and a half of these things. She had a self-imposed limit, but that hadn't stopped her from racing toward it.

She shook these musings away like cobwebs clinging to her brain. "Well, I've already found an admin and an acquisitions and supplies lead."

"You have?" Lauren's eyebrows rose. "Already?"

"Yup. And an IT team lead."

"Wow." Rae nodded. "Impressive."

"Well?" her friend demanded. "Tell us about them."

Angela smiled, satisfied by the enthusiasm and interest. "Well, the IT guy was fired from his last job for failing to meet deadlines and streaming porn on the job."

Rae wrinkled her nose. "Eww."

Lauren laughed though. "Perfect."

"And the supply specialist was forced out under a cloud of suspicion because she's a kleptomaniac."

Rae shook her head, and Lauren chortled and clapped her hands together. "Oh my God. Remind me never to piss you off, Angela."

The comment had been offered in humor, and Angela's grin deepened. "As far as the admin, well...he's rude, short-tempered, and impatient."

"Perfect qualities in an administrative secretary."

"Right?" She laughed. "And he seems to think the job will be easy."

Rae groaned. "Right. Let him actually do it, and then see what he thinks."

"Especially when he's working with George. Mr. 'I won't tell you about my meetings until I yell at you because I'm late getting to them.'"

For a while, the three women discussed these picks and laughed about how delightfully awful they were.

"But what about the others? There are still a few more positions you need to fill, aren't there?" Lauren asked.

Angela nodded again. "That's right. Sutherland still needs a PA. And I need to find the right Strategic and Business Development Leader."

"Any prospects?"

"A few. I mean, a few of the candidates have the usual weaknesses—miserable spelling, inattention to detail, damned by faint praise from their last jobs. But..."

Again, she paused for dramatic effect.

"Dammit," Lauren snapped, laughing as she said, "Enough. I've been waiting since last week for this. No more suspense."

"She has, too," Rae sighed. "She couldn't believe you wouldn't tell her last weekend."

"I was busy. Anyway, I had to get my ducks in a row."

"To hell with ducks. I'm your best friend. You tell your friend about your damned ducks."

Angela didn't quite know what to do with that mangled metaphor, so she let it go. "What I mean is, it had to be perfect. I wasn't even sure I could pull it off."

"Yes, yes, I've heard these excuses. I don't agree, and I'm not sure I'll ever be able to look at you the same." Lauren cracked a grin. "But, if you've any hope of earning my forgiveness, telling me everything is a good start."

"Please," Rae beseeched, "so she can find something else to talk about. Not that I'm not interested too. But I'd like to talk about something else sometimes."

Lauren shushed her wife and prodded Angela to continue.

"My prize PA candidate got arrested for slugging his boss," she said. "On the job."

This was too much even for Rae's cool composure. Lauren hooted and clapped, and she barked out a laugh. "Damn, girl. You're going to get that man killed."

That gave Angela a moment's pause. She'd read the few news articles she could find. They'd been sparse on details, but it sounded like Matt Kilbourne—the candidate—had finally had enough and snapped. He seemed like exactly the kind of guy she wanted in close, constant proximity to George Sutherland, Jr. "No, of course not. He's not *dangerous* violent. Just, apparently, the boss liked to harass people. And he knocked him out cold."

"That's brilliant," Lauren said. "Perfect. Oh, I'd love to hear about George getting knocked out cold."

"Me too," Angela admitted. "But the candidate probably learned his lesson. Still, if he was willing to clock someone before, even if he'll keep his hands to himself now...well, he's not going to be easy to work with."

"No."

"He sounds perfect," Rae said.

"I do have a few other interviews lined up, in case he's not. But," Angela added with a smirk, "I've got high hopes."

Rae shook her head and took a sip of her beer. "Dare I ask what you have in mind for the other spot? Strategy or whatever?"

"Strategic and Business Development Leader."

"Right," Rae said. "What's he? Ex-con? Part-time pyromaniac?"

Angela laughed. "No. Actually, my top candidate—on paper anyway—is a woman for that one. She's been working as an independent contractor since leaving her last job."

"Oh? I assume there's a story there."

Angela smiled. "Oh, yes. She'd applied last year, and there was a red flag on the application, but not much detail. Just said 'interpersonal issues.' I had a very nice chat with the HR lady at her last job. Her work, from the sounds of it, is all right. But her personality is anything but. Even to her bosses."

The actual conversation had been an interesting one. The woman on the other end of the phone, a sweet-voiced, youngish-sounding person called Caroline, had sighed when she tried to describe the reasons for Heather Bradshaw's departure. *"Well, imagine yourself working with a drill sergeant. Or a Nazi. Only, less friendly. That's what being around Heather was like. Not that I personally worked with her. But—well, suffice it to say, there were plenty who were relieved to see her go. And not just her peers or subordinates.*

"But I can't fault her work. She was, by all accounts, reasonably proficient and very punctual. I heard very few complaints on that front."

Caroline in HR had covered the whole spectrum of putdowns in their short conversation, from klaxons-blaring, *Danger Will Robinson*, to damning with faint praise.

But Angela owed Caroline, and her retinue of slams. If Heather was half as promising as she sounded, she'd make George's life a living hell.

She couldn't tell her friends all of this, of course. There were some degrees of confidentiality that even she had to respect. But she told them what she could, and they all agreed that Heather was, indeed, a promising prospect.

"And what about your dad?" Rae asked after a while.

"Oh, he's ecstatic about the whole thing. He wants me to quit sooner rather than later. He's sure I'll be happier when I'm 'out of the rat race.' I tried explaining that llama races weren't any better..." Angela shrugged, and her friends laughed.

Llama racing was one of the children's attractions at her family farm. The llamas didn't actually race. Half the time, they didn't even walk. But, if they felt cooperative, they'd start at one end of the minitrack, and race, or saunter, or make their way a few steps at a time, toward the carrots or apples at the other end. It didn't particularly matter if they ran or plopped down. They provided endless, adorable entertainment for spectators.

And, like any other animal, a lot of poop for the farm workers to clean up.

Again, Angela shook herself. She didn't want to think about that. She didn't want to think about animal poop, or farming, or anything else. She had a mission right now. And that was to make George Sutherland pay for forcing her into this situation. If she was going to have to muck out stables, well, dammit, he was going to have to deal with shit on a daily basis too.

"Oh," Lauren exclaimed, pulling her from her thoughts. "I almost forgot."

"Oh, no," Rae groaned, as if she knew what her wife was about to say.

Lauren frowned at her. "*You* were supposed to remind me."

"Oops."

"Oops my ass." She shook her head, turning back to Angela. "Anyway, no thanks to her, I have good news."

"Sorry, Angela. I tried," Rae said.

"Oh, no. Now I'm really worried."

Lauren shushed her wife with a playful smack of the hand. "You stop it. And you haven't even heard what I'm going to tell you, Angela."

"No, but I've got a good idea. You're just like your mother." Mrs. Ellis was the world's sweetest busybody, always trying to solve other people's problems. Whether they wanted them solved or not.

"She is," Rae exclaimed. "I told her that this morning."

Lauren frowned at first one, then the other. "You shut your mouth, Rae Grant, unless you want to be sleeping on the couch. And you, Angela McCormack, shut yours, too, and listen to me. We met someone at church yesterday."

Angela groaned, but Lauren paid her no mind.

"She's a lesbian, I'm sure of it. I could tell by looking."

"You mean, you Facebook stalked her," her wife put in.

"Well, that too. But only after I guessed. And her profile is covered in queer stuff. She's definitely a lesbian. But the best part is—"

"Don't," Angela protested. "We've had this conversation already."

"Yes, but that was before. Her name is Nikki Fulton. She's single, and she's about your age—"

"She's younger," Rae put in.

This earned her a fierce look from Lauren, and Angela shook her head.

"You know I don't date younger women."

"You can't say that. You haven't even met her."

"Nor do I plan to."

"Come on. You can't isolate yourself forever. You can't be alone forever."

Angela considered for a moment, and then shook her head. "Actually, I can. I've got my friends and—even when they *are* pains in the asses—that's more than enough."

"Oh bullshit. That's never enough."

Rae started to speak, and Angela flashed her a grateful glance for what was, she assumed, an intervention on her behalf. The relief disappeared though, when Rae continued. "Look, Angela, I know Lauren can be quite a pain in the ass about this—"

"Hey."

"But she's not wrong."

"Oh, God, not you too?"

"All I'm saying is, She-Who-Shall-Not-Be-Named isn't worth it. She never was, she sure as hell isn't now."

Angela glared at her two friends. "It's not about Carrie. I've told you how many times, I'm over that. I'm over—her."

It was true, more or less. Carrie was her ex, and she was as over her as anyone ever could be over someone they'd loved and thought they'd be spending the rest of their lives with. She'd gotten over the lying, and the cheating, and the feeling of betrayal too. But that didn't mean she was ready to risk her heart again. It didn't mean she'd *ever* want to risk that again.

"Then what?" Rae asked.

"I just...I don't want to deal with it all again."

"Oh, Angela." Lauren took her hand. "It's been five years. You've got to start living your life again."

"Look, I'm in the middle of changing jobs. Sabotaging my shithead boss. Don't you think my life is complicated enough without *inviting* trouble?"

Lauren started to speak, but Rae touched a hand to hers, and she paused.

Rae said in slow, measured tones, "Maybe it's not the right time. But, hell, it wasn't the right time for me, either, when Lauren and I met. I was trying to finish my degree. And I still wasn't a 100 percent over Jacklyn."

Lauren leaned into her wife's arm, smiling tenderly at her. "She wasn't either."

"But here we are. And I'm damned glad I didn't listen to the voice that told me it was the wrong time."

Angela drained her margarita. "Look, maybe once this is all done you can introduce us, okay? But I can't be thinking about dates and shit now."

Lauren smiled broadly and nodded. "Deal."

She grimaced at her friend's exuberance. "I didn't say you *could*. I said maybe. I'll think about it."

"Too late. No backing out now. Once you're out of there, I'm setting something up."

Rae smiled. "Oh, Lord. Season One of *The Matchmaker*, starring Lauren Grant-Ellis, is about to commence."

Chapter Seven

She knew Lauren meant well. But Angela would have preferred not ending her night with Carrie on her mind. Hell, if it was up to her, she'd never think of Carrie again.

They'd met in college in her junior year and dated for a year and a half before they graduated. Carrie had gotten a degree in graphic design but had never managed to find the right employment fit for her skills. Companies either didn't pay enough, or didn't respect her artistic vision, or weren't the right *feel* for her. That was very important. The *feel* of a company told her all she needed to know, and if she got a bad feeling, well, she couldn't work there.

When Angela had landed a good job in her hometown, Carrie moved with her. They talked about getting married, although her girlfriend wanted to wait awhile, just long enough to really establish herself.

She worked on and off as a barista—while she searched for the right job—at Lauren's coffee shop, or a few of the local diners. But they never quite worked out either. There were always reasons why: hostile coworkers, or bad auras, or the work just didn't inspire her.

It was bullshit. On some level, Angela had always known that. But she didn't mind. Carrie was smart and gifted, and she loved her. If her girlfriend hated the day-to-day grind, well, they didn't need the money.

Would it have helped, especially with all the money her fixer-upper historical home needed? Sure. But they didn't *need* it. The projects could take a little longer. And she was in a position to support them both, so why not?

If Angela had any complaint on that front, it was that she'd have preferred honest communication. But Carrie struggled with that. She didn't always express herself. She kept her thoughts and feelings bottled up, and close to the vest. It was just part of who her girlfriend was, and she'd accepted that, even when it bothered her.

So when Carrie reconnected via social media with an old high school flame, Angela didn't immediately notice anything out of the ordinary. The first clue had been the change in her texting habits—the way she'd shield her phone when Angela glanced at her, or smile at the screen when a message popped up.

But Angela loved her, and when she'd asked about it and Carrie had assured her that nothing was up, she refused to think about it anymore. She trusted her girlfriend. Relationships were built on trust, weren't they? Of course she'd trusted Carrie.

She'd trusted her when she had to take three trips to Los Angeles in as many months to meet up with old friends. *"No partners allowed, just the old group getting together."*

Lauren and Rae hadn't believed her. But Angela did. Because she trusted her girlfriend.

The emotional distance wasn't so easy to ignore though. It started slowly. Carrie withdrew, a little at a time. It got worse after each trip. But when Angela asked if everything was all right, Carrie would assure her it was. Sometimes, she'd get annoyed by the question.

It hadn't been long until there was a wall between them, which no amount of Angela's affection or love or trying could get over.

And not soon after, Carrie was moving out, with recriminations about being dragged to the middle of nowhere. She didn't see herself as being in the wrong. She might have been the one cheating, but Angela had ruined her life. Angela had dragged her to Fenwood—*Fenwood, for God's sake!*—away from her friends and family, away from civilization. She had sunk their money into *a piece-of-shit house.* And it was Angela's fault she'd never found steady employment because there was nothing decent in Fenwood. It was a *goddamned Podunk town. Who the hell is going to find design work here*?

No, as far as Carrie was concerned, she'd spent years suffering and sacrificing for Angela, and she was done.

Carrie left to move in with her ex, a doctor living in Los Angeles. Unsurprisingly, she was the person she'd been flying out to meet for those "no partners allowed" trips. They were engaged within six months and had been married for four years.

And as far as Angela knew, their lives were perfect. Carrie had a nice, new penthouse apartment, a sports car, and an endless supply of entertainments and occupations. Carrie was happy.

And Angela? Well, Angela had made good strides at not being miserable. She'd spent a lot of time in the beginning wondering how the woman she loved could have changed so much, and how she could rationalize all the things she'd done.

But then she'd come to the conclusion that it didn't matter. It didn't matter if Carrie had changed somewhere along the way, or if Angela just hadn't seen who she really was. What mattered were the choices her ex had made, not the internal motivations behind them.

And once Angela understood that, she stopped pondering the what-ifs. She stopped trying to figure out how she might have changed things, if only she'd done this differently or that differently.

She didn't hate Carrie. She'd loved her too much for that. Hate would have been a darker, uglier face of those old feelings. She didn't want to hang on to any of them. She wanted to be free. She'd moved on. But moving on didn't mean she wanted to think about it. There was no sense opening old wounds.

Still, sleep had been long in coming that night as her mind took a detour down memory lane, lingering on times-gone-by that she would have much sooner forgotten.

When Angela rose the next morning, she had dark circles under her eyes. *I've got to stop doing margarita night. Even when I don't end up with a hangover, it's hell.*

After arming herself with a full thermos of coffee and donning her favorite flats—Angela was in no humor for anything but sensible footwear—she headed out the door.

George was in a good mood. He was early, too, which was a frightening combination. To be happy and eager to be at work usually meant he was up to something awful. Angela wondered vaguely who would get the chop today, and if it would be her. There'd be something ironic in that, wouldn't there? If she'd spent these last few weeks plotting against him while he was really coming for her?

But it seemed no one was getting the chop. George glanced up when he saw her. "Good morning, Angie. You look a little rough." He winked. "Margarita night?"

She forced a smile. "Am I that predictable?"

He laughed at that. "You are. But you know I love it. I'm a whiskey guy myself. But, maybe one of these nights I'll have to join you for margaritas."

She made a lukewarm comment about that being "great," and tried to escape to her own office. But George ambled over from the coffee maker and blocked her path.

"I brought donuts."

"Oh? Any special occasion?"

He shrugged. "Just felt like it."

"Oh. Well, uh, thanks."

"Yeah. Make sure you grab one. I made sure they put a maple long john in there. That's your favorite, right?" She blinked at the question, and he shrugged again. "I remember you mentioning it when Steve brought donuts in."

"Oh. Well, uh, yes, it is. Thanks."

He smiled. "Well...I guess I should get back to it. The day beckons."

"Right." She sidled past him and felt his eyes on her. She made a point to stop by the box of donuts and select the one he'd picked out for her. "Thanks again."

"Of course."

She was glad to round the corner and escape his gaze. *What in God's name has gotten into him?* She had many complaints about George Maxwell Sutherland, Jr., but creepy wasn't usually one of them. Yes, she'd caught him staring at her ass once or twice or glancing down her blouse. Still, for the most part, he kept his creepy side to himself.

But whatever the hell had been running through his mind this morning? Well, the whole thing had been creepy.

She set the donut aside as soon as she reached her office and shut the door after her. Hopefully, that would be signal enough for him to keep away.

It wasn't. He'd stopped by twice that morning, ostensibly to inquire about the candidate recruitment process the first time, and to ask her advice on a business lunch meeting the next day.

But he'd lingered longer than necessary both times and mentioned more than once what a good day it was. She came no closer to discovering the source for this suddenly cheerful—and creepy—side of her boss.

But she was grateful when her first interviewee arrived.

Matt Kilbourne was a mountain of a man, with a neatly trimmed hipster-style beard, and a shoulder span that would have shamed the average quarterback. He stood well over six feet tall and wore a cheap but well-fitting suit.

He was probably five years younger than her and called her "ma'am." She didn't hate him for it, even if it did make her feel a bit like a grandma. He was polite almost to a fault, and she couldn't tell if his manners were genuine or practiced. They seemed at odds with the picture she'd formed in her mind of the man who'd beaten his boss senseless.

She led him to a conference room with the usual pleasantries and got him talking.

He'd had a good trip up. "Thank you for asking."

He lived about two hours away, but if he got the job, he'd find a place to rent. He'd already done some scouting of the local apartments and found some good prospects.

No, he'd never been to Fenwood. "Drove past it a few times, but never been."

Yes, it was a beautiful day. "Feels like summer already."

He'd wondered how her day was going, in turn, and if she could recommend anywhere to eat in the area.

They settled into easy conversation in this manner, and she steered it back toward his credentials and the job.

He'd served in the army prior to pursuing a corporate career. "Medical discharge, purple heart." He tapped his leg. "We got hit by an explosive. I was jettisoned from the vehicle. Broke my femur in five spots, but I lived." He grinned. "Magnets love me now, but not airport security."

"That must have been terrifying."

"Little bit. But I was lucky. We all were. A few broken bones, some shrapnel wounds. But no fatalities that day."

His motives for being a PA were simple—*a little too simple for George's liking*. "To be honest, I kind of stumbled into the work. One of my buddies knew a guy who was hiring, and he recommended me for the job. I thought I'd hate it, but I actually didn't. Turns out I was pretty good at it."

Not exactly a glowing recommendation. "Why did you leave that job?"

"It was a temporary position. Like this one."

"What about your time with Vita Health?" Her tone hadn't fluctuated at all, but she watched him with an eaglelike sharpness. "Would you like to tell me about that?"

He shifted. "Well, I was Mr. Smith's personal assistant. He was the chief information officer."

"So I gathered."

"And...well, I suppose what you're really asking is why I got fired?"

She nodded. "And arrested."

"I punched him in the face. Broke his nose and knocked out a tooth."

She blinked. "Okay. And...any reason?"

"Yes. A good one. But...well, I'd rather not talk about it."

Angela crossed her arms. "I don't really think that's an option, Mr. Kilbourne. Not if you want to work here. Or, anywhere really."

He sighed and ran a hand through his hair. "He...he used to harass a friend of mine. Make inappropriate comments, joke about her appearance in a—well, in a sexual way."

"And you couldn't report that to HR? You thought hitting him was the most appropriate response?"

"I did report it. They must have talked to him because he made her life a living hell for weeks. But nothing came of it. He kept his job. And he kept harassing her."

He looked away from Angela and swallowed. "Well, one day, he grabbed her by the... Well, he put his hands on her posterior. And I clocked him."

Angela was almost disappointed. He was definitely not shaping up to be the erratic loose cannon she'd hoped. "Really?"

He nodded. "I can get you the police report. It'll verify everything I'm telling you."

"Tell me what happened after that."

"Well, I ended up getting arrested. My friend was going to press charges against Smith, but agreed not to if he dropped them against me. The company—finally—let him go, with a nice severance package. I lost my job on the spot. And a few months later, they *downsized* my friend's position."

Dammit. This wasn't going at all the way she wanted. She'd hoped to find someone erratic and irrational. Instead, her candidate was shaping up to be a perfectly decent guy who'd broken the rules, sure, but in good cause. And she, of all people, certainly could not fault someone for taking matters into their own hands.

"Well, I'm sorry. Very sorry."

He nodded. "Me too. She found a job in New York, and she loves it. Which is good. But she shouldn't have had to."

Angela shifted in her seat uneasily. She contemplated the odds that he was lying. Lying would be good. Lying would mean he was capable of spinning an elaborate story and telling it convincingly. She imagined George dealing with that for a while, and the imagery sat quite nicely.

But something told her Matt wasn't lying. Sure, her background check results would be available by midafternoon, and she'd be able to confirm or deny several of the salient points. But everything she'd read corresponded to what he'd told her. And everything she knew of the corporate world, and the way it worked? Well, it couldn't confirm his story, but it surely didn't raise any red flags either.

All of which made her uncomfortable. She wanted to find terrible candidates. Matt Kilbourne wasn't a terrible candidate. On the contrary, she was disposed to consider him a very good applicant, all things considered. He had the requisite experience and skillset. And he didn't think twice about slugging a predator, even if the predator was his boss. He could have been better at talking himself up, but she wasn't going to hold not being a good liar or bullshitter against anyone.

No, all of that recommended him highly to her. Except, she wasn't looking for a good candidate. *Dammit.*

She decided to try another tactic. "Well, you know, this is only a temporary gig? A year or less, depending on how long Mr. Sutherland is required at this branch."

He nodded. "I know. I understood from the ad, though, that there might be the possibility of staying on long-term, when Mr. Sutherland's position is filled with a permanent candidate?"

"Yes…" She shifted. "But that's up to the discretion of the new CEO. You know how it is—sometimes they like to bring in their own staff, or find a new candidate. Everyone's work style is a little different."

"Ah. Gotcha. Well, I'd still like to apply. To be honest, after the Vita Health business, finding work hasn't been easy. You're the first callback I've gotten in six months. Which, I suppose, I probably shouldn't tell you. But that's the truth of it. I'd be good for the job, Miss McCormack. I've got the experience, I know what I'm doing, and I'm a hard worker.

Matt looked Angela directly in the eye. "I know a lot of people see that arrest and think I don't deserve a chance. But..." He scrutinized her for a long moment. "You gave me an opportunity to explain. I'm not sure why. But I appreciate it. And if Sutherland Research gives me a shot, too, well, you won't find a better employee."

Chapter Eight

Angela McCormack sat scowling at her desk. Matt Kilbourne's background check bore out his story. And that, frankly, pissed her off. She wanted a reason to give the job to someone who didn't deserve it but who would suit her purposes.

Try as she could, she couldn't quite justify denying the job to a qualified candidate who'd only lost his previous employment by defending another employee. *And a wounded vet, on top of that. Dammit.*

She'd given him a few pointers on how to present his case to Sutherland. George was one of those men who flattered himself that he wanted nothing but the truth. But like everyone, he wanted truth to reflect his own reality, and he expected a degree of happy horseshit.

He wouldn't want to hear that his PA fell into the work. He'd want to hear that a grown man who'd served his country had, in turn, felt compelled to be his personal assistant as a kind of higher calling.

He'd want to hear that Matt Kilbourne couldn't think of a better way to make the world a better place than to bring him his coffee and arrange his schedule and draft his letters or run his errands for him. He'd want to hear how helping him furthered the company's goals and brought lifesaving innovations to the world. He'd expect the whole unicorns and rainbows spin.

Matt had accepted her feedback—filtered rather heavily from her brain to her mouth—with a solemn nod, and a few *Yes ma'ams*.

Now, Angela stewed on the prospect of her perfect scheme being disrupted. *Dammit. Why'd he have to apply at Sutherland's? Why not somewhere else?*

It would have been one thing to lose a position like acquisitions specialist. Sure, Kathryn would deliver her own brand of hell. But the PA would be one of the most critical roles in her sabotage.

And yet, for all that, she couldn't bring herself to deny the job to Kilbourne. If she hadn't met him, if she didn't know what she knew, it would have been a different story. She might well have already turned away a dozen Kilbournes in her stack of rejected applications.

But it was different to *know* that she was doing it. She couldn't knowingly, in good conscience, reject an applicant in these kind of circumstances. Which was why she was good and pissed off.

Still, Angela's mind reasoned, there could be advantages. It would allay suspicion if at least *one* of her hires wasn't absolutely awful. It would make it harder for Sutherland to guess her purpose in that case. And if he guessed her scheme, he'd probably fire the lot of them. This way, it would be a protracted paring down of his staff, one bad actor at a time.

It was cold comfort, but it was all she had. So, feeling somewhat sullen, she headed to her next interview. This was Heather Bradshaw, she of the impeccable résumé and appalling personality.

And that prospect, at least, improved her mood. If hired, Heather would be working closely with George. And if she was half as bad as Caroline from HR had made out, that would be quite the punishment for Mr. Sutherland.

Angela found a tall woman, impeccably dressed in a tailored suit that did nothing to diminish her fine figure, and short heels that achieved the holy grail of women's footwear: practical yet stylish. She glanced up with cool blue eyes that rather took Angela by surprise. They were probably her best feature but certainly not the only remarkable one. Her nose and cheekbones were delicate in their proportions but sharp in their angles. When she smiled, dainty lips parted to reveal perfect, sparkling white teeth. Her jet-black hair was pulled back in a stylish way that was at once flattering and very professional. She was remarkable, not with an effusive, warm kind of beauty, but with an aloof, frosty allure.

She wore no nail polish or rings. Indeed, she wore no jewelry at all, except a pair of tiny diamond studs in her ears. She was the picture of understated elegance, and cool confidence.

She stood and extended a hand to Angela. "Ms. McCormack?" Her voice was firm but congenial.

"Call me Angela. You must be Heather Bradshaw?"

The dark-haired woman smiled. "That's right. A pleasure to meet you."

Without meaning to, Angela found herself smiling too. There was something disarming about the other woman. If she hadn't already had some idea of what to expect from Caroline, she might have formed a very different picture of Heather Bradshaw. As it was, though, she reminded herself of what she was dealing with.

A Nazi, but less friendly. That was what Caroline had called her. "The pleasure's all mine. Welcome to Sutherland Bio Research."

★

The interview ran long. Angela could not fault Heather's experience, and, to her credit, the other woman maintained a cool and collected demeanor throughout the interview. Unlike the other candidates, those she'd had to coach and lead, Bradshaw needed no such help.

She spoke with confidence and ease about her past work, and had no problem making a case for why she was right for Sutherland.

Indeed, her pitch was so perfect it left Angela a little discombobulated. She'd expected some kind of tell, some kind of giveaway that she was dealing with someone who was less fun to work with than a drill sergeant. But she'd gotten none.

The closest she'd come was when she asked, "Tell me, I see you've been working as a freelancer for a bit. But before that, you'd been at Northwest Medical Research for five years. Why did you leave?"

Heather crossed her legs and sat back in her seat. "I moved, for personal reasons, and I needed a position with a little more flexibility." Then she smiled, but the expression seemed to be more practiced and less natural than before. "Northwest needed us to be onsite all the time, and that wasn't practical for my new situation."

"Ah." Angela studied her for a moment. There was evasiveness in those cool blue eyes. Heather didn't want to divulge more than she'd already said. For half a second, Angela thought about leaving it there.

But leaving things alone wasn't her role. She was in human resources. Her job was to sniff out the problems before they became her company's problems. Or, in this case, so that they could become her company's problem. "Do you have family in the state, then?"

She nodded. "My parents and my brother."

"Ah." That was disappointingly not sinister. "Well, it's good to be around family."

"Exactly. I'm excited about Sutherland for a lot of reasons, but personally—selfishly—one of the big perks is how close it brings me to my family. I'm within a hundred miles of all of them."

"Oh. Well, that's awesome. My parents actually live in Fenwood."

"Oh? Really?"

"Yes."

"That must be wonderful."

Angela considered, then nodded. "Yes, it mostly is. I mean, it's a mixed blessing sometimes. It means I get a lot more of those, 'Angie, why won't The Netflix load?' questions."

"'The Netflix'?" Heather repeated with a laugh.

"Yes. My dad is convinced everything to do with his TV or phone should be preceded by a 'the.' 'The Netflix,' 'The ESPN,' and so on."

Heather laughed again. "That's pretty awesome, actually. My dad won't even try. He's got his own TV, and he watches one channel, and that's that."

Angela laughed too. "See, I think that's what my mom would do, if Dad didn't forge ahead, and at least *try* to figure things out." Then she shrugged. "Although, to be honest, she probably wouldn't even leave it on a channel. She'd probably still be watching her VHS collection."

"Oh, God. Your mom and my dad sound like twins. He was quite upset when my mom upgraded to DVDs decades ago. He still talks about it."

"Mom too. She was sure Dad had made a terrible mistake."

"Every time one of his discs scratches, he points out that 'VHS didn't scratch. If I had my old videos, this wouldn't be a problem.'"

Angela nodded along. It was a familiar refrain. "When her dog was a puppy, it grabbed a Blu-ray disc off the coffee table and chewed it up. She insisted that wouldn't have happened with a video because they're stronger."

Heather smiled, and Angela sat back in her chair, staring at this seemingly perfect model of a woman. She tried to ignore the weight in her stomach, and the little voice of warning in her head.

Something was wrong—but that was okay, wasn't it? She wanted wrong, didn't she?

Chapter Nine

She wasn't sure how, but Angela had lost sight of her original line of inquiry. When the interview was over, she promised to be in touch within the next few days.

Heather flashed her an endearing smile and shook her hand warmly. "I look forward to hearing from you. Have a great day, Angela. It was a pleasure meeting you."

Angela had to remind herself that Heather was a drill sergeant. A charming one, perhaps, but underneath that professional exterior was a devil to work with. All of which, of course, was exactly what she wanted. The interview with George would be a breeze. Heather had the expertise and professionalism to ace that. It'd only be after that, once George got stuck working with her, that her true colors would come out.

No, Heather Bradshaw was the perfect candidate. Which meant Angela had her dream team picked out. All that remained was getting them past the last hurdle: George Maxwell Sutherland, Jr.

Angela had scheduled the first interview for eight o'clock in the morning on Friday. That was Kathryn's interview. George yawned into his hand as he arrived, but straightened his suit when Kathryn Myers walked in. He was all smiles, but not quite alert enough to care much about background questions.

She was pretty, she laughed at his jokes, and she had the experience he needed. He extended an offer on the spot, and she took it.

"Welcome to Sutherland, Ms. Myers."

One down.

The ten o'clock spot was Casper's. He showed up in a suit and tie, and rumpled shirt. Angela sighed to herself, but George didn't seem to mind. He shook the young man's hand, then wiped his palm against his leg.

She couldn't blame him for that. Casper did seem to have perpetually moist hands.

"Casper Caspersen, eh? Your folks put a lot of thought into that name, huh?"

Casper laughed awkwardly and avoided the question. "Technically, I'm Casper Caspersen IV."

"No kidding?" George shook his head. "Not the most creative in the naming department, I guess."

Casper repeated the laugh, and Angela cringed. He'd remembered her advice about laughing at George's jokes. But she was pretty sure she'd never heard such a fake laugh in her life. It was like canned laughter from a seventies TV show. But, somehow, worse.

Mercifully, the rest of the interview went better than the fake laugh. George's eyes glazed over when they got to the industry terms, but in a good way. Casper threw out just enough jargon to impress his future boss that he was dealing with a genius.

The real victory came, though, when Casper spotted a picture of George on the wall. It was one of the windsurfing photos he'd hung around the building, ostensibly to "brighten the place up." That it featured him, apparently, was a happy coincidence.

That had led to a discussion of George's hobbies—a topic George particularly loved to indulge since all of his hobbies were expensive, and they all involved his *favorite* topic: himself.

But when they touched on kite surfing? Well, Angela had never seen a friendship forged that quickly.

"No way, man—you kite surf too?"

"That's right. But you're a kite surfer?"

"You bet. Every year, we head up to Lake Superior."

"Superior? God, that's got to be cold. That water's always cold up there, isn't it?"

"Pretty much. But you want to talk cold? One year, we were up there at my buddy's cabin when it froze over. He had his kite. We went kite *skating*. Which was in*sane*. I would definitely do that again, in a heartbeat."

And just like that, George and Casper were friends. Casper got the job by noon and an invite to lunch with the boss.

Angela didn't escape either. "Come on, Angie. It's been a while since we've had a team lunch. We need to get back into the habit of that. Especially now that we're going to have our core team."

God, I can't get out of here soon enough. But, that's two down. So she went along with it and suffered through a conversation that had turned entirely to surfing. George paid, which surprised her—not least of all since he still owed her a good chunk of change.

Then it was back to the office, and back to interviews. She'd left Conrad for after lunch for two reasons. She figured he would have already eaten by then and had his morning coffee. Any caffeine shortage or hunger-related grumpiness should, by then, be gone.

But she'd also counted on after-meal sleepiness helping. She wanted George to want to get through the interview as quickly as possible. She didn't want him asking too many questions or getting too much of a preview of Conrad's personality. She just needed him to go through the motions and sign off on his new administrative secretary.

And, just in case a full meal and a long day weren't enough, she cheated. She'd switched out the regular coffee for decaffeinated about halfway through the morning. For the last three hours, George had been drinking decaf.

And, his stomach full and his interest waning, her planning paid off. He yawned his way through the interview with Conrad. He asked a few questions, nodded when he got his answers, and seemed generally satisfied.

Conrad Walters, for his part, seemed to be on his best behavior. He managed multisyllabic answers most of the time and dropped a few of the key words Angela had given him into conversation now and then.

In the end, Sutherland was satisfied and offered Conrad the job. "We'd be honored if a patriot like you decided to join us. What we do here is different than what you did in uniform. No bones about that. But we're on the same team. Our research keeps the folks at home safe. In a way, it's a continuation of your mission—protect and serve."

For half a moment, Angela thought Conrad might blow his shot. His lip curled, and he seemed about to say something. Something nasty and unprofessional. But instead, he smiled. It was more a baring of teeth than a proper smile, and she saw George shiver at the sight. But Conrad said, "Well, how can I say no to protecting and serving?"

George clapped him on the back and extended a hand.

The older man took it, shaking so hard he left his new boss wincing. "I'm in."

Once the requisite forms were signed, Angela showed the office's new administrative secretary to the door. "We'll see you Monday, Conrad."

He nodded, then frowned at her. "He does know I was in the marines, right? Not a cop?"

She chuckled. "Yes. I'm not quite sure he knows the difference, but he knows."

The old man snorted. "'Protect and serve.' You could have warned me he was such a dumbass. Then again, maybe it's a good thing you didn't. I might not have showed up today. You have yourself a good weekend, Miss McCormack. I'll see you on Monday."

"You, too, Conrad."

Chapter Ten

Today was shaping up to be a good day. George's payment from Gilmore had cleared. Not that he'd ever had problems on that score. But, still, it was nice to see those dollars show up as expected in his secret account. He was feeling a lot more forgiving toward the other man, now that he was that much richer.

And the day was looking up. He had never understood why people bitched about Mondays. He liked the workweek. There was more to do then, especially in a place like Fenwood. The weekend hours here were crazy. Even on Saturday night, only the bars stayed open past eleven. But Sunday was a joke. The coffee shop closed by six. The movie theater was done by ten. Half the businesses on the main drag didn't even open on Sundays.

And, if you wanted to eat out on a Sunday, timing was crucial. Anything between nine to noon meant dealing with the church crowds—the hordes of old ladies and bad perfume and whining children.

No, George hated the weekends in Fenwood. He got out of town as often as he could, flying back home at the slightest excuse. The weekends, when he had nothing to do elsewhere, he spent bored out of his mind.

So Monday was good news to him. Monday meant what little the town offered was open most of the day. And he was the boss. His hours were flexible. If he wanted to head out at nine in the morning and not be back until two in the afternoon, well, he was the boss. He could do that.

It didn't cure Fenwood of its insufferable lack of variety, or its ridiculously early closing hours. But at least it gave him more options.

Today promised to be a more interesting Monday than most though. Angie McCormack had done a stellar job of recruiting candidates. She'd had three of her top picks in, and every one of them had knocked it out of the park. They were going to do great things for Sutherland. Plus, she'd been smart in her recruitment.

Conrad wouldn't need health insurance, which meant cost savings. Plus, he'd be another warm body meeting his father's ridiculous veteran's quota.

Casper was young, and he accepted less than a more seasoned professional might have expected. That was one thing George loved about millennials. Older generations had grown up in a different economy, before the upward consolidation of wealth. They expected Clinton-era benefits and pay. Millennials knew better. They'd entered the workforce during or right before the Bush economy and spent their entire working lives in the shadow of it. If a millennial could pay their bills and see the doctor, they were doing better than most of their peers. And they knew it. They weren't grateful, exactly, but they knew how things worked nowadays.

Kathryn Myers had been another good find. Her résumé was solid, and she was very pretty. George considered himself to be a man of the future, a man with the vision to lead his company forward. But some old-fashioned ideas were worth holding on to. And women being pretty? Well, that was one of them. He knew it was unrealistic as a general expectation, but for his core team? It was one thing for a hag to fill orders or test samples or write up emails. But no one wanted to do business with one. No, Ms. Myers would fit in perfectly.

He was pretty sure he was going to like this week's candidates as much. Angie had mentioned their bios and résumés last week, and though he only half remembered what she'd said, that was enough to satisfy him it would be another good day.

One of their prospects, a Matt or Mark-something, had been a veteran. It did seem a little ridiculous to have that many military guys around, but George Sr. would like it. And, again, they'd save a fortune on healthcare. Plus, this one was younger, which George felt was necessary in a personal assistant. Not only did he want the vigor of a young person, but a PA represented his employer in a way. He didn't want an old, crusty face in that role.

The other guy, a Brad-somebody, had been the corporate strategist for a handful of healthcare and research facilities over the last decade, during critical points of their growth. He'd led them out of dark periods, onto solid ground. Unless he weighed a thousand pounds or didn't believe in baths, the interview was just a formality at this point: the job was in the bag.

No, today would be a good day. George was sure of it. And maybe, once he'd wrapped up the interviews, he'd give Kendall a call and see if he and Tommy wanted to do something this weekend. *Hopefully without Ralph.*

George stretched in his seat. The first interview was at nine, so he had half an hour left. Well, he had some emails he needed to get through. *God, we can't fill that PA spot fast enough.*

He'd just pulled up his email client when his phone sounded. George cringed at the tone. It was a sad clown noise, a kind of comical, melancholy horn sound. He'd assigned that ringtone to one person: George Sr.

And suddenly, George's day was not looking so bright. Still, he affected a happy tone as he answered. "Hey, Dad. What's up?"

"I need to talk to you, George."

The younger Sutherland cringed. "That's what we're doing, isn't it?"

His father didn't laugh at his joke. "I mean, are you alone?"

George glanced around his office, as if the other man could see his actions. "As far as I know."

Again, George Sr. didn't laugh. "Good. Because we need to talk about what's going on over there."

"Oh?" He tried to keep the aggravation out of his voice. But he had a pretty good idea of what was coming next. His father was about to find fault with something he'd done. Because that's what George Sr. lived for: to find reasons to second-guess his actions. "And what's going on?"

"Exactly what I wanted to ask you. I'm looking through a list of terminations, and I'm wondering what the hell is going on over there."

"What terminations?"

"You laid off dozens of people, George. What do you mean, 'what terminations?'"

He clenched his jaw at the impatience in the other man's tone. "I mean," he said, a bit sharply, "what's bothering you about them?"

For a moment, George heard nothing but silence. He almost hoped the line had dropped. But, no such luck.

"You're kidding, right? You got rid of people who had been with that company for years."

"Yeah, I did. And?"

"And? Why the hell did you do that? We promised Tillerson we wouldn't be firing his people."

Greg Tillerson had been the previous owner of Fenwood Bio, and George didn't really care what promises his father had made him. He said as much now, adding, "He had his chance with the company. He fucked it up."

"I gave my word, George."

The younger Sutherland rolled his eyes. His dad was fond of saying his word was his bond. *A man lives or dies by his reputation. Don't ever forget that, George.* God, how many times had he heard that growing up? He decided to try another tack. "Right. Which is why I didn't fire anyone. Those positions were redundant. He can't expect every employee to stay on whether they're needed or not."

"IT is redundant? Did I miss a memo somewhere along the way? Have computers started running the way they're supposed to? Have phones? Do help-desk tickets solve themselves?"

"What I mean is, if we're going to bring them under the umbrella of Sutherland, they don't need their own IT department."

"What, we're going to dispatch someone from Philadelphia every time a printer goes down?"

George stared daggers at the wall. He didn't have an answer to that, and he refused to cede the point. Instead, he sat in sullen silence until his father spoke again.

"And if they're redundant, why did you sign a new IT team lead Friday, after letting the last guy go?"

Shit. The nosy son of a bitch really was keeping close tabs on him, wasn't he? "That's a different position."

"Bullshit. It's a different title. But we both know that 'IT Team Lead' and 'Information Technologies Lead' are functionally the same thing."

George clenched his jaw and said nothing.

"Well? Are you going to deny it?"

"What's the point? You've already made up your mind."

"Tell me one difference between those roles. And give me a reason you had to fire the old lead instead of transitioning him into the new position?"

"Because I didn't, okay?" George snapped. "Because you sent me here to do things my way, and dammit, that's what I'm going to do. You know damned well how hard it is to come into a place and implement changes with existing staff."

"So what? It's easier to fire people?"

"I didn't fire anyone."

"Don't give me semantics. You came into a business that's been around for a hundred years and started letting good employees go. What do you think that does for morale? I can tell you what I see, looking at the turnover rates."

"I don't give a shit about turnover. That's the trash taking itself out. Listen, Dad, you told me to do this job. Well, I'm doing it. You don't like how I run things? Well, that's your right. Send someone else to babysit your pet projects. But you want me to do something? You have to let me do it my way."

"That's not the Sutherland way."

"I'm a Sutherland, and it's my way. You're not hearing me. I have to be able to make decisions and know I have your backing. I can't have you second-guessing every damned thing I do. If you want me to make calls, well, you need to fucking back off and let me make them."

For a long moment, there was only silence on the line. Then, very quietly, his father said, "Well, I guess that's the sixty-four-thousand-dollar question, isn't it? *Do* I want you making those calls?"

"What the fuck is that supposed to mean?"

But his father made no answer to that. Instead, he said, "Well, I have to get to a meeting. We'll talk about this again."

That had been enough to irrevocably sour George's mood. He sat in his office, staring at the wall and thinking of more than a few unpleasant things to tell his father. Mostly, they involved the old man's opinions, and all the things he could do with them. There was a lot of shoving and cramming and sticking up one particular orifice.

He didn't hate George Sr. most of the time. He loved his father, in a way. But there were days, like today, when he felt a lot further from love and a lot closer to hate.

So, when Angela McCormack poked her head into his office with a smile and a "Good morning, George," he was in no mood. Not for pleasantries, or smiles. She smiled too often, as far as he was concerned.

This is a workplace, not a goddamned circus. "What do you need?" He said it with a brusqueness that, he hoped, would wipe some of that unwarranted cheer out of her expression.

"Just reminding you of the interview. We're in conference room *C*."

He scowled at her. He still had plenty of time, didn't he? With a glance at the clock to ascertain how much time, his scowl deepened. It was five past the hour. "On my way."

She smiled again. "Great."

"Go on without me," he decided. "I need coffee. I'll be right there."

She acquiesced and left him in peace, and he sighed. He should have stopped for coffee on the way in. But the office stuff would have to do in the absence of anything better. He grabbed his mug and filled it and took a long sip.

His scowl returned. It was garbage. He wondered how these people could drink it. Granted, he'd been the one to change the office coffee. But if Fenwood Bio had been run more competently, he wouldn't have needed to put so many cost-saving measures into play.

I need to get a brewer for my own office. Even if I am out of here by midsummer. He wavered between leaving the mug behind and taking it with him.

But George had a headache setting in, and caffeine would probably help. If he could manage to choke down enough to reap the benefits anyway.

Angela was waiting for him in the conference room as she'd said. He cursed the woman for scheduling interviews on a Monday morning but pushed ahead anyway. Then he frowned.

There were two women here—Angela and some other he didn't recognize. She was a knockout, and the frosty blue of her eyes as she turned to him rather put his sour thoughts of earlier out of his mind.

But he was confused. Turning to Angela, he said, "I thought this was the Strategic and Business Development Leader interview?"

She smiled. *Again.*

"That's right. Heather Bradshaw, allow me to introduce George Sutherland, Jr., interim CEO of Fenwood Bio. George is overseeing the transition of the company to Sutherland Bio Research. And George, this is Heather Bradshaw."

They shook hands and assured each other it was a pleasure to meet. George had to admit the view only got better as Heather stood. Long legs, an ass at least as nice as Angie's, and a rack to go with it. Even under a blazer, there was no hiding those melons. She had a nice face, too: good skin, attractive smile, and killer eyes.

Still, he struggled to figure out what was going on. They'd talked about a man last Friday. He was sure of that.

He couldn't remember the name, but she'd called him Brad. *Bradshaw*. He understood then. He'd only been half listening, he supposed, and had caught part of the last name.

Now, though, he ran a critical eye over Ms. Bradshaw. She was young, at least for the position. She was probably in her midthirties. And by some measures, that was old—it put her in the upper bracket of his dating range, for instance. But to decide the strategic direction of his company? Thirties was pretty young.

The truth was, George had been expecting a young candidate. Angie had mentioned something about the interviewee bringing a "youthful energy" to the position that had been lacking under the Tillersons. He'd liked the idea.

But that had been when he was expecting a Brad-something. Not a Miss Bradshaw.

It might not have been the most politically correct sentiment, but somehow, this changed things for George. He couldn't say why, exactly. Ralph would have had some hogwash explanation, had the other man been privy to his internal musings. He would have made it about gender and sexism and that sort of thing.

It wasn't. Of course it wasn't. George was a feminist. Not one of those fourth-wave feminists, or whatever those women called themselves nowadays. He didn't get bothered by things like equal pay and Me Too, except that the *movements* bothered him. Radicals, he was sure, were ruining the nation. He had plenty to say about modern feminism. And none of it good.

But George was still a feminist. He'd tell anyone who listened that he was a *real* feminist. So it wasn't that Heather was a woman. Of course not.

There was just...something. He couldn't quite put his finger on it. But there was something about her.

She lacked the gravitas, maybe. *Yes, that's it.* Someone setting the course of a company needed that certain something, the kind of gravitas and authority people would respect at a glance.

He didn't doubt her résumé or her accomplishments—what he recalled of them anyway. But it wasn't enough to *be* the part. She needed to look it too. Clear vision without a broad set of shoulders that could carry the weight of those decisions? Well, that just wouldn't inspire confidence.

No, in the course of fifteen seconds, George had made up his mind. She just didn't have the *something* he needed.

Chapter Eleven

Heather Bradshaw handled herself well. He had to give her that. She had the right answers to all of his questions and a kind of confidence that couldn't help but impress. She spoke with ease about her past experience and what she'd bring to Sutherland. As the day wore on, he found himself almost believing in her himself, so good were her powers of persuasion.

She was almost the perfect candidate. *If only…*

But he didn't quite know how to finish that sentence, so he didn't, not even in his mind. When the interview wrapped up, he promised they'd be in touch soon.

Angela was surprised. She didn't say so, but he could tell from her expression. She had very chatty brows, even when she meant to keep her thoughts to herself.

She inquired as to his thoughts on the interview, and he answered halfheartedly. The truth was, his mind wandered. He found himself wondering what it would be like to play poker with Angela. *She must have no game. Those brows would give her away every time.* He had a devil of a time explaining his sudden laughter at that thought.

"Sorry, Angie," he said after a few false starts. "I just thought of something my dad said this morning on the phone. Completely unrelated. Just popped into my mind."

"Oh."

It was a shitty save, but it did have the desirable effect of flummoxing her for long enough to steer the conversation in a different direction.

"No, she was very impressive. I just...I'd like to try a few more interviews before we make any decisions. It's one thing with the head honcho of the nerds or the secretaries. But this is a big role. We have to make sure we get it right. And we've got time."

He'd flashed his pearly whites and moved on. "But what about the next interview? That's the guy for the PA position, right? Mike somebody or other?"

Angela nodded. "Um, yes, that's right. Matt. Matt Kilbourne."

"Great, when's he going to be here?"

"Nine o'clock tomorrow morning."

"All right. Well, I'm going to take an early day. See you tomorrow."

George didn't think about Heather much more after that. He didn't think about work, either, or his father. He spent some time on one of his favorite games, winning a little and losing more than he liked, and working his way through more whiskey than he probably should have had in one sitting.

He was, as a consequence, annoyed with life in general and not altogether rational when his phone rang a few hours later. The same sad clown noise he'd started his day with sounded again. "Jesus fuck," he muttered into the darkness of his gaming room. "Not again."

But he answered, like the dutiful son he was. "Dad. What a pleasure."

"I assume you're not at work?"

"You are, as ever, quite right."

"Good. Because I want to have a serious talk with you, George."

He groaned and didn't realize he had let the sound *outside* of his head until it was too late. "Didn't we already have one of those today? I think I hit my limit."

"This is no time for your smartass shit."

George just laughed though. "Oh? You're the one who always says 'there's no time like the present.'"

"Are you drunk?"

He bristled at his father's accusation. "Of course not."

"Jesus, George. It's not even six o'clock your time."

"I'm not drunk."

"Bullshit. I can hear it in your voice. You must have been hitting the bottle as soon as you got out of work. You sure as hell better not have been doing it on the job."

The more his father spoke, the more indignant he felt. This, finally, was too much. "Fuck you, Dad. Of course I didn't drink at the office. I left early."

A moment of silence followed, then George Sr. spoke in a cold, calm way. "I've warned you before about using that kind of language."

"And I've warned you before about treating me like a goddamned infant. But here we fucking are again, aren't we? What is it this time? You didn't chew me out enough earlier? Find something else to second-guess me on? More decisions to undermine?"

"What the hell is your problem, George?"

"What the hell is *my* problem?" He was practically shouting now, his whole body trembling with rage. "*My* problem? What the hell is *your* problem, Dad? You want me to do shit for you, and you never—never—let me do it. You always second-guess me. You always have to police my work, micromanage my shit."

"It's my company," his father snapped, "not a damned class project."

"And I'm your son. You care so much about that god-damned company, all you ever do is shit on me. That's all you've ever done."

"That's bullshit, and you know it. I've given you opportunities most people would die for."

"And what about what I've given you?" he shot back. "I've invested my whole career in this fucking company. Only to get shot down every time I try something my way."

"You're not the CEO yet, George Jr.," his father said, and the edge in his voice could have cut glass. "You don't set the course of this company. And until you can prove you're ready, that you've got the maturity for that kind of responsibility, you never will. You understand me?"

"And how in fuck am I supposed to do that when you never let me make decisions on my own?"

"You know what'd be a good start? Not cutting out of work early to get shitfaced. Not laying off good people and triggering massive turnover just because you're on a power trip. Not ruffling feathers just because you can."

"I told you the turnover was a good thing. We got rid of people who weren't loyal to the company."

"You got rid of good employees because your sorry excuse for leadership inspired nothing but apprehension and fear. That's nothing to be proud of. That's a complete and utter failure of leadership—yours, and mine, for ever trusting you with the responsibility. For ever believing that you had what it takes to do this."

A kick to the gut probably would have stung less than that. It didn't happen often. But George didn't know what to say, so he remained silent.

For a long moment, the silence stretched out between them. Then George Sr. sighed. "Look, George, I need to go. There's not much left to say. It's too late now. What's done is done. And you're drunk anyway."

"I'm not drunk."

"Right." His father's voice came across the line quietly, resignedly. "We'll talk some other time. Good night."

George heard the call drop, and for a moment he sat in the dimness. He let loose a scream of pent-up frustration into the evening air—and the game controller, into the gaming room wall. It shattered loudly, and dark splinters of plastic flew this way and that. It felt cathartic in a way.

Fuck him, the old prick. What did George Sr. know? Not a goddamned thing. He was a dinosaur. If he'd been left to his own devices, Sutherland Research would have gone the way of Fenwood Bio. And for the same reason: old men who didn't know how to operate in today's market.

So fuck him.

George poured himself another glass of whiskey and dug around for a second game controller. He had a feeling the other one was irreparably damaged, and he didn't want to confirm that. It'd only piss him off more.

He slipped his headphones back on and returned to his game. The match had already ended, and his team had lost. Someone must have noticed he'd gone MIA because he'd been booted from the server too. "Fuck you guys too," he muttered.

He'd just selected a new round when his phone rang again. *Really? Again*? He was about to let into George Sr. for real this time when he noticed the ringtone was the default ring.

He looked before he picked up. If he didn't recognize the number, there was no way in hell he was answering. Not with the mood he was in. But he did recognize the number.

And for half a second, he considered not answering precisely for that reason.

The number was Andy Gilmore's. And after a moment of indecision, George switched audio between the console and the phone. "Hello?"

"George," Andy's voice came through, a smarmy smile evident in the words. "How are you doing?"

"Great. Couldn't be better. How about you?"

Andy ignored the question. "Everything okay?"

"Yeah. Just another call from Dad. You know how it goes." If George hadn't been drunk, he might have been more circumspect. Confiding in Andy was what had gotten him ensnared in the other man's web in the first place. But, for all he'd told George Sr., he was drunk, or as good as. And, what was more, he was angry. And anger made him rash.

"I'm sorry, dude. I was hoping you two were getting back on good terms again."

"Yeah, me too. But you know Dad. He's a visionless prick."

"He's from another generation."

"That's what I just said, isn't it?"

Andy had the decency to laugh. "Fair point. Listen, you need to talk? I'm actually going to be heading down there—if you're okay with that, of course."

Warning sirens went off in George's head. "Wait, what? You know you can't come down here. If my dad gets wind—"

"I didn't mean Fenwood. I was thinking we could meet in one of the cities nearby."

George scoffed. "What cities? There's nothing for a hundred miles."

"You don't mind a little drive, do you?"

The sirens sounded again, and he asked, "Why? What do you need to meet in person for all of a sudden?"

Andy laughed lightly. "Partly to catch up, of course. And partly—well, I've got a proposition. I think you'll like this one. We both have the opportunity to profit big."

"I'm listening."

"It'd be better if we talked about it in person."

George considered, then laughed. "I've seen that movie. That usually ends up with someone getting knifed or shot or something, doesn't it?"

Andy laughed too. "Maybe in the movies. But I'll leave Caruso behind, if it makes you more comfortable. The only thing you get out of this is a mountain of untraceable cash. If you're game?"

George considered again, for a good long minute. Something told him he should pass. Something told him the reason Andy wanted to meet face-to-face was to sell him something he couldn't do over the phone. "I suppose my father would lose his shit if he knew we were doing this?"

"A very safe assumption."

"All right. I'm in."

Chapter Twelve

Angela had been ready for another rejection. She couldn't fathom why Sutherland didn't want Heather Bradshaw. Her résumé was impeccable. So impeccable, in fact, that if not for the red flag in her file, Angela never would have considered her. She was not only a good candidate on paper, she was one of the best she'd ever run across. And with the interview? Well, she had to keep reminding herself of what Caroline from Northwest Medical Research had told her.

So, what her boss was thinking, Angela couldn't begin to understand. He'd been particularly evasive on that score too. He hadn't flat out said he wouldn't hire her, but his hesitation and talk about other candidates spoke volumes. And he'd made no efforts to explain what was causing it, despite her gentle prodding.

So, going into an interview with a candidate who'd lost his previous job for knocking his boss out? She'd been prepared for another failure, more pronounced than the last.

But George had loved Matt Kilbourne. He'd laughed out loud at the story of his last job and nodded vigorously. "Good man. Good man. No man has the right to be putting his hands on a woman. I'm something of a feminist myself, you know."

He'd clapped Matt on the shoulder, rather vigorously, and commented a few times about the other man's stature. "God, you look like you could stop a tank with your bare hands. I'll bet those bastards didn't know what hit them when they sent you out there, eh?"

Matt had seemed uncomfortable with the questioning. "I'm made of flesh and blood like anyone else, Mr. Sutherland."

"I don't know. I'm thinking you might be titanium under there or something." George had laughed but followed the laughter up with a few faux punches to the chest, as if to verify he wasn't actually talking to a metal man. Matt grimaced a little more with each hit but laughed it off in turn.

Still, the interview had gone well. George had made an offer, and Matt accepted it. *One more position filled, and one more to go.*

★

Angela conveyed the story to her friends the following Tuesday night. They'd gone out for food at Tres Amigos instead of drinks at Marty's. Rae was happy for the change.

"Means I get steak, and I don't have to be the designated driver." She pecked her wife on the cheek. "Your turn, my love."

Lauren shook her head. "You may be the only person I know who goes out for Mexican food and orders the steak and fries."

"I like fajitas as much as anyone," Rae said, referencing Lauren's order, "but no one in town makes a steak like they do. Not even you."

"Oh, my God. You want to go there?"

Rae nodded resolutely. "It brings me no pleasure. But the truth is the truth. Someone has finally bested your cooking."

"Angela, you're a witness to this. When I file for divorce, and our friends ask why, you're my witness."

"Oh, no. She's on my side," Rae decided. "Aren't you?"

Angela laughed. "Don't bring me into this. I would never say a bad word about Lauren's cooking. But I'm also not going to take sides against Tres Amigos."

Lauren threw her hands in the air in an exaggerated fashion. "Both of you? I don't believe it. And I thought we're friends, Angela."

They shared a laugh, and then Lauren said, "I think I'm getting cheese sauce. You know, to cope with all this betrayal."

"Ohh," Rae said, "good idea."

Tres Amigos served tortilla chips and fresh salsa with every meal. It was good. But with their signature cheese sauce? They weren't chips anymore. They were manna from heaven when dipped in that melted cheese. Angela never bought it unless she was with friends who could help her devour it. Because it never made it to a to-go box, much less stayed behind in the serving bowl. Right now, she agreed this was an excellent plan.

Lauren, though, scoffed at the pair of them. "And when did I say I was going to share?"

"We're married," Rae reminded her. "What's mine is yours—like my fries. But what's yours is mine too."

Lauren grinned. She was a notorious fry thief who would power through her own fries, and then pick off Rae's plate. "Fine. And I suppose I'll share with you, too, Angela. Even after that."

For a few minutes, they talked about food and teased one another. Then Rae brought the conversation back to Sutherland Research. "But what were you saying about the interview?"

Lauren nudged her. "See? You're as invested in this as I am."

Rae harrumphed, but urged her friend to continue the story anyway. Angela obliged.

"I don't know what it was. Heather—that's the candidate—was incredible. Like, seriously, I couldn't imagine a *better* applicant, other than the drill sergeant thing. But he doesn't know about that. Her experience, her vision..." Angela shook her head. "I don't know what his deal was."

"She's a woman," Rae offered matter-of-factly.

Angela frowned. "I don't know. He's a prick, for sure, but he's never had a problem hiring women before. The new acquisitions lead, she's a woman. And I'm the only one on the HR team he kept."

"Yeah, but your team was *all* women. As for the new hire, what's her role? Ordering office supplies and software. This is something else. This is one of the top positions in the company."

Rae shook her head. "I've known plenty of guys like George Sutherland. Their father's generation was okay with women as secretaries. They think they're more progressive than that because they'll hire women into management. But it's always low-level management. They never make it past the bottom tiers, or mid if they're really lucky. Guys like Sutherland are okay with women ordering supplies for them and interviewing candidates. They're not okay with women making business decisions."

Angela considered for a long moment. "You could be right. Damn, every time I think I figure out just how shitty he is, he surprises me. And never in a good way."

Their cheese sauce arrived, with the promise their food would be out shortly. They dug in and made obscenely short work of the cheese.

"This is why I never order this stuff." Angela sighed. "I can't stop eating it."

"I don't even care today," Lauren said. "Not after the day I've had."

"Tell me about it," Angela prodded.

But her friend shook her head. "Not yet—finish your story. What are you going to do since he rejected Heather?"

"He didn't reject her. Not outright. He says he wants to see more candidates before making any final decisions."

Rae shrugged. "So, let him meet more candidates. You said you had a list of terrible applicants, right?"

Angela nodded. "Yeah. But...Heather was perfect."

"Yeah. But if you send him a parade of incompetency, who knows? He might just decide it's okay to hire a woman after all."

Angela snorted. "Just my luck, he'll hire one of them."

"Either way, that's a win, right?"

She considered. She wasn't quite sure why she had her heart set on Heather. She supposed it was because it was part of her plan, and everything else had worked out so nicely. The stars seemed to be aligning for her hire too. Ms. Bradshaw had applied to Fenwood Bio a year ago. She'd been surprised but pleased when Angela explained they'd kept her résumé on file.

"We didn't think the position you applied for was a good fit at the time. But we were very impressed with your résumé. I hope you don't mind me reaching out like this, but we'd love to schedule an interview if you're interested." That's what she'd told Heather. And everything fell into place afterward.

Everything, except the George factor. She hadn't accounted for that. "I suppose," Angela said. "I can't make it too obvious."

"No, of course not. But there's got to be a lot of bad candidates who aren't glaringly bad?"

"That's what I'm going to have to do, I guess. But enough about that. Lauren, tell us about your day. How are things in customer service hell?"

Lauren laughed. "Oh, you know how it goes. Sarah called in sick, so we were short-staffed in the morning. The drive-through line was backed up to the street. People were honking their horns and screaming at us. I took the window, so none of my people had to deal with that. One guy literally threw his money at me."

"Jesus. People."

"You'd think that they were dying, having to wait an extra two minutes." She shook her head, and Rae wrapped an arm around her.

"I'm sorry, babe. That sucks."

Lauren munched another chip, and for a moment, seemed lost to her thoughts. Then her expression brightened. "Oh! But I didn't tell you my good news."

"No, you didn't," Angela agreed. "I could use good news."

"Me too," Rae said.

Her wife shot her a dirty look. "I didn't tell *you* because you're a tattletale."

"What?"

But she ignored Rae's confusion and smiled broadly at Angela. "Guess who I saw again today?"

"Uh...no idea."

"Nikki Fulton. You know, the lesbian from church? The cute, *single* lesbian?" Angela and Rae groaned at the same time, and Lauren elbowed her wife playfully. "See? This is why I didn't tell you."

"That is not good news, Lauren. That's some serious false advertising."

"It is good news. Because she was complaining about meeting people. She had to drive an hour and a half for a date on Saturday. And..." Lauren grinned. "It didn't work out. They had no chemistry. I told her I might be able to set her up with someone. Someone local."

The other two women groaned more deeply.

"I told you..." Angela began.

"I know, I know. But opportunity knocked. And I had the chance to talk you up. She was really interested."

Angela sighed. "I am not thinking of relationships right now."

"I know. But you don't argue with the universe's timing."

"The universe? It has nothing to do with the universe. The universe isn't trying to set me up on blind dates."

"I," Lauren declared airily, "am but the humble messenger, doing the universe's bidding."

"So humble." Rae shook her head and laughed. "I should have known something was up. You were too deviously happy earlier."

Lauren ignored her wife. "Seriously, Angela, this is Fenwood. We're probably the only lesbians in a hundred and fifty miles. And here comes someone else, out of the blue? You can't tell me that's not the universe."

"Good God. You're already picking out wedding music, aren't you?" Rae sighed.

"Of course not. I'm not saying it *will* work out—"

"Just that Nikki will have no choice since I'm the only lesbian around? Now that's flattering."

Lauren frowned at her. "Don't be ridiculous. I mean, the universe is sending you a sign. It's time to move on. Maybe with Nikki, maybe not. But you've got to put yourself out there again, Angela. It's time."

Angela promptly forgot her friend's dating advice. She had bigger fish to fry at the moment, and no particular desire to subject herself to another failed relationship. Instead, she focused on the job.

Fifteen interviews in as many days—it was damned good work, while simultaneously being *awful* work. That she'd managed it in conjunction with new employee orientation was a feat for which she did pat herself on the back a little.

These hadn't been random interviews, after all. She'd put as much care into selecting these candidates as she would have good candidates.

George's despair was palpable. The first candidate, a young man named Martin Blakely, had held six similar titles over the past five years but hadn't lasted more than six months in any job but one. He'd made it all the way to seven and a half months there.

And despite the fact that Martin was a very smooth talker, not even Sutherland could miss those implications.

The second interview had been with an older man who spent the entire time complaining about technology. His vision, it seemed, was to return to precomputer and smartphone days. This, of course, was a clear no.

The next had been a woman with a fairly solid, if not extraordinary, résumé, and no actual failings. Angela had called her in as something of a control sample. She was the only normal candidate of the lot—but female. Angela felt fairly certain Rae was onto something, but this was the only way to really test it.

George had given the last two candidates—even the "dinosaur," as he'd termed him after the interview—his undivided attention. But he'd yawned his way through the day with her and decided they'd "be in touch."

That was confirmation enough, and it pissed Angela off. She'd resigned herself to the fact that Heather, for whatever reason, wouldn't be her poison pill. But to know that the reason got down to sexism? She seethed at the idea.

But there was nothing she could see to do about it. So she kept arranging interviews. And candidates kept crashing and burning.

George had plenty to say on the matter. "It's this damned place. No one wants to move to the middle of bumfuck nowhere."

"It does make recruitment quite the challenge," she'd demurred. "We were lucky with the other positions."

"Yeah, but it doesn't take any brains to be a secretary. Those positions are easy to fill. We've got to lure someone out here, to the sticks. Someone good."

Angela forced a smile. "Well, the good news is, Sutherland's reputation is stellar. The right person won't mind the location, if it means they get to work here, under your leadership."

George considered her words, then smiled. "That's true. You know, I don't know if I've told you today, Angie, but you're doing a hell of a job. Keep up the good work."

Chapter Thirteen

George met Andy Gilmore at a real restaurant, not one of the crappy mom-and-pop diners or middle-class eateries he'd been surviving off for the last few months. He'd had to drive almost two hours to get there, but he felt a bit like a man crawling at last out of a desert and emerging again into civilization. "Fenwood really is the armpit of the world." He sighed and took a sip of his drink.

He'd ordered a scotch, neat; and he was working his way through it quickly. Andy was taking longer with his bourbon on the rocks, but George didn't care.

Andy was paying, after all. If George needed a second glass sooner rather than later, well, that's how it went.

"So I hear," the other man said. "I don't envy you that."

"No. I half suspect dad sent me there just to get me out of the way." George smiled as if he was joking. He hadn't been. Then again, he'd only just started drinking. And it took more liquor than this to get him to confide in Andy Gilmore.

The other man laughed. "My dad was the same way. You never quite knew what he was thinking." He paused to take a sip of his bourbon. "But you probably won't be there much longer?"

"I hope not. Two months, I'm figuring. If we can get the team together soon."

Andy nodded. "That's an aggressive timetable. You think you'll be ready to hand it over to a new guy that quickly?"

George finished his drink and flagged the waiter down for another. "I'm ready to hand it over now. But—"

"George Sr. says otherwise," Andy finished for him.

"That's right." He watched the other man, trying to get some read on him. But his bland features were arranged in as inscrutable and placid a fashion as ever. Whatever he was up to, George couldn't guess. "But I don't think you called me here to talk about that."

Andy smiled. "True. Not entirely anyway. I have a business proposal."

"You mentioned that. What kind of proposal?"

Andy smiled and sipped his bourbon. "The kind that will make us very rich. You know the research you sent over?"

"The last batch?"

"That's right."

"What about it?"

"Sutherland is developing immunizations from that work, yes?"

George nodded. "Yes. Like I said. They're probably six months away from market. Trials have been extremely successful. They show 99.5 percent effective protection against all known tick-borne diseases." He crossed his arms. "But, like we agreed, that's off the table."

Andy raised a hand to stem his concerns. "I know. I told you, George, I'm a man of my word. But they're looking at the human potential, right?"

George nodded again. "Yes."

Gilmore shrugged. "Tick-borne diseases aren't just a human worry, George. The Lyme vaccine alone is regularly recommended for pets."

"I know. They're looking into the feasibility of extending the research in a few years. But right now, my father's concern is human impact."

The other man smiled. "Very benevolent of him, of course. But there's a market for this. It'll be smaller than the market for the human vaccine, of course. But..." Andy shrugged. "On the other hand, we don't have the research costs. Our overhead is going to be a lot less."

"So you want to use the research for vaccines after all?"

"Not to cut into Sutherland's market."

"Bullshit. It's not our first target, but it'll happen eventually."

The waiter returned with George's refill, and Andy waited with a patient smile as he took another sip.

"*Eventually*, in our business, is nothing. You know that. For all we know, there's another company out there doing the same research. If your father waits five years, or ten years, to move on this, someone else might have already stepped in."

George drank again and tapped the rim of his glass with a finger. "Maybe."

"There are about seventy million pet owners in the United States, George. There's about ninety million dogs, just in this country. There's eight to ten million in the UK. About twenty-seven million in China—and a hundred million pets total. Thirteen million dogs in Japan."

George considered that, then shook his head. That was a lot of dogs. "People are nuts."

"Yes. But, luckily for us, the nuttier they are, the more likely they are to take their dogs in for their shots. And their cats. Which means, if we get this to market…"

"That's a lot of revenue."

"Exactly. Hundreds of millions of immunizations, requiring a yearly booster."

George shook his head. "No. Our research finds the vaccine remains effective for at least a decade."

Andy smiled and took a long sip of bourbon. "Oh?"

"Yes. You read the data, right?"

"I did. But…" His smile broadened. "I'm not sure that's the best approach."

George frowned. "What do you mean?"

"Come on, George. You're thinking like your father. Do you want people to buy the vaccine once in a decade—once in the lifetime of many dogs—or once a year?"

He was about to protest the comparison with his father. He was about to protest that it didn't matter what he wanted: the vaccine lasted for a decade regardless. But then he understood. "You mean…we say it's required once a year."

Andy raised his glass in a mock salute.

"What if there are side effects?"

"From what?"

"From overmedicating?"

"We've developed models to determine what happens if we decrease the potency. As far as we can tell, the vaccine should retain about 85 percent effectiveness, with no side effects."

George drummed his fingers against the table, mulling this over. "That's a significant decrease. We're almost at a hundred."

"Sure. But no one but us knows what *could* be. The consumers will only know that an 85 percent chance is a hell of a lot better than 0 percent, which is what they've got right now."

George shifted in his seat. It made good sense, from a purely business perspective.

On the other hand, it was unethical. He wasn't a stickler for the rules. God knew, he'd broken them often enough where money was involved. But to withhold a more effective treatment to increase his bottom line? That was a line he hadn't crossed. Yet, anyway.

He wasn't sure he wanted to or could. And he told Andy as much.

Gilmore listened patiently, nodding now and again as he expressed his objections. "I hear you, George. No, I really do. But the thing is, we're still bringing something huge to the market. Is it as good as it could be? No. But it's a hell of a lot better than nothing. And if we don't turn a profit—because, at the end of the day, that's what keeps us doing this—then the shareholders lose interest. And all of a sudden, we're not bringing *anything* to market. Not just animal vaccines, but nothing."

He concluded with, "A lower success rate may mean a handful of animal deaths. But if companies like yours and mine shut down, or don't get the investment to take risks? How many millions of *people* end up dead?"

George considered. He wanted to agree. As they'd been talking, he'd been running the numbers. Andy had mentioned a lot of millions. Global immunization rates would vary and fluctuate, of course. There'd be hesitancy to try something new. It'd be years before they got full buy-in from veterinary doctors across the world.

Even so, that was a lot of millions. And they had the research. George Sr. was just sitting on it, wasting the potential. Wasting the money they could be earning.

The money *he* could be earning.

And yet...there was something that just didn't sit right about producing an inferior product to maximize profits. "I don't know, Andy. To knowingly sabotage our own work..."

"It's not sabotaging it. We're ensuring that we make ten times the profit."

George blinked. That was a hard lure to resist. "That doesn't change what we're doing though."

"No. But maximizing our profit means we can keep saving lives, George. And that's what you're worried about, isn't it? You're worried that doing this compromises our mission. But our mission is to do everything we can to save lives. In a perfect world, we wouldn't have to do this. But we don't live in a perfect world. In our world, a yearly vaccine instead of a ten-year one means we make ten times the profit. It means we can be ten times as effective."

And make ten times the money. "I assume I'd be paid on an ongoing basis?"

Andy grinned. "Your standard commission. Plus, a 2 percent bonus. For being flexible on this."

George licked his lips and downed his scotch. "Make it 5 percent, and you've got yourself a deal."

Chapter Fourteen

George reached for his mug of coffee and lifted it to his lips. But he froze halfway between the desk and his mouth. His mug was empty.

He sighed. *For the love of God...* "Conrad?"

No answer reached him, so he tried again. And again, he was met with only silence. *Dammit. What's the point of having help if they don't actually help?* Normally, he would have called Matt for this kind of thing, but Matt was at the dry cleaner's picking up his suit.

He pushed to his feet and stalked out of the office. Conrad's station was just down the hall from him, and he expected to see it empty.

But it was not empty. The other man was staring intently at his screen, with an expression that seemed more suited to murder than a day at the office. For half a second, George's courage failed. He thought of retreating to his office and making his own coffee.

But no. Conrad had to have heard him. He had no excuse for ignoring his boss. They weren't even twenty feet apart. And without a PA in the office, he could step up to the plate.

George squared his shoulders and marched over. "Conrad, dammit, answer me when I talk to you."

The old man started and glanced up at him, his expression not much more softened than earlier. "Mr. Sutherland, did you say something?"

"Did I say something? I've been calling you all this time."

Conrad plastered a very thin smile onto his lips. "I'm sorry; I was having some difficulty with the schedule. I must not have heard you."

"Didn't hear me? How the hell can you not hear me? We're barely a hallway apart."

The smile shifted so that the ends of his mouth pointed downward rather than upward. If George didn't know better, he'd have said that was a scowl.

"I lost about 40 percent of my hearing overseas, sir. When I was serving our country. I'm sorry for the inconvenience. How may I assist you?"

George blinked. "Well, uh...I, uh...well, I wanted coffee."

"Coffee?" Conrad tightened his jaw, and his entire face flexed with the movement.

"That's right."

"Well, of course. Let me leave your schedule for the week and get right on that."

George couldn't tell if the other man was being obliging or sarcastic. He supposed it must have been the former. He was a bit brusque and straightforward in his presentation; he was ex-military, after all, and a marine at that. They tended to be a little...well, tighter wound than the rest.

But Conrad had been too excited about the job to be a smart ass. So, George nodded. "Right. Thank you."

"Oh, my pleasure."

Again, there was a hint of something that George almost misinterpreted. Almost, but didn't. "You might as well make a pot. It's going to be a long day. Another one of those goddamned daylong interviews. I can't believe it's so hard to find a quality candidate."

"Me either. I'd imagine people would be lining up in droves to work here."

George nodded. "Exactly. I know Fenwood kind of sucks, but the job is a good one."

Conrad made no response. He headed to the communal area behind his station and busied himself with the coffee maker. "Do you want cream or sugar?"

"Yes and yes." Then, George remembered to add, "Thanks."

"Of course." Conrad flashed him another tight-lipped smile.

George shivered at the sight. He wouldn't have told the other man, of course. He couldn't help what his face looked like. But he was positively ghoulish when he tried to smile. Still, the room started to smell like coffee, and before long, he had a steaming mug full of it in his hands.

He took a sip, and then smiled. "You make a mean cup of coffee, Mr. Walters. Well, don't let me keep you from your scheduling."

The older man departed with another one of his scary smiles, and George returned to his work. His workload had lessened considerably since he'd hired Matt.

Matt Kilbourne was a very competent PA. George had checked his first emails carefully. Not that he doubted the other man's abilities, exactly. But he had been an enlisted man, not a commissioned one, and he'd graduated from a public university after all. He looked more like a football player than a businessman.

But Kilbourne's grammar was excellent, his attention to detail unflinching, and his work ethic really admirable. No sooner than he'd gotten out of orientation, he'd stayed late every night to work his way through the backlog of emails George had left for him.

If he had any complaint with Matt at all, it was that he was a bit too jumpy. That, he'd said, was PTSD. He didn't care to be touched without his foreknowledge. Which meant no spur-of-the-moment slaps on the back, or similar friendly gestures.

George hadn't thought to ask about PTSD. He probably couldn't legally anyway. He rather wished that wasn't the case.

He liked Matt. He appreciated his work. Still, PTSD in the workplace? He wasn't sure he cared for that. But it was too late to second-guess his decisions.

Anyway, Dad'll love to hear it. Not just hiring a veteran, or even a wounded veteran, but a fucked up one? How philanthropic.

Like an evil spirit conjured up by mere thought, at that moment, his phone announced a call from George Sr. in its familiar clown trumpet.

George Jr. felt a shiver run up his spine. That was a little uncanny. He answered the phone with all the wariness he might have responded with had he actually summoned a demon. "Dad?"

"George?"

"That's me. What can I do for you, Dad?"

"Just calling to check in."

Great. "About what?" He couldn't entirely keep the aggravation from his tone.

"Come on, George. I don't want to argue."

"I'm not arguing."

His father sighed. "Okay. Good. I'm not either."

"Fantastic. This is probably a first for us."

"How's the team coming?"

"Great. Everyone hired but one."

"Which one?"

George hemmed and hawed for a few moments, before revealing that it was the most important role. He expected an angry denouncement, or some lengthy criticism. But instead, he heard only silence. "Dad?"

"I'm here. That's good work. No, really. Keep it up. The sooner you get that team together, the better."

They didn't have much to discuss beyond that, and George Sr. ended the call shortly thereafter. *Well, hell must have just frozen over.* George sat in place, pondering this strange turn of events until Matt Kilbourne returned.

"Your suit, Mr. Sutherland."

"Excellent. Good work, Matt. Well, I'm off to the interview. I've flagged a couple of emails for your review."

"I'll get right on them."

"And get some lunch catered here, will you? I don't feel like heading out today. Anyway, if we eat here, it'll end sooner."

The younger man laughed. "You bet."

George poured himself another cup of coffee and headed to the interview. Today's idiot of the hour was a man with a heavy accent called Oliver Fischer, who worked *vision* into just about every sentence he uttered. He'd left Germany because the companies there didn't have the *vision* of American corporations. He believed the *vision* of the head of strategic development was probably his most important quality. He had himself worn many hats in his career, but he relished the opportunity to formulate a forward *vision* for growth. He wanted to work at Sutherland because he admired the *vision* the company displayed.

Angie had tripped him up good when she asked, "What vision, Mr. Fischer?"

He'd gone very red at that. "Well, the uh, that is, the company's vision, strategically, insomuch as an outsider can ascertain, that is."

George had driven the knife home by asking, "And what would you say our vision is, Mr. Fischer?"

"Well, the, uh, vision of any company, but especially a company like yours that is, how do you say it? Built from the ground up? No, self-made. Yes. The vision of any self-made company, and particularly one so successful and forward-thinking, is, uh, quite remarkable motion."

That was all George needed to hear. He appreciated a bullshitter as much as anyone, but he expected quality bullshitting. Oliver hadn't even bothered to make a study of the company he was applying for. Hell, the applicant the day before had regurgitated the company's mission statement word for word. And that was a better showing.

He was about to call an end to the farce when a knock sounded on the door. Matt Kilbourne poked his head and half of his barrel chest inside.

"I'm sorry, Mr. Sutherland. But you have a call. An urgent call."

Bless the man. "Oh. Well, I need to take care of that. Angie, you continue the interview. I'll be back when I can."

He stepped outside, shutting the conference room door after him. Matt was waiting. "Is it on my office phone?"

"Yes. It's—well, it's from your mother."

George raised an eyebrow. "You pulled me out of a meeting because my mom wanted a chat?"

"No. I mean, yes, but...she said it was important."

George groaned. "Matt, everything is important to my mom. If her eggs are over salted, that's important to my mom."

But Kilbourne didn't respond to the witticism. "I believe something serious may have happened, Mr. Sutherland."

This, at last, got his attention. "Why? What did she say?"

"Nothing. Only that she needed to talk to you urgently. It was her tone." The military man shook his head. "I could be wrong, sir, but I think something's happened. Something bad."

George pulled out his cellphone. He'd muted it for the interview, but now he checked. *Five missed calls. Fuck.* That was too much drama, even for his mother. "Right. I'll take it in my office."

He ran the full way and lifted the phone to his ear before he'd even reached his seat. "Mom?"

"Junior?"

He could hear the tension immediately in his mother's tone, and his heart sank. With a wave of his hand to shoo Matt, who hovered in the doorway, George said, "Get the door."

"What?"

"Not you, Mom. Tell me what's going on."

"Your dad: he's in the hospital again. I had to call an ambulance. I don't know what's wrong with him."

"Where are you?"

"I'm on my way there now. Stuck in traffic."

"Okay, listen. You probably shouldn't be driving, ma. Can't someone from the office take you?"

"Did you hear me, Junior? Your father is in the hospital. He could be dying."

George pinched the bridge of his nose. "I heard you, Mom. You just...you know how you get when you're worried. It'd be safer—"

"It'd be safer for you, George Maxwell, if you dropped the topic."

He sighed. "Right. Okay, tell me what happened."

"Your father was in his office. His home office. He was working remotely today. He came out, saying he couldn't breathe right. I've never seen him so pale."

He sighed again as he listened to his mother's sobs. She sobbed for a long time. Once or twice, he tried to interject with a question. "Mom, did they say anything?" or "Mom, why didn't you ride with the ambulance?"

But they were all ignored until she'd had her cry. He waited rather impatiently.

"Junior," she said after a space, her voice still breaking now and again. "Junior, you need to get back home."

"I can't just leave, Mom. I've got a team to build. Dad wants me to—"

"Your dad might be dying," his mother shot back.

He grimaced at her tone. His mother's penchant for hysteria was really grating on his last nerve. "Mom..."

"George, listen to me. I know you and your dad have been fighting lately. If he dies, and you're still at odds...well, you don't want that. Do you?"

He blinked. Sometimes, his mother's insight surprised him. This was definitely one of those times. "Oh. The business..."

"Exactly. I want you out here on the first flight. Do you understand?"

"Yes."

"You promise?"

"I promise, Mom."

They parted with a few words of solace.

George stared for a moment at his office wall and the photos of his kite sailing adventures. *Dad in the hospital. Dad...dying.* He couldn't quite wrap his head around that.

Love him or hate him, George Sr. had been a part of his life since he'd taken his first breath.

And the company. What happens to Sutherland Research?

No, his mom was right. He had to get there sooner rather than later. But not without wrapping up the business at hand. He'd come so close to finishing the team. And these interviews were going nowhere. It was one clown after another.

He sighed, going through the list in his mind of everyone he'd seen so far. It had been a carousel of jackasses though. The ones who'd looked good on paper bombed in person, and the ones, like Martin Blakely, who seemed great in person bombed on paper.

He'd like to face George Sr.—if there was still time to face him—with this part of the task completed. But he couldn't in good conscience hire anyone who'd come through those doors. None of them had the experience or know-how to get the job done.

None of them... He sat bolt upright in his seat. That wasn't entirely true, was it?

He was on his feet at that and barreled out of his office. He almost careened into Matt, who only just escaped by pressing his oversized frame against the wall. "Mr. Sutherland?"

But George didn't stop to chat. "I need a flight to Philly, Matt, as soon as possible. Within the hour, if possible. But by tonight at the absolute latest."

He raced past him and down the hall, back to the conference room. He didn't bother to knock. Bursting in, he interrupted Oliver midsentence.

"And so," the other man was saying, "I think that is the kind of vision—"

"Oh shut the hell up. Take your vision and get out of here, Mr. Fischer," George said. Angela gaped, and so did their interviewee. So he threw in an, "Are you deaf? Go. You're not getting the job. You didn't even bother to research the damned company. Get out."

Angela started to make some kind of conciliatory statement, thanking Mr. Fischer for his time. But the other man gathered his belongs and let loose a few swears and a detailed recommendation for which pieces of his anatomy George could perform unsavory acts upon.

George shooed him like a fly, and ordered Angela, "Make sure he gets the hell out of here."

She did, and when she came back, she stared at him in mute surprise.

"Well, don't look at me like that, Angie. The man's a moron."

"I'm sorry, Mr. Sutherland. His résumé—"

"I know. I'm tired of this. My father's in the hospital again."

"Oh, no. I'm so sorry."

He held up a hand to stop her. "Well, life catches up to us all, I'm afraid. My point is, we need to wrap this up. I asked you to set up more interviews, well you did. I think I've made up my mind."

George nodded behind his desk. "I'm going to be on a flight within the hour, if I can help it. I need you to get me any paperwork you need me to sign before I go. I want to extend an offer to Heather Bradshaw."

Chapter Fifteen

Angela didn't know exactly what was going on with George Sutherland Sr. No one did. Matt had heard from their boss, George Jr., a handful of times throughout the past week. Mostly, it was direction on emails to send or follow-ups that had to be made by such-and-such time. But very few details about the elder Sutherland's condition trickled down.

All they knew was that George Sr. had been rushed to the hospital for the second time in a year. Whether he'd make it out alive this time or not, they could only speculate. A kind of cloud hung over the office, not only of sympathy for the old man, but of fear for the future.

Even the newest arrivals had some idea that George Jr. wasn't the leader his father had been. Whatever reputation Sutherland Bio had for being a good place to work was coupled rather tightly to the older man's stewardship.

They waited in tense expectation. The days passed slowly. In the beginning, Angela found herself busy. She still had paperwork related to the new hires, and their remaining benefits. Every time one confirmation would roll in from corporate, there would be another form to process, or another approval to grant.

Plus, Heather started on Tuesday of the week after being hired. Angela coordinated her orientation as she had the other new hires, handling some of it herself. The rest was done remotely, via videoconference with the Philly branch.

Heather Bradshaw must have been on her best behavior, Angela thought. The other woman was all politeness—and quite charming at that. She had a quick wit and tempered a playful sense of humor with a brisk professionalism.

Still, Angela wasn't fooled. She remembered Caroline's words. And she was glad she'd be out of here, sooner rather than later. Before Heather and everyone here got comfortable enough in their roles to let the fur really start flying.

As it was, the office atmosphere was all right at the moment. Conrad was his usual short-tempered self, but he'd buried himself in redoing the filing system. So, as long as no one bothered him—which included greetings or communication of any kind—and everyone made sure the coffee pot got refilled, he was no trouble at all.

Casper shut himself in his office most of the day. He was, he told them, "Getting acquainted with the Sutherland systems."

On the few occasions when Angela had walked by his closed office door, she heard audio playing and never lingered long enough to determine what, exactly, he was watching. She had a pretty good idea, and no need to confirm her suspicions.

Matt and Kathryn were more congenial. Matt, finding he had less to do now that he wasn't fetching coffees and lunches, made himself useful to the rest of the office. He went on coffee runs and lunch runs for the staff and generally helped out where he could.

Kathryn had already familiarized herself with the vendors and contracts she would be dealing with, but with the moratorium on new spending, didn't have much to do until the boss was back and lifted it. She wandered from office to office, chatting with everyone about every and any thing. Everyone but Conrad, who firmly rebuffed any overtures of friendliness from anyone.

For her own part, Angela found her work winding down too. George had put a hiring freeze in place, other than the positions she'd already filled. Performance reviews weren't due until the end of the year. Once he was back with new direction, she would have more to occupy her time. But for now, he'd put a halt to almost everything. Her business consisted of concluding the new hire process, and that was pretty much it.

She found herself chatting a lot with Heather in the second week of George's absence. She'd only met her new boss once and had had no guidance other than what she could glean from that interview.

Angela, of course, couldn't provide much. She acquainted Heather with the company policies, and various materials George had flagged for her consumption. But their conversation usually turned more personal. Not that it ever got *too* personal.

But she did learn that Heather was having some difficulty finding an apartment that allowed dogs.

"There've been a few that let small dogs in. Twenty-pound limit and that kind of thing. But Ragnar's almost a hundred pounds over the limit."

Ragnar was a giant, snowy-white Great Pyrenees who, according to his mistress, loved giving kisses and pretending to be deaf.

"He's really the nicest dog. He does bark a little. It's a Pyrenees thing. But he loves everyone. But he will absolutely pretend he can't hear you if he doesn't want to."

For now, Heather was renting a hotel room. "Mom's boarding him. But I know she'll be happy when I do find something. She's getting tired of his shedding."

This was another feature of Great Pyrenees, Angela learned: They shed rather abundantly. Heather had proffered pictures, and she understood why when she saw him. The dog was huge, and he had a veritable mane of long, fluffy fur. His tail was enormous, and the fur around his legs billowed out in great, puffy pantaloons.

"He's gorgeous."

Heather smiled. "Yes. He's my baby."

Angela laughed. "That might be the biggest baby I've ever seen."

"Oh, he doesn't know that. He thinks he's a lap dog."

She wasn't quite sure that that sounded ideal to her. A large, loud, shedding dog who liked to climb into your lap? Angela loved dogs, of course. But her idea of a big dog was the Labrador she'd grown up with. This thing looked about three times as big as Maxie had been.

"Well, let me talk to one of my friends—Lauren. She knows some people, through her church, who are renting out their mom's house. She had a dog there. A golden or something. So they might accept Ragnar."

Heather beamed. "Thanks, Angie. I'd owe you one."

By midweek of the second week of George's absence, an idea had struck Angela. She'd assembled the new team. They were all settling in well. If their boss had still been around, she would have tried to persuade him to hold some kind of welcome event.

But she did have a company card and a little bit of discretionary spending for human resource–related events. And George had given her the go-ahead to wrap things up.

Anyway, I'm going to be gone a few weeks after he gets back. Even if he's pissed, what do I care?

The matter thus settled to her satisfaction, Angela began the arrangements. It was time to welcome the new team. She considered taking them all out to lunch. Tres Amigos was her first choice. But Conrad couldn't abide spicy food and wasn't placated by the promise of other items on the menu. "Don't worry about me. I'll just stay here."

Of course, she couldn't have a team lunch that didn't include a member of the team. She cycled through the list of reasonably decent eateries in town. And one by one, someone objected to something. Kathryn had read a review that mentioned food poisoning at the family restaurant. Matt was trying to keep his cholesterol down, so the steak house was out. Casper couldn't stand sushi. The very sight of it made him sick.

She was about to give up in despair when a new thought occurred to her. *Brunch.* And she knew exactly where she'd go. Tealeaves.

Lauren was delighted with the idea. "We can bring breakfast or lunch—whatever you want."

"Great. I think we'll do some quiches—those should stay warm on the way over—and cold lunch sandwiches. And coffee."

"I've got a better idea. Why don't I bring one of my portable toaster ovens over, and we make the sandwiches there on demand, so people can choose what they like from our catering menu? And I've got my catering espresso machine, so we can make whatever coffees people want. Lattes, americanos, whatever. No extra charge. Just pay the menu price."

Angela had protested that this sounded like a lot of extra work, and she didn't want to impose on her friend.

Lauren replied first with a snort, then, "Come on, Angela. I've been dying to meet those whackos. I want to put names to faces. This'll be my chance."

Chapter Sixteen

She couldn't argue with reasoning like that, and so she didn't. They chose that Friday as the appointed day, and Lauren showed up at seven in the morning to set up.

"I really feel bad about this," Angela said. "You've got a business to run. You can't be hanging around here."

Lauren grinned at her. "Like I'd miss this? Trust me, they can handle themselves. I'm not even on the schedule today. And I need to meet the team."

Angela rolled her eyes. "You're worse than I am."

"That's what Rae said this morning. But..." She shrugged. "I think she's just annoyed she couldn't figure out a reason to be here too."

"At least let me help you set up. I'll feel a little better about it then."

Lauren allowed it, setting her to work on the coffee bar. She'd brought over a dozen syrups. "Including lavender." She grinned. "Couldn't forget that."

"I'd certainly hope not," Angela declared. "We've been friends for a long time."

They'd made use of the two empty reception pods in the hall. Prior to Sutherland's acquisition of Fenwood Bio, there had been three admins: One full-time, and two part-time. Now, Conrad sat nearest the door, and the other two pods remained empty.

For the time being, those empty desktops served as breakfast and coffee stations. Angela brewed two types of regular coffee, and Lauren set out an array of piping hot breakfast quiches and fresh pastries. Then they swapped spots.

Angela hadn't told anyone what to expect—only that they should "come in hungry tomorrow."

Conrad was the first to enter, and he cast a critical eye over the setup. "I hope that thing doesn't make too much noise," he said, gesturing to the espresso machine. "I'm going to be working over there."

Lauren only smiled though. "You must be Mr. Walters?"

He frowned at her. "That's right. How'd you know that?"

"Angela's mentioned your work ethic—'always the first in the office.'"

"Ah." His features relaxed at that, and he shrugged. "It means I get in before he...that is, I can get started without distractions."

Lauren nodded and offered to make him a coffee.

"What kind of coffee?"

"Whatever you like. We've got breakfast blend and dark roast in the carafes, and I can make anything on the menu there."

Conrad read through the offering, harrumphing at the variety. "Coconut? Lavender? Hmph. I remember when coffee was supposed to taste like coffee. Not some kind of botanist's shop. Well, I guess I'll have a latte. No sugar."

"Any flavor?"

"Nope. I like to taste my coffee. Not sure why folks drink it if they don't want to taste it. Doesn't make much sense to me."

"Make sure you grab some food," Angela encouraged. She could tell Lauren was struggling to keep the smile off her face, so she figured she'd intervene to help her friend.

"What do we got?"

"Quiche and fresh fruit and a variety of pastries," Lauren put in. "And bagels over there."

"Quiche, eh?" Conrad studied the plates suspiciously for a long moment. "Nothing with bacon?"

"There's a bacon quiche." Lauren smiled sweetly. "Right beside you."

"Bacon, huh?" He eyed the egg dish for another long while, then shrugged. "Well, I suppose I'll try it."

Matt arrived next, and he was considerably less finicky. "Damn, Angela. You weren't kidding that we should come in hungry. This is a lot of food."

He loaded a plate with several bagels and a pile of fruit and stopped at the coffee station. "You really can make a latte right here?"

"That's right."

"Sweet. Well, I'll take vanilla caramel, extra tall. Extra shot. Extra sweet."

Conrad harrumphed emphatically from across the room. Matt ignored him, and Lauren smiled. Angela, meanwhile, helped herself to a slice of tomato quiche.

It was now that Heather entered. She wore a crisp navy-blue pantsuit with a white blouse, and Angela almost dropped her plate at the sight of her. She felt a little ridiculous. But, damn, if that woman didn't get more beautiful every time she saw her.

Shit. What the hell is wrong with me? Even if they weren't coworkers, and even if she didn't already know that the other woman was a lowkey psycho Angela had no idea if she was even single, much less a lesbian. And none of it mattered anyway, she reminded herself. *Because she is psycho*.

Heather turned those frosty-blue eyes her way, and they lit up at the sight of her. And Angela's insides did a stupid little dance at the change in expression. *What the hell*?

Maybe Lauren was right. Maybe the universe was sending her some kind of message. It had been years, after all. Maybe she should see if Nikki was interested in meeting. *Maybe...*

"Angie," Heather's voice pulled her from her reverie. The other woman was crossing the distance between them, and still beaming. "I talked to Lauren's friends. I signed the lease last night. I'm going to pick Ragnar and some of my stuff up tonight."

"You must be Heather," Lauren cut in. She'd abandoned the coffee station and was pressing between them with her hand extended.

Heather took the proffered hand with obvious confusion. "That's right."

"I'm Lauren."

"Oh. I should have recognized your voice."

Lauren glanced between Angela and Heather, explaining, "We talked about Franna's house. But just on the phone. I'm so glad to meet you in person."

"Likewise. Thank you a bunch. I owe you—both of you. The place is perfect."

"Oh, I'm so glad you liked it. It's been nicely kept up, but it is a little older."

Heather waved that away with a brush of her hand. "I don't care about that. It's a roof over my head and a nice place. And, they let me bring Ragnar."

"Ragnar...that's your dog, right? He's some kind of giant breed?"

Heather nodded. "That's right. Great Pyrenees."

Lauren shook her head. "Not sure I could deal with a dog that big. I'd be afraid he'd sit on me wrong and crush me to death."

"Careful," Angela teased, "that's her baby you're talking about."

Heather's cheeks pinked, and she laughed. "In fairness, he will try to sit on you. But he hasn't crushed anyone yet."

Lauren laughed, too, although her eyes seemed to be focused on Angela rather than Heather. "Well, I'm still not sure I'd be up to it. Angela, on the other hand, will probably love to meet him. She's a big dog lover. Always has been, since we were kids."

"You two knew each other growing up?" It was Heather's turn to glance between her peers with a curious gaze.

"That's right. Next door neighbors."

"Oh." Heather nodded. "That's...great."

Lauren held up her ring finger. "She was my maid of honor. Walked me down the aisle with my mom."

"Oh." Heather's expression brightened. "That's—that's awesome."

"It was." Lauren smiled. "But she tells me you're a big coffee drinker?"

"Oh, yes. Complete addict." Heather shot her a faux suspicious glance. "Although, I'm a little worried. What else has she said?"

"Only that you're the smartest person to walk in Fenwood's doors in a long time." Lauren shrugged.

Conrad harrumphed again, more loudly than before, and Heather threw a glance Angela's way.

Angela flushed. She had no idea why in hell she'd have repeated that. "Well...uh..."

"Wow. I'm flattered."

Lauren smiled, seeming to miss the awkwardness she'd just created. "So, what'll it be?"

"Oh. Um...what do you have?"

Lauren tapped the menu. "Whatever's listed. And if it's not here, well, I can probably still make it."

Heather glanced over the choices and exhaled. "That's a lot of options." She glanced back at Angela. "What do you recommend, Angie?"

Lauren's eyes flashed up at that, and Angela's cheeks grew hot. No one ever called her Angie. No one except George, because he was an asshole, and Carrie, because it had been a term of endearment.

Except, somewhere along the way—probably after overhearing it during the interview—Heather had picked it up. And it felt perfectly natural when she said it.

"Careful now," Lauren said, the faintest hint of amusement in her tone. "You will never get an unbiased opinion from *Angie*."

Angela scowled at her friend and all the absurd conclusions she knew she was jumping to. "Well, uh, she's not wrong there. I always recommend the lavender. But I'm biased."

"Biased? She means obsessed. She won't even try anything else."

Heather smiled. "Well, that's recommendation enough for me. I'll try the lavender."

Lauren smiled, more to herself than either of them. "Well, a lavender latte coming right up."

"So," Heather said to Angela, "lavender? In coffee? Does it actually taste like the flower? Or…?"

"It does. I know it sounds weird."

"Weird doesn't begin to cover it," Conrad offered.

They exchanged covert smirks, but otherwise ignored the comment. "It tastes exactly like lavender smells," Angela said.

"And that's…a good thing?"

"Very. It's…it's hard to explain. You have to try it to know what I'm talking about."

Heather nodded. "All right. I'll give it a shot."

Chapter Seventeen

Angela waited as Heather made up her mind. It took several sips, but she declared the lavender latte a winner.

"You're right. It *is* hard to explain. But it's good. Very good."

Conrad harrumphed, and Matt declared he'd give it a try. Kathryn, meanwhile, had arrived, and she wondered, "What are we trying?"

"They're having soap-flavored coffee," Conrad explained.

Kathryn wrinkled her nose. "Eww. What?"

"It's not soap," Heather said. "It's lavender."

"That's what my soap smells like." Conrad shrugged.

Matt laughed. "Really? I wouldn't have guessed you were a floral soap kind of guy, Conrad."

He snorted. "I'm a whatever-soap-the-Missus-buys kind of guy. And the Missus happens to like lavender. In her soap, and her hand lotion, and in her candles. But not..." He frowned at them all. "In her coffee."

Heather smiled. "Well, she does not know what she's missing."

"Hear, hear," Angela agreed. The pair raised their mugs in a mock toast, and then found a table.

For a few moments, they said nothing. And as the silence began to feel awkward, Angela asked, "So, Ragnar...how old is he?"

"Six and a half."

"Ah."

"But I've only had him for two years." Heather smiled. "He's a rescue. Used to be a livestock dog. His owners sold the farm and left the dogs."

"Oh, that's awful."

Heather nodded. "A few of them were so old or feral they ended up being put down. But Ragnar was more social, and young enough. They were looking for a foster home. He's what they call, I suppose, a 'foster fail.'"

"How so?"

"Well..." She shrugged, "We couldn't give him up."

Angela blinked. "'We'?"

"Oh." The other woman's cheeks pinked. "Me and my ex, Caroline." She smiled in a careful way. "We were fostering him together. It was supposed to be a kind of trial run before we actually adopted a dog. But we fell in love with him."

"Ah. Well, that, uh, worked out well for him."

"I like to think so." Heather smiled.

So she is a lesbian. And single, from the sounds of it. "So, umm, you said he was a livestock dog. How does he like living in the house now?"

"Like it? He loves it. He sleeps on the sofa all day long, until it's time for his walks. He'd be a permanent couch potato if I let him, I swear."

"Oh, wow—" A voice distracted them from further conversation. "Is that real coffee? Like, good coffee?"

Casper had just entered the building, and he was standing in the doorway taking in long lungsful of air.

"You mind shutting that thing?" Conrad snapped. "I don't want flies getting in. There's food out."

Casper obliged, stepping over the threshold. "Oh my God, that smells so good. What do we got here?"

"What about you?" Heather wondered, drawing Angela's attention back. "Lauren says you love dogs. Do you have any pets?"

"Oh, no. Once we got the house, Carrie didn't like dogs on the wood floors."

"Carrie?"

"Uh, my ex."

"Oh."

"And I just haven't had the time since. Not with helping out at my parents' farm on the weekends."

Heather nodded. They'd talked about Angela's family farm before. "I don't know. I'll bet a dog would love that."

"Maybe. But he'd have to be well trained, so he wouldn't run off after people or anything. Especially during hayride season."

"There's tons of adult dogs looking for homes. Already trained and everything."

"I know. I just...haven't really got around to it."

"Got around to what?" Casper wondered, plunking down in a seat next to them. His plate was piled high with food, and he carried a steaming mug of a light-brown coffee and milk mixture.

"Getting a dog," Angela said.

"Oh. Dogs are the best. But so much work." He took a bite of quiche and proceeded to speak before he'd finished chewing or swallowing it. "Mmm. This was such a good idea, Angie. I haven't had breakfast all week. Never have time. This is so good."

Angela felt her appetite waning in direct proportion to her colleague's enthusiastic conversation. But she smiled politely and agreed. "Tealeaves' food is always top-notch."

"And Lauren was saying she's going to be making sandwiches later in the morning for us?"

"That's right. She'll be here until one."

"No way." Casper took a gulp of coffee. "Lunch too?"

She nodded.

"Damn. You're the best, Angie." He popped another bite into his mouth. "Hey, I've been meaning to ask you. Have either of you seen my umbrella? I brought it in the other day when they said we might get rain. It was at my desk when I left for lunch, I would have sworn. But when I got back, it was gone."

Heather shook her head. "Sorry, I don't think I have."

"You'd know it when you saw it. It's got the bat symbol all over it. You know, from Batman?"

"I haven't seen it either," Angela said. "But if I do, I'll let you know."

★

Lunch was every bit as good as breakfast.

Matt had broken his low cholesterol diet, declaring, "After spending all morning staring at eggs, my willpower was done in." He'd gone for the Philly steak and cheese.

Conrad had too. "No mushrooms. Onions on the side. And I'll take a grilled ham, too, if you have that."

Matt came back for a second Philly, and Conrad decided he needed a piece of coffee cake for dessert.

Casper went back and forth between the tables so frequently Angela wasn't sure if he was having trouble making up his mind, or if he was coming back for sixths.

Kathryn bemoaned the lack of variety among the soups. An employee had dropped off only two pots of freshly made, piping hot soup. And she didn't care for chicken and wild rice. "And cream of cashew pea soup? Hard pass for anything with peas. No, I'll just have to work off the carbs from my sandwich."

"Or you could pack your own lunch," Conrad muttered. "If nothing here is good enough."

Heather chose the wild rice soup, and Angela got a bowl of pea soup. "You want to split a sandwich?" she wondered. "I'm not sure I could eat the whole thing and one of those bear claws. And I'm definitely going back for a bear claw."

Angela laughed and agreed. "What do you want?"

"Oh, anything. It all looks excellent."

She considered for a moment, then flashed a grin. "Do you trust me?"

Heather squinted her eyes suspiciously. "You know that's exactly the kind of question that is going to inspire *mis*trust, right?"

"It's another weird suggestion. But, it's divine."

The other woman considered for a long moment, then nodded. "All right. You didn't steer me wrong on the lavender latte. I'll go with your recommendation."

"Okay." Angela nodded and added as they both headed to Lauren, "We're going to get the popper."

"Wait, what?"

"You do like jalapeños, right?"

"Yes. In small quantities."

"All right. The popper it is, then."

"Oh God. Is it too late to change my answer?"

Angela shook her head. "So much for trust."

"Fine. Fine, but if I end up with indigestion..."

Lauren laughed. "It's very mild; don't worry. Two jalapeño poppers coming up."

"Just one," Heather corrected. "We're going to split it."

"Oh." Lauren's eyebrows quirked, but her tone didn't change. "Of course. That'll be done in a jiffy."

Heather watched with an obvious mixture of curiosity and fear as Lauren spread some kind of cream cheese mixture on a baguette.

"That's the jalapeño cream cheese," Angela explained.

Next, Lauren layered it in strips of bell peppers and slices of fresh mozzarella cheese and popped it in the oven. "You want any coffee or tea to go with that?"

"Another lavender latte," Heather decided. "I'm afraid Angie's gotten me hooked on them."

Lauren smiled. "And what about you, *Angie*? Do I even have to ask?"

"No. It'll be the same."

By time their coffees were finished, the sandwich was ready.

Heather turned to Angela after a cautious first bite. "I have to admit, this is excellent. Well, you're two for two today."

They'd just sat down to eat when Lauren joined them with a plate of food of her own. "You don't mind if I sit with you, do you Heather?"

"Not at all, please. You've been on your feet all morning."

She waved this away though. "No different than a day at Tealeaves. Actually, that's not true. No screaming customers today."

Angela laughed. "The worst we did is complain about a lack of variety for soups."

"And too much variety for coffee."

"That's right. I forgot about that."

"So, really, you've been outstanding customers, all things considered."

Heather shook her head. "Those are some pretty sad standards."

"It's customer service. What are you going to do?"

The three nodded contemplatively, nibbling at their food.

Lauren looked up. "Hey, I had an idea."

"Oh?" Angela asked.

"Heather, you said you were going to be moving this weekend?"

"That's right. Picking up my dog and some of my stuff tonight. I'll probably borrow my dad's truck to get the big things tomorrow."

"You got anyone to help you?"

"Well, Dad'll help me load everything."

"What about unloading?"

Heather shrugged. "I'll manage."

"You sure?" Lauren dabbed a crust of bread in her soup. "Rae and I would be happy to lend you a hand."

The other woman hesitated. "You sure? I don't want to ruin your Saturday."

"Oh, no. It's no worry at all. Hell, I'll bet we could get a whole posse together. Get it all done in no time." Lauren glanced at Angela, who was a little too stunned by her friend's sudden chumminess to think of much else. "You're not busy tomorrow, are you?"

"Me? Uh, no."

"You don't have to, Angie. I wouldn't dream of imposing—"

"No, no, it's no imposition. I'd be happy to help."

Heather eyed her dubiously. Angela's hesitance had clearly not gone unnoticed. "I know you have commitments with your family farm and all that. I can handle it."

"No, really, I'd be happy to help. Especially..." Angela flashed a grin. "If you promise me that I get to meet the famous Mr. Ragnar."

Chapter Eighteen

It had all been arranged with not much hassle. Indeed, as soon as the rest of the team got wind of Heather's predicament, they had more movers than they knew what to do with. They all promised to be there, except Kathryn.

"I'm babysitting my boyfriend's cat," she said.

"I'll come," Conrad decided. He shrugged at their surprised stares. "My wife's got the grandkids tomorrow. Son and daughter-in-law are heading out of town."

Angela stayed behind as Lauren packed up and helped her carry everything to the catering vehicle. Her main motive was, of course, to help. But she had another goal too. "What are you doing?" she asked as soon as they were outside.

Lauren, though, ignored the question. Eyes sparkling, she hissed, "Then *that's* why you're not interested in Nikki."

Angela blinked. "What?"

"Heather. She's the reason you're not even interested in meeting Nikki."

Angela groaned. "Good God. I knew you were going to jump to conclusions."

"Why? Because you two were inseparable and blushing and flirting together all morning?" She set the warmer she'd been carrying down and spread her hands in the air. "Come on, Angela. Oh, yeah, that's another thing. Since when are you 'Angie'?"

Angela groaned again. It was exactly as she'd predicted. "I'm 'Angie' because that idiot George calls me Angie, and everyone heard it."

Lauren took the crate from her hands and loaded it into the back of her vehicle. "Right. That still doesn't explain the flirting."

"We weren't flirting."

"Oh, my ass you weren't. What? Were you just not going to tell me about this?"

"Yes. Because there is nothing to tell." Angela exhaled in exasperation. "Nothing at all. I literally didn't even know she was a lesbian until a few hours ago."

"Really?" Lauren frowned at her. "She told me in, like, fifteen minutes of us meeting. Then again, I wasn't tongue-tied. And you're a little tongue-tied around her."

"I am not."

Lauren had no time for her denials. "That's why this moving thing is a good idea."

"Wait, is that what you're doing?"

"Um, obviously."

Angela facepalmed in a theatrical fashion. "Are we forgetting that she's a crazy lady, Lauren?"

This, at last, wiped the enthusiastic grin from her friend's face. "Are you so sure about that, Angela?"

"Yes. When I talked to HR, they said that's why she left."

Lauren made a skeptical face. "I don't know. She told me it was because her ex worked there. In HR, actually. And it was just getting too awkward."

"Wait..." Angela blinked. "What? When did she tell you that? And since when the hell are you two on such chummy terms?"

"She came back for another lavender latte after breakfast. And being a barista is like being a bartender. People tell you things." Lauren grinned. "Plus, I'm adorable. Who can resist my small talk?"

"You mean, your nosy grilling."

Lauren shrugged. "Call it what you will. I still got the answers I wanted. And I'm a good judge of character. Nothing about her says 'crazy lady.'"

Angela snorted. "You're just saying that because you're obsessed with being a matchmaker. Whether I want one or not."

"No. You know I'm a good judge of character. And I may be concerned about you being alone." She ignored Angela's scoff. "But if I really thought there was something up with Heather, I'd tell you."

The two stood in silence. Angela crossed her arms, and Lauren added with a smirk, "Anyway, that'd just mean I could go back to my original plan—getting you and Nikki Fulton together."

"You do have a good track record," Angela conceded. "And...she is pretty cute."

"Cute? She's a knockout."

"Well...all right, I'll give you that one too. But I still think you're wrong on this."

"Why?" Lauren seemed at a loss to comprehend.

But to Angela, it was obvious. "Because, I'm telling you, I talked to Northwest's human resources department. Caroline said..." She trailed off, her eyes going wide. "Wait a minute. You said her ex worked in HR, right? At Northwest?"

"That's right."

"Fuck."

"What's wrong?"

"Earlier, Heather told me she and her ex adopted Ragnar—the dog. She mentioned the ex's name—Caroline.

"The woman I spoke with in HR was..."

"Caroline," Lauren concluded, her own eyes going wide. "You don't think..."

"That it was the same Caroline?" She nodded, sinking into the back of her friend's vehicle. "I'm thinking it'd be a hell of a coincidence if there were *two* Caroline's working in the same department, who both had an axe to grind against Heather."

Angela had spent the rest of the afternoon trying to devise a means of confirming her theory. Ideally, she needed to know Caroline's last name. Finding out wasn't difficult. It was listed on the Northwest company website: Caroline Miller.

There was no nonchalant way to ask what Heather's ex's last name was though. In the end, Angela resorted to a deeply unprofessional but far more effective tactic—social media snooping.

She found Heather's profile. It was pretty locked down. None of her posts were visible. Her friends list was, though, and Angela searched it for "Carolines." There were two. One in her late seventies, and one a middle-aged, married woman a coast away. Neither of those seemed like the Caroline in question. Neither were Caroline Miller.

For a minute, it seemed like she'd struck a dead end. Then she headed back to Heather's page. From there, she scrolled through her profile pictures. These were all public. And while there were none of her with Caroline—any Caroline—after about fifteen minutes of searching, Angela found what she was looking for.

Three and a half years earlier, Caroline Miller had commented, "So proud of you, babe," on a picture of Heather accepting a leadership award.

Angela rested her head in her hands. *What a fuckup I am.* So, all that nonsense about Heather being a drill sergeant, and a monster to work with? That had been sour grapes from an ex. Not the unbiased opinion of a human resources professional.

Knowing what she did, Angela didn't put an ounce of stock in the other woman's word. If Caroline had been a professional, she would have handed the call on to someone else in her department. That she'd trashed Heather with no hint there'd been a prior connection between them? No, that was deeply unprofessional, and unethical.

Not that Angela was herself in a position to be too particular about ethics. Her current disappointment stemmed mostly from the fact that she'd been so utterly played. But part of it related to something else entirely. Her revenge had been sabotaged.

She'd hired not one but *two* good candidates. Both Matt and Heather were excellent in their roles.

And their roles were the most critical for the company's success. *For George's success. Good God, I'm a fuckup.*

She confessed her failings and findings to Lauren and Rae, who took them far better than she did.

"Hey, look on the bright side," Lauren said. "She's not a crazy lady."

"She's got a point. From the sounds of it, you two are really hitting it off. You don't want her to be crazy."

"Rae, you know I love her, but don't listen to a word Lauren says on the matter. She's a gossip."

"I knew that already. Doesn't mean she's wrong though."

"She is."

Lauren rolled her eyes and sipped her margarita.

They were sitting at the bar at Tres Amigos, waiting for a table to open up. They hadn't made reservations—a rookie mistake in Fenwood, as this was the premier eatery, and Friday nights were always packed. But, in the present instance, it was a result of the emergency nature of their meeting.

"She is in denial," Lauren said. "I'm telling you. There's so much chemistry between them, you could cut it with a knife."

Angela frowned at her friend. "That doesn't even make sense."

"Don't distract with semantics. You know what I'm saying, even if I don't. You like her, she likes you. That's obvious."

Rae grinned. "I don't know. The judge has spoken. Sounds like it's wedding bells and happily ever after for you two."

Lauren frowned at her wife. "You hush, you beautiful brat."

Rae's grin broadened. "Now who is being bratty?"

Angela sighed. "Okay, slow it down. You're going to need a room before they even find us a table."

The other two women exchanged a few whispered phrases and giggles, but then returned to the conversation. Rae's cheeks had gone positively crimson, and she attacked her glass of water with gusto. Whatever Lauren had said had, apparently, been good.

Angela shook her head. She almost couldn't fathom a love that evergreen. She'd long ago given up on ever finding it. Hell, if she didn't see it with her own eyes, she probably wouldn't have believed it.

Lauren, meanwhile, turned back to her friend, looking quite pleased with herself. "Where were we?"

"You were making me gag into my martini."

The other woman's grin broadened. "I remember. What I'm saying is, Angela, let's just see where it goes. Yeah, your plan to fuck George over might be hosed. But who knows…" She took another sip of her margarita, then flashed a wicked smile. "You might end up fucking someone far more deserving."

Chapter Nineteen

"I hear things are quiet on the home front?" Andy asked.

"For now." George nodded. He glanced around from under his sunglasses, shifting in his seat. "But what was so urgent we needed to meet?"

Andy smiled a half smile. "Relax, George. No one's going to notice you."

That was probably true enough. They were seated in an outdoor café in the Italian market. Andy had picked the spot, but it didn't surprise George. The other man had an unhealthy attachment to all things Italian, from his choice of muscle to cuisine. Something to do with an Italian grandmother. *Or was it great-grandmother*? He'd heard the story once but hadn't really paid much attention.

Still, there were many heritages to get wrapped up in. But Italian? What had Italians ever given the world, except pizza and olive oil and organized crime? He appreciated all three in their spheres. None of them were particularly worth getting bothered about though.

The other man was still trying to make his point for some reason. "These people are here to get a taste of the heart of Philly. They're not interested in us."

Ninth Street and the marketplace were always bustling. Tourists loved it for the cheesesteak, the *Rocky* movie connections, and the colorful vibe of the place. Andy was right, on some level. Most of the people here probably couldn't tell him from Adam.

Still, this was his backyard, where he'd grown up. And while it might have been a massive yard, someone, sometime, might spot them. That was why he didn't like open-air meetings.

Andy was less concerned, and George began to fear he'd keep on making his point unless he was interrupted. So, he nodded.

"Right. Still, I have to get back."

This, at least, silenced the other man's monologue. "How's your dad doing?"

"Good. His heart rate had spiked. One hundred and sixty beats per minute."

Andy whistled. "Jesus."

"They put him on meds to get it under control. But it keeps slipping back into strange rhythms."

"Atrial fibrillation, then?"

"That's right. They're talking about a procedure, some kind of targeted heat to the part of the muscle that's misfiring."

"Ablation." Andy nodded.

"I think that's it, yeah." George remembered looking up the rates of complication. They were disappointingly low. But he didn't recall the name.

"Joey's mother needed it a few years back. He had to take a few weeks off to be with her."

"Ah." George threw another glance around. "Speaking of Caruso, where is he?"

Andy smiled. "I have no idea. Gave him the morning off. Seeing as how he's basically a pilgrim in the Holy Land."

George shook his head. "I don't know how you can stand that guy."

"Joey's a good guy. A bit...colorful. But a good guy."

George took that to mean that Caruso broke skulls on command. A moment later, his colleague confirmed his suspicion with a shrug.

"He gets the job done and doesn't ask too many questions. And good help? Well, that's damned hard to come by."

Here, at least, he could agree. "Don't I know it. Before he had his episode, Dad had me building a team for the newest Sutherland facility."

"The Fenwood one, right?"

"Right."

"How'd that go?"

"Well, I got the team. But my God, I've never met so many imbeciles in the process."

Andy laughed. "Like I say—good help is hard to find nowadays. Everyone thinks they're entitled to something. No one's got a work ethic anymore."

George nodded. "And it doesn't help that it's in the middle of absolutely nowhere. Who in their right mind wants to move to Fenwood?"

The other man laughed again. "I don't know. Joey seemed pretty keen on the place."

He snorted. "I said, 'who in their right mind.' Caruso doesn't qualify."

Andy smiled. Whether he was offended or not, George couldn't quite tell. He didn't quite care either. He might have made more of a secret about his feelings toward Caruso if Andy hadn't deployed him to Fenwood. But he had, so George didn't feel the need for too much discretion.

"Well, maybe. But I'm glad George Sr. is on the mend."

"Me too," the younger Sutherland lied. He wasn't glad. He didn't want his dad to die, of course. But, on the other hand, he didn't want him restored to full health either.

A nice middle ground, something that would prompt George Sr. into a well-deserved retirement, would have been just perfect in his book.

Still, he hadn't lost hope on that score. His father might look better, and the doctors might be optimistic, but he talked about being tired a lot lately. George's mom was an asset here too. Dorothy Sutherland had never taken an active role in her husband's business. She had no head for figures and declared so with almost a kind of pride.

But she did play a very active role in her family. And a husband who worked himself into an early grave had always been a fear of hers, articulated whenever George Sr.'s business kept him from his family.

She'd been articulating it with more frequency lately. "That business is going to kill you, my love," she'd tell him. "You've given it years of your life. Let Junior deal with it now."

He hated being called Junior, as if his existence was some shadow of his father's, as if he was some lesser copy. But that mindset played a role in his mom's advocacy. Her husband had done his part and given years to the company. Now it was time for her son to take over, to fill his father's shoes.

He didn't mind the weight of that expectation. Not one bit. He just hoped his father would see reason and be willing to hand the reins over. Some part of him feared George Sr. would stubbornly remain at the helm of his company until he died—or killed Sutherland Research.

"George?" Andy's voice cut through his thoughts.

"Sorry, what?"

"I was asking how you were doing?"

"Me? Oh, I'm fine."

"You sure?"

"Fit as a fiddle."

Andy smiled again. "Well, that's good."

George sighed. "Look, I'm happy to catch up, Andy. Old times and all that. But I really do need to get back. What's this about?"

The other man nodded. "Right. Okay, so the research you sent over, the tick-borne illnesses?"

"Yeah?"

"It's incomplete."

George cocked an eyebrow at the other man. "What? I got everything. I told you that."

Andy raised his palms upward in a placating fashion. "I don't doubt you, George. But...it's still incomplete."

He crossed his arms now. "What are you playing at? If you think you can cut me out of the vaccine profits—"

Again, he was preempted by a calming gesture. "Of course not. Never. I'm not talking about cutting you out. We've *both* been cut out."

George frowned more with every word. "What in hell are you talking about? Cut out? By whom?"

Andy sighed. "Okay, I'm going to tell you something you probably know already. You're going to pretend to be pissed off, as if you don't do the same thing. But we both know we both do it. So let's skip that part and get straight to business."

George scoffed. "What the hell?"

"I have someone planted in Sutherland, just to keep an eye on things. No espionage. Just to watch over my investment."

"What the fuck?"

"Come on, George. We agreed to skip the faux outrage. The point is, he says there was more to this. Your dad's team, they found something. Something that scared George Sr."

For a moment, George forgot his wrath. "What are you talking about?"

"They were looking for a way to stop tick-borne illness. They found a way to make it fifty times as potent."

George blinked. "What? That's not possible."

"It is possible."

But he shook his head. "No. No, if they found something like that, my dad would have told me."

Andy shifted in his seat, projecting an uncomfortableness that said what his absence of words didn't: *You sure about that?*

George's cheeks flamed. "He wouldn't have hidden it from me."

"My source says..."

"Your source? You mean, your goddamned spy."

"Let's not do this."

But George wasn't about to be silenced this time. "What? Call you on smiling to my face while you put a fucking spy in my midst?"

"Like you don't have people in Gilmore?"

Of course, he did. But that was only because Andy was a snake. Andy was the devil, and George knew it. You don't do business with the devil without covering your ass. So, of course, he had people in Gilmore.

But he wasn't about to admit it. He wasn't the one who just got caught. "This isn't about me. This is about you."

"This is about *us*, George, and our investment. Our partnership."

"Partnership? You've got a spy in Sutherland."

"Lower your voice, dammit," Andy hissed. "And he's not a spy. I told you. He's just there to make sure I'm getting the full returns on my investment."

"You son of a bitch."

The other man smiled as if he'd just been paid a compliment. "The point is, your father is holding out on us. On *you*. As soon as they knew what they'd found, he shut down that part of the research. Had all the files sent to him, and everything wiped from the lab."

"Bullshit. He would have told me."

Andy ignored his protestations. "Some of the scientists on the project were pissed. They didn't like giving up their research. Which is how my guy first heard about it."

George ran a hand through his hair and stared out at the bustling street, at its colorful stalls and picturesque cafés. He watched the tourists mill past, through air heavy with the smell of food and the ring of laughter and conversation. The tranquility and inanity of it all juxtaposed with the turmoil in his mind and bothered him in a way he couldn't quite describe. He turned back to Gilmore, nostrils flaring.

"No. Dad wouldn't hide something like that from me."

"Your father was concerned about what would happen if the research ever went public. He reminded everyone on the project of their NDAs and confidentiality agreements. That their work belonged to him. Because he plans to bury it."

"How do you know all this?"

"My guy dug into it once he caught wind of what was going on."

"And you didn't tell me because...?"

"Because I needed confirmation. And now, I have it."

"Even if any of this is true, what do you expect me to do about it?"

"Get the research, of course."

"Get it?" George laughed, a harsh laugh. "I don't even know if it's real. I didn't hear about it until just now. If what you're saying is true—and I have my doubts—Dad didn't bother to confide in me. He hid it from me too. How the hell am I supposed to get my hands on it?"

Andy shrugged. "I don't know. But if anyone's got a shot, it's you. You're his son, after all."

George frowned at him. He didn't need to point out that that didn't, apparently, count for shit. "And why do you want it, anyway?"

"Don't you?"

"If my dad buried it, he must have had his reasons."

"Sure. He was worried about what would happen if it fell into the wrong hands. But we're not the wrong hands, are we?"

George studied the other man. Andy's bland features were pressed into a reasonable facsimile of a congenial smile. But there was something wicked in his eyes. Something avaricious. Something that sent a shiver up his spine. "Look, even if someone's not yanking your guy's chain, maybe this stuff is better wherever Dad has it. We already have what we need for the vaccine. We're in the business of preventing illness and curing it. We don't want more potent tick-borne diseases. No one does."

Andy nodded slowly. "Well, we surely wouldn't want it in the public's hands."

"Exactly."

"But we're practical businessmen, George. Who knows what we could learn from that kind of research? Whatever trigger they discovered, maybe it's reversible."

"I'm sure Dad would have taken that into consideration."

"Maybe. But there's another aspect he wouldn't have thought of. Or, if he did, he wouldn't have considered it long."

George felt as if he shouldn't ask further. But something compelled him to anyway. "What?"

"The potential for weaponizing it."

"Jesus," he spat out. "See? This is exactly why he buried it."

Andy smiled again. "I'm not saying we'd do the weaponizing. I'm saying we'd leave that in the capable hands of those in the best position to make the calls about when to use it, or if it should ever be used."

He watched the other man suspiciously. "Who?"

"The military. That's where the real money is anyway. We sell it to the Department of Defense, and walk away with a big, fat paycheck. And they decide if it ever sees the light of day."

George shook his head. "Military? Why would they need that?"

"I don't need to tell you how lethal tick-borne diseases are. It's your company that's been doing the research.

"But imagine how effective it would be if you could reduce an entire army to a shivering heap of misery? Think of the symptoms of Lyme disease, but fifty times more potent?

"Think what could have happened if we could have fed that shit into the caves in Tora Bora? Our guys could have strolled in without firing a shot. The bad guys would be incapacitated."

"That's all kinds of illegal."

Andy smiled. "It's war, George. Anyway, we wouldn't be the ones making the call. The question of legality would be up to our nation's best legal minds."

George shook his head. "No. We develop cures. We don't build weapons." He was no philanthropist. He didn't do this for the feel-good aspects. But still, at the end of the day, Sutherland saved lives. It didn't end them.

Andy—the devil—seemed to be able to read his thoughts. "Think of all the lives you'd save."

"What? By devising more effective means of killing people?"

"It wouldn't have to kill anyone. Our guys could incapacitate entire towns. Stroll in, arrest the hostiles, administer the cure. No one dies then. Not us, not them. No innocent civilians, no bystanders, no collateral damage. Hell, not even terrorists."

"War doesn't work like that. It's never worked like that."

Andy shrugged. "Maybe not. But people are already dying. The point is, we'd reduce the casualties." George was about to offer a new round of objections, when Andy added, "And make serious bank in the process."

George sighed. "Look, not only would that violate all kinds of international laws, we don't even know if the research is real."

"The legal part isn't our concern. We wouldn't be doing anything to violate the law."

"We still don't know that it's real."

"I'm pretty sure it is. But, that's the first step, right? You get confirmation from George Sr. And find out where it is."

"I don't know, Andy. I don't like it."

"It's your company, too, isn't it? Shouldn't you at least know what it's doing?"

That was a good point, and George didn't have anything to counter it. "I should. Dad shouldn't be hiding shit from me."

"Exactly. Even if you decide you're not in, at least you know what's yours now. At least you have the information you need to make a decision."

George sipped the soda he'd been neglecting all this time and wrinkled his nose. He hated Italian sodas. He'd never comprehend Andy's obsession with that damned country.

"Well?"

"All right. I'm in. I'll do some digging. But I make no promises."

Andy smiled. "That's good enough for me, George. I don't want you doing anything that makes you uncomfortable. As long as you have all the facts and you're the one making the call, not your dad? Well, that's good enough for me."

Chapter Twenty

Heather had brought back a pickup truck and trailer full of furniture and boxes of belongings.

From what she could see, Angela thought she had good taste. The pieces were a coordinated blend of vintage and modern, hitting the right mix of sophisticated but chic.

Lauren picked up on the fact at once. "You're into antiques?"

When Heather answered in the affirmative, she smiled. "Oh my God, you *have* to see Angela's place, then. It's a historic home, and she's done such great things with it."

"Really?"

"Oh, yes. It was in such humble shape when she bought it, but Angela put so much work into restoring it. It looks amazing."

"So you're a handywoman?" Heather asked, turning an appreciative gaze her way.

For some inexplicable reason, Angela flushed to the roots of her hair.

Rae, who'd come along ostensibly to lend her muscle to the endeavor—and so been there to witness the entire spectacle—smiled. "Quite the handywoman. That place was a dump before she bought it. And now—"

"It's beautiful."

Angela shot them both a dirty look, but Heather seemed intrigued. "Really? Now I'm interested. I love historic homes."

"Well, it's *Fenwood*-historic," Angela cautioned. "It belonged to the son-in-law of the town's first mayor. Its historical import is very...well, small town."

"Oh, small-town history is my favorite."

"Really?"

"Yes. There's so much to it. It's the perfect blend of charming quaintness, and merciless drama."

Angela laughed, and Lauren nodded emphatically.

"Well, that sums Fenwood up pretty well," Lauren said. "There's a story about Angela's house too. But come on, let's get this furniture moved, and she can tell you all about it."

That had proved a pretty good model for the rest of the afternoon. Lauren took every opportunity to bug her. When the scowls proved ineffective, Angela had tried mouthing, *Don't make me murder you.* Her friend only laughed and winked at her.

Rae was no better. At the first opportunity to get her alone, she took one end of an awkward cardboard box Angela was lugging into the house—but paused to lean in and whisper, "Damn, girl."

Her friends and their ridiculous matchmaking notwithstanding, the afternoon passed pleasantly enough.

The whole team arrived as promised, and they made short work of the furniture. Matt probably moved more than everyone else combined. Before long, Heather's house looked quite homey—except for the piles of cardboard boxes lined against the far wall.

Meeting Ragnar was every bit the delight Heather had promised. He was the friendly, loveable monster she'd said—with a little more drool thrown in. But Angela didn't really mind. He was a sweet dog and took to everyone immediately. He followed them back and forth through the house with each trip, tongue lolling out and tail moving slowly side to side.

He demanded attention from everyone too. When he was ignored, he'd put a great paw on the malefactor. If this failed, he'd snuffle and lay his head on the offender. Even Conrad had to finally comply. And he didn't seem to object. On the contrary, Angela was pretty sure she saw her colleague crack a smile when the dog rested his giant fluffy head on him. But she couldn't say for certain. If it had been there, it was gone in the next instant.

And soon enough, the work was done.

Matt clapped his hands. "Good job, y'all."

Casper seconded this. "Right. Good work, everyone." He had been noticeably absent for most of the afternoon but had joined the group as the work wound down.

Conrad sighed dejectedly. "I suppose this means I have to go home."

"Not yet," Heather smiled. "I owe you guys lunch at least."

"Lunch? How about drinks?"

She nodded. "Sure. Drinks, too, if you want them."

Conrad nodded briskly. "I do. Especially since I'm due home afterward."

★

"So, you got the Ragnar seal of approval." Heather smiled, slipping into a seat beside Angela.

They were at the bar in Tres Amigos, their lunch orders already placed. Angela and Rae were the only ones who'd opted for something other than an alcoholic beverage. They'd all clustered together, and by design—she was sure of it—Rae had grabbed a seat on the other side of Angela, only to go sit in the place Lauren had reserved for her.

Meaning the only seat left for Heather was by Angela. Could her friends be any more obvious if they tried? *Probably not.*

Angela tried to ignore her embarrassment at their heavy handedness. She hoped her cheeks weren't as colorful as she supposed they might be, judging by their warmth. "He's awfully sweet. You weren't kidding when you said he's a big baby."

The other woman laughed. "I'm pretty sure he was in doggy heaven today. He got to meet all kinds of new people." She tapped Angela's glass. "Refill?"

She'd been drinking a strawberry lemonade, and had downed it rather rapidly. She was hot and tired and nervous, once she'd realized what Lauren and Rae were up to.

Still, it was a little too early in the day for anything with alcohol, so she'd stuck to lemonade. But she shook her head. "Not right away, thanks. It was good, but I probably don't need that much sugar before lunch."

Heather laughed. "Come on, you earned it. You did a lot of the heavy lifting today."

Angela smiled. "I don't know. If I drink too much now, I won't be able to eat."

The other woman nodded, glancing down at her own drink. "Fair enough."

An idea was floating around in the back of Angela's mind, and she wished now she'd had some kind of liquid courage. But it was too late for that, so she forged on anyway. "But...uh...if you wanted a lavender latte later, I'd probably be game for that?"

Heather grinned. "You got a deal."

Angela grinned too. "Great. Cool."

For a moment, they settled into an awkward silence. Angela felt a bundle of nerves. She'd only asked her for a coffee. That was safe, and not date-ish. She tried not to date coworkers. There was no policy against it, but she'd seen enough office romances go sideways to know it was generally better avoided.

No, they were hanging out socially. *Friends*. That was all.

Still, there was a warmth in Heather's eyes that she rather liked, and an ease in her manner toward Angela that didn't extend to her peers.

But was it comradery between the only two lesbians in the office, or two professional women of a similar age and interests, or something more personal? Angela didn't know.

It was probably nothing. And she didn't mind. She wasn't interested in dating anyway. *But if...* Well, if

Heather was interested in anything more, Angela would leave the asking to her. Not that she would. *And that's okay.*

Angela was really wishing she'd opted for alcohol, as her thoughts were doing nothing to relax her, when Heather's voice interrupted her jumbled reverie.

"So there's a story with your house?"

"What?"

"Lauren said there was some kind of story with your house."

Angela had to fight the urge to grimace at the memory of yet another clumsy attempt by her friend. "A murder mystery, really."

"Ohh, even better." Heather paused and laughed. "Does that make me a terrible person, that I'm excited to hear about a murder mystery?"

Angela laughed too. "I'm probably not the best judge. Because it's one of the reasons I bought the place, so, for obvious reasons, I'm biased toward 'no, of course not.'" She paused to flag the bartender down for a glass of water. "Fenwood was first settled in the eighteen-thirties. A couple of families moved out here and built farmsteads."

Heather nodded. "I figured it had been farming country. Still is, really."

She nodded too. "One of those families was the Stewart family. The eldest daughter came with them, but two years later, her beau followed. And he was a McCormack."

"Really?"

Angela nodded. "They were my dad's grandmother and grandfather, a few generations removed."

Heather's eyes widened. "*They* weren't murdered, were they?"

"No."

"Oh." She blinked. "Well, uh..."

Angela laughed at her hesitance. "They weren't the killers either." But she couldn't help adding, "At least, as far as anyone knows."

The other woman grinned but let her continue.

"So, a few decades later, there's an actual town. One of the early families, the Hallisters, had accumulated a lot of wealth from trade. We had a lot of trappers coming and going then, and new settlers.

"Anyway, their son ended up practicing law. Became one of the town's foremost men. Eventually ended up being elected mayor—the first mayor of Fenwood. And this is where things get interesting.

"David Hallister had several kids, including one daughter, Rebecca Hallister. She married another lawyer, Andrew Logan.

"Andrew Logan wanted to build a perfect home for his new bride."

"Your house?"

Angela nodded but, despite the interest in the other woman's tone, would not divert from her narrative except to say, "That's right. Andrew picked a plot of land near the river."

"Wait, your house is on a river?"

"Not anymore. They diverted it decades ago for the mill."

"Oh."

"But stop interrupting," she half chided. "We're almost at the best part—mysterious death."

"Sorry." Heather grinned. "I'll be good."

"At the time, this is a prime piece of real estate. Best spot on the river, with a huge backyard and good elevation for springtime flooding. Plus, it's well-situated relative to the rest of town.

"But the problem is, it's not for sale. It's owned by one of the original farmers, a Thomas McGill. His wife is dead, his sons have moved out of the area, back home to live with their mom's family. His daughter's married to the postmaster. Thomas is in his late fifties now, and he runs the farm on his own."

Heather took a long sip of her drink and nodded. She seemed to be getting into the narration, though, because she didn't interrupt, not even with questions.

"Andrew tries to buy the spot he wants. Thomas isn't selling. Andrew makes him a very generous offer. Thomas *still* isn't selling.

"They go back and forth for a couple of months, and by now, the whole town knows about it. Andrew's told a few of his friends that 'bad things' are going to happen if McGill doesn't 'see reason.'

"Thomas hears about that, and it makes him more determined than ever. It's probably Fenwood's first 'blood feud.'

"Then, Christmas Eve eighteen fifty-five, Thomas McGill disappears.

"Andrew Logan has a rock-solid alibi. He was at his soon-to-be father-in-law's house celebrating. Two dozen people saw him there. Whatever happened to McGill, he couldn't possibly be involved.

"Then, two weeks later, they find Thomas's body in the river. It's in bad shape, but the cause of death is clear—his skull had been battered in."

Heather gaped. "He *murdered* him for his land?"

"Officially, it's an unsolved case."

"Oh bullshit."

"Remember, Andrew had an airtight alibi. There were a lot of folks who were suspicious, of course. And he didn't do himself any favors. He basically crowed about Thomas's death. 'Well, he loved the river so much, he got to spend the rest of his life there,' and stuff like that. But nothing could ever be proved.

"Thomas's son-in-law sells him the property, and he builds the house—*my* house.

"But then, decades later, when Andrew is dead, and Rebecca is dying, she tells her kids a story. Some of them believed it, some of them insisted it was old age and what-not.

"Anyway, she says Andrew hired one of the local farmhands, a kid named Jorgen Miller, to off Thomas that night."

"While he had an alibi."

"Exactly. Jorgen was in trouble a lot. Drunk and disorderly, that kind of thing. He'd beaten a guy pretty badly the summer before in a barfight. He got worse after that. More drinking. More fighting.

"No one was surprised when he died a year later. Someone had put a bullet through his skull and took his wallet. They never figured out who, but everyone assumed it was someone he'd crossed, at cards or over cups.

"Only, Rebecca said it was Andrew. Jorgen had started demanding money to buy his silence. Andrew offed him to shut him up for good."

The other woman whistled. "Jesus. That is quite the story."

Angela nodded. "Yes. The family buried it for a while, keeping it a secret known only to themselves. But eventually it came out—long after anyone involved could be brought to justice. The Logans and Hallisters insist it's bullshit."

Heather laughed. "I'm sure they do." She took another sip from her drink. "You're a hell of a storyteller, Angie. I could practically *feel* myself back there. But you know what this means?"

Angela shook her head. "What?"

"Now I really do need to see this murder house."

Chapter Twenty-One

When George entered his father's office, the old man closed his laptop hastily. But it was too late.

"I thought you weren't working today?" he snarked to the older man with a wry grin. "Since it's Saturday and all."

The older man smiled too. "You know how it is. No rest for the wicked, and all that." Now, though, he glanced past the door. "Don't tell your mother, okay?"

"I won't. I'm pretty sure another one of her lectures would be at least as bad for you as sneaking work in. But you really do need to learn how to step back, Dad."

"I know, I know." Now, the elder Sutherland surveyed him. "But you didn't come here to catch me working. At least, I hope you didn't. Because *you* clearly don't have enough to do, if that's the case."

George Jr. laughed. "No, I didn't. Actually..." He glanced behind him at the door and hesitated for a moment. Then he closed it. "I need to talk to you."

The other man raised an eyebrow. "Oh?"

"I need to ask you about something."

George Sr.'s expression lost none of its quizzicalness, but he gestured to a seat. "Then you'd better sit down. Want anything? Coffee? Something stronger?"

"Dad," he chided, "you know damned well the doctor said no coffee for you. Not until he gives the all clear."

This concern, however, was met with a brisk wave of the hand. "It's half-caf. Relax."

"It's supposed to be *no*-caf."

"Yeah, yeah. But I don't function without caffeine. I was getting these damned awful headaches."

"That's because you're an addict. You need to break the addiction."

George Sr. frowned at his son. "Is that a 'yes' or a 'no' to coffee?"

George Jr. sighed. "Fine. It's a 'yes.'"

The elder man smiled and poured a fresh cup for his son. He topped his own off and returned to his seat. "All right. What do you need to talk about?"

George Jr. found himself shifting uncomfortably in his chair at the question. He'd planned his line of inquiry. He was going to be friendly but direct and cut right to the chase. Only now...

"Come on, George," his father prompted. "Whatever it is, it'll be easier to tell me. It'll be better when the air is clear."

He puffed his cheeks in a slow exhale of breath and nodded. "Right. Okay, I heard a rumor. And I need you to look me in the eye and tell me it's not true."

George Sr. frowned. "What kind of rumor?"

"The kind I don't like to hear, Dad. The kind that makes me feel like an idiot because I can't say 100 percent that it's bullshit." His father's frown deepened, but he didn't acknowledge it. "What I hear is, the vaccine project found something—something dangerous."

George Sr. was a good liar. His son had learned that over the years. He tended not to lie directly, but he kept his own counsel and lied by omission where he—for whatever reason—decided not to confide in his son. And lately, that was more and more frequently. He had a few telltale tics though. He'd move his leg in a certain way or pay extra attention to his coffee cup or glass if he had one. He'd fiddle with his reading glasses if he was wearing them.

At the moment, George Sr. seemed to find his coffee cup absolutely riveting because his attention shifted to it. And he began to move his foot, up and down, in a repetitive motion. "Oh? That's a pretty vague rumor. Anything specific?"

George Jr. felt his heart sink. *So, it's true.* "Yeah, there were specifics. But I'm not here to talk the science so much as why you decided to hide it from me."

The elder Sutherland glanced up. "I didn't *hide* it, George."

At least he's admitting the rumors were right. "Then why don't I know about it?"

"Because...well, I didn't tell you. But not because I was hiding it from *you*. I didn't tell anyone. Not even your mother. Only those who already knew."

"That's, by definition, hiding it from me..."

The two men stared at each other for a long moment. The elder sighed. "I mean, it wasn't about you."

George Jr. laughed, a touch bitterly. "It never is, is it?"

"What I mean is, I still haven't made up my mind what to do about all this. I thought, the best thing to do for now, was to just sit on it. And keep it as hush-hush as possible until I had time to think about it."

"Ah. So, you weren't going to consult me at all?"

"I...I don't know. Look, George, I had a lot going on. I didn't know what to do with it, and I...I didn't have the capacity to deal with that on top of everything else. I thought I'd hold off for a bit."

"That's because you never delegate, Dad. You've got an entire team of overpaid staff, and you still handle everything yourself.

"And," George Jr. added, more pointedly, "you've got a son, who works his ass off for you, and you don't trust him with the time of day. Everything has to stay in your damned head. Even if it kills you."

George Sr. raised a hand palm upward to his son. "I'm not saying I was right. Maybe I wasn't thinking clearly because of...well, because of this damned heart."

His father's atrial fibrillation and related hospitalizations were serious. Of course they were. But it was a new phenomenon. And this concealment and refusal to confide in him? George glared at his father.

Well, that was anything but new.

"Or maybe, old habits die hard," the old man continued. "I don't know what to tell you."

"The truth. You could start by telling me what the hell they discovered, and why you decided to hide it from the world."

George Sr. nodded slowly. "All right. They found a way to amplify the effects of most tick-borne diseases, making them as much as fifty times as potent. We're talking almost instant lethality in some cases. Which is why I pulled the plug on the research. Our models show the worst of it could kill within hours. And they'd be excruciating hours—pure agony in every joint, every muscle, every breath."

George Jr. felt a shiver run up his spine at these words, and he forgot some of his anger. "Okay. So you pulled the research?"

"That's right. I wiped all records related to it and pulled the researchers on to new work." He frowned at his son. "But I'm curious how you learned about it. They're all bound under NDAs."

The younger man shook his head. "We're not having that conversation. Until I don't need spies to find out what's going on in our company, you don't get to question where I get my intel."

George Sr. frowned at him. "Spies are dangerous. They may answer to you now, but if they'll lie to me, they'll lie to you. They can't be trusted."

"Are you really the one to be sitting in judgement about someone else's trustworthiness?"

He said it archly, and his father laughed and replied, "Just because I'm not trustworthy doesn't mean they are. But the point is well taken. I shouldn't have concealed it from you." George Sr. leaned in toward him. "But to tell the truth...well, it scared me, George. That kind of research, if it fell into the wrong hands? You could wipe out cities, or even nations, if you manufactured enough infectant."

"You should have told me."

He nodded slowly. "Maybe I should have. I'm sorry."

George Jr. sighed. "So, you destroyed the research?"

His father shifted and began tapping his foot again.

"Well?"

"No. I probably should have, but I didn't. I pulled it from the research computers. I wiped the server. But..."

"But?"

"But I printed a copy of it before I did."

"You printed it? Like, paper?"

"Yes. I didn't want a digital copy. That's too dangerous. Our firewall is supposed to be impenetrable, but we both know that's bullshit. Nothing's impenetrable. And I didn't want some hacker stumbling on what might be the most devastating biological weapon in the history of mankind."

"You could have transferred it to a private server. Something not connected to the company grid, or the cloud."

But his father shook his head. "No. That lowers the risk, sure. But still, anyone with physical access could go retrieve it. I didn't want that either."

"But a single copy of the research, and on paper? Jesus, Dad. A fire or—hell—a paper shredder could permanently destroy all that work."

George Sr. nodded slowly. "I know. And, frankly, it'd probably be for the best. I couldn't bring myself to destroy it. Not completely. I don't know if I have the right to just erase knowledge."

"But you'll keep it buried, so it never sees the light of day?" George Jr. was flabbergasted. His father's illogic seemed incomprehensible. "What sense does that make?"

"None, maybe. I just...it felt wrong to destroy it. But we can't let anyone have it either."

He groaned. Some part of him wished his father had made the call. This was too terrible a discovery to trust to anyone, no matter what they were paying. But to just sit on it without pay? That seemed even worse because there was still a degree of risk for absolutely no payoff. "Jesus, Dad. You can't make a hard call and yet waffle. Either you're burying this, or you're not. Either you want it destroyed, or you don't."

"This is why I didn't want to tell you."

"Because you wanted to be indecisive?"

"No. Because it's my burden. I didn't want to make it yours too."

"What the fuck? I'm not some kind of glorified secretary, Dad. We're in this together, aren't we? This is Sutherland Research. Your burdens are mine."

George Sr. considered for a long moment, then nodded. "You're probably right."

"You know damned well I'm right."

"What I mean is, I should have told you."

George Jr. wasn't about to let his dad off easily. "You're damned right you should have."

"I put the files in my safe. The one in my office."

He blinked. "What? Why are you telling me that?"

"Because it's too late to consult you beforehand. But you're my son, and this is your business too. Those decisions are going to be all yours to make, maybe sooner rather than later if this damned ticker doesn't straighten itself out." He smiled, but it didn't hide the haggard look in his eyes. "Now you know. If you want to look at it, you know the combination."

"You don't mind?"

George Sr. shook his head. "You're my son. You'll be head of Sutherland Research someday, probably soon."

"Don't talk like that, Dad. You've got years left ahead of you."

His father smiled again. "Maybe. If those damned doctors know what they're talking about anyway. But that doesn't mean I can keep doing this forever. If your mother had her way, well, I'd have retired years ago."

George Jr. shifted in his seat. He'd thought the same thing, if the truth was to be known. But he didn't want to appear overly eager. "You've got to do what's best for you, Dad," he said at length. "You've given a lot to the company."

"I regret how much, sometimes. Sometimes, it feels like it's gotten my whole life." The older man nodded.

"You did a hell of a job," George demurred. "You kept us afloat when the economy went to shit. When other companies were going under."

"I know. But there's always something else. Some reason for me to stay on. Some reason not to hand things over." He scrutinized his son. "But you're a grown man, George, with a good head on your shoulders. And maybe...well, maybe it's time for me to walk away and leave the hard calls—all the calls—to you."

Chapter Twenty-Two

"You sure you don't mind?" Heather asked. "He's awfully big. And he sheds a lot."

They were standing on the steps outside Angela's house, and she seemed to have caught just enough of a glimpse of polished wood beyond the stained-glass windows of the door to have second thoughts about bringing Ragnar inside.

It had started with a drink. *Lauren's idea, of course.*

"Come on; we did incredible work," Lauren said. "We deserve a margarita."

Rae had acquiesced so quickly Angela knew it was part of some scheme. But she'd spent an entire meal side by side with Heather. She needed a drink, and she'd had one. They'd all had one.

The guys, finding the drinks a little too fruity and the atmosphere perilously close to a "girl's night," excused themselves. Matt had unspecified "stuff" he needed to do.

Conrad decided he probably should head home. "Make sure the Missus is still alive. They're little gremlins after snacks."

Casper hung around a little longer, asking, apropos of nothing, "So, you're all lesbians? Like, all of you?"

When or how he'd figured that out, no one was quite sure. But it was obvious he'd spent some mental energy pondering the implications. He had the air of a man who—somehow—thought he'd won the lottery. He'd tried to seat himself between Heather and Angela.

But, here, Rae had proved an invaluable friend. She'd eased in between them, ostensibly to talk to Angela. "Hey, you got a tampon?"

Casper blanched and turned wide eyes to his drink.

Angela hadn't expected the question. "What?"

"A tampon. One of the extra-strength ones, preferably? My cramps are off the charts, and you know what that means. Heavy bleeding."

Lauren made a sound of agreement. "I told you, babe, you need to switch to the cup. The cramps are so much better with the cup."

"Yeah, if you think I'm collecting my blood in a cup and then hauling a dripping cup to the sink every few hours, you're out of your mind."

Casper looked like he'd seen a ghost—an observation that brought the women no shortage of amusement when they remarked on it after he'd left. Which he did shortly, slamming back the rest of his drink and declaring, "Well, I have to get too. Got a server I'm building. See you all later."

They'd laughed at Angela, too, when she'd fished out a tampon from her purse.

"Geez, I don't actually need one." Rae said. "I just wanted to get rid of that guy."

Angela had *really* needed the drink after that. But despite the embarrassing start, they'd had a good time.

When Lauren decided it was time for her and Rae to go, and the other two women had started to remark that they probably should get going as well, she'd declared, "You should show Heather your place, Angie."

Angela flushed, as much from the unsubtle remark as the amusement in her friend's voice at the use of "Angie." For a moment, she didn't know what to say.

Heather must have taken this as unwillingness because she demurred, "Oh, I've got to take Ragnar for a walk anyway."

"Walk him to Angie's place," Lauren persisted. "That's a good, long walk."

Without two margaritas under her belt, Angela might not have been ready for a comment like this. But she'd drunk them, and she was. "You could. I could show you the tower. I mean, if you're not too tired after everything today."

Heather hadn't been too tired. On the contrary, she'd assented with a readiness that triggered significant looks between Lauren and Rae—and an unsteady feeling in the pit of Angela's stomach.

And now, Heather was here, on her front doorstep. And looking damnably hot, at that. She'd changed out of her moving clothes of earlier. The baggier work T-shirt had made way for a fitted one, and the jeans had given way to jean capris. She'd looked good earlier.

But now? Damn. The new outfit accented her curves a little more, and the blue of the T-shirt emphasized the blue of her eyes.

Angela was struggling to remember what they'd been talking about. *Dog. Shedding.* "No, I don't mind at all. Bring him in."

Heather nodded, albeit dubiously, and followed her host inside. For his part, Ragnar didn't seem overly disturbed by the change in scenery. He'd apparently worked up a pant on the way over, and now focused on steadily puffing in cooler air, his tongue lolling out of his mouth.

"Let me get him some water," Angela decided.

The other woman apologized and thanked her. "If I'd known just how gorgeous your house was, I wouldn't have brought him. There's going to be dog hair everywhere."

Again, Angela assured her it was no trouble at all. "I've always meant to get a dog myself. And one of these days, I will. So don't worry about it."

They left Ragnar with a giant bowl of water, and he settled quite happily onto the cool tile floor. Then the tour of the house commenced. It began with a return to the outside.

Angela's house was a three-story Victorian-style home with a wraparound porch and a tower that extended above the highest point of the roof. The exterior had required the most intense restoration, and much of the original millwork had needed to be replaced. The vergeboards were original, with only a small section needing to be recreated.

"They'd taken a lot of damage, and they just couldn't be restored," Angela said. "But I found a place that would recreate them exactly, so you can't really tell that it's new."

Heather smiled. "I can't tell at all."

Angela had gone with a mild color scheme of two-tone beige with blue accents. "When I have to repaint, I might try blue and white," she said.

The other woman had only praise for the home, for the current look, for its possible future, and for all the work she had done. She loved the tower and its tall windows. "The view must be amazing."

"It is—I'll show you."

She loved the porch, too, and its carved columns and ornate railings and spindles. "This is really beautiful, Angie."

Her praise only increased when they returned to the interior, and Angela fished out her old photo album of before-and-after photos. The house had been in humble condition indeed when she'd bought it. It was solid, and its essentials in no immediate danger of decay. But all the finery had begun to break down. The paint had long ago faded and begun to chip. The roof was overdue to be replaced. The wooden interior, bare and worn in spots, had been subject to too much abuse, and too little tending.

Heather flipped through the book, glancing around her when they reached the sitting room shots—where they were now standing—and marveling at the change. She whistled at the difference between the original exterior and the current, and smiled at the tower. "That is pretty cool."

Angela beamed at her appreciation and promised that the real view was much better. "You'll really be able to see the town. You can't make it out in the pictures, but you can see the river too."

When Heather got to the last page, though, Angela flushed. It was a shot of herself and Carrie standing in front of the house, arms wrapped around each other and beaming. It had been taken the day of her housewarming party, when the first and most necessary work had been completed.

Heather glanced up at her, and she only flushed deeper.

"Oh, that's, uh, from my housewarming party." Angela laughed, hoping she sounded nonchalant. "I threw a big thing. You know, to celebrate the house being livable again. And that's, uh, Carrie. My ex."

"Ah." Heather nodded. "Was she an old-house aficionado, too, then?"

Angela laughed, a little more sardonically than she'd meant to. "Not really."

"Ah."

Somehow, the exchange had only gotten worse.

"I, uh, need to update the album. New pictures. Get rid of that one. Add some shots of how things look now. I've made a lot of changes since those were taken. I just keep forgetting."

Heather nodded and put the album back in place. "What was she like?"

"What?"

"Carrie."

"Oh...well, um, she was into computers. Graphic design, mostly."

"Sounds interesting."

"Yeah. She was really good. Really gifted."

"I can see that. She looks kind of artsy."

Angela smiled. "Artsy" was pretty much Carrie's aesthetic. It didn't matter how much her style evolved; she always put an artsy spin on it. "She was. Is. Last I knew anyway."

"That must have been really handy. Someone with an eye for that kind of thing, I mean, when you were remodeling."

Angela almost laughed again, so far from the truth as this was. Carrie had had as little to do with the project as possible. Carrie had hated the restoration and how much time and money it took. But Angela demurred on the point. It wasn't really worth rehashing.

Heather smiled and changed the topic. "That was really impressive. But I need to see this tower for myself."

Ragnar found them soon after, and tagged along as they saw the rest of the house. The dog followed dutifully, but Heather was duly impressed. She loved the woodwork, she appreciated the layout and plethora of nooks and cubbies, and she grew rapturous about the view from the top floor of the tower. Everything impressed, and as far as Angela could make out, it *genuinely* impressed.

Once or twice, the conversation had come back to Carrie. Angela couldn't tell if Heather had engineered it that way, or if it had been the natural progression of things. It had seemed natural enough at the moment. This was a house they'd shared for several years, after all.

Heather gleaned from their conversation that Carrie had left the state and moved to LA. "Sometimes that's for the best. When Caroline and I broke up, I left the state too. Hell, I left my job, and I really liked working at Northwest. But it was just...weird. Seeing her every day, you know?

And I was lucky enough that I could move, and freelance for a bit."

"So...Caroline," Angela ventured, "she was in HR, right?"

Heather blinked, seeming surprised by the question. Then she nodded. "That's right." They were downstairs, back in the sitting room turned living room, drinking coffee. She took a sip and, eyes twinkling, added, "Why? Are you implying I have a type?"

Angela was midway through explaining that she might have talked to Caroline during the reference check when she processed the other woman's words. She fell silent midword, flushed, and stammered out, "Uh, what? A type?"

Heather surveyed her for a moment, then shrugged with an affectation of nonchalance that almost worked. "Maybe I do."

"Oh. Well..." Angela's mind raced. Heather was nothing like Carrie. She was cool and professional, where her ex had been warm and laid-back. She was collected where Carrie had been chaotic. She was structured and controlled where her ex had been artsy and free. "I, uh, don't think I do."

"Really?"

She couldn't tell if Heather took her meaning. So she added, "Except, I do seem to have a thing for blue eyes."

The other woman smiled. If she'd missed it before, she understood her now. Angela's heart raced. Her mind screamed that she'd just made an incredible blunder. This was a coworker, and someone she'd hired to sabotage her company at that. What was she doing hitting on her?

Not that there were any rules prohibiting dating coworkers. She'd have to recuse herself from anything related to Heather's performance or remuneration. But she wasn't going to be at Sutherland long enough to worry about it anyway. And her information about the other woman's personality had come from an ex. She couldn't take that as reliable, much less when it contradicted everything she saw for herself.

Still...this is a mistake. The timing—

Her thoughts trailed off as Heather set her cup of coffee down and slid across the sofa seat until she was close to her. Very close.

Now, her thoughts were far too addled to allow any further rumination. At this point, Angela had to remind herself to *breathe*. "I...uhh..."

"Yes?" Heather smiled, leaning toward her until their upper bodies and faces were almost touching.

Their legs already were, and the heat of their thighs, side by side, drove away the power of cogent speech.

"Umm...you're...beautiful. Your eyes, I mean. All of you, but..."

Heather leaned forward even more until their lips nearly touched. Angela found herself unable to speak at all. "Can I kiss you, Angie?"

Even if the thought hadn't been at the forefront of her mind, feeling the other woman's breath wash over her, smelling her soft perfume, feeling the press of her leg, would have put it in mind. Swallowing, she nodded.

Heather's lips touched hers, carefully and almost hesitantly at first. They were soft and inviting, and Angie closed her eyes and kissed back.

The other woman seemed to need no further encouragement than that. She wrapped an arm around Angela and pulled her into the kiss, gentle still, her hesitance long gone, and in its place a rising passion, a heat that seemed to be building and building between them.

Heather tasted sweet, like coffee and desire. Or maybe Angela was just projecting that desire. But the other woman's kiss was sending shivers through her entire body.

She moaned as Heather slipped her tongue into her mouth. She didn't mean to. It just—well, *happened* before she could stop it.

Heather's breath quickened at the sound, and she growled into the kiss. She was on top of Angela now, with the passion of a woman who hadn't been kissed in years, the pair of them leaning into the sofa back.

In Angela's case, at least, that was true. She'd sworn off dating and even casual sex after Carrie. She hadn't kissed or been kissed since then. *Until now.* And for half a second, the realization almost pulled her out of the moment. But Heather's fingers running along her side, Heather's tongue devouring her mouth, brought her back.

They stayed there for a long time, kissing and feeling and holding and now and then moaning. Angela's every nerve seemed awakened by the other woman's touch, any thoughts of earlier long gone. No, this probably wasn't prudent. Yes, maybe she was being weak.

But she didn't care. All she cared about in the moment was the fire coursing through her veins, the too-long dormant desire Heather's touch had awakened. She was trembling with it, weak with it.

When the other woman pulled back from their kisses, Angela felt disappointment wash over her. She didn't want the touch to end.

"Hey," Heather said, her voice a breathy whisper. "You know what you didn't really show me?"

Angela tried to collect her thoughts. She was lying on her back, staring up into Heather's blue eyes. "What?"

"Your bedroom."

She blinked. She'd opened the door and the other woman had peeked inside, but it hadn't been a stop on their informal tour. "Oh. That's true."

"How'd you like to show me now?" Heather purred.

Angela grinned. "Is that what this is about, then? You're just trying to get inside my bedroom?"

Heather grinned too. "Among other things."

Goddammit. The words, and the expression in the other woman's eyes as she'd said them, seemed to speak straight to Angela's clit. It took an effort to ignore its input and nod with some semblance of control.

"All right. Well, uh, it was kind of thoughtless of me to leave that off the tour."

"Yes, it was." Heather leaned forward to kiss her and nibbled on her lower lip as she pulled away. "Very thoughtless."

Angela shivered and let Heather pull her to her feet. They made their way back upstairs, but it was slow going. They paused in the doorway, Heather pressing her into the polished wood frame to kiss her again.

They paused a second time by the great staircase for the same reason, and again on the landing midway up. Angela was moaning with need from these interruptions.

She loved the feel of the other woman's lips on hers, her hands on her body. But she needed more. So much more.

Finally, they reached her room, and Heather shut the door after them. She threw a glance around the room as if to get her bearings and pulled Angela into another kiss.

Guiding her to the bed, she ran a hand under her shirt. Angela trembled at the touch. "I want to see you," Heather breathed. "All of you. Can I?"

Swallowing hard, Angela nodded. The full weight of every insecurity she harbored about her body lingered in her thoughts. She was reasonably fit and in shape, but every stretch mark, every bit of flab and everything that had sagged with age, stood out in her mind as Heather's hands reached for the hem of her T-shirt. She'd been five years younger since anyone had seen her body.

And now...

She shivered as Heather lifted the shirt over her head, only breaking eye contact as the fabric passed over her eyes.

Then, when the shirt was gone, she was there again, those cool blue eyes fixed on hers with an intensity that made her weak at the knees. Slowly, deliberately, Heather broke her gaze and let her eyes wander.

Angela wished she'd dug out one of her sexier bras earlier. This one was pure function, simple and matched to her skin tone. But she hadn't anticipated things going— well, like this.

Heather didn't seem to mind. "Fuck. You're gorgeous."

A blush reached from the roots of Angela's hair and spread over her face and chest. But she didn't have long to contemplate it. The other woman had her in her arms, kissing her, running her fingers carefully, slowly up her back.

Her lips left Angela's and started to make their way down her neck.

She shuddered and grasped the bedpost to steady herself. Heather kissed and licked and now and then nipped until she'd reached the fabric of her bra cups.

Here, she reached around to the clasps and paused to catch Angela's eyes. For a minute, each panting with desire, they held the other's gaze.

Angela didn't want her to hesitate. She hadn't forgotten those insecurities, but she didn't care about them right in the moment. She wanted to be here. She wanted to be naked before this woman, to let her see her. To let her touch her, feel her, take her...

Heather seemed to take her cue from her gaze because she slipped a finger under the band. And the next instant, the fabric fell away, and a rush of cooler air hit her.

Heather's eyes followed the descent of the bra, and she groaned. Every nerve in Angela's body seemed to respond to that sound, but none as forcefully as those in her clit, which was pulsing.

And the pressure only built as Heather traced her fingers down the curves of her breasts, letting her fingertips dance gently over her nipples.

Angela couldn't repress a full-body shudder. Heather's eyes blazed with desire, and she wrapped an arm around her, lowering her onto the bed.

For a moment, she hovered over Angela, their eyes locked. Then she lowered her attention. Her tongue traveled where, so far, only her fingers had ventured, laving her nipples with gentle caresses, first on one side and then the other.

Angela's breath came hard and fast now, and she squirmed under the attention. It felt good—*so fucking good*—but the rest of her was aching for similar attention.

She cried out when Heather sucked one of her nipples into her mouth, hard. Her hips bucked, and Heather kept sucking.

With one hand, she rolled the other nipple between her fingers. And with the other, she fiddled with the buttons on Angela's pants.

Angela groaned with pleasure and impatience. "Oh God." She wanted to beg, but she didn't dare. How needy and pathetic would that have sounded?

Still, she was pretty sure her clit was going to explode if it didn't get some attention soon. As Heather pulled the jeans down, Angela hoisted her hips, grinding into the other woman's palm.

Heather left the nipple to grin at her. "So that's how it is, huh?"

And then she slid a finger into her panties, between her lips, and grazed her swollen clit.

Angela gasped and shuddered, and Heather's grin remained. So, mercifully, did her finger, running back and forth as Angela gasped and trembled and moaned.

Then, almost without warning, her orgasm came, crashing over her with a wave of pleasure that left her shuddering. Heather had remained in place the entire time, their eyes locked as her hand took her over the edge.

Now, she slipped her fingers out of Angela's panties and slowly, deliberately, into her own mouth.

Angela groaned, all the pressure that her orgasm had just relieved surging back as she watched the other woman suck her juices off her fingers.

"Oh God," she breathed.

Heather smiled as she finished, then glanced down. Angela lay there with her jeans still draped around her thighs, panties still on, if a little disheveled.

"Well, that was nice. But I still haven't seen all of you."

Angela trembled with a hundred sensations as Heather slipped her pants off, then her panties, leaving her naked, exposed, and very wet.

The other woman stood at the edge of the bed, surveying her with a hungry look for a moment. Angela shifted to her elbows. She had the idea that she should be doing something too. She wanted to see Heather, to feel her—to taste her.

But Heather seemed to sense something of her thoughts because she shook her head. "Oh, no. I'm not done with you. Lie back down."

Angela knew she could have said no. She knew she could have objected if she'd wanted to. But the truth was, watching Heather devour her with her eyes had left her desperate for the more physical thing.

She wasn't left disappointed.

The other woman sank to her knees and, grasping Angela's thighs, pulled her toward the edge of the bed.

Draping her legs over her shoulders, Heather groaned, "God, you're so fucking wet. Do you have any idea how hot that is?"

Angela shivered as Heather's breath, hot and quick, hit her. A moment later, her tongue grazed her clit.

This time, Heather wasn't about to let her have an immediate release. She licked and nibbled, lapped and sucked her to the edge of orgasm more than once before she let her come.

And as she crashed down from that plateau, hips bucking, Heather slipped a finger inside her. Angela barely had time to catch her breath when, gasping and moaning, she was riding a new wave toward orgasm.

Heather added another finger, and then another, until Angela lost track of how much of her hand was inside her. All she knew was that she'd never felt so full, so satisfied, so ready to explode with pleasure.

And then, fists full of her bedspread, she came again, clutching the other woman's hand inside her, riding it to orgasm.

Chapter Twenty-Three

It had taken a few minutes before Angela caught her breath enough to get Heather undressed. But the wait had been worth it. Heather Bradshaw was every bit as beautiful as Angela had supposed she might be.

They'd made love for several hours, then realized they were both hungry again.

"Starving," Heather declared. "Not that I'm complaining. I always like to eat dessert first."

Angela blushed, which earned her a kiss.

"I mean, I'm kind of a hobbit like that."

"What?"

"I'm always down for second dessert."

Angela's cheeks flamed hotter. "Me too. But I want actual food first."

Heather grinned triumphantly and kissed her again, nibbling on her lip as she pulled away. "Sounds good to me."

They decided on an Irish pub-style eatery in the center of town for two reasons. The first was that its seasonal seating on the patio would allow them to bring Ragnar along too. The second was that, of the two establishments in Fenwood that allowed pets, the other was Tealeaves. And there was no way in hell Angela was marching in there with Heather on her arm.

She didn't care if it was well past when Lauren was supposed to be working. She had no doubt that at least a few of the baristas had heard something of her scheme. And word would get back to Rae and Lauren before they'd taken their first sip of lavender latte.

No, Angela wasn't letting a word of this reach her friends—not until she knew what *it* was. That was a conversation they hadn't had yet. Hell, by time she'd even known there was an *it* to inquire about, she'd been a little too distracted by Heather's tongue in her mouth.

Not that she was complaining. Whatever it was, it had been...well, incredible didn't cover it. A month ago, she'd had no interest in a relationship. But now?

She was of a different mind now. She wanted to pursue it. She hoped Heather did too.

But if nothing came of it all, if it had been a moment of bliss and nothing else, the filling of their mutual needs...well, she surely would not complain about that either.

Nor would she tell Lauren. Not until she was good and ready to anyway.

Right now, her brain was a little too saturated with oxytocin to be making rational choices. And she wasn't going to risk subjecting herself to a lifetime of teasing on a chemically induced bad decision.

So, they settled into a pair of patio chairs at a corner table of Aberdeen's. Ragnar surveyed their surroundings for all of thirty seconds, paying more heed to the scents in the air than to any persons passing by. Then he plopped down under the table and promptly drifted off to sleep.

"What's good?" Heather asked.

"This is the first time I've been here."

"Really?"

Angela nodded. "They opened a few years back, and I've always meant to check it out. I just...never have. It had been a cupcake place before that. I never went there either, actually."

"Good God. Neither cupcakes nor a pub could lure you? Just how strong is your will, anyway?"

She laughed. "I wish I could say it was willpower. To be honest, I just never get here when I'm in the mood to eat, or if I do, I go somewhere I know."

Heather laughed rather heartily. "So you'll buy a dilapidated Victorian house, but you're risk averse about changing up your burger order?"

"I'm not risk averse. I just...get what I like."

"Set in your ways?"

"No," she protested. Then shrugged. "Maybe a little."

Heather grinned at her. "Never would have pegged you for a *dinosaur*."

She laughed. "Technically, you're older than me. I'd be careful who you call prehistoric, Miss."

"Which is totally not a dinosaur thing to say," Heather needled. "Anyway, I'm talking about mindset, not age. I'm what the kids call 'young at heart.'"

"Whatever." Angela shook her head. "And what kids say that, exactly?"

Heather was smiling. "Okay, that was a bit of a dinosaur thing to say too. Maybe we're both prehistoric. But seriously, if you don't try anything new, how will you really know what you like?"

Angela studied her for a moment. The other woman's smile was lighthearted, but she seemed earnest at the same time. "Are we still talking about food?"

"You tell me."

It was then, mercifully, that a waitress came out and ran through her script welcoming them to Aberdeen's. Had they been here before? *No.* She beamed. "Well, welcome!" Then she ran them through the list of beverages, many of which were imported from Ireland. "Our domestic list is on the back page."

The foods got the same treatment, and they learned that Aberdeen's beef was locally sourced, and so were their vegetables when in season. They also learned that the pub had routinely been named one of the best pub eateries in the area by the local chamber of commerce. "Three consecutive years now."

They put in their drink orders, and Heather smiled as the waitress left to give them a moment to peruse the menu. "See? Best pub eatery in Fenwood. And you would have missed it."

Angela snorted. "You realize the competition is, like, three other places, right? Fenwood's not exactly a metropolis."

The other woman laughed. "Fair point. Still, I'm glad we came. Sometimes..." She glanced up so that their eyes met. "It pays to take a risk."

Angela folded her menu and pulled a faux frown. "Ok, I'm not sure how to take that. Are you saying I'm the risk? Or you are? Or, that you really just love variety in your burgers?"

Heather's cheeks colored a little. "All of the above, I guess. I do love burgers." Then her expression sobered. "But mostly, I'm talking about me. I've been thinking of asking you out for a while. And your friend, Lauren, told me you hadn't dated in a bit. You were just kind of getting back into the 'dating scene.'"

"Wait, she told you that?"

Heather nodded. "Why? Was she not supposed to?"

Angela sighed. "No, it's just...well, she's been pushing me to date again. I think she thinks she's some kind of matchmaker."

"Oh, I figured that out the first time we met."

"Jesus. It was that obvious?"

Heather grinned. "Oh, yes. But I'm glad, in a way. I wasn't sure...well, if you even were a lesbian for a while. But what I'm saying, I guess, is...well, I like you. A lot. And I don't know what your plans are, or what you're open to now. And I hope it doesn't make things weird, with us working together and everything. But I'd like to ask you out, if I could?"

Weird? They'd eaten each other an hour ago, and *now* she was worried about workplace impropriety? Angela might have laughed if she hadn't been so distracted by the point at hand. "I'd love that. Although, aren't we kind of going out now?"

The other woman smiled. "No, I mean a proper date. Not just getting food because we're starving. Like, I want to take you somewhere. It can be nice or casual—whatever you want." Her grin took on a more bashful aspect. "But you'll have to help me pick it out. I'm still getting used to Fenwood."

Chapter Twenty-Four

George Sutherland Jr. whistled as he strolled into the office that Monday morning. It was about two weeks after he and his father had had their heart-to-heart. And what a change clearing the air had brought about.

George Jr. had reviewed the documents his father had hidden. He wasn't a scientist. That's how George Sr. had gotten his start, but the son's wheelhouse was business, not science. Still, you didn't need to be a scientist to understand the implications laid out in those papers. Lethal arrhythmic heart conditions, excruciating joint pain, loss of muscular control, intense nerve pain—and then, death. Those were some of the highlights.

George didn't need to understand the mechanisms that made it possible. The results and implications were enough.

And in the end, he'd drawn the same conclusion as his father. The risk was too great, the reward too low. The legal implications alone were staggering. Weaponizing this research would almost certainly constitute crimes. The creation of biological weapons was prohibited by international law.

There were loopholes, of course. Good lawyers could argue that the weapon had been created for defensive or peaceful capabilities. And, anyway, if they sold the research to the government, that would be an ethical and legal quandary for other people to navigate, not Sutherland Research.

Andy hadn't been able to see past the dollar signs he imagined. But George was a little more pragmatic. Even if the government bought the data, and even if they made a serious profit out of it, and even though the legal repercussions of misusing the find would be on the heads of others...this was Sutherland's data. He didn't want the name of Sutherland to wind up attached to biological weapons.

No, Sutherland Research made plenty of money and kept its name clean in the process. Even if there was bank in Andy's schemes, it wasn't worth the risk.

Andy had tried to get ahold of him once or twice—or maybe it had been three times—in the intervening weeks. But George had let the calls go to voicemail and hadn't bothered to read the texts. He'd told his associate at the time that he wasn't keen on the idea. And Gilmore had left the call to him to make.

Well, he was making it. The research would stay where it was.

George's motives weren't as pure as he considered them. He knew that, on some level. On some level, his newfound loyalty to Sutherland Research sprang from something much more self-serving.

George Sr. had all but promised to hand the company over to him within the year. In the last two weeks, he'd taken an increasingly lighter workload. He spent more time at home, and less time in his home office. He talked a lot about things that would need to be tended to—*in the future.*

Dorothy Sutherland had been all smiles at this. It was clear she knew she was getting her husband back. It was clear she knew her son was getting what he'd earned after so many years. She'd told him as much the night before he left. "I want you to wrap that Fenwood business up as soon as you can, Junior."

He'd tried to explain that it wasn't as easy as that, that they still needed to set the company's goals and directions, to review projects, and so on. But she'd waved it all away.

"I know there's work to be done. But I also know I don't want your father to slip back into old habits in your absence. So, get it done." She'd smiled in an imperious way—a way that rather irritated her son. "This will be a good opportunity to show that you've learned a skill your father never really had—delegation."

He loved his mom, of course. But her ignorance about the demands of his job, and her just-get-it-done attitude drove him up a wall. Then again, she wasn't wrong.

George Sr. was nothing if not a creature of habit. If left too long to his own devices, he'd fall back into the same patterns he'd always known. And if he kept getting better as he did it, well, he'd probably convince himself he could manage the company for another two or three decades.

No, George had to get back to the home branch as soon as possible.

Yet, he saw no cause for immediate alarm. He had a competent team that, with a little whipping into shape, could make the Fenwood branch run like clockwork in no time. And then? Then, he could catch the first flight back to Philly. For good.

Things were finally falling into place for George Jr., so it was only natural that he returned to work with a light step and a song in his heart. He felt good. The sun was shining, the morning was bright, and he was about to get his due. Yes, he felt damned good.

"Good morning, Conrad," he declared.

The older man glanced up from under furrowed brows and grunted out a reply.

"It's good to be back. I've missed your smiling face."

"Mr. Sutherland," Matt said, heading out of his own office. "How's your father?"

"Matt—long time, no see. He's doing well. Very well. They've got him scheduled for an ablation two weeks from now. They don't foresee any complications. And once that's done, well, he should be back on his feet in no time." He clapped the younger man on the shoulder and ignored his grimace. "Thanks for holding down the fort in my absence. I've been checking in on your work. It's all top-notch."

"Of course, Mr. Sutherland. Happy to be of assistance."

"George," he reminded Matt. "Call me George." The other man nodded his acquiescence, and he clapped him on the back again. "Hey, you want to grab me a coffee and then brief me on my schedule for the week? But not right away, say, ten o'clock?"

"You got it."

"I'll take the coffee now though."

Matt nodded. "Of course. But, uh, why don't you check out our options? We've changed things a little."

George almost frowned. He didn't really want to be bothered—that's why he had a PA, after all—but his curiosity did get the better of him. The coffee expenses had been one of his first cuts. What had they been up to in his absence?

He followed Matt around the corner, to the spot where he indicated. At least, he would have, except half a dozen bodies sprang out before he reached it.

"Welcome back, George."

"Welcome back, Mr. Sutherland."

"Good to see you back, George."

"We're glad your father is on the mend."

Even Conrad's monotone called out behind him, "Surprise."

George smiled. He was genuinely affected. They had a whole table of breakfast food—and a container of good coffee—waiting for him. And the rest of his new team was all there—Kathryn and Heather and Casper and Angela. Even Richard Kaplan from the lab had joined them. Not that that surprised him too much.

If there was free food, the lab techs would find their way to it. They were worse than college students. Still, he appreciated the gesture, and he told them as much.

"It was Angela's idea," Matt said.

"But we all pitched in," Kathryn hastened to add.

"Well, I appreciate it. It's been a rough couple of weeks. It's good to come back to my Sutherland family." It was the kind of thing underlings expected to hear, especially after they'd gone out of their way to kiss a little ass. It was bullshit, of course. They were employees, not family. But happy employees made better workers.

And these particular employees had made him happy, so he felt no compunction in returning the favor. Loading up a plate and a mug, he stayed for a while to talk and reassure everyone that George Sr. was fit as a fiddle. Then he retreated to his office, feeling even better about his day than he had earlier.

Casper followed him a few minutes later, and he was surprised to see the young man. Not that he didn't enjoy his conversation. He was the only other kite surfer in the building, as far as he knew. But he had work to catch up on.

"So, you have a chance to talk to Angela or Heather yet?"

George frowned. That sounded ominous since one represented human resources and the other was intended to be his righthand woman. "About what?"

Casper grinned and threw a glance behind them. "They're a thing now."

George blinked. "What?"

"You know, a couple? They hooked up a few weeks ago. Been dating since."

"Wait..." George's mind was racing to keep up. "You mean...dating *each other*? Like..." He lowered his voice to a whisper. "Lesbians?"

Casper laughed. "I know, right? Why do the hot ones always end up lesbians?"

George had a feeling the other man's experience had more to do with himself than women or lesbians in general. But he kept those thoughts to himself. "Wow. I never guessed."

Some part of his mind now scanned his mental archives for any indelicate comments he might have made in the months of their acquaintance. He was pretty sure he'd offered a few politically incorrect witticisms about "the alphabet community." Which, of course, if he'd known Angela was a member of, he probably would not have done. Not because they weren't funny, but because that community tended to be oversensitive and humorless. And he didn't need another lawsuit. Especially not now. "You're sure?"

"Oh, yeah. Check out their Facebook pages. We're not friends—they must not have seen my request yet—but they've got all kinds of pictures up."

George cleared his throat and tapped his fingers absently. He felt a kind of betrayal, as if in withholding this information from him, Angela had compromised him somehow. "Wow."

Casper threw another glance over his shoulder and lowered his voice even more. "Nice food for thought, though, eh?"

George blinked at him. "What?"

"You know? Those two?" Here, the other man made a gesture with his two hands, and Sutherland realized it was a crude attempt to depict scissoring.

And, despite himself, he laughed out loud. "I hadn't thought of that. But, yes, it is."

Casper grinned. "Right? Two hottest women in the office, going at it?" He shook his head. "Day-um."

★

Heather smiled up at her as Angela brought their coffees from the counter. "Thank you, beautiful."

She'd stayed with their purses and order tag. The food had come in the interim.

"Of course. Oh, that looks good." Angela had ordered a tomato mozzarella panini, and the sight of melted cheese and the tomato and spinach that peeked out of crisp, golden-brown bread made her mouth water. She set their lattes—lavender, of course—down and slid into her seat. "So, how's your day so far?"

Heather shrugged. "Not much different than any other day. I've barely had a chance to talk to him."

The "him" in question was George Jr., of course. It was his first day back at the office in almost six weeks.

"He's probably got a lot to catch up on."

Heather nodded. "Yes. But he sure seemed to like the breakfast thing. That was a good idea."

Angela shifted uncomfortably. The truth was, she'd been motivated more from a guilty conscience than anything else. She'd done everything she could to make life miserable for George Jr.

But his dad almost dying? She hadn't accounted for that.

And then, of late, she found herself questioning her earlier plan. Sure, he was a self-centered, egotistical jerk who had ruined her workplace.

But maybe she'd gone overboard too. Maybe it wasn't her call to make. Maybe, she should have just walked away.

Lauren said her doubts were just because she was happy. "You're getting laid. You're in a better mood." She hadn't cared that her proclamation made her friend blush to the roots of her hair. She'd gone full steam ahead. "But that doesn't mean you weren't right to fuck him—in the metaphorical sense, of course. He's a prick. He deserves it."

She still wasn't sure. But what was done was done. And things certainly hadn't gone according to Angela's plan anyway. Despite her best efforts, she'd hired two exceptional employees with Heather and Matt. Conrad was far from personable, but he still excelled at his work.

Kathryn and Casper were another story. Casper took forever to complete a simple task and retreated into technobabble when called on it. And Kathryn? She performed her job admirably. But, as with her previous workplace, things had started to go missing.

Conrad's stained-glass suncatchers had gone missing twice, and he was ready to call the police on the cleaning crew. He was convinced they'd taken them. "My wife made that, dammit."

It made perfect sense, somehow, to his mind that the cleaning crew would leave behind the cash in his desk drawer, his tablet, and other assorted valuables but take a homemade craft.

Casper had complained about his missing umbrella and a handful of video game figurines that had vanished. Matt noticed his staplers and hole punch had gone missing. Heather had lost several lip glosses and a day planner. And Angela found herself chronically short of pens these days.

She was convinced the thefts were attributable to Kathryn and her kleptomania, but of course, she could say nothing on that score without revealing her own duplicity in hiring the other woman. So she left it alone.

"What's wrong?" Heather asked, drawing her from her thoughts.

"What?"

"You got quiet all of a sudden, when I started talking about work. Everything okay?"

Angela stared at her latte. Then, after taking a sip, she said, "Actually, Heather, there's something I need to tell you."

Consternation crossed Heather's features, but her tone was lighthearted as she said, "Oh, no. That sounds worryingly like 'we need to talk.'"

Angela laughed. "We do. But, not about—well, anything like that. It's about work. About *me* and work."

Heather cocked her head to one side. "What's going on, Angie?"

She let loose a long sigh. "The thing is...I've told you I think Sutherland is an asshole."

"Yes. I'm still not sure I forgive you for not giving me full warning before I took the job. But go on."

Angela smiled at the other woman's teasing but didn't lose track of her thoughts. "I've been planning to leave the company for a while."

"To leave?" Heather's face fell.

Angela felt a touch warmed by her reaction, and she hastened to assure, "I'd still be in the area."

"Oh." Heather's brow relaxed. "Uh, that's not so bad then."

"No. My dad wants me to work for him."

"On the farm?"

"That's right."

Heather nodded. "That makes sense."

"Yeah. It's not—it's not my first choice. But I don't like working at Sutherland. And I feel like now's the time to leave. I probably should have told you earlier."

"I will miss seeing you at work. But..." Here, the other woman grinned. "I won't say I'll be sorry to see you get out of HR."

"Oh?"

"It felt a little weird, is all I'm saying, falling for the HR lady again."

Angela laughed. "I suppose. But listen, don't tell anyone, okay? I haven't decided when I'm going to give my notice. It'll be soon, probably."

"Don't worry; I won't say a thing."

"Thanks, babe."

"Of course. And hey—thanks for confiding in me."

For a moment, they sat there, gazing into each other's eyes and smiling. Angela wasn't quite sure what to say. She found sometimes that words failed her when she was with Heather. There was something so much more intimate in a tender glance than the prettiest poem.

A flash went off, and both women started.

Lauren's voice hit them. "Sorry. I didn't mean to startle you, or interrupt. But you looked too damned cute to let the moment go by."

Blinking, Angela saw that her friend had her phone out. She groaned. "We need to start meeting somewhere else."

Heather laughed. "Yes, Tealeaves is clearly not safe."

Lauren brushed this off with a dismissive gesture and a good-natured laugh. "But you won't. No one else in town makes a lavender latte."

"She's got us there."

"Yes," Angela conceded. "But that doesn't mean we can't complain."

"On the contrary, I intend to. As a matter of fact, I demand to speak to the manager."

Lauren grinned and pulled up a chair. "I don't need a second urging. Sally, cover the register, will you? So, how have you two been?" She threw a faux scolding look in Angela's direction. "If it wasn't for your addiction to lavender, I wouldn't have even known if you were still alive."

Angela made a show of rolling her eyes at her friend's exaggeration. It was true she and Heather had been spending a lot of time together lately, and that didn't leave much room for anything else. Still, it wasn't *quite* that bad. They'd all gone out for margaritas last Wednesday. *Or had it been the Wednesday before?*

"That's my fault," Heather said.

Lauren scoffed. "Believe me, I know."

Angela's cheeks pinked, and Heather laughed. "I mean, she's been helping me at my place. Finishing unpacking things."

"Mhmm. I'm sure that's what you two have been doing. Unpacking." Then Lauren's expression morphed from skepticism to excitement. "But anyway, Rae and I want you over for dinner sometime this week. You can choose what night, but don't tell me you're too busy. You have plenty of time to *unpack* the rest of the week. We're claiming you for one evening."

Chapter Twenty-Five

George had taken an early lunch, and let it last a long time. He was finding it difficult to settle into his work again, and the patterns of before. So, he'd had a drink over lunch, and now he was feeling a little better about things.

He spotted Heather and Angela coming back to the office together, and he shook his head at the sight. He still didn't like that Angie hadn't been upfront with him. He still feared what he might have said.

Of course, it would be her word against his. But that was not the sort of thing he needed at a moment like this. Not with his dad so close to handing the company over.

Then again, he was probably worried about nothing. Angie seemed like a girl with a sense of humor. And he'd been good to her. She was the only one in her department who still had her job—and she had only him to thank for that.

No, the more he thought on it, the more he was sure he had nothing to worry about. So, thanks in part to his own reasoning, and in part to a neat whiskey, he walked back into the office in tolerably good spirits.

He seemed to be the only one, for he stumbled onto a scene of chaos. Heather and Angie were talking in calming tones to Conrad, whose shouting was anything but calm.

Matt, meanwhile, was telling him he needed to calm down. Casper was watching the entire spectacle with wide-eyed surprise—and a touch of amusement. And Kathryn was wringing her hands in a distressed fashion.

"I'm calling the goddamned cops," the older man shouted.

This seemed to be the right cue for George to make his entrance. Assuming his most managerial tones, he said, "Hold on; who is calling the cops? And about what?"

It commanded the attention he expected because everyone turned. Conrad seemed to have sparks flying out of his eyes, and George immediately doubted the wisdom of his interference.

"I've been robbed," the other man declared hotly. "Again."

"Robbed?" George's consternation only increased.

Angela cleared her throat. "One of his drawings has gone missing."

"One of my grandson's drawings," he corrected. "And it isn't 'missing.' It was stolen. And I know exactly who did it. Housekeeping."

George might have laughed if the other man didn't look so serious—serious and slightly dangerous. "Um, sorry; I'm not sure I'm following. Some kind of...artwork is missing?"

Conrad turned to point to a handful of papers secured to the wall, bearing colorful but otherwise awful crayon drawings.

George couldn't check his expression in time, and a little hint of amusement seeped out. "You mean, you think someone stole one of those?"

"I *know* they did. I brought it in last Thursday, and now it's gone. And I know who took it. The cleaning staff has been robbing me blind."

"Okay, dude." Casper laughed. "First of all, that's insane. No offense, but nobody wants your grandkid's crappy artwork."

George glanced over in surprise. He couldn't disagree, but he couldn't commend the other man's tact either.

Casper continued, "And even if they did—which they didn't—what do you care? You were complaining about finding room for it anyway? I mean, *you* didn't even want it."

This launched a heated war of words between the two men, and had George not feared it might end up a more physical confrontation, he might have let it continue for a few more moments. As it was, he intervened with, "Gentlemen, please. Casper, your reasoning is sound, but remember—we're a team here. There's no need to disrespect our team members. Or the art skills of their grandchildren.

"And Conrad, while nobody is disputing the sentimental value of such a treasure, you have to admit it does seem *unlikely* someone would want to steal that." When Conrad stared daggers at him, he shrugged. "I mean, why would they?"

"I don't pretend to know the motives of the criminal mind, Mr. Sutherland."

"Well, uh, that's fair. Still, these, uh, crimes do require motive. And as far as I can see, there is none."

"Maybe they're just thieves. Maybe they're messing with me."

"Or maybe it fell when they were cleaning and ended up in the trash. Isn't that possible?"

"No."

George tried to keep the impatience out of his voice. He appreciated absurdity as much as anyone, but not on company time. "Look, I'm sorry the picture's lost. We're all sorry. But there's no evidence this was theft."

"That's why I want to call the police. Because they can dust for fingerprints. You've got a bunch of thieves on your payroll, and I want them found and brought to justice."

"Jesus, Conrad. Nobody is going to dust for fingerprints over a missing scribble. No offense, but..." George gestured at the remaining pictures. "Your grandkids aren't exactly little da Vincis. The cops would laugh at us—and probably bill the company for wasting their time."

"If someone is stealing my property, I have a right—"

"No one is stealing your property," he snapped. "Enough already. Fuck. What is wrong with you?"

The two men stared daggers at each for a moment.

Matt cleared his throat. "Sir, I'll mention to housekeeping to pay particular attention to avoid wall hangings. I'll let them know we've had a few things disappear lately."

George nodded. "Good. There, problem solved. Right?"

He didn't wait to see Conrad's expression. He had a feeling it wasn't going to be a pleasant one. And he didn't want to have to fire the other man—which, if his attitude kept on its current trajectory, would be the only course of action left. It had taken too long to find an admin, and he didn't need turnover now.

He stalked back to his office and shut the door after him. *What in the hell is wrong with people?* Conrad was a grown man, a reasonably intelligent one. And though he wore spectacles, his eyes couldn't be *that* bad. How could he possibly think someone was going to steal his grandkid's scribbles?

Throw them away? Sure.

But steal them? "Jesus."

He sat at his desk for a while, alternatively shaking his head and trying to concentrate. The latter was not going well. He'd already been distracted today, but the absurdity of a few minutes ago was just too much.

He decided to text the story to Tommy. *He'll get a kick out of it.*

His prediction proved accurate. Tommy wanted pictures of the missing artwork and full details on the alleged heist.

He was smiling when a knock sounded at his door. Matt answered his summons to come in by poking his head inside.

"Sir? There's an Andy Gilmore on the phone for you."

George frowned. *What the hell?* Andy knew his personal number. What was he doing calling the office, much less his PA? "Why did he call you?"

"He didn't. I had your calls forwarded while you were gone, and I forgot to unforward them."

"Oh." That, at least, made sense. "Well, I don't want to talk to him. Tell him I'm in an all-day meeting."

Matt nodded. "Sounds good."

The door closed, and George glanced back at his phone. Tommy had said something about calling in SWAT, but the jokes didn't draw his attention now. He'd hoped Andy would take the hint inherent in his silence.

But obviously, that wasn't going to happen. *Dammit.* He was going to have to do this the hard way.

Not that George minded confrontation. He'd never shied away from that with his inferiors or even his equals. But it was a different thing to argue with the man who had enough dirt on you to put you away for a long, long time.

You've got just as much dirt on him too. It's your company, and your research. Stand your ground. There's not a damned thing he can do.

It took a few moments of consideration on this point to restore his equilibrium of mind. But then, satisfied that the worst Andy could do was pitch a fit, George shrugged. That was coming sooner rather than later anyway. They'd have to have the conversation about Sutherland and Gilmore parting ways. Andy wasn't likely to take that well. But they'd both known it would come eventually, whenever it was no longer in George's best interests to keep doing business with him.

He was just making up his mind to call Andy—*Tomorrow. I'll block some time in my schedule*—when a knock sounded at his door. "Come in," he called, adding to himself, *He better not be on the phone again.*

But it was Conrad, and not Matt, at his door. The older man surveyed him with unfriendly eyes. "Mr. Sutherland, there's someone here to see you. He's not on your schedule, but he says you'll want to see him."

George frowned. "What? Did he give a name?"

"Yes. Gilmore. Andrew Gilmore."

Chapter Twenty-Six

George had nearly had a full-blown panic at those words, but he'd managed to keep his cool. A nervous laugh that didn't escape Conrad's attention, to judge by the upraised eyebrow, was his only giveaway. Otherwise, he'd been quite collected when he told him to send the visitor in.

He'd managed a reasonable facsimile of cordial surprise when the other man entered his office too. "Andy, wow. Imagine seeing you in Fenwood."

To his credit—and George was very hesitant to give him any credit all—Andy played along masterfully, at least until they'd shut the door. Anything Matt and Conrad would have overhead would have given the impression that Andy Gilmore was passing by on the interstate when he saw a sign for Fenwood and decided to stop in on an old friend.

Of course, had they been privy to the council that ensued, that impression would have been short-lived indeed. Nothing friendly happened once the door closed.

George was in the other man's face before he'd crossed half the office. "What in God's name do you think you're doing here?"

Andy feigned an ignorance that only furthered his irritation. "What do you mean? Jesus, what's the matter, George? We'd been having so much trouble getting ahold of each other, I thought it would be easier to see you in person."

"What's the matter? Are you fucking serious? Are you *trying* to give us away?"

Gilmore frowned at him. "By stopping in for a chat?"

"A chat my ass. You know why you're here."

"But your dad doesn't. And that's what you were worried about, wasn't it?"

George scowled. He wasn't wrong—that was his immediate concern. If George Sr. found out that he and the head of Gilmore Pharmaceuticals were in league at all, well, he'd be lucky if losing everything was the only price he paid. But the other man's nerve in showing up uninvited chafed too.

Still, he tried to stay on topic. "You don't think he's going to find that, I don't know, a little suspicious? That the head of a rival corporation shows up for a private tête-à-tête with me?"

"Come on. He knows we used to hang out." Andy passed him to settle in a chair, and George followed to his own seat.

"Yeah, socially. Not in business meetings."

"So, tell him I was in the area and stopped by."

George managed to stop himself from swearing, but only just. "In Fenwood?"

"I was on the interstate. Which, technically, I was." Andy's lips slithered upward into a smug smile. "Of course, that was to see you. But he doesn't need to know that part."

"What do you think you're accomplishing by showing up here?"

The other man ignored the question, casting a lazy glance around the place before answering. "Nice office. Think you have enough pictures of yourself, though?" His smile returned. "I'm just giving you a hard time. They're great shots. But why am I here? I told you. We kept missing each other. It was simpler than playing phone tag."

George ignored the lie that they'd been "missing" each other. There'd been no attempts at contact on his part, and he knew Andy was perfectly aware of it. "And what's so urgent that it couldn't wait?"

Andy shrugged. "I was just checking in on the research. Seeing if you found anything."

For a long moment, George didn't answer. Part of him wanted to lie and say the whole thing had turned up a dead end. But, somehow, he didn't think that would help him in the present. After a pause, he nodded. "I did."

Andy's eyes twinkled with a rare spark of excitement. "Excellent. And?"

George shifted in his seat. "And...look, I'm sorry you wasted a trip out here, Andrew. But—for once—my dad was right."

The other man's brow knit with concern. "What do you mean?"

"I mean, the research isn't going anywhere. It's too dangerous. I'm not going to risk attaching Sutherland's name to something that might end up—well, who knows what. I'm sorry. But my mind is made up."

Andy steepled his fingers and seemed to be considering his words. For a long moment, a silence that was at once awkward and ominous settled between them. "I don't really think that's your call to make, George."

George's eyes blazed. "What the hell does that mean?"

Andy shrugged in a slow, casual fashion. "I mean, we had a deal. I paid you for the research. All of it. Not for you to pick and choose which pieces you delivered. Now, I've kept my end of the bargain. And you're telling me you don't intend to keep yours."

"You told me I could decide what we did with the research," George reminded him. "If I wanted it to stay buried, it stayed buried. That's what you said."

"Did I? I don't think so. Anyway, if I did, I spoke in error. We had a contract. You took my money and didn't deliver my product."

"I gave you everything I knew there was."

"And yet, that's not what we agreed on. Now you know there was more. You owe me it, George. And I—because *I* keep my word—will pay your share of whatever profits we make. Like I've always done. Because, to me, a deal is a deal."

George shifted again. Something in Andy's unruffled manner set his teeth on edge. He almost would have preferred screaming and raging. That, at least, he could counter. But this cool, collected blackmail?

It made his skin crawl. "Andy," he tried in his most placating tones, "in all the years we've been doing business together, I've never once asked you for anything like this. Have I?"

"No, you haven't."

"Exactly. So I'm asking you now. Let this one go. Please. This is way too big, way too dangerous."

Andy smiled again, studying his steepled fingers. "Well, you make a good point. And if this was just friendship, of course I'd do it. But you know it's not that easy. This is business. It's nothing personal. I bought the research. You owe me what I bought."

"Fucking hell, are you listening to me? This is too dangerous."

"I know you believe that. Really, George, I do. And I wish I could let it go. You're a good friend. Really. But a deal is a deal. And you know how it goes. If I make exceptions for you, what about the next guy who wants to back out of a deal? What about the one after that? What stops me from caving to them, but exempts you?" He shook his head. "You know that's no way to run a business."

George ran a hand through his hair. "Look, what if...what if I give you back some of the money?"

Andy sat in silent thought for a moment. "*All* of the money."

He recoiled at the very idea. "Jesus, are you kidding? You know I can't afford that." He'd already started spending his payoff. "Anyway, you owe me for the research you have."

Andy smiled patiently. "You know it doesn't work like that. You don't get to make a deal and renegotiate the terms midway through."

"I won't do it," George declared resolutely. "I won't."

Andy raised an eyebrow and watched him. "Be careful, George. Don't say things you'll regret."

George swallowed but stood his ground. "You heard me. I've crossed a lot of lines for you, but I won't cross this one. I'm sorry, Andy. I really am. But this is for the best. For both of us."

"Really?" He smiled again, and his eyes had suddenly become very flinty. "I wonder, do you think your father would agree?"

George wasn't falling for that. "Don't bluff, Andrew. You're not very good at it."

"I *never* bluff."

"Really? You're going to what? Run and tell my dad that we've both been profiting from corporate espionage for years? You're going to prison over something that might not come to anything anyway?"

The other man sighed. "You never were very imaginative, George. But no, I wouldn't do anything that drastic. I wouldn't have to. All I'd have to do is send some of my people—you know, my 'spies'—to have a chat with Daddy. They wouldn't have to mention half the laws you've broken. Just enough to give him an idea. You think you'd end up head of Sutherland Research after that? You think you'd ever see a dime of your father's money?"

George swallowed. His mouth had suddenly gone very dry. "You...you wouldn't."

"Wouldn't I?"

"That's blackmail."

"Is it blackmail if you're just getting back your own property?"

"It's not yours, you son of a bitch. Sutherland discovered it."

"And I paid for it. The exchange of goods. Fundamentals of commerce. Come on, George. You know how it works."

"And if you do, what's to stop me from telling what I know? You think I don't have enough to put you away forever?"

Andrew Gilmore laughed, a long, deep laugh. Then he leaned forward, peering at him across the desk. "Well, that's how we're going to play, is it? All right then. Let's put all of our cards on the table. You have compromising information on me. I have compromising information on you. It would be to both of our advantages to conceal the worst of it—because if I go to prison, so do you."

"And if I go to prison," George countered, "so do you."

"I don't doubt it. So, as I say, since neither of us wants that, we sit on the worst of it. But I don't have to send you to prison, do I? I just have to let your father find out a fraction of what you've done, and you're fucked."

Andy sat back now, smiling with satisfaction. "Now, that's not a play you can match. I'm head of Gilmore. And anyway, my dad's only problem would have been that I was stupid enough to compromise myself. We don't all have Goody-Two-Shoes for fathers. So, no, you will comply. Because you have too much to lose by not complying."

George swallowed again, trying to think of some way out of this, something he could say to shake the other man's belief that he'd won. But his mind was blank. "You son of a bitch" was all he could come up with.

And Andy just laughed at that. "Flattery will get you nowhere. But you will comply, won't you?"

George nodded miserably.

"Excellent. I knew you were a man of reason. And don't worry. Our old agreement holds. You will be compensated accordingly."

"Go to hell."

"Now, George, there's no cause for that. It's just—"

"We're done," George interrupted.

"What?"

He was gratified to see the flash of surprise on Andy's face, and he pressed forward. "We're done—you and me. You say I owe you this. Okay, I'll get you it. But it's the last thing. Final. Finito. Done."

He got to his feet now. "No more business between us after this." Gilmore opened his mouth to speak, but George cut him off. "And save your threats. You want to tell my father? Fine. You do that. But remember something, Andy. A cornered animal will act in desperate ways. I'll give you a bit of advice. Take your victory and get the fuck out of my life forever. Because as much as you think you can fuck me over, I swear to God, I will fuck you up so much worse."

Then he pointed to his office door. "And get the fuck out of my office. Don't ever let me see you on Sutherland property again."

Andy smiled, a soft, resigned if not satisfied, smile. "Well, as you see fit, George. I'm sorry it's come to this."

"Out."

The other man headed to the door but stopped to turn before he opened it. "I'll expect you to retrieve the files within the week."

"What are you talking about? They're still in Philly."

"That's why you're going to retrieve them."

"I was just there. I can't go back."

"George, you seem to think I'm negotiating. I'm not. You will get the files this week. And when I call, you will answer the phone. Are we clear?"

George wanted to tell him to shove his ultimatums up his rear. But the dead, flinty expression in the other man's eyes gave a measure of caution to his words. "Crystal."

"Good. I'll be in touch. Have a great day." With this, Andy showed himself out.

"Yeah, fuck you too," he muttered under his breath.

Chapter Twenty-Seven

George's good mood lasted all of half a day on return-ing. Angela knew the type of boss he was, but she was still surprised to see just how quickly he'd turned foul tem-pered. Conrad and Matt bore the brunt of his wrath, for they were in the closest proximity. Nothing either man could do was sufficient to please him.

The coffee was too hot or not hot enough when Matt brought it. His schedule was a mess, his planner a disas-ter, and the business waiting all completely out of order.

Conrad, meanwhile, needed to get his hearing checked. And he should work on his attitude. Would it kill him, George wanted to know, to smile now and then?

It wouldn't kill Conrad, but Angela had her suspi-cions about what it might do to George's health and well-being to press the issue.

He was curt to the rest of the employees too. None of Heather's ideas were good enough.

Casper needed to remember that he was on company time, and company dime. Irrelevant conversations about kite surfing could happen on his own time.

Kathryn had ordered too many paperclips and too few pens. And what in God's name were they going to do with all that bathroom tissue?

As for herself, Angela should have been working on the lab hires in his absence. Her politest reminder that she'd been expressly forbidden to hire anyone under George's hiring freeze had invoked a greater degree of his wrath. And it existed well into the middle of the week.

Everyone was walking on eggshells. Heather confided that she might quit, too, if his attitude didn't change soon. Kathryn broke down in tears twice. Casper stayed locked in his office, talking to no one. Matt took every opportunity to be out of the building. There was no task, no matter how mundane, that he wasn't eager to perform if it meant getting out of the office. And Conrad?

Well, Angela was pretty sure Conrad was either going to quit or strangle George. Or maybe both. The job wasn't turning out to be as easy as he'd anticipated, not least of all as it involved working in close proximity to his boss. She told Heather as much, and the other woman laughed.

"If he's going to leave, I hope he has the decency at least to take George with him, for all our sakes."

But all joking aside, the week solidified now more than ever Angela's desire to quit. It was time to leave Sutherland behind and move on to greener pastures. That they were *actual* pastures just proved that the cosmos had a sense of humor. Or so her dad informed her anyway.

Regardless, she wrote and rewrote her letter of resignation during the week. It started with a list of all the reasons why she was leaving. It ended up short, simple, concise, and devoid of any reasons why.

This was George Sutherland, after all. He wouldn't give a damn why his employees left. He'd never admit fault or consider her reasons why. All listing her grievances would do was ensure she ended up with a miserable recommendation if she ever tried to use Sutherland as a reference in the future.

No, she would leave without burning bridges.

It helped that George took an unexplained absence on Thursday. Late Wednesday afternoon, he'd dropped to Matt and Conrad, "I'm going to be gone tomorrow."

The older man blanched. "But your schedule—"

George waved his concerns away with a brush of his hand. "Take care of it. Clear it. Reschedule what you need to. Cancel what you can.

"And, Matt, I've got a bunch of follow-ups I need to do. I've flagged them in my inbox. Get me some drafts together. I'll look them over when I'm back."

"When will that be?"

"Friday, maybe. Or Monday. Hell, I don't know. Whenever I'm back. Just do it."

Thursday passed in relative tranquility. Matt found that his stapler had gone missing again, and Conrad talked about bringing in surveillance equipment. "To catch those bastards in housekeeping once and for all."

Angela had to remind him that that went against corporate policy, and he nodded. "Of course. I was only kidding. If I was actually going to—and I'm not, of course—I'd bring one of those cameras that look like something else."

"You mean, like a nanny cam or something?" Matt asked, an eyebrow raised.

"Exactly." He glanced at a keychain set on his desk, with one of the storage closet keys attached. And smiled. "Not that I'd do that, of course. Still, if I was going to, that's how I'd do it."

"I don't know, dude. That's kind of creepy."

"So is robbing people."

"Both," she reminded him, "are against company policy. I really hope you wouldn't do that, Conrad. Because you'd end up getting yourself in trouble too."

"That's only if I told anyone and didn't take matters into my own hands." He smiled again. "Which, of course, I wouldn't do. Because that would be against policy too."

"Yes, it would. Very much so."

Other than this exchange, the day went off without a hitch. Angela finished her resignation but held off on submitting it. *Just to be sure.*

Then she and Heather spent the night at her house, cooking dinner together and making love. Thoughts of work couldn't have been further from her mind.

Friday passed less pleasantly, despite the fact that George Jr. was still absent. On Friday, Conrad found that someone had stolen the key from off of his keychain. "The son of a bitch reached over the counter, too, so the video didn't show anything."

"Wait," Angela said, "the what?"

Conrad scowled at her. "Did you hear what I said? Someone stole the supply closet key."

"I heard you, Conrad. I also heard you say you had a camera here. Which is expressly against our policies. You know that. We talked about it yesterday."

His scowl deepened. "So you're going to what? Write me up for trying to stop a thief? A thief that you're all ignoring?"

Another time, Angela might have had to write him up. But she reminded herself she was leaving Sutherland. *Not my problem anymore.* And she was responsible, in a way, for his suffering. She'd hired Kathryn to make George's life miserable. But so far, the other woman had only tortured her coworkers. And that got back to Angela, and her desire for revenge.

So, she said, "No, Conrad, I'm not going to write you up. But, if I see any kind of surveillance equipment in this office after lunch, I will have no choice. Do you understand?"

He started to protest, but she raised a hand. "It's not up for debate. I'm doing you a favor. Take it or take a write-up."

Conrad had been in a proper huff for the rest of the morning. But the keychain did disappear shortly thereafter. And to judge by his attitude, he wasn't planning to bring it out again.

Angela stopped by Kathryn's office later that morning and closed the door after herself.

"Angela." The other woman smiled. "Can I help you?"

She seated herself. "Let's cut to the chase, Kathryn. I know about your last job, and why you left it. I know you're the one taking everyone's shit. And if you don't leave Conrad alone—and Matt and Heather and Casper too. And me, for that matter. If you don't leave us alone, you're going to be looking for a new job."

Kathryn's face went very red, and she released a long string of protests and indignant sputtering.

Angela ignored it all and got to her feet. "You heard me. Leave Conrad the hell alone, and we can pretend this conversation never happened. Keep stealing from him, and you'll be looking for new employment."

Professional? No, of course not. But she wasn't planning to be here long enough to care. On the contrary, she was more determined than ever to submit her resignation. And at four forty-five that afternoon, she pressed submit on her voluntary termination form.

She sighed with relief. That was it. She'd given her two weeks' notice. She was free. Or, as good as.

Sure, George would be a monster to work with over the next two weeks. *But what's the worst that could happen? He'll fire me?*

After work, she and Heather headed for Heather's house. Ragnar needed a walk, and they took him for a long one. Then, at six thirty, they joined their friends for dinner and drinks. Lauren and Rae were so excited by their relationship news that work never came up. And it was just as well.

She'd told Heather, but with the relief came a feeling of sadness. She'd worked at Fenwood Bio since she'd graduated. She hadn't planned to leave like this. She hadn't really thought of leaving at all. It had been a good job, an ideal job. Fenwood was the sort of workplace where people passed their entire working lives. Sure, there was more money to be made elsewhere. But Fenwood paid enough, and they'd been a good employer. And she hadn't had to leave her hometown and family.

But, of course, that was all in the past. Her time with Fenwood was over.

Chapter Twenty-Eight

Angela and Heather stayed out late and rose late the next morning. They were at Angela's place again. So was Ragnar. They'd stopped on the way home to pick up the great, slobbery pooch, who seemed to have no problem adjusting to either home. As long as there was a warm welcome and a lap or two to crush with his pretentions at being a lapdog, he was as happy as could be. They'd already brought a bag of his kibble and a set of bowls to Angela's house since he was by now a fairly regular visitor.

On Saturday morning, Heather rose first. Angela yawned as she got out of bed, and the other woman leaned over and kissed her on the forehead. "I'll get coffee on and breakfast started."

Angela murmured a reply and drifted back to a semi-sleep. She was roused a few minutes later by the sweet smell of coffee. And as she ebbed back into awareness, yawning and stretching and blinking into the midmorning sunlight, she smelled something else. *Eggs, maybe? Pancakes?* She wasn't sure, but her stomach started to growl.

It was definitely time to get up. So, she did, stopping to brush her teeth and hair, and wash her face. A full shower would wait until after breakfast, but she did dress for the day. They'd have to take Ragnar for a walk, and she'd probably shower after that.

She came down to find Heather in the kitchen and discovered with surprise that both of her earlier guesses were correct—eggs *and* pancakes were on the griddle. "Jesus, wow. That smells divine."

Heather smiled up at her. "Grab a plate, beautiful. It's almost ready."

Angela complied, grabbing plates and silverware for the pair of them. Wrapping an arm around the other woman, who was still in her pajamas and a light house robe, she kissed her on the neck. "Thank you for this."

Heather craned her neck around to peck her on the cheek. "Of course." Then she turned back to the eggs. "You like yours over medium, right?"

"That's right. Hey, I'll get us coffee. Milk in yours?"

"Not today. Thanks."

They busied themselves with their respective tasks. Angela had just brought the mugs to the kitchen island when a booming bark sounded.

"Oh boy," Heather said. "Can you check on Ragnar? He's still on his tether."

"Of course."

They'd put a tether in the yard for the dog. He was a complete couch potato in the heat of the day, but he enjoyed sitting outside in the early mornings and late evenings when it was cool. Ragnar hadn't had a chance to learn the boundaries of her yard, but a propensity to wander, apparently, was a breed trait. Heather had asked early on if she could bring a tether so the canine could enjoy his morning watch in safety.

Usually, he was quiet on patrol. This, Angela had learned, was not entirely common for the breed either.

"I'm just lucky he took to living in town," Heather had told her.

Now, however, he was barking with a fury that would certainly rouse the neighbors to anger if she didn't check it soon. The dog weighed well over a hundred pounds and had a deep, barrel chest that could produce cacophonous noise when he had a mind to do so.

And as Angela raced out to the porch, she found he was very much of a mind to do so. The reason why became immediately clear as she stepped outside.

A visitor was standing on the lowest step. Ragnar had ascended to the highest and was warning him off with loud, fierce barks.

Angela couldn't quite place the man. He was older, with thin gray hair and a vaguely familiar face. But she couldn't put her finger on how it was familiar. And, at the moment, she was more concerned with Ragnar. "Hey," she told the dog, who immediately retreated to her side at the sight of her, "it's okay. Calm. Good boy."

Ragnar stopped barking, bracing himself against her leg in a defensive stance instead.

She addressed the stranger, "Can I help you?"

"Are you Angela McCormack?"

"I am."

The older man smiled, and Angela blinked. She recognized that smile. At least, it seemed very familiar. *George Sutherland.* This old man smiled with George Sutherland's smile. "Excellent. My name is George Sutherland. I'd like to talk to you. If your pup will allow it."

He smiled again, but Angela hardly noticed. She could have, as the saying went, been knocked over by a feather.

"George Sutherland? You mean...*the* George Sutherland?"

"Of Sutherland Research, yes. May I come in?"

"Oh." Suddenly, she remembered her manners. "Uh, of course." She unhooked Ragnar's tether and turned to the house, guiding both dog and visitor inside. "This way."

Then she remembered that Heather was in the kitchen in her pajamas. "Uh, will you take a seat?" She gestured to the sitting room. "I'll just, uh, get us coffee."

She didn't wait for him to voice a preference, lest he should decline coffee, and practically raced for the kitchen.

Heather glanced up. "Thanks, babe. I don't know what gets into him sometimes, but—" She cut off as she got a good look at Angela. "What's wrong?"

"Nothing. But—we've got a visitor."

"Oh." Heather's eyes fell to her bedclothes now. "Crap."

"George Sutherland."

"The boss?"

Angela shook her head. "Not that one. George Sutherland *Sr.*"

Heather seemed as amazed as she'd been. "What? Here? Why?"

"I have no idea. But I need to get back there."

"Of course." Heather again glanced at her clothes. "I'll, uh, go change. See if he wants any breakfast."

"Okay." Angela turned toward the sitting room but stopped as she recalled her reason for racing off. After grabbing two cups of coffee, she made the trek back. Ragnar sat in the entryway, watching the newcomer.

For his part, George Sutherland was glancing around the room with unmasked curiosity. At her return, he smiled again. "Ah, Miss McCormack. I'm just admiring your house. This is a very pretty place you've got."

She thanked him and handed him the mug.

"Oh, thank *you*. It's been quite a few days since I've had real coffee. My wife and son—they keep me closely guarded against the evils of caffeine."

He said it in a lighthearted fashion, but Angela paused. She hadn't thought of that. "Oh, I'm sorry. I can brew decaf."

"No. No, please don't. I've been craving real coffee." He took a long sip and sighed. "They say you can't taste a difference. But you can."

Angela didn't know what to say to that. So she changed the subject. "How can I help you, Mr. Sutherland?"

"I'm sorry," he said. "I know this is completely unexpected, and you must be wondering what in the hell I'm doing here."

It was a pretty fair summary, and she laughed and said, "I am pretty surprised."

"I saw your resignation yesterday."

"You did?" She blinked. The idea of the head of the entire company noticing her resignation seemed a little...well, strange.

"I did. I've been keeping an eye on the Fenwood branch. I've got my reasons. You've been with the company for a while now. Longer than anyone on my son's core team. You're the only one left of the old HR team."

"Yes, he let the rest go," she said, a touch more bitterly than she'd meant to.

"I know." His tone was flat and unemotive. She supposed he hadn't appreciated her own tone. "But the reason I'm here is to ask...why are you leaving, Angela?"

She blinked. Was the CEO of Sutherland Research really sitting in her sitting room to conduct his own exit interview? On a Saturday a few weeks before his heart surgery, no less? "Uh, I'm going to be starting work on my parent's farm."

"A farm?" Sutherland studied her for a moment. "That's quite a career change."

"You know what they say about greener pastures and all that."

He smiled. "A farming joke. I like it. But you know what farming and my line of business have in common?"

"What's that?"

"A lot of bullshit, if you'll pardon my French."

Angela blinked. She had no idea at all what to say to that, so she said nothing.

George Sr. continued, "The turnover at our Fenwood branch has been four times as high as any other facility under our umbrella. I doubt very much they're all taking up farming, Miss McCormack."

"I didn't say they were."

"No. But I doubt that a career professional like yourself is leaving the company from any deep love of agriculture. So, I ask you, why are you leaving Sutherland Research?"

Angela shifted in her seat. She didn't like the questions, and she didn't like the old man's presumption in asking them. She particularly resented his insight in cutting through her lies. And for half a moment, she considered being brutally honest. Then again, she didn't plan to work on the family farm forever. Chances were, she'd need references in the future. So she cleared her throat. "Mr. Sutherland, why don't we just leave things where they are? I am joining my family business. I'm sorry about any inconvenience to you, but I'm sure you'll find someone to replace me soon enough."

George Sr. took a long sip of his coffee. "I've gone over your performance reviews since you started with Fenwood. They're extremely consistent. They speak very highly of your commitment to the job, your team spirit, your willingness to go above and beyond, your leadership. You are a model employee."

Angela's cheeks colored with anger. Yes, she had been a good employee, hadn't she? She had loved her job, and her coworkers. She'd loved the good they were doing in the world. She'd loved playing a part in that.

And George Sutherland Jr. had taken it all away. George Sutherland Sr., the man who sat before her studying her with inquisitive eyes, had taken it all away when he'd sicced his irresponsible, petty, vindictive man-child of a son on their office.

It was everything she could do to keep those thoughts bottled up inside as she answered, "People change. We move on."

"Miss McCormack," the elder Sutherland said, and his tone was sharper now, "you may have resigned, but I'm still your boss. Stop lying to me. I want to know why you're leaving the company. We both know it isn't to shovel manure. If that had been your goal, you would have done it years ago."

Angela stared daggers at her boss and replied in an icy tone, "Don't call me a liar."

"Then don't lie to me. Why are you leaving?"

She laughed. "Do you really have to ask?"

"I'm not a man who wastes time, Angela. If I didn't feel it necessary, I wouldn't have asked."

This, at last, was too much. There was a shade of patronization in his tone that reeked of George Jr.

"Why? Because you handed over a prosperous, successful business to the most conceited, petty, power-hungry asshole in the business. You promoted someone whose ambition, without your name, would have probably propelled him to middle management somewhere, but whose personality, ego, and incompetence would have ensured that he never rose above it. Because you let him fire dozens of good people who had been here for years, decades even, just so he could make a point that he was in charge. You let him fuck up dozens of lives and flush employee morale down the toilet to save a little bit of money. And he walks around thinking he's doing a great job, and that he's a great leader."

She shook her head. "You want to know why I want to get the hell out of Fenwood Bio? Because your son is a condescending, bigoted asshole, and I can't stand working with him. Nobody can. That's why I'm getting out."

"Everything okay, babe?" Heather's voice started the pair of them.

"It's fine," Angela said. "Mr. Sutherland was just leaving."

George Sr. made no move to go though. He glanced over at Heather and smiled. "You must be Heather Bradshaw."

She glanced between him and Angela. "That's right."

"A pleasure to meet you."

Angela glared at him. "You can go, Mr. Sutherland."

"I can," he answered. "But I hope you'll let me stay, Miss McCormack. I asked you why you were leaving because I wanted to know the truth. And you have told me."

"That's right. And what are you going to do about it? We both know, not a damned thing."

George Sr. lowered his eyes. "You misjudge me, Angela. Although, I suppose, I have brought that on myself. I have, as you say, allowed my son to do these things. Not deliberately, but I have not stopped him. And in the end, there's not much difference. But I do plan to do something about it. That, in a way, is why I'm here."

Angela frowned at him, not quite sure she understood what he was saying. "What do you mean?"

He glanced between her and Heather. "Miss Bradshaw, would you join us? What I have to say—well, I was going to consult you both individually, but this is more fortuitous."

Heather looked at Angela for reassurance and, getting it in a moment via a nod, joined her on the sofa. "What's going on?"

"I don't think I introduced myself. I'm George Sutherland."

Heather nodded. "I gathered. But...why are you here, Mr. Sutherland?"

He turned from one to the other, then sighed. "I'm going to tell you something. Something I wish very much I never had to say. But I have reason to suspect that my son is stealing from my company."

Angela blinked. "What?"

"I won't get into specifics—it'll preserve your cover if you know nothing of that. But I believe he's selling research to a rival company and has been for some years now."

"Wait, why would you tell us this?" Heather asked. "Why wouldn't you go to the police, or to him?"

"Because I need proof. If I confront him, he'll deny it. You know my son pretty well, I think. If he meant to convince you that the sky wasn't blue, he could be quite persuasive in his efforts."

"Or at least shout you down until you agreed." Angela nodded.

"Precisely. If my suspicions are correct, I need proof of them. Which is why I'm here. I want to ask you—both of you—if you would help me."

Angela and Heather exchanged glances. The former laughed out loud. "Are you seriously asking us to spy on your son?"

"No, nothing so drastic, Miss McCormack. I just want you to keep an eye on him. Let me know if he gets any peculiar visitors, or if his behavior is out of the ordinary."

Angela snorted. "Have you met your son, Mr. Sutherland? His behavior is always out of the ordinary. He came to work all smiles on Monday, and then spent the rest of the week screaming at everyone."

"That," George answered slowly, "is perhaps not as inexplicable as you think. And more relevant to what I'm asking."

Again, the two women exchanged glances. "Oh?"

"I believe he had a visitor that afternoon?"

"I don't know," Angela admitted.

"He did," Heather said. "I heard Conrad and Matt talking about it. Guy in a suit."

"Yes. His name isn't relevant, but he represents another entity. An entity I believe my son is doing business with. And this brings me to my point—will you help me?"

Angela shifted in her seat. It wasn't that she was opposed to catching George Jr. in the midst of something illegal. She rather liked the idea of that. But she didn't know if she could trust his father. And, more pressingly, she was going to be gone in two weeks. "I already turned in my resignation."

"Yes, you did. Which is why I came out here as soon as I could get a ticket. I deleted your resignation. Junior will be none the wiser. No one will."

She blinked. "You...what?"

"Forgive me, Miss McCormack. If you choose to resubmit it, I will not interfere. But I didn't want to leave it out there for someone to spot, on the chance that you would assist. We don't need those problems later on."

"I'm still not clear on what you'd be asking us to do," Heather put in. "I mean, I'm not sure what your son is up to or if your suspicions are justified, but I do need to be clear. I won't do anything illegal."

"Of course not," the old man said, then snorted. "I would never approach you if I thought you would. But I suspect my son is doing quite a few illegal things. What I need from you is very simple. Keep an eye on him and report anything suspicious to me."

"So...spy on him?" Angela summarized.

"It's not spying. It's more...surveillance."

"How is that different?"

"Because you'll be surveilling him at my request."

Chapter Twenty-Nine

George Sr. stayed for breakfast with the two women, and they ate and discussed his plan. Angela was skeptical. She knew the son well enough to hold the father in the highest suspicion.

Heather was more amenable, but even she insisted on having the scheme in writing.

The old man nodded. "Cover your ass. I completely understand."

"There's one more thing I should tell you," he continued. "And maybe I should have mentioned it first. I didn't want to scare you off though. George has lately stolen something very dangerous. Some research that we had agreed will never see the light of day. He came to see me two days ago. Ostensibly to see me, at least.

"But he accessed and photographed something he should not have been taking with him. He thought I did not know, but I had my suspicions that he might try it. I had cameras installed.

"And, to my everlasting disappointment, he did exactly as I feared he would."

"Shouldn't you call the police?" Heather wondered, her brow furrowed.

George Sr. shook his head. "No. I cannot prove that he did steal it. He took it, certainly. He should not have. I know he stole it. But he? He could very credibly claim he was just taking a copy to study on his own, or some such nonsense."

"How do you know he wasn't?" Angela asked. "I mean, I can't stand your son. But isn't it possible that that's all he was doing?"

He smiled ruefully at that. "Possible? Yes. But I know my son, Miss McCormack. The timing of his business meeting earlier in the week, and his temper. His sudden return, and his secretive copying of the files..." He shook his head. "No. I wish I could explain it away, but I can't. And I still can't prove he was actually stealing it. I know he was, but that's not the same thing.

"And there are two other reasons I won't call the police. The first—selfishly, perhaps—Mrs. Sutherland would never forgive me. She would believe Junior and abhor me for ruining our son's life."

Angela was about to protest that this was a very poor reason indeed, much less if the research was as dangerous as he was suggesting.

But he continued before she could, "And the second, perhaps better, reason is that even if I did have him arrested, it would do nothing to stop his partner. I would destroy my son—whether he faced any legal consequences or not—while someone at least as guilty walked free." He shook his head. "No. I will not do that. I would sooner quietly cut George free than let Andrew Gilmore get away with all he's done."

"Gilmore?" Angela's ears perked up. "You mean, of Gilmore Pharmaceuticals?"

Heather's eyes widened. "Wait, Conrad mentioned an Andy-somebody when he was talking about the visitor. I didn't hear the rest. But was that who visited him? Andy—or, Andrew—Gilmore?"

A shadow crossed George Sr.'s face. "I'm sorry. I shouldn't have mentioned names. It would be easier for you to know less—"

"Bullshit," Angela interrupted, then, remembering who she was talking to, added, "I mean, that's not true, sir. It'll be easier if we know what the heck is going on."

"You understand that these are—at this point—only suspicions? I can't prove anything. I may be impugning the character of my son needlessly."

"It won't go further than us," Heather promised.

"Good. Because my wife would kill me. And Andrew Gilmore, if his name was attached, would sue me into the next millennium."

In the end, the two women agreed. They would help George Sr. discover the truth. "As long as we get those written assurances that this is all at your direction, and we will suffer no employment consequences as a result," Heather said.

"Of course. And, you'll be under the standard NDA," he'd returned, referring to the corporate nondisclosure agreement they'd signed on employment. "Unless there's a breach in our agreement on my side. Which will all be specified in the document."

He thanked them profusely, complimented Heather on her cooking, patted a still suspicious Ragnar on the head, and took his leave.

Heather closed the door after him, and Ragnar sounded a few half barks at the change. He settled down, and the two women stared at each other.

"Are we insane?" Heather asked.

"I'm not sure," Angela admitted. "We might be."

"We must be. What the hell did we just agree to?"

"But what were we supposed to say? 'No, we won't spy on your son so you can call the cops on him for selling off sensitive information'?"

"Jesus. What a mess. This was supposed to be a straightforward job."

"I was supposed to be getting the hell out of there. Now..." Angela trailed off, then exclaimed, "Shit. What am I going to tell my dad?"

"The truth?"

"That I'm playing corporate spy for the CEO?"

"Good point. That sounds a little hokey."

"And we agreed not to say anything."

"Right. Although, who knows if we're even going to have jobs come Monday. I mean, I wouldn't put it past George to cook something like this up to test our loyalty or some such shit."

"You think his father would go along with it?"

"Probably not," Heather conceded. "But who knows. If he's anything like his son, maybe."

"I don't know. Why bother?" Angela shook her head. It didn't make much sense. But then, this whole business didn't make much sense.

They settled for a few minutes into contemplative silence. Then Heather laughed out loud.

"So, uh, you think your dad needs anyone else on the farm? Just in case this does go sideways in a hurry?"

Angela's conversation with her dad went well, all things considered.

He laughed. "Well, kiddo, I can't say I'm surprised you're staying. You always loved that place. And now that that Heather chick is working there..."

"I swear, Dad, I'd put in my resignation. But..."

"But?"

"You're not going to believe me if I tell you."

"I will."

She sighed. She wasn't convinced, but she owed him some kind of explanation. "Okay. But you can't tell anyone. Not even Mom. Because she'll say she won't tell anyone, and—"

"She'll tell everyone," he agreed with a smile. Angela's mom was notorious for breaking confidences. She didn't *mean* to. She'd never have done it maliciously. But it just somehow happened. Whether in casual conversation, or under a pledge of absolute silence, or even forgetting that she'd promised to say nothing: she would spill the beans to someone, somewhere. "All right, not a word."

"My boss's dad—the CEO of the company—asked me to stay."

Angela's dad was absolutely silent for a long moment. Silent, and unmoving; and Angela wondered if the video call had frozen. Then he blinked. "What now?"

"I know it sounds crazy. But he really did. There's—well, problems. I can't tell you much, but there's problems at the company, and he wants me to stay on while he figures something out."

"So, you're staying for good? Or...?"

"To be honest, Dad, I don't know. I'm not really sure what's going on. I'll find out more on Monday, hopefully. But, for now, I'm going to stay. I think just to help him out. But maybe longer. It's probably too much to hope for, but things might actually be changing there."

Chapter Thirty

George Jr. returned to Fenwood late Sunday evening. His flight had been delayed twice, and the drive from the airport seemed even longer and more onerous than usual.

Or perhaps it was the situation. He'd done what Andy Gilmore had demanded. He'd expected to make the tradeoff then, when he'd been in Philly.

But Andy hadn't returned his calls or texts. And George hadn't dared stay away longer than he had. As it was, George Sr. had dropped hints that he'd be "better doing your job than fussing about me. I've already got your mother to babysit me."

He supposed Andy was making a point. Their business would be done when he said so, and not a moment sooner. George had half a mind to *miss* Gilmore's call when it finally came.

But some wiser part of him cautioned against it. Discretion was the better part of valor, after all. And discretion told him to play along until their mutual business was done for good. Then he could terminate the acquaintance forever.

Still, George Jr. was in a foul temper when he reached Fenwood. A poor night's sleep did nothing to alleviate it the next morning. Everyone in the office irritated him.

Heather's cheerful smiles, Conrad's scowls, Matt's helpfulness, and Casper's absence; Angela's all-business attitude and Kathryn's mousey tendencies; the lab's bookish scientists, and obsequious head: everything around him grated.

His own mother was little better. She'd sent him a message again imploring him to finish his business sooner rather than later. "Your father needs you by his side."

He was doing everything he could and dealing with Gilmore too. Did she really think the constant reminders were remotely helpful? *Goddammit, why doesn't that woman take up a hobby and get the hell out of my business*?

That he got the official RSVP to Ralph's wedding over lunch only further soured his mood. He didn't want to think about Ralph Pearson or his ridiculous bride-to-be. They annoyed him enough in the best of times. Now, they were salt in his already wounded mood.

But the final cut came on Tuesday, just after nine.

Conrad knocked on his closed door and poked his head in a moment later. "There's someone to see you, Mr. Sutherland. Someone who isn't on the schedule, but insisted I check anyway."

Andy. That son of a bitch. "Send him in."

Conrad seemed surprised. "Are you sure? I mean, right away."

But it wasn't Andy Gilmore who stepped into his office a minute later. It was someone even more detestable, if that was possible: Caruso.

George blinked, stunned by the gall of the man to show up here, on his property. And stunned worse by the idea that Andy would have dared send him here.

Caruso wisely got the door behind him. "Mr. Sutherland," he said in an accent that might have been nails on a chalkboard translated to speech. Joey didn't pronounce *th*'s. They were *d*'s. He didn't usually pronounce *r*'s either. They sounded like *ah*'s. It was just one more thing he detested about Joey Caruso. "A pleasure to see you again."

"What the hell are you doing here?"

"Mr. Gilmore sent me, of course. He did mention it, didn't he? Oh, no. I hope it didn't slip his mind." Joey plopped into a seat and grabbed a chocolate from the bowl on George's desk. "You know how it goes though. He's a very busy man. Sometimes things slip."

"You're here for the research he's extorting from me, right?"

Joey recoiled, as if offended by the words, tossed the candy into his mouth, and chewed it with a deliberate slowness. "George, please. What kind of clown do you take me for? I wouldn't embarrass you at your place of employment like that."

"I own this place," he reminded the other man through gritted teeth.

"Really? I thought it was your dad's? Never mind. My point is, I'd never do that to you. You're Mr. Gilmore's friend. And his friends, are mine.

"But extortion? I'm insulted. I'm insulted for myself, and I'm particularly insulted for Mr. Gilmore. I'm here to talk about picking up what Andy is owed. What you were paid for. That's the furthest thing from extortion."

George didn't bother to argue the point. He hadn't prevailed on Andy. He certainly wasn't going to prevail with one of his minions—much less this one, who had probably already choked out the few brain cells he did have with hairspray anyway. "I don't have it with me."

"Of course you don't. I wouldn't expect that. Like I told you. I'm here just to verify that you have what Mr. Gilmore is owed."

George scowled. "Of course. Which he would have known if he picked up his goddamned phone when I was calling him."

Joey spread his hands. "What can I say? Mr. Gilmore's a busy man. He asked me to check for him. And here I am. And, anyway, I was happy to do it. I love this place. So many cows."

George was in no mood to be laughed at by this insolent man. "You tell that son of a bitch that if he wants to deal with me, he can call me himself. No more sending his goons here. People are going to start noticing."

The other man shook his head and smiled, flashing his absurdly white teeth. "I see you're still as paranoid as ever, eh? All this farmland, it's not doing you any good, my friend. Must be something in the water."

George ignored the other man's taunts. "I can get it to you tonight. We can meet at Tres Amigos."

Joey held up a hand. "Mr. Gilmore will tell you where and when to make the exchange. I'm just here to confirm that you have his property."

He grimaced at the phrasing but nodded. "Of course I have it. I told him I'd get it."

Joey nodded briskly. "So you did. So you did. You're a good man, George. A man who keeps his word. That's everything in our line of business, isn't it?"

Getting to his feet, George straightened his jacket. "We're not in the same line of business. We're nothing alike. Don't pretend we are." Joey smiled but said nothing. George gestured to the door. "You got what you wanted. Now go."

Caruso nodded slowly, pushed to his feet, and grabbed a few more chocolates. "All right, all right. I'm going."

"When will I hear from Andy?"

"When you hear from him. See you around, George."

Two days later, when George thought he couldn't possibly bear the suspense of finding out what in the hell his erstwhile partner in crime was up to, he did get a call.

"Gilmore," he said as he picked up, and his tone was frosty.

The other man's voice exuded warmth. "George. I'm glad I caught you. I hope you're well? Joey had mentioned you seemed a little out of sorts last time he saw you. He thought you might be coming down with something."

"I'm fine."

"Good, good. Well, I was very glad to hear you were able to get the rest of my order."

"When are you coming by to get it? Or are you going to send that goon of yours?"

"I'm out of the country at the moment, actually. In the EU, looking at ways to expand our global reach. The hustle never ends, does it?"

George wasn't interested, and he grunted in a way that, he hoped, conveyed just how little he cared.

"It'll be a few weeks before I can meet you."

"What a shame," George said dryly. "I was looking forward to seeing you again."

Andy laughed as if he wasn't at all offended by the other man's sarcasm. "I'm sending you a time and location now."

George pulled the phone from his ear to read the text message that popped up. He frowned. Returning to the conversation, he demanded, "What the hell is this? *The White Rose*?"

"Yes, it's a boat."

"I gathered. What the hell am I going to be meeting you on a boat for?"

"Because I have business in the Caribbean. *The White Rose* is a tour boat you can charter to take you along the Haitian coast. It will intersect with me at one of its ports of call."

George stared into the emptiness of his office, sure he'd misheard. "What? You can't be serious?"

The other man's tone took on a slightly patronizing tone as he answered, "Don't worry, I'm sure the accommodations will be more than adequate."

"Accommodations? What the hell are you talking about? You can't expect me to charter a fucking boat and meet you somewhere on the Haitian coast."

"That's exactly what I expect, actually."

"What the hell are you playing at, Andy? I can't just up and leave, much less on an excursion to the Caribbean. What the hell am I going to tell my dad? He's expecting me to finish—"

"Look, George, I'm really on a schedule here. You're a smart man, with an active if underused imagination. And you're an adult. If you want to go to the Caribbean, your father can't stop you."

"No," George said, shaking his head though the other man wouldn't see the motion. "No, I'm not doing it. You can tell me where to meet you."

"I will tell you, along the way. You get on *The White Rose* on the eighth, and I'll give you more details as time goes on."

"No. You can tell me here and now, and I'll meet you wherever the hell it is you're going to be. That's already a huge pain in my ass. But if you really think I'm going to be wasting my time on a cruise, waiting on a phone call from you—"

Andy's voice interrupted, and his tone was pleasant but icy, "You're not understanding me. This isn't a request. You will be on the ship, and I will send you a meeting place and time when you're there."

"What the fuck is your problem? You think you can just order me around like some kind of monkey?"

"Not that I need to explain myself to you, but at the moment, my schedule is a little in flux, and I don't know for sure where I will meet you, or when.

"And, frankly George—and no offense intended, of course—the way you've been acting doesn't inspire a lot of trust or confidence. I would never think of you so ungenerously as to assume I couldn't trust you when you give your word, but you understand that it wouldn't be entirely prudent on my part to give you weeks to prepare. Joey did mention that you used a very ugly word—extortion. If I didn't know you so well, I might be afraid that the extra time would give you the opportunity to try to set something up to frame me.

"But we're friends. And I respect that friendship. So, of course, I don't think anything of the kind. But this is business. I'll send you the details when the time arrives."

George started to protest that this was outrageous, that when he had agreed—under duress—to hand over the documents, it was with the understanding that the meeting would not be so absurd.

But Andy spoke over him, declaring that his next meeting was about to start. "Sorry, George, got to run. I'll text you more details later."

The details came as promised. They included a name and number. "She'll help you manage everything."

For a while, George sat fuming. There was no way in hell he was going to comply with such outrageous demands.

But the longer he thought on it, the more the alternatives stacked up in his mind. Was Andy being a vindictive prick? Absolutely.

Was it still in his best interests to comply with him? Probably.

The situation hadn't materially changed, except that Andy had thrown this ridiculous hurdle into the mix. So after some back and forth, he called the number.

A pleasant female voice answered, and as soon as he mentioned the dates Andy had given him, it took on an even more pleasant aspect. "Ah, you must be Mr. Sutherland."

"That's right," he answered cautiously.

"Excellent. Mr. Caruso said we would be hearing from you today. Everything has been arranged at his suggestion. We really only need the requisite forms signed—and payment, of course—and everything will be ready to go."

Though he tried, he could ascertain little from the woman. Their itinerary covered a large strip of the Haitian coast and some surrounding islands. *The White Rose* was a yacht for hire and could house as many as ten guests in addition to the captain and crew. Meals and entertainment were part of the package.

But as for meeting anyone along the way, she had no idea about any of that. The foreign gentlemen hadn't made a mention of it, although he had said Mr. Sutherland was keen to take in some of the ports along the way.

She was very excited for his trip and hoped he would enjoy it very much. Yes, it was off-season, but the weather had been especially mild for this time of year. And off-season, she always said, was the best time to avoid the crowds.

In short, George learned absolutely nothing. She faxed the forms he'd need and discussed payment. And he was left to decide what to do—and what excuse to give his father when the inevitable questions arose, if he chose to pursue this madness.

Chapter Thirty-One

Mr. Sutherland's signed assurances arrived, and they seemed straightforward enough. What's more, he sent along his contact information, and instructions to let him know whenever anything strange happened.

"If you can discreetly take pictures of any unusual visitors, that would be outstanding. Remember, though, that you cannot be apprehended. Don't do it if he'll catch you."

Heather and Angela were more convinced than ever that it was madness. But they'd agreed. "Which, I suppose, makes us even crazier than him," Angela decided.

They were understandably apprehensive when Monday morning rolled around. But, aside from an ill-tempered boss, nothing seemed out of the ordinary. Kathryn was a little more skittish, but Angela attributed that to their conversation the week before. Casper hid in his office more, but the cause was plain enough: George's angry behavior.

Conrad was sullen, Matt tried, and mostly failed, to avoid his boss's claps on the back, and Heather and Angela worked hard to appear nonchalant. For all their expectations of doom, Monday came and went without incident.

Tuesday proved to be a little more interesting. A man with a bad tan, nice shoes, and a gaudy suit showed up, insisting in a loud, East Coast accent that George was expecting him.

Apparently, he hadn't been lying, because George did see him, and they remained in conversation with the door closed for a few minutes. Heather managed to snap a profile picture as he passed on the way out, and Angela got a good front view.

These, they texted to the number George Sr. had provided. Angela also asked, *Anyone of interest?*

A few minutes later, she received: *One of Gilmore's associates. Did he leave with anything that you could see? An envelope, or a drive?*

Not that I could tell. If it was a data card or a thumb drive, he might have slipped it in a pocket though.

Thanks, Angela. Keep your eyes open for anything else out of the ordinary.

Wednesday proved mostly uneventful. Conrad noted that "the housekeeping thieves must have learned their lesson" since nothing new had gone missing.

Casper had to come out of his office when one of the printers went down with a paper jam that Conrad couldn't fix. After aggressively tapping the side of it, he declared, "This is bad. We're going to have to call the manufacturer's support line. Find the contract for that, will you Conrad?" Then he disappeared into his own office and left Conrad to deal with the manufacturer tech.

Thursday was only remarkable in that their internet connection seemed incredibly slow, and George Jr. seemed to be in a worse humor than usual by time the day wrapped up. The two, Angela speculated, were probably linked, for it certainly put *her* in a foul mood.

And the fact that Casper didn't bother to respond to her questions about what was happening only further annoyed her. It wasn't long before Richard was messaging her.

Hey, is that IT guy in?

As far as I know...

Internet's slow. We're getting a lot of timeouts.

Same here.

Can you check with him?

Will do.

She'd stood but hadn't yet left her office when Conrad appeared in the doorway.

"Do you know why I can't get my email?" he asked.

"Because...we're having internet problems?"

He scowled. "Still? I sent Casper a message half an hour ago."

"I'm going to talk to him now."

"Why do we even have an IT guy if he doesn't fix anything?"

"I'll go talk to him, Conrad," she said as patiently as she could manage. *And there I thought I was so clever hiring Casper.* This must be some kind of penance, she decided: stuck at the job she'd meant to quit, left to deal with all the miserable employees she'd hired out of spite. *Dammit.*

Casper didn't answer the door when she knocked. After the third knock went unanswered, she rapped with a ferocity that made her knuckles ache. This, finally, did the trick. A moment later, the young man poked his head out, a large set of earphones around his neck. "Hey, Angie, what's up?"

"Didn't you hear me knocking?" she snapped. "I almost broke my knuckles."

"Sorry." He tapped the headphones. "I was listening to music."

She shook her head. "You know the internet is giving everyone problems, right?"

"The internet?"

"Yes. We've all been messaging you about it."

"Oh." His glance darted to his computer and then back to her. "Well, uh, I was working on something. You know how it is, you get in the zone, and you lose track of things."

"Like basic communication?"

He ignored the question. "So, umm, what kind of trouble? I mean, it's working fine for me."

"Slowness, mostly. Some of the lab applications are timing out. I've had a few timeouts too."

"Oh." He scratched his head, shrugged, and said, "Well, uh, you know, I was downloading something. It might have throttled the bandwidth a little."

She frowned at him. "You realize that's for work functions, right?"

"Of course. Hell yeah. You didn't think?" He laughed awkwardly. "That I was, like, what? Downloading movies or something? Hell no. It's an update. For the, uh, mainframe servers. The code build is out of whack, you know, and we have to get on the latest update. This build includes lots of bug fixes and security loopholes. Critical stuff."

Angela scowled at him. He was full of shit, and she knew it. But she limited her response to, "Great. Well, I hope it doesn't have much left."

"Oh, no. I'm sure it'll be done soon."

"Good."

A few minutes after Angela returned to her desk—and found that the internet had quite miraculously come back at full capacity—Conrad appeared again. "You're a magician, Angela. I owe you one."

Friday started a little more interestingly, in that George was late. Once nine o'clock rolled around and he still hadn't showed up, a few people began to speculate—hopefully—that he was going to be gone for the day.

But, disappointing them all, he showed up shortly after nine. He went first to his office and closed the door after him. Angela had been grabbing another cup of coffee and witnessed his entrance—and the anxious glance Conrad and Matt exchanged.

They'd taken from it what she had—their boss was in another mood. *Why didn't I just tell George Sr. to go to hell? I would have only had one more week left of this crap.*

The morning progressed slowly. She'd been working on posting the positions George had indicated and reviewing applications as they came in... But it had been a long and wearying week, and she struggled to give the work her all.

Then a meeting invite came into her inbox, marked *urgent*. Her heart leaped into her throat when she saw the sender: George Sutherland, Jr.

The subject did nothing to relieve her fears. *Department heads meeting, ten o'clock. Mandatory.*

Chapter Thirty-Two

A quick text to George Sr. revealed he had no idea what was planned either. "Keep me posted."

Matt and Conrad were talking in whispers when she left her office at five to ten. They glanced up, and the former said, "Angela, you know what this meeting's about?"

"Not a clue."

"I'm not a department head. Do you think he meant to include me?"

"If you're on the invite," Conrad declared, "you better go. Technically, I'm head admin. I have to go too."

"And I'm head of HR, the department."

"But if you don't know...I guess it can't be bad news, right?" Matt persisted.

"What?"

"I mean, it won't be layoffs or anything. You'd know if those were coming."

Angela wished with all her heart she could tell him something to put his mind at ease. But this was George Sutherland Jr. She had no idea what was going through his mind at any given moment, even in the best of times.

Was he capable of firing people without a hint? Of course. That's what he'd done when he came into Fenwood Bio. Was he stupid enough to bypass HR to get it done?

Maybe. Especially if the HR department-of-one was on the chopping block too. "To be honest, Matt, I have no clue what's going on, or why."

The young man nodded grimly. "I hope it's not layoffs. I really need this job."

Conrad nodded, too, even more grimly. "I'll go nuts if I have to spend the rest of my summer listening to my grandkids."

Angela found a seat next to Heather. They'd already exchanged questioning texts, and having ascertained that neither knew anything about the meeting, all that remained was apprehensive glances.

They were joined in this by the rest of the room. No one spoke except in hushed whispers. A general air of apprehension hung over the group and seemed to intensify as the minutes rolled by.

When ten o'clock came and went, and George made no showing, the quiet made way to a general shuffling and renewed exchange of glances. Still, no one spoke.

Ten-oh-two came and went without a sign of George. Another two minutes passed. Angela could feel her palms slicking, and she could see great beads of perspiration dotting Matt's forehead. Conrad dabbed his forehead now and then with a handkerchief. Casper pulled at the collar of his shirt, fanning himself with the fabric.

"Maybe someone should go check on Mr. Sutherland," Kathryn offered, glancing pointedly at Matt.

Kilbourne scoffed. "Don't look at me."

She shrugged. "I just thought, since you're his PA and all..."

"He told me to be here. And that's where I'm staying until he tells me otherwise."

"You could go check on him," Conrad offered.

Kathryn scowled at the two men, and for a moment, silence returned. Richard Kaplan started to drum his fingers along the tabletop. Casper bit into his nails with a terrible ferocity, disturbing the relative quiet with loud, sharp cracks.

Still George didn't appear. Angela had half made up her mind to go looking for their errant boss when the door opened. Everyone jumped.

George's expression did nothing to relieve the nervous sweating of his assembled department leads. His lips were pressed together in the kind of upside-down smile that seemed designed to inspire rather than quell alarm. He barely looked at anyone.

Instead, he marched to the lectern at the far end of the room and addressed them with a peculiar preamble. "Thank you all for coming on short notice. You're probably wondering why I asked you here. Well, here's why—to thank you."

If he noticed the blank stares this pronouncement caused, he made no sign of it. "As you know, this has been a challenging year for Sutherland Bio. Like myself, some of you are new to the company. But we've been in this together, from day one. All of us, whether we were Sutherland for a decade, or hired after the merger."

The words seemed so odd, so disconnected from his stony manner and mechanical delivery that Angela felt at a complete loss as to what was going on. Layoffs? Another reorganization? That's what his manner suggested. But his words seemed to indicate something else. And that's what really confused her.

"You know, when my dad first opened Sutherland Research, he started the company with him and three other people. They didn't know if they were going to be able to keep the lights on until the end of the month. He didn't know if they'd be able to put food on the table.

"But he made them a promise. If we make it through this, we are family.

"I hadn't been born yet, but that's a story I've heard more times than I can count."

He smiled now, and though it didn't come across as entirely genuine, at least he was putting a little more effort into his delivery now than he had been before. "Family. That's what Sutherland is.

"One team, one family—all of us together.

"Now I know the past few months have been challenging. We've seen some of our family go their own way. That's never easy. We've seen a lot of changes. That can be hard too.

"But through it all, we have always been there for one another. We are a team. We are—I know, as my dad would say, I'm a broken record on this—a family. We've stood together, and we've made better progress in our short time together than I ever would have imagined. When I had to go away, when my dad was in the hospital, you kept this place running. When I came back, you were all ready to hit the ground running again.

"Because you're my family. I'm yours. We are there for one another."

He flashed another smile, this time complete with teeth. "And that's why I scheduled this meeting. Because for all we've been through, you have reminded me again and again that we are in this together.

"And I appreciate that. Sutherland appreciates that. And to demonstrate just how much it means to us, we've chartered an all-expenses paid Caribbean cruise for all of you as a thank-you."

Angela blinked in unconcealed astonishment. The power of speech seemed beyond her as she tried to process what had just happened.

Her companions were not so afflicted though.

"A cruise?" Conrad repeated skeptically. "Do we have alternatives? Can we take the cash value instead?"

George shot this down. "The cruise is already booked. No refunds or exchanges. We wanted it to be a surprise, so everything's all set."

"Jesus," Casper said. "That's terrific."

"Booked? For when?" Heather asked.

"Next month. We'll be leaving Port-au-Prince on a privately chartered vessel on the eighth. You'll all be getting emails soon with ticket information and whatnot."

"But that's only about three weeks from now. Not even," Richard Kaplan objected.

"Yes. But all arrangements have been made. You won't have to do anything but show up."

"But I don't even know if my passport is still valid. That's not enough time to get a new one if I need too."

George scowled at the dissenter. Then he addressed the group more generally. "I know it's short notice, but I wanted it to be a surprise. And you know how these things go; the longer the delay, the more likely someone will get wind of it."

"Loose lips sink ships." Casper nodded.

Conrad shifted in his seat. "Yes, well, let's hope there's no sinking of ships. Not when we're planning to be on one."

"Anyway, as you know, my time here isn't indefinite. And I wanted to make sure this was a memory I could share with my family." He smiled again and spread his hands to gesture at all of them. Something about the expression made Angela's skin crawl. "All of you."

Chapter Thirty-Three

George shut the door and blew out a sigh of relief. It had taken all of his considerable ingenuity, but he'd hit upon it at last: a plausible cover story.

The lab rats would resent it, he knew, since they weren't included. But Kaplan, as head of the lab, was on the list. That would do. As for the rest of them? Well, he'd never seen them that damned grateful.

If I'd known my ass was going to be kissed that much, I might have showered this morning. He laughed at his own sardonicism. The truth was, George Jr. was happy—or as happy as he could be in the circumstances.

He wouldn't have minded letting his fist get intimately acquainted with Andy Gilmore's teeth—or his boot with Joey Caruso's ass. But short of such pleasures, at least he'd hit on a good cover story. His department heads were too excited to be suspicious. And as for George Sr.?

Well, this was the kind of stupid thing his father would have thought up, back in the day, and for all the absurd reasons the younger Sutherland had espoused. Only, George Sr. would have meant it.

But, on the off chance that the older man had finally picked up a little more business sense, and started to appreciate the cost of such indulgences, he had good reasons lined up. This was an investment in employee morale after a tumultuous year. Without a Sutherland on the premises, this would ensure the loyalty of the leadership left behind.

Whichever way George Sr. approached it, he was ready.

Yes, George was feeling pretty good about himself. There might be a few hiccups. That fool Kaplan and his passport might leave their party one short. And Conrad's reluctance to go at all, and whining when he found out spouses were not invited, didn't bode well.

But Conrad wanted his job. A well-placed comment about the importance of this trip to the Sutherland family would probably convey the point. And if it didn't, he could always remind the other man of the alternative: a summer spent babysitting.

No, Conrad would go. Heather and Angela had already admitted that they had no other plans. He'd wrung that out of Matt too. Casper and Kathryn had gladly volunteered it.

Even without Kaplan, their group would be large enough not to attract his father's suspicion. George didn't know where Gilmore meant to meet, but *The White Rose*'s itinerary included plenty of port stops, and plenty of time for passengers to disembark and enjoy the delights.

Whenever the message came, he could slip away long enough to make the exchange and return before anyone was the wiser.

Indeed, the worst part of it all as far as he could tell was the expense. Not that it mattered much to him. It was a mere drop in a very large bucket. Still, on principle, it rankled. He didn't particularly care for any of his employees. He liked them well enough, he supposed, but not enough to merit such attention.

And what would happen when other branches caught wind of it and started expecting similar treatment?

Those were problems he'd put off dealing with for some other time. In the meantime, George would simply celebrate his victory.

His self-congratulation lasted all of four days. It lasted through Friday, over the weekend, and until about halfway through the following Monday. His father's approval bolstered it.

"There you go, George. You're thinking like me. One team, one family."

It survived through Conrad's repeated and pointed comments about not letting spouses accompany the team. "At least, *some* of us aren't able to bring our significant others. I guess Heather and Angela were exempt from that decision?"

If George had needed the other man less, he might have fired him on the spot. His ingratitude was hard to take. But he smiled as benignly as he could and reminded Conrad that Heather and Angela were going on their own, and their relationship status was immaterial.

It hadn't prevented Conrad from muttering under his breath, but George pretended not to hear.

His good humor made it through Richard Kaplan's nervous confession that his passport had expired two years ago. How anyone could let their passport expire, George didn't know, and he didn't bother to hide the fact from his subordinate. Kaplan had blinked at the sharpness in his tone.

"We just...haven't had a chance to go anywhere. Not since Kyle and Kayla were born."

George remarked rather sourly that he completely understood. "Family takes precedence. I get it. Well, your *Sutherland* family will understand, I'm sure."

Kaplan apologized again, assuring him that he would do everything he could to procure the document in time. George waved him away with a dismissive flick of the hand.

And still, through all of these trials, his good humor prevailed.

But then, shortly after he returned from lunch, the call from Andy Gilmore came. George groaned at the sight of the number and didn't bother to keep the annoyance from his tone. "What?"

"Well, good afternoon to you too."

"I'm busy, Andy. What do you want now?"

"Straight to the chase, eh? All right. Well, the truth is, I'm a little puzzled by your arrangements. Caruso says the *Rose* staff are preparing for a whole guest roster. What are you up to, George?"

George scowled into the empty air. "What the hell do you think I'm up to, Andy? Covering my ass, in case my dad wonders why in the hell I'm up and leaving without a reason. They're my reason."

Andy groaned. "I know I encouraged you to use your imagination. But I meant for you to use your brain too."

"Fuck you."

The other man seemed unperturbed by his outburst. "I thought you wanted to be discreet? How does inviting half your office help with discretion?"

"We'll be stopping at ports along the way. That's what your goon scheduled, right?"

"You shouldn't talk about Joey like that. He's a good man."

George snorted. "So that's how the wind blows? How cute. Where should I send the wedding presents?"

"Oh, George." Andy's tone dripped condescension. "Humor never was your forte, was it? But what happens if some of your people get suspicious about you disappearing?"

"They'll be too busy taking care of whatever they want to do. Trust me, Andy. I can get away from my employees if I need to."

The other man sighed. "This is complicating things unnecessarily."

"Complicating things unnecessarily was being a paranoid asshole, and insisting I meet you halfway across the friggin' world," George snapped. "Complicating things unnecessarily is giving me an absurd deadline to be in Haiti. That's what's been complicating this.

"What I'm doing? That's covering my ass, so my dad doesn't wonder what the hell I'm up to. And you know what, Andy? I'm getting sick and tired of your shit. I've complied with all the bullshit you've foisted on me. And now you want to question the hows? Maybe it's time for me to reevaluate whether I should be complying at all."

A long, pregnant pause ensued. Then Andy sighed.

"All right, all right. Do it your way. Just, for the love of God, don't get yourself caught. We don't need any more problems."

Chapter Thirty-Four

Angela didn't much believe in miracles, but this trip was about the closest she'd ever come to seeing one in real life. That George Sutherland—the same George Sutherland who had laid off so many of her coworkers—was paying for his team to take a Caribbean cruise astonished her to a degree she couldn't quite articulate.

George Sr. had either had no insight, or chosen to share nothing, because her queries came up empty. He assured her he was as much at a loss as to his son's motives as she. And then his ablation surgery happened, and while it had gone off without a hitch, she felt it better to leave him in peace. Their undercover work could wait until the man was fully alive again.

As for her and Heather, well, things only seemed to get better as time passed. The other woman spent most nights at her place now, and on the nights she went home, Angela went with her. Ragnar had taken to sleeping in their room and even, unfortunately, jumping onto their bed in the middle of the night.

The big dog seemed to fancy himself a lot lighter than he was, and a lot sneakier, because he would creep up the bed until he was lying with his back to one or the other of them, as if he hadn't just woken them both.

Still, Angela didn't mind terribly. He was a sweet dog, and she found herself loving him rather quickly.

And, though she refused to dwell on the point, he wasn't the only one. Angela's heart had opened to Heather with a speed that surprised her. Maybe it was loneliness. Maybe it was just being ready for the right person.

She didn't know. But somewhere along the way, what had started as exciting and sexy had taken on a depth she hadn't anticipated. Not that it lost the sexiness or excitement. That only increased as she got to know her lover's body, and Heather got to know hers.

But she found that knowing Heather's mind was a pleasure not unconnected, but distinct from the more physical side of things. Angela was in real danger of being very much in love very soon.

She wasn't sure how she felt about that. She'd been in love before, with Cassie. It had ended badly—so badly, she thought she'd never love again, or want to.

And yet, here she was.

Lauren and Rae were over the moon. Lauren was already planning her wedding, and not even Rae's level-headedness could quite keep her in check.

Angela's parents took to Heather with almost as much eagerness as her friends. Her dad, Dave, decided Heather was, "Very smart. You two seem good together."

Her mother Carla was a little blunter. "Thank God. I was afraid you were going to die an old maid."

"Thanks, Mom. You know we're just dating, right? We're not engaged?"

Her mother hadn't let a trifling detail like that get in the way of her plans though. "Of course you're not. Not yet. But Lauren and I have been talking about it..."

She didn't pay much attention after that. She'd been too busy groaning. Still, the first meeting had gone better than she dared to hope, and Angela's parents volunteered without being asked to board Ragnar while they were on their cruise.

"We'll take good care of him."

So it was settled, simply and with very little hassle. Angela could hardly believe it. Nothing was ever this straightforward. And George Sutherland Jr. was never generous. As the date of the cruise neared, a kind of anxiety settled in the pit of her stomach. She couldn't fully articulate why.

Maybe it was Conrad's constant complaining that his wife wasn't able to come, and the hostile turn his behavior had taken toward her and Heather. As if, somehow, they had something to do with it.

She'd almost convinced herself that was all it was when George, in a half rage, declared that Conrad could take his wife, "If it shuts your goddamned mouth." Richard's passport wasn't going to arrive in time, and George had an extra seat. Conrad's ill humor instantly vanished. He practically walked on air the rest of the week.

And yet, the uneasiness remained. Heather had her own theory.

"You don't like that he's being generous when we're spying on him."

"You think that's it?"

Heather pulled her close. They were lying in bed holding each other and talking. "I do. I've been feeling it too. But we didn't ask to do it. His father approached us. Whatever's going on, it's above our paygrade."

Angela sighed and leaned into the other woman's arm. "I know. Just...something feels so strange about the whole thing."

Heather considered, then nodded. "Yes. But there's nothing we can do but go and keep an eye on George when we can. More importantly, let's actually enjoy ourselves."

"I suppose you're right."

Heather kissed the top of her head. "It happens now and then. Come on, my love. Let's try to put aside any of that, and just really focus on having fun. When's the last time you've been to the Caribbean?"

"Never."

"Same here. So let's enjoy ourselves."

"Okay," Angela sighed.

Heather laughed. "You're going to have to do better than that."

"I'll try. It's just...something's bugging me about it."

Heather ran a hand up her thigh. "Really?" Her tone was lower and huskier than a moment ago. "Maybe we should see what we can do to take your mind off work."

It did the trick. Angela smiled, and for the rest of the evening her thoughts and attention were directed in an entirely different, and far more pleasant, direction.

And the nearer they got to the day of departure, the more preoccupied she was with other things to worry about than the why's. She packed and repacked several times. Her suitcase and carryon were crammed with what she deemed the bare essentials, and she still felt certain she was missing something. Heather, by contrast, packed one item of formal wear, a few shirts and pairs of shorts, some toiletries, and swim wear: one bag, lightly packed, with room to spare.

"How are you able to pack so little?"

Heather had no real answer, except to laugh and wonder, "How are you *not*?"

Angela was convinced her girlfriend was going to find she'd left behind something she needed.

Heather scoffed at the idea. "We're going on a luxury cruise, not a survival trek."

"Just remember that when you're asking to borrow something because I came prepared and you didn't."

"You mean, because you overthought it, and I didn't?"

"I'd rather be overprepared than under."

"Well, my dear," Heather said, kissing her playfully, "you should be happy—because you are way overprepared."

When it came time to leave Ragnar, they hugged him and promised they'd be back soon. The great canine watched them head back to their vehicle without him with doleful eyes, as if he had some inkling of what was at hand.

"Poor baby," Heather said. "Mommy'll be back before you know it."

"Don't worry about him," Carla called. "We'll keep him so preoccupied he won't even notice you're gone."

And then they were off to the airport. The flight was scheduled to take nearly sixteen hours, with two layovers. George Jr. had booked everyone's ticket together, with the exception of his own. He was flying first class. Still, Angela couldn't complain about a free trip, even if it meant flying with her coworkers.

At least, that's what she thought. Then she took her seat. Heather and she had snagged a pair of seats near the window, and Angela gladly ceded the window to her girlfriend. Takeoffs and landings put her heart in her mouth, and she wanted to enjoy this trip.

But the aisle was three seats wide, and no sooner had they sat when Casper crowded in beside them.

"Angela." He smiled. "This sure beats any Monday I've ever had, eh? Well, these are close quarters. Good thing we all know one another. You're practically sitting in my lap." He laughed, and she cringed.

Kathryn, Conrad, and Mrs. Walters found their seats in front of them a few moments later. This was Angela's first glimpse of Mrs. Walters. She and Conrad had boarded late—so late, that the rest of the group began to speculate they might not be planning to show at all.

Angela saw a fresh-faced older woman who was all smiles. And, even more surprisingly, her husband seemed happy too. He wasn't smiling, exactly. But he was frowning *less* than usual.

"Angela," he greeted, "Heather. This is Bess, my wife." The older woman was fiddling with her carryon, but glanced up. "Bessie my love, these are my coworkers, Angela McCormack and Heather Bradshaw."

The women exchanged handshakes and greetings, and Casper piped up, "Well, the infamous Missus. It's good to put a name with a face." Again, he laughed. And again, he was alone in doing so. "I'm Casper, by the way. Casper Caspersen."

Conrad grunted. "He works with us too."

"Ah. Well, a pleasure to meet you too, Mr. Caspersen."

"Likewise. I feel like I already know you, you know. Conrad talks about you all the time. You and the grand-kids."

Here, Bess smiled, and her eyes lit up. "Oh, little Elsa and Justin are the lights of our lives. Aren't they, my dear?"

Conrad grimaced but answered, "Yes they are."

"Our home was so quiet before they were born."

"Yes, it was," her husband sighed, a bit wistfully it seemed to Angela.

Mrs. Walters took his melancholy remembrance quite another way though. Smiling at him fondly, she squeezed his arm. "We were both bored to distraction. Nothing but time on our hands."

"That sounds...kind of nice, actually," Casper said. "I mean, as long as you've got a good internet connection..."

Bess Walters brushed this thought aside with a brisk sweep of her hand and settled into her seat. "I don't use the internet. I unplugged five years ago, and it was the best decision of my life."

Casper blanched. "Really? Like, no internet at all?"

She turned in her chair to face him. "Not a bit of it."

"Not even email?"

"Nope."

"Or YouTube?"

She shook her head. "Nothing. I don't even text."

Conrad glanced over at his wife. "I've tried to convince her to get a smartphone. So I know she's okay."

She shook her head with more energy this time. "I don't want anything to do with it. Everyone is so tied to their phones these days. I was, too, before I retired. But I want to be free in my old age. No technological fetters."

Casper stared at her as if she had two heads. Kathryn pulled out a sleep mask and glanced askew at her companions. Angela had the impression she was calculating how soon she could put the mask on and shut everyone out without seeming rude.

Heather, meanwhile, was nodding. "I wish I could do that."

Angela laughed. "What, and not be able to take pictures of Ragnar every two steps?"

Her girlfriend grinned at her. "That's a fair point. Without my phone, how could I capture his adorableness?"

"Ragnar?" Bess asked.

"Her dog," Angela answered. "And be careful—if you don't avoid the topic like the plague, she'll never let you be."

But Heather had already whipped out her phone, and offered, "I've got pictures."

"Oh, I love dogs. We had a dog, years ago. You remember, my love?"

Conrad nodded. "Good old Bailey."

They smiled in unison. "Before our daughter was born, we adopted him. Never ended up having time for another dog after he passed away. But he was such a good boy."

Conrad wrapped around her. "Yes, he was."

"I used to say he was my first baby." The older woman's eyes glistened. If she didn't know better, Angela might have said that Conrad's eyes were glistening too. But he blinked back any moisture that might have gathered there with an energy so fierce she didn't dare look longer.

"I'm sorry," Heather said. "Losing a pup is so hard."

"It is. But come, let me see your baby."

For a few moments, the two women passed the phone back and forth, Heather pulling up choice photos of the canine, and Bess *oohing* and *aahing* over him.

After the fifth or sixth exchange, the older woman paused and glanced at first Heather and then Angela. She said, "Oh."

Angela glanced at the phone. She couldn't see the full picture, but she could make out enough. It was one of the shots they'd taken at her parents' farm the other weekend, with her, Heather, and Ragnar together. She looked up as a sudden deer-in-the-headlights look crossed the other woman's face.

But, in the next instant, Bess smiled. "You two must be the..." She lowered her voice to a confidential tone. "Lesbian couple."

"Uh..." Angela and Heather exchanged glances. "I guess so."

Bess's smile broadened, and she nodded. "Conrad told me about you. I'm glad. It's about time that you folks can be...what's it called? Out of the cupboard?"

Heather shifted in her seat, and Angela smiled. "Closet."

"That's right. My niece's daughter is a lesbian, you know. She's married to a woman. And one of the deacons at our church—Dan? He's married to a man. A very nice man. What's his name, dear?" For this, she appealed to her husband.

"Mike."

"That's right. I always forget his name. He doesn't come to church very often. But when he does, he's very polite. And he dresses so smartly, like people used to when they went to church. In his Sunday best. Not like you see nowadays."

Angela murmured that he sounded like a very nice man indeed.

Bess nodded. "He is. And I'm glad he's *out*. It's about time, I think, that people can be who God made them."

They agreed that it was, indeed. Reaching an arm over the seat back, Bess squeezed Angela's hand in her own. "That's right. Good for you, my dear. Live your truth."

★

It was a long flight. Not just because—once he'd recovered from the shock of someone choosing to live without internet—Casper talked nonstop, but because it was quite literally a long flight. Sixteen hours of either hustling from one terminal to the next, or crammed in beside her fellow travelers.

They transferred planes at both stops, but Angela's seating arrangement didn't change. It seemed that the group, having settled into a pattern, was in no hurry to alter it. She was stuck between Bess Walters' well-meaning—if a bit indelicate—conversation, and Casper's much less well-meaning—and much creepier—queries.

And he took every opportunity to be creepy. When Angela began to nod off, he'd yawned. "I think I might have to take a nap soon too. Hey, bet you didn't see that coming."

"See what coming?"

"The three of us…" He gestured at himself, her, and Heather, who had already slipped into a light slumber. "Sleeping together."

Her cringes didn't deter him, either, any more than the fact that he was the only one who laughed at his jokes. He didn't seem to notice. He still droned on about tanned bodies and skimpy swimsuits and sunny beaches at every opportunity.

"You know how there's the theological debate about whether God is male or female, right? I don't know, bro. You go to the beach and see all those ladies in bikinis? It seems pretty clear to me. God's a dude."

"Or a lesbian," Heather offered.

Casper considered, then nodded. "I can't argue with your reasoning. That's 100 percent legit. But either way, I'm thankful."

A very long flight indeed. Still, when they arrived in Port-Au-Prince, the sun was shining. It was morning, but the day was already excessively hot. George seemed impatient and out of sorts as he explained that he had hired cars, and they should be waiting to take them to the yacht.

A middle-aged man met them after they passed customs, introducing himself as Charles Abbé. George took lead now.

"Yes, nice to meet you too. I assume you're our driver?"

Charles confirmed that he was, and that he'd come on behalf of Haitian Rose Tours to take them to the yacht. Furthermore, he'd brought an assistant, a deferential and much younger man named Andre. Andre busied himself with the bags, and before long, they were packed into the back of a comfortable vehicle.

"You picked a good time to land," Charles informed them. "Two days ago, the rain was very bad."

"That's what I was saying," Conrad put in. "This is the rainy season. Would have made more sense to come later in the year, once the rains ended."

"July is a good month, for the season. Less rain."

"Is the humidity always this bad?" Casper wondered. He'd already taken a few puffs on his asthma inhaler.

"Yes," the other man declared matter-of-factly. "When it rains more, it is worse."

"But it'll be better when we're at sea," Matt assured him.

"This is very true. As long as you bring plenty of sunscreen, this is a very pleasant time to explore the coast. The storms are not bad, and if bad weather is on the horizon, you will not be so far from land that you cannot find a safe harbor."

Once they were underway, Charles took the opportunity to point out the landmarks as they passed them. "Over there you can see the historic area. During the earthquakes, we lost many buildings. The old Presidential Palace and our legislative and judicial buildings were all destroyed."

Casper laughed. "Sounds like God doesn't like politicians much either."

"Many people died," Charles replied. He didn't address the comment directly, but his meaning wasn't lost on Casper, whose chuckling faded into awkward silence. "Over two hundred thousand. Our seaport was also damaged, and the airport as well."

Casper at least had the good sense to look contrite. George sighed and checked his watch. Charles changed the subject, moving on to reconstruction efforts, surviving buildings, and the residential districts.

It was when he delved into the history of the area that he really caught everyone's attention though. Even Bess Walters was all ears when he mentioned buccaneers.

"Oh, yes. Buccaneers prowled the coasts of Tortuga and Hispaniola, preying on Spanish shipping and coastal towns. Some of them were pirates, and some worked for other governments. The French and English and Dutch would sanction attacks."

"With a letter of marque," Casper nodded. "I played a video game about that."

"But eventually, they got greedy, and not even their own governments could trust them. Many buccaneers were hung before the trade ended."

"Like Calico Jack," Kathryn piped up. "And Mary Read and Anne Bonny."

"Yes, the lady pirates." Charles nodded.

Bess shivered. "It's very exciting, isn't it? Kind of like that movie. What was it called? With the attractive pirate who wore a lot of makeup?"

"*Pirates of the Caribbean*," her husband sighed.

"That's right."

Charles nodded. "Yes. On your tour, you will see some of the ports and towns that buccaneers used to frequent."

Bess thrilled a little more and grinned broadly. "I can't wait."

★

The White Rose was a large, elegant, modern-looking yacht. The truth was, Angela didn't know much about boats. But, to her untrained eye, this was a luxury vessel, with spacious guest cabins and a large sumptuous dining hall. It even had a pool on the deck.

Captain Tennison—a smiling American—welcomed them onboard and introduced several members of the crew and staff. Charles and Andre carried the bags onto the gangplank, and Tennison's crew took it from there. "Martha here will show you to your room, ladies," he told Heather and Angela, introducing them to another American.

The young woman smiled and showed them to their cabin, conversing just enough to make them feel welcome, but not overwhelmed.

They could hear Casper, who was a little ways ahead, bombarding his guide—Frank? Fred? Angela couldn't remember; but he too was definitely an American—with questions. "What time is breakfast?" and "Can we swim any time?" and "Do we have any live music? I've read about that. I know this isn't a cruise, but it's kind of like that, right?"

Martha's questions were less excited, and more practical. "How long have you been in Haiti?" and "Is this your first time here?" and "Do you need any sunscreen or protective clothing? We do stock extra if you run out. Just let one of us know."

By time they reached their room, the suitcases had already been brought and stacked neatly. Heather shook her head at the sight of Angela's great, bulging case, and her small, neat one.

"I'll leave you two to it, then. If you need anything, there's a comm right here," Martha told them, pointing out a comm on the wall.

"Well," Angela said when she'd closed the door, "this is something else."

Heather wrapped an arm around her and pulled her down onto the bed.

Giggling as she lost her balance and landing in a heap, Angela demanded, "What the hell are you doing?"

"Kissing you."

"You could give me some warning next time," Angela protested. But not too heartily.

"Hmm. I could. Then again, where's the fun in that?"

Chapter Thirty-Five

The White Rose remained at port until evening. This was for the benefit of her passengers, to give them time to explore the city at their leisure. Conrad and Bess were the only ones who availed themselves of the opportunity, though, coming back with arms full of touristy trinkets. They were laughing and giggling, too, which was Angela's first clue that they'd been drinking. Bess seemed like the laughing and giggling type, but she knew well enough that it would take something strong—something like chemical intervention—to get Conrad to loosen up that much.

The heavy whiff of vodka that assailed her nostrils as the pair passed confirmed her theory.

For their part, Angela and Heather had stayed in their cabin for several hours. Ostensibly, this was because they were exhausted after the long flight and needed a nap. There was some truth to that. They did spend *some* of the time sleeping.

When they emerged, they were giggling as much as Conrad and Bess. Casper spotted them first when they reached the deck. He was in his swim trunks and drinking a large, beachy-looking drink with layers of orange and red in a tall, clear glass. He grinned at the sight of them. "Good nap, eh?"

Heather ignored the question and, instead, gestured toward his drink. "Where can I get one of those?"

Casper pointed to a bar at the opposite end of the pool and a man behind it. "You see him? His name's Jack. And Jack can fix you up just about anything you want to drink." He tapped his glass. "But you definitely want to start with a White Rose Sunrise. That's a Jack Special. And it's excellent. This..." He tapped his glass again. "Is my third. Or maybe fourth."

"Well, we'll, uh, definitely keep it in mind," Angela declared, squeezing past her coworker.

"You won't regret it," he called after them.

Heather smiled. "No need to guess what *he's* been doing. What do you want, babe?"

"I don't know. Hell, I'll try one of the White Rose Sunrises."

The other woman laughed. "After such a recommendation, I suppose I'll have to too."

They put their order in, and Jack—a man with a crooked jaw but an ever-ready smile—obliged. "Tell me if it's too sweet."

It wasn't. "Damn. This is really good," Angela declared.

Jack flashed a set of pearly-white teeth. "What can I say? It's a Jack Special."

"What's in it?"

"That would be telling." He grinned again. "But, for a pair of pretty ladies, I can give you something anyway. Pineapple juice is the secret weapon. There's sweet, there's bitter, and there's pineapple juice. That's the key."

"Ah. I wasn't sure if it was orange or pineapple." Heather nodded.

"Pineapple all the way. Al—he's the morning guy—makes something similar. But he uses orange juice." He shook his head. "Nothing compared to mine. You want one of these tomorrow? You tell him to make you a Jack Special. Okay?"

The two women assured him that they would, though Angela was fairly certain she wouldn't be drinking in the morning anyway. *Then again, we're on vacation. What happens in Haiti, stays in Haiti.*

They headed over to the beach chairs. There were two rows, one on either side of the pool. Casper had returned to his chair and was stretched out sipping his cocktail. They headed to an unoccupied spot on the other side, near Kathryn.

The other woman glanced up at their approach. "Oh, no. You're drinking those things too?"

Angela glanced down at her glass. "The, uh, Jack Special?"

Kathryn rolled her eyes. "Yes. The 'Jack Special.'" Lowering her voice to a whisper, she added, "Casper hasn't left me the hell alone about it. I told him I don't want one."

"Don't blame the drink," Heather advised. "That's his personality at fault. The drink is actually pretty good."

"Excellent," Angela corrected.

Kathryn rolled her eyes. "Here we go again."

Angela laughed, realizing they had both inadvertently done exactly what she'd asked them not to. "Sorry. Not another word about it."

"How's the water?" Heather asked. The pool wasn't huge. It was on a ship, after all. But Angela expected it would be warm.

"No idea. I'm just sunning myself. I tried to take a nap, but my bed is hard as a rock. I have no idea how I'm going to get to sleep tonight."

Casper, meanwhile, having realized he was the only one on his side, decided to fix that. He ambled over and plunked in a chair near Angela. "I don't know about you three, but *my* vacation is starting out exactly how I imagined it—just me and a bunch of hot women."

"Jesus, Casper, if you don't knock it off, I'm reporting you to HR," Kathryn warned.

"I *am* HR," Angela reminded him.

He flushed and laughed nervously. "Come on, ladies, you know I was only kidding."

"You're always 'kidding.'"

"Yeah. I'm a funny guy."

"No, Casper, you're not. You're not funny at all. Funny means you make people laugh. Other people. Not just yourself. You're a creepy guy. Not a funny guy." Kathryn had gotten to her feet, and she turned to Angela and Heather. "I'm going to go get ready for dinner. Good luck dealing with the creep."

She left a deeply awkward silence in her wake. But Angela felt no compunction to break it. Nothing she'd said had been wrong. And she certainly wasn't going to make it easier on her coworker. He didn't deserve easy. He *was* a creep.

Finally, he laughed. "Well, uh, so these Jack Specials—amazing, right?"

★

The next three days passed in a whirlwind of sea and ports and beaches. *The White Rose* travelled largely at night, moving from place to place while her guests slept—or ate and drank and danced the night away, as the case might be. Captain Tennison joined them at dinner most nights and would give them a little preview of what to look forward to the next day.

They stopped at several incredible beaches, and Heather and Angela felt the thrill of walking on hot sand and swimming in the most sublime blue-green water. It was a little slice of paradise, and they got to share it.

The markets and ports were incredible, too, and Angela felt like a month in each town they visited would barely begin to scratch the surface. They were very much tourists in the moment, taking in the sights and making memories. And then stumbling back to bed to make love. There was something about making love on the ocean, with the world far away and nothing but empty sea and night and coastline outside.

Maybe she'd seen too many movies or read too many romances. Maybe it was the fact that there was no alarm clock waiting—nothing but more beaches and more sun and more pleasure. But surrendering to Heather's touch here, or touching her in turn, seemed almost magical.

Angela almost forgot how much she detested George Jr. She almost forgot she was a spy, employed by his father to surveil him. She almost forgot she'd tried to sabotage him. It might have been that he kept largely to himself, and so his absence and the trip increased her fondness. But she didn't even mind his short temper when he did appear. George was George. Happy or sad, jolly or angry, he was who he was. She was on vacation.

And she was too busy enjoying herself—and applying copious amounts of sunscreen—to remember or remark anything else.

Chapter Thirty-Six

George's patience quickly waned as time passed. He didn't think much of it when the first day ended. He sent Andy a text to let him know they'd arrived on schedule and got a thumbs up emoji in return.

And he grimaced. He hated emojis. Then again, he hated Andy, too, so it seemed somehow apropos.

The second day, he checked his phone a lot. The morning was better than the afternoon, and the afternoon was better than the evening. He had the unhappy idea that Andy—*the damned fool*—might message him when they were getting ready to depart one of the ports. He didn't doubt that Tennison would stay if he asked, but delaying would bring attention to the matter. And George didn't want attention.

Of course, his worries were in vain. No call came on the second day, and no text message either.

On the third, he sent a reminder, with the port they were at and their departure time. Andy didn't reply, and as the day wore on, George grew increasingly more anxious. What if Andy had changed his mind? What if this whole thing was just to make a monkey of him? What if...

The scenarios were endless, and George ran through them all. He barely noticed the beauty around him. He had no time for beaches or tourist traps.

In other circumstances, he might have enjoyed himself—if he didn't have that weight on his shoulders, and if he wasn't surrounded by this gaggle of imbeciles.

And he'd suffered much on that account these last few days. Angela and Heather had the decency to mostly leave him alone, but their public displays of affection were a little too much. If he'd been in a better mood, he might have found them sexy. But he wasn't in a good mood, and watching the two women giggle and flirt and paw each other on their way back to their room made him scowl.

Matt, the great ape, seemed to have grown allergic to clothes. Because not a day had passed since they'd boarded that he'd bothered with a shirt. Seeing the other man's absurdly sculpted pectorals and increasingly deep tan did nothing whatever to improve George's mood.

Casper's physique put him more at ease. He was thin and pale and covered in freckles. Matt was the kind of man who would make a fitness freak feel self-conscious. Casper was the anti-Matt: a good, solid ego boost for the most average of figures. George almost appreciated him for it. Except that Casper Caspersen never shut up. *Ever*. And he'd discovered the bottomless bar on his first day.

And Casper Caspersen got ever chattier, the more alcohol he downed.

If there was a disappearance at sea, George planned for it to be Casper who vanished. Not that the Walters weren't doing everything they could to recommend themselves for the honor. On his best days at the office, Conrad was an ill-tempered, scowling recluse.

On vacation, he was another man entirely: laughing and smiling and annoyingly social. And, somehow, it was worse than his office persona. Bess wasn't much better. She encouraged his worst instincts, teasing and flirting with him in a way that made the grizzled old bastard stammer like a teenager.

And their displays of affection were even more stomach-turning than Angela and Heather's. Was there anything worse than watching old people dirty dance, or grope each other? George was pretty sure there wasn't. He was pretty sure the whole experience had left him scarred for life.

Of all of his employees, only Kathryn comported herself well. And that was mostly because she'd taken seasick the first night and rarely made an appearance on deck since. She apparently refused to take medicine for it and would only come out of her berth—looking gray and miserable—when they reached land.

The situation, he had to admit, rather amused him. Why anyone would refuse a treatment and suffer for no reason, he couldn't fathom. *Oh well. It may be my circus, but I'll still laugh at the monkeys.*

Still, aside from this minor consolation, the trip was a bust for him. Captain Tennison proved deferential and respectful, and the ship, thankfully, seemed staffed entirely with Americans. George rested easier on that score and didn't feel it quite as necessary to lock his door when he left his cabin.

But none of that made up for the constant anxiety of waiting for a call that didn't seem to be coming.

By the middle of the third day, George had sent another half a dozen messages and tried to call twice. He'd received no answer to his texts, and his calls had instantly been diverted to voicemail.

When dinner rolled around, he was in a truly foul humor. Tennison made a point of inviting him to share the captain's table when they dined, which seemed right, seeing as how he was paying for everything. But he would have preferred a little less hospitality. He would have preferred to be left to stew in his own thoughts and not to have to attend to the other man's conversation. Even if he did only offer the most perfunctory nods and grunts.

Tennison was droning on about the next day's schedule. "We're headed to Carrington's Island. It's one of the few privately owned islands in the area. Like Navassa, both the United States and Haiti claim it as being under their jurisdiction. But both recognize the private ownership." The other man paused, and George glanced up, wondering if he'd missed some cue. But Tennison had only stopped to smile. "And luckily for us, *Haitian Rose* has an arrangement with the owner. When he's not using it, the island is one of our stops. And in return, we pick up passengers for him.

"Which, I should mention—we will have a few guests tomorrow. Just temporarily, until we get back to a mainland port. But wait until you see this island. Such pristine beaches. The place is hardly touched by humans."

Tennison droned on and on. George lost the thread of his words and returned to his own thoughts. He had the idea that if Andy was just wasting his time, if this was some prank or joke or trick, he was done. *He can threaten me with whatever he wants. He'll never see those files.*

He survived the rest of the meal and sent yet another text to his erstwhile partner before bed. Then, more annoyed than ever, he drifted into sleep.

The next day brought no relief from his misery. They'd reached Carrington's Island, and his idiotic employees were already preparing to disembark, chattering and buzzing about like a swarm of insects.

George stayed on board. George could see pristine beaches whenever the hell he wanted. He didn't need to tag along with this gaggle of nuisances for the pleasure. Now, he availed himself of the pool, and the bar, and drank away some of his misery.

Morning became afternoon, and he was starting to care less about the whole business when his phone rang. Starting in his lounge chair, he almost sent his drink and the phone into the pool. But, collecting his wits before either catastrophe occurred, he accepted the call.

It was Andy Gilmore. "Jesus, dude, I told you I was busy. You've been blowing my phone up."

"What the hell is going on, Andy?"

"What do you mean?"

"Where are you?"

"I told you, I had business. I told you, I'd let you know when to drop the data off."

"Well?" George demanded.

"I've got a guy getting onto the ship soon. You'll know him when you see him. Give him the data."

"Wait, what? I thought you were going to pick it up?"

"Me too. But things aren't wrapping up as quickly as I'd hoped. And I had to improvise. You know how it goes."

Klaxons blared in George's mind. He wasn't sure if it was the copious amount of booze he'd been downing, or the days of pent-up anxiety, or a real problem. But something was wrong. Something was off.

He started to protest, but Andy interrupted, "Look, George, I'm really busy, okay? I don't have time for this. We're almost done. All you got to do is hand over the data, and we're both free. Why complicate it?"

George continued to argue that this wasn't what they'd agreed on, and that he'd part with the chip to no one but Andy. The other man let him rant for a few moments, but then sighed, long and loud into the phone. "Sorry, man, I got another meeting. I got to get. Just make the transfer, all right? Talk to you later."

"Goddammit," George snarled as the line disconnected. He hurled his phone across the deck, and it landed with a satisfying crack of glass. A stupid thing to do, maybe. Then again, let Andy try to contact him now. *Fucking bastard.*

"You need another, my man?" a voice called.

It was Jack, the bartender. George nodded. "Damned right I do. Keep 'em coming, Jack."

"You got it. Another whiskey? Or you want to try a Jack Special?"

George asked what a Jack Special was, and though he was generally opposed to fruity drinks, he had enough whiskey under his belt to give it a shot. He wasn't sorry. The drink was the right combination of bitter and sweet, with a strong kick of alcohol.

He'd made his way through several of them before the passengers reembarked. He heard their prattle before he saw them. The women were giggling, the men were laughing. He scowled at the sound but couldn't help but keep an eye out for Andy's man, whoever it was.

But they embarked alone. George waited and watched and drank some more. His employees went back to their quarters to change. He'd almost given up on Andy's man when a figure emerged—a figure in a gaudy suit and polished leather shoes.

George's heart skipped a beat. *Joey Caruso. What in the fuck?*

★

It was indeed Joey Caruso and a small cadre of less expensively but no less gaudily attired clowns. Joey smiled as he caught sight of George and, with a quick but indistinguishable word to his goons, sauntered over.

"What in the fuck are you doing here?" George sputtered.

"Mr. G. told me you had something to deliver."

"He sent you? My people already saw you at the office. They'll recognize you. They're going to know something's up. This is going to get back to my father."

"Relax, George. You're going to give yourself a heart attack, you know that? No one's going to be any the wiser."

George poked a finger into Caruso's overdressed chest and began to explain in forceful terms how imminent their discovery was due to his presence.

Joey took a step backward, adjusted his jacket, and said, "We're heading to our cabins. Your people aren't going to see us. I'll meet you in your room tonight at eleven. You're number fifteen, right? Good. I'll see you there. We'll disembark after your people are gone tomorrow." He spread his hands. "No fuss, no muss. Yeah?"

Despite the insanity of the plan, George could see no way around it. He couldn't throw Caruso overboard—not that the idea was anything short of appealing—so hiding him out of sight was the only possible solution. "I swear to God, if anyone sees you..." he warned.

But Caruso waved the threat aside with a sweep of his hand. "Respectfully, Mr. Sutherland, save it. I've heard better threats from worse people."

Then, without another word, Caruso headed below decks.

George started as a voice beside him asked, "Another one?"

Glancing up at the speaker, he saw Jack at his elbow, a fresh Sunrise in hand. "You know it. Fuck my life."

George had had a little too much to drink by the time dinner rolled around. Captain Tennison didn't seem to mind. He didn't mind when George declared he'd had better lobster in Fenwood than what they were eating at the moment. "And let me tell you something about Fenwood—it puts the shit in shithole."

Tennison laughed heartily and said he'd speak with the cook in the morning.

"Fire the fucker," George advised.

"I may do that."

This point settled to his satisfaction, George glanced around the dining room. "That bastard Caruso staying in his cabin?"

Tennison's smile took on a more measured aspect. George noticed it immediately. He might have been drunk, but he wasn't blind. "I believe our guests are taking their meals in their cabins. I'm sure they won't interfere with your run of the ship at all."

George snorted. "They better not. It's too bad keelhauling went out of fashion, you know that? I'd have you keelhaul the lot of them."

The captain laughed, and encouraged by the response, George went on. "Or maybe walk the plank. That'd be worth watching. That gaudy son of a bitch taking his last steps in those godawful shoes."

"Tell me," Tennison said. "I've heard about Sutherland Bio, but I'm not sure what you do."

This was a subject George could wax damned near poetic on. And he did, for some hour and a half as they ate. He talked about his father and his timidity. He talked about the branches they had around the country, including Fenwood. And he drank a little coffee and sobered up a little. As the night wore on, his conversation grew more agreeable.

Then, at around ten thirty, Tennison interrupted, "Well, it's getting late. You probably want to turn in."

"I don't," George said obstinately. Turning in meant dealing with Caruso. He wasn't sure he wanted to do that. "I might head back up to the pool for another Sunrise."

"Well, there's always tomorrow for that, isn't there?" Tennison smiled. "Probably best to sleep the day off."

Grumbling, George indicated that he would. This, though, was a lie. George didn't head directly for his bedroom. As soon as he was out of the dining room, he headed back to the poolside. Joey could wait. *God knows I've waited long enough.* Joey would wait until he'd had another drink or two.

But Jack, on whom he'd relied these last days for his whiskey and now Sunrises, was nowhere to be seen. For a few minutes, he waited, assuming the other man must have been on break.

But when he didn't reappear, George slipped behind the bar and helped himself first to a glass, then a bottle. *What the hell. Might as well.*

Whiskey in hand, he settled into one of the pool loungers and stared up at the sky overhead. There were no stars out tonight, and the moon was barely visible under cloud cover. He tried to remember if Tennison had mentioned anything about rain. It was the rainy season, he knew, in this part of the world.

Somewhere between sips and studying the sky, George fell asleep. He woke sometime later to something cold and hard against his cheek.

"Huh?"

"Wakey wakey, George," a voice said.

He grimaced, although he didn't know why exactly. Something about that voice bothered him. But the deck was dark. The pool lights cast the figure in shadow, and all he could see was the dark silhouette of a man in a suit.

And then he understood. There was only one person stupid enough to wear a suit in heat like this. "Caruso." He tried to sit up, but felt the force of cold steel again, biting into his jaw. He glanced down and froze quite still.

Caruso had pressed a pistol into his lower cheek.

"What the fuck?" George sputtered out.

White teeth, seeming almost pale greenish in the dark, flashed in front of him. "Come on, George. You can't be *that* unprepared for this."

George was entirely unprepared for it though. He drew back as far as he could until he was squeezed firmly against the arm supports of his lounger. And even then, the pistol seemed far too close to his face. "What's going on? What the fuck do you have a gun on me for?"

"You owe me something. Rather, you owe Mr. Gilmore something. Time to pay up."

Sputtering and protesting that he had every intention of paying up, and that there had never been an excuse to bring guns into it, George added, "You think Andy won't hear about this?"

Caruso laughed. "God, you're not that bright, are you George? Come on, on your feet." He gestured quickly, and two sets of hands reached from behind him and dragged him to his feet.

George threw a frantic glance around him, only to see that Caruso had brought two of his roughs with him. It was they who had pulled him up. "What the fuck is going on here?"

"Where are the files?"

George reached for a pocket but froze as Joey tutted. "Uh-uh. No hands in pockets."

"What, do you think I'm packing? Fucking crazy bastard."

The comments didn't sway Joey, who fished around in the pocket George had been reaching for until he found a tiny plastic case. He drew it out and took a step back. "Keep an eye on this idiot."

George watched as he examined the case and its contents—the data card, containing the files Gilmore wanted—in a flashlight beam. George had thought it unwise to leave such a sensitive item in his room. Now, he wondered if keeping it on his person had been as clever as he'd first supposed.

"This all there is?" Joey asked. "This one little card?"

Despite the presence of two other toughs and a gun, George scoffed. "Are you stupid? Those things can hold more data than your primitive chimp brain."

Joey flashed his teeth again, in a grin or a snarl George couldn't quite tell. "All right. You better be telling the truth. You know Mr. Gilmore's going to be pissed if you're not. Let this clown go, boys."

George launched into a diatribe about how it was him, not Gilmore, who had the right to be pissed, and Joey laughed.

"God, you're really stupid, man. I can't believe you haven't caught on yet."

George blinked as the other man whipped out his pistol again.

"It's game over, *amico*. Fin. For you and your friends."

Chapter Thirty-Seven

Angela grinned, pinning Heather's hands above her head. They'd headed back to their room after dinner, "for dessert" as Heather had put it.

"Oh, no. Tonight, I'm going to take my time." Angela leaned in, growling softly as she nibbled Heather's ear. "I'm going to make you beg."

This was too much for her girlfriend, who, giggling, tried to rise. "You want to bet?"

But Angela held firm, hoisting more weight onto her hands to keep Heather's in place. "I'll take that bet."

For a few moments, they struggled, giggling and promising to make the other suffer. Angela had learned rather quickly in their relationship that, despite a lifetime of no interest whatsoever, she actually had a latent fascination with wrestling, of the erotic variety anyway.

Finally, Heather flopped back onto the mattress with a sigh of defeat. "Goddamn, you're beautiful when you're feisty. What if I surrender? Will that lessen my suffering?"

Part of Angela wanted to strip the clothing off the gorgeous woman before her right then and there and indulge her every desire. She wanted to make her come, to hear and feel and taste her pleasure, over and over.

But no. She was going to make this last. She'd been staring at this gorgeous woman all day, planning tonight. She'd spent more time on the sunny beach thinking about being back in this room, envisioning the sights and touches and tastes she was about to indulge than actually enjoying the sights and smells of the beach.

"Please?" Heather prompted when she didn't immediately answer.

By way of answer, Angela kissed a line from her ear to her neck, nipping and nibbling along the way.

Heather groaned and squirmed under her. "God, you're terrible."

Angela ducked under her collar with her lips and teeth and nipped a little harder.

Heather yelped. "Fuck. You're killing me."

"Mhmm." She traced one of her hands down Heather's arm, toward her breast. Even through her bra and shirt, she could feel her nipples. "Oh. Now what do we have here? Shall we take a look?" When she received no answer, she asked, "Well?"

Heather whimpered. "Yes."

"Yes, what?"

"Are you really going to make me say please?"

Angela grinned. "Yes."

Heather grinned too. "Oh, you're going to regret this."

"I hope so." She pressed a kiss against Heather's lips. "But aren't you forgetting something?"

"Yes, *please*," Heather growled.

Angela moaned. All of a sudden, she wasn't sure she was going to be able to hold out as long as she'd planned. Not if the pressure building in her pants was any indication. Still, she tried to collect herself. *Focus. Nipples.*

It didn't really help relieve tension, but at least it gave her direction.

She was just slipping Heather's shirt toward her neck when a noise arrested her. It sounded like someone jiggling the lock. She turned quickly, glancing at the door. And to her mortification, saw the lever depress. "Wrong room. Occupied," she called.

Heather sat bolt upright too. "What the hell?"

Then both women froze as the door burst open, and they found themselves staring into the business end of a pistol. Angela blinked, and she heard Heather gasp.

A voice from the other end of the pistol laughed. "Jesus, don't let me interrupt, ladies."

Another voice, this one coming from the hall beyond their room, said, "Get a move on it, Chuck."

The speaker to whom the first voice belonged sighed. "Well, I guess we'll have to forgo the show. Sorry, girls. On your feet." He was a tall man, and Angela recognized him as one of the galley workers—though it took a moment to place him outside the kitchen and in this nightmare scenario.

"What's going on? What the hell are you doing?"

But he didn't seem to be in a communicative mood. After pulling Angela off the bed so brusquely she had to catch the side of a dresser to avoid plunging headfirst downward, he yanked Heather up too. "On your feet, I said."

Heather tried, and failed, to get him to give them some clue about what was happening.

"You'll see soon enough. Move."

Clutching Heather's hand, Angela marched at gunpoint into the hall. There were others out there. For half a second, she almost hoped. She spotted Martha, the smiling American who had welcomed them onboard. But she was carrying a weapon, too, and had it trained on Conrad and Bess.

Conrad was taking things far less quietly than they had. "What in God's name is going on here? Who the fuck do you think you people are? You point that gun at her, and I swear to God, I'll pull your head off with my own hands."

"Onto the deck," Chuck ordered.

Martha was similarly guiding Conrad and Bess upstairs. A few other armed escorts were leading some of their coworkers. She saw Casper trembling at the end of a military-style weapon. Kathryn was wailing a few doors down while a sneering man trained a pistol on her. Over this scene of managed chaos, a few rifle-bearing men and women watched.

Wherever Matt and George were, Angela didn't know. They weren't, at the moment, her first priority. Whatever was happening, she knew they needed a plan, and soon. Any possible reason to be woken at gunpoint on the open seas wasn't a good one. Whether these people were smugglers, traffickers, pirates, or plain old murderers, she couldn't guess—and didn't want to wait to find out.

"What are you doing?" Heather demanded. "You don't think people will come looking for us? You can't think you'll get away with this."

Chuck laughed. "You think this is our first rodeo, sweetheart? Why don't you shut up, so I don't have to mess you up?"

"All right," one of the overseers called, "get 'em on deck."

Someone poked their head out of a cabin farther down the way. "He's not here, Dave."

"Martha's seen him on the top deck at night. Go look for him. Call Jack for backup and check in with Caruso's guys. He's ex-military, remember. Don't take chances. Shoot if you have to."

Angela craned her neck to search the full group of their captors. She counted six armed personnel, plus the one who was leaving to look for Matt. Four seemed to be crew, but two, she'd never seen before. If they were crew, they must have stayed out of sight. And if not, they were clearly working in concert with the crew.

Mutiny? Piracy? Is Tennison a prisoner too? Or are they working for him? The captain had been nothing but smiles and cordiality, so she had a hard time imagining him as part of this plot. *Whatever it is*. Then again, Martha had been all congeniality too. And she'd stuck a gun in Conrad's ribs, and was currently making some very ugly threats to the old man.

Angela tried to think worst-case scenario. Worst-case scenario was that the entire crew—and whoever these goons were—was against them. That was over a dozen people, obviously well-armed.

Against a handful of sleepy, unarmed people, half of them drunk and in pajamas. *Fuck*.

Worst-case scenario seemed a little too grim, so she tried to consider better ones. If this was a mutiny, Tennison and his loyalists would be on their side. That would even the odds a little. And hopefully, the captain would have some kind of weapons too. *Which will also improve our chances of survival.*

Heather squeezed her hand and asked as Angela glanced up, "You okay?"

Angela nodded and whispered back, "You?"

She nodded too.

"Hush," Chuck said. "Start walking."

They marched to the deck, and Angela's heart sank. Tennison was there, and he grinned as he caught sight of them. "Good work."

"They're still looking for Kilbourne," the leader of their escort said. "He wasn't in his cabin."

"We should have locked the doors," Tennison said. "But it's a small ship. We'll find him."

The cutthroat in charge nodded. "I've got Jack and Terry on it. I told him to check in with Caruso's people."

Angela's legs started to tremble now. This was worst-case scenario. This meant no allies, no heroic rescues or last-minute saves. Whatever the hell was planned, there'd be no escape.

With no hope of escape, she focused on what was in store for them. Death? Were they being taken up here to be shot? And if so, why? Or did these bastards have something worse in store? Were they human traffickers, maybe?

She felt in the moment very small and very afraid. In the worst points of her life, she'd never been powerless. No matter how bleak things had seemed, she could always walk away, or start over.

But now, she had nowhere to run, and no option to hide. She had, as far as she could see, two plays. One was to wait and let whatever happened, happen. She wasn't particularly keen on that option.

The other was to do something that would make them stop her—with lethal force, hopefully. She couldn't hope for better. Not with the odds stacked against her people the way they were. But some fates were worse than death.

She was surveying the deck, trying to make out what she could in the near darkness, when a voice called, "I've got the target."

She turned in the direction of the speaker. They all did. The night was overcast, and the ship lights were out. She could see almost nothing. In a moment, though, a pair of dark forms grew visible. She couldn't tell who they were, but they were approaching.

She didn't need to wait until she could make out the figures to find out who at least one of the forms was.

"I swear to God, you're going to regret this, Joey," a voice said. An annoying, grating, mortifying voice.

George. An idea popped into her head. This newcomer, this Joey, had said he had the target. "Target?" Angela repeated aloud. "You mean...you're after *George*?"

Tennison smiled. "Very clever, Miss McCormack."

"Look," Conrad said, "I don't know what your beef with him is, but you'll get no argument from us. We work with the son of a bitch. We don't need to be involved."

"Sorry," Tennison answered. "Those aren't our orders." He shrugged almost apologetically. "It's nothing personal. But our contract is Sutherland and his associates."

"Wait, why us?" Casper demanded, his tone high and desperate.

"Don't know. Not my business to know." Tennison seemed to be tiring of the conversation already because he shouted toward the approaching forms. "Hurry up. Let's get this over with."

"What are you going to do?" Angela asked. "Kill us all?"

Tennison glanced back at her, and his eyes seemed very cold in the darkness. "It's nothing personal."

"It feels pretty fucking personal," Casper snapped.

"Leave my wife out of it," Conrad demanded. "Do what you want with me, but let Bess go. She won't say a word. Will you, darling?"

"Like hell. You better kill me if you touch him because I'll kill you all."

Kathryn, meanwhile, began to sob out a refrain of, "I can't die. I can't die."

Tennison groaned. "For the love of God. I hate civvy disposals."

"Muss *and* fuss," Martha agreed.

George, meanwhile, had reached them. Angela recognized the man guiding him as the same one who'd visited George a few weeks earlier, the man whose photo they'd sent to George Sr. He wore a suit and a very satisfied grin. Every now and then, he jabbed George in the back with the barrel of his pistol.

"All right? We ready to do this?" the newcomer wondered in tones that were so casual and lighthearted they made Angela's skin crawl.

Tennison nodded. "Get on with it."

Kathryn responded by wringing her hands and shrieking and sobbing violently. And while she was ugly crying, Casper released an explosive stream of vomit. Tennison almost dodged it but wasn't quite quick enough.

Two of the thugs, seeing the young man and their boss both lurch in unison, jumped forward. One of them, Martha, had no sooner directed the business end of her pistol away from Conrad then he leaped forward. Two quick cracks of bone—first her elbow as he wrested the gun from her hand and wrenched her arm, and the second, her neck, as he twisted her head in one direction and her body in the other—finished her.

Angela barely had time to blink in surprise before the old man whipped the pistol up and started firing rounds. *Crack. Crack. Crack.* They rang through the dark, echoing off the water.

Chuck moved his attention to Conrad, and Heather grabbed Angela's hand and pulled her downward, out of the line of fire. George, meanwhile, shoved the man in the suit and bolted for the railing, screaming as he went.

Tennison went down right in front of Casper, and the young man vomited again. Kathryn screamed even louder than the gunshots. Conrad kept firing, and the thugs kept dropping.

Angela saw Chuck level his pistol at the old man's head. And without stopping to think about what she was doing, she leaped to her feet and crossed the distance between them. She grabbed for the gun, and her fingers and his grappled for it as they went down. He landed first and hardest. She brought her knee down as hard as she could into the soft, fleshy bits between his legs. He screamed and loosened his grip on the pistol.

Angela wrenched it out of his hands and turned it on him. She didn't pause to consider. She just pulled the trigger as he rose. Once, twice, and thrice.

He fell backward hard against the deck, but silently. It was Angela's turn to throw up. Before she knew what was happening, someone pulled the gun out of her hand. She tried to struggle, but he was fast and strong. Hot tears stung at her eyes, and her throat burned. Still, she pushed herself up, fists balled.

But it was Conrad. He'd tossed his own pistol down, and she saw the slide was open. *He's out of ammo. Ammo. I need to get ammo.*

She scrambled for Chuck's body as gunfire sounded all around her. Again, someone grabbed her hand. Heather's voice pulled her from her thoughts.

"We need to go."

"We need to help," she said.

"We need to get off the ship, Angie."

She glanced up and around. There was nowhere to go. And yet...half of their party was already gone. George and Casper were gone, and she realized they must have both jumped overboard. Kathryn was making her way to the railing, covering her head with her hands. Matt still hadn't appeared.

Only she, Heather, Conrad, and Bess remained—and a group of bad guys that seemed not to have diminished much in size, despite the deck being littered with corpses.

Wherever they were coming from, apparently, they had more than a handful of reinforcements.

Part of her wanted to follow Kathryn and leap over the side of the boat without a second thought. But there was nowhere to go. In the water, they'd be sitting ducks. *At least here, we've got some kind of chance.* She grabbed the magazine pouch on Chuck's belt and fished out a handful of full magazines. Then she scurried toward Conrad's dropped pistol. He'd moved back to Bess's side, and left it on the deck. As quickly as possible with trembling hands, she dropped the magazine and replaced it with a new one. Then she started firing too.

Her shots were not so accurate as Conrad's. She was pretty sure she didn't hit anyone. But the man in the suit—the one who had been escorting George—ducked out of sight.

Her success came at a cost though. One of the men with a rifle spotted her. And she might well have died if a new voice didn't join the commotion.

Matt Kilbourne broke onto the scene in a blaze of bullets, screaming at the top of his lungs, "Overboard. Abandon ship. Get overboard. Go, go, go."

The man with the rifle went down even as he trained the barrel onto her, his head evaporating in a cloud of tissue and blood. This time, she didn't hesitate when Heather pulled at her arm. This time, she raced to the railing. Before she leaped over, she threw a glance over her shoulder.

Conrad and Bess were following her, the old man shooting and his wife carrying a magazine pouch. Matt was shooting, too, picking up the rear. There were a lot fewer bad guys now. She saw the man in the suit poke his head out now and then, and two others make a showing once or twice before ducking behind cover.

Satisfied that she'd done all she could, and that they were going to make it, Angela hoisted herself over the barrier and jumped. She didn't look. She knew herself well enough to know that looking would mean hesitating. And she'd hesitated long enough.

The water washed over her, cold against the heat she'd built up sweating for her life. Water filled her nose, and she lost the pistol. Coming up sputtering, she glanced around for Heather. Her girlfriend was beside her, in a similar state—sputtering and gasping.

"We need to get out of the way," Angela said. The others, she knew, would be close behind them, and they needed to make room. "Swim, babe."

They did, and none too soon. A second later, a series of heavy plunks sounded in close succession. Turning, she saw the dark heads of Matt, Bess, and Conrad peeking above the water.

"Go," Matt yelled. "As fast as you can."

"They're going to kill us," she said. "We'll never outrun them."

"The ship's about to blow. Go, Angela."

Chapter Thirty-Eight

Angela had never swum so fast or so hard in her entire life. Her muscles burned and her lungs felt like they might rend. They'd barely covered any distance at all when the first confirmation of Matt's prediction came—a rumble, deep in the belly of the ship.

The White Rose rocked. One of the gunmen who had reached the rail toppled over. He screamed as he went down and hit the water heavily. The men onboard screamed too.

She swam harder. A wave washed over them, and it seemed to carry a terrible chill. Or maybe that was her nerves, and her premonition that—somehow—something was about to go down.

A few bullets hit the water with a sharp *whiz* around them. She forgot about the ship and the rumble. All she could think of now was how their escape had been for nothing after all. They'd made it overboard just to get gunned down in the water. *Fuck*. And it was all George Sutherland Jr.'s fault. *And that son of a bitch just might make it.*

She didn't want George to die. But he was the reason they were in this mess in the first place. And he—*the miserable son of a bitch*—had been the first overboard. He was the farthest from the ship. He was the most likely to get away, if anyone actually got away.

And, as angry and scared as she was, Angela didn't stop to wonder where he'd wind up. All she could think of was the unfairness of it all. And every regret she'd ever had, every thought that maybe she'd overreacted in pursuing her revenge, vanished. Her only regret now was that she'd settled for so little.

And then a bullet whizzed over her head, and she forgot her anger. Fear filled her instead. The next shot, she felt, wouldn't miss. They were getting closer and closer. The next shot would find its target. And she'd be dead.

Then another rumble sounded, louder and deeper, like a monster rising from the depths of the great, dark sea.

Something compelled her to turn, and what she saw stunned her into incomprehension. A great plume of fire shot into the sky with an earsplitting roar. The thought of a sea monster hadn't entirely left her mind, and it seemed that one was swallowing *The White Rose* whole. Fire engulfed the yacht in a great, orange envelope. Then it vanished, and all but the water was eerily still for half a moment.

Then the final roar sounded, and Angela yelped. *The White Rose* rent in two, and the upper deck flew high, breaking apart like so many splinters—all black against a backdrop of red fire.

"Go," Matt yelled. "Go, Angela."

"Babe," Heather said, "we need to go."

Their voices brought back her senses, and Angela swam. Flaming debris fell all around them, splashing into the water, hissing as the fire extinguished. Somehow, it missed them. Somehow, she managed to keep her head above the tumultuous wake of the disaster.

Somehow, through it all, she'd survived. They all had. And, too numb to stop and ask questions, they swam on.

She swam for a long time before a dark shape began to take form on the horizon. "What is that?" she gasped. Whether they'd been swimming in silence for hours or minutes, she couldn't tell. To judge by her heart rate, or the burning of her arms, it had been hours. But her mind was in no state to make that call.

"It's the island," Matt answered.

"What?"

"Carrington's Island. We never left. We moved offshore and stopped."

She didn't ask more. She focused her energy on swimming instead. They kept at it for what seemed like hours after that, but probably wasn't. The sky was still dark when they reached land. Somehow, it seemed to have gotten *darker* since they'd been on board *The White Rose*.

Angela dragged herself, gasping and wheezing onto the sand. Heather dropped beside her, and Conrad and Bess followed a few minutes later. Finally, Matt reached them. All five lay on the sand, just breathing.

Angela couldn't think for some minutes. Not until she'd caught her breath. Then, pushing up on an elbow, she glanced over the beach at the four dark forms by her. "Conrad, Bess, you okay?" They were the oldest of the party by some decades. And while they were in good shape, she was impressed that they'd managed the pace they had.

"Alive," Conrad grunted. "How are you, my love?"

"Alive too. But I lost the magazine pouch."

"You're all right. That's what counts." The old man dragged himself over to his wife and wrapped an arm around her.

"What about you, babe?" she asked Heather.

"Uh, completely at a loss for what the fuck happened there. But drawing breath, if that's what you meant."

"I'm fine," Matt put in. "Thanks for asking."

Angela ignored his sarcasm. "What the hell happened back there?"

"They tried to kill us," Conrad offered.

"Well obviously. But why?"

"How the hell do I know?"

"What happened to the ship?" Heather wondered.

"I happened," Matt said.

"What?" Angela asked.

"Didn't you notice we'd stopped moving?"

"Well...uh...no."

"We were supposed to be heading back to the mainland. But we stopped as soon as we headed down to dinner. I asked one of the guys about it. He straight up lied to me. Said the engines 'run real quiet.' I knew something was up."

"You should have told me," Conrad said. "My wife was on that damned boat. You should have told me, dammit."

"If you'd drunk less, you would have noticed."

"You should have told all of us," Heather said.

"I didn't want anyone panicking. And I wasn't sure if you were too drunk to help, Conrad."

"Too drunk?" the old man sputtered.

"Drunk?" Bess repeated. "He barely had a drink or two, Mr. Kilbourne."

Angela found this quibbling to be beside the point. "We almost died, dammit."

"But you didn't. I didn't have time to tell anyone. I slipped away and kept a watch out. I saw them start milling around with guns. I saw the guy in the suit—the guy that came to see Sutherland at Fenwood Bio, Joey Caruso—take him hostage. I slipped into the engine room while they were all mobilizing."

"Wait, was that *you*?" Heather asked.

"You're the reason the ship blew up?" Conrad said.

She saw his head bob, dark against the sandy shore.

"I cut the fuel line. Figured it would be a matter of minutes before..." He slapped his hands together suddenly.

Angela jumped.

"Fuck," Conrad hissed, "don't do that."

"Come on," Matt threw a glance around the darkened beach. "We need to get a move on it. We need to find Kathy and Casper, if they made it."

"And that son of a bitch George," the other man agreed. "I owe him a knuckle sandwich."

"Me too." Angela nodded.

"Get in line," Matt said. "But if any of those bastards lived, they'll be heading here too. The fact that they stayed close to the island makes me think this place has something to do with their attack."

"What do you mean?"

"I don't think they were planning to just dump us in the ocean. If they were, it would have made more sense to be farther out. I'm thinking they meant to run us back here. Once we were dead. Did you see the plastic on the deck?"

"Plastic?" Angela repeated.

"Yeah, the big rolls."

"Oh. No." She felt a bit silly for missing a detail like that. But the truth was, she had been a little too preoccupied by the guns pointed at her to notice anything much that wasn't moving or wielding a weapon.

"They were going to drop us and contain the mess," Conrad declared, a little too matter-of-factly for her liking.

"I'm guessing we were headed back here. After the killing bit, I mean," Matt said.

"Which means, if any of those fuckers survived, they'll be heading back here too," Conrad agreed.

"Yes. But there's a good possibility they've got men here already."

"Shit."

"And if they don't, whoever they're working for is going to send people here to look for us."

"Dammit," Angela said. "So, we might have survived getting shot just to get shot anyway."

"Yes. If we're lucky, someone heard the explosion. Hopefully, it sent a distress signal before it vanished."

Angela glanced back at the utterly black horizon. *The White Rose* had sunk below the waves and left no trace behind.

"And that's not all," Matt went on.

"There's a storm coming in," Heather offered. "The wind is picking up. So are the waves."

"That's right. And this island is only a few miles across. We need to get inland. The shore isn't going to be safe if it ends up being a bad storm."

"Well fuck me," Conrad muttered. "This just keeps getting worse."

"How many bullets do you have left?" Matt asked.

"I don't know. I lost count. I think seven. But I didn't check to see if the mag was full or not."

"I've got two extra mags, and five left in this one."

"That's something anyway."

"Yeah. It's still two of us against everyone else."

"We don't know if there is anyone else," Angela reminded Conrad.

"No. But we should operate under the assumption that there is," Matt cautioned.

"Plan for the worst, hope for the best," Conrad agreed. "All right, let's get our asses in gear. Matt, you take point. I'll take rear guard. You girls know how to fight?"

"I took hapkido," Heather answered. "But it was years ago."

"You might need to remember it in a hurry. These guys aren't kidding around. If we run into them, kill. Don't ask questions. You will be dead. What about you, Angela?"

"Well..." She remembered Chuck, and the holes she'd put in him. "I..."

"You shot someone," Conrad said.

"Yes."

"You did?" Matt sounded impressed. "Good. Excellent. Here." He handed her a pistol. "I grabbed a spare. You can have it."

She hesitated. "I...don't want it."

"You know how to shoot, don't you?"

"Yes. But..."

"Look, Angela, these guys will kill us. If you can't use a gun, okay. But know that you might die if you don't."

She swallowed and pushed the image of the dead man out of her mind. "All right."

"Good." He nodded at her and pressed a reassuring hand on her shoulder. "Better to have it and not need it than not have it and need it."

"Right."

"Okay, let's go. When we were here earlier, there was a path a little ways north of here. Let's try to find it."

They pushed to their feet, and Heather wrapped an arm around her. "I didn't know you could shoot."

"My dad taught me."

Heather squeezed her. "You did the right thing, darling. You saved our lives. Conrad's—all of ours."

"I know. But...I killed someone."

"I know." Heather held her tight. "I know, my love."

They walked along a lengthy stretch of beachfront in silence. Angela didn't know if they were headed in the right direction. She had no idea where they were and could only hope Matt's sense of direction was less dysfunctional than hers.

Chapter Thirty-Nine

George's mind was a mass of confusion and anger. *The White Rose* had gone down somehow. Andy Gilmore meant to kill him. Joey Caruso—*that goddamned snake*—had almost killed him. And yet, he'd escaped.

He'd dived overboard the instant he had a chance. George was a good swimmer, and he felt very comfortable in the water. It was one of the reasons he'd taken up kite surfing.

But he'd never hated the water quite as much as he did tonight, swimming, and swimming, and swimming for dear life. He didn't know where he was going, except away from the yacht. He might have stopped, except that he heard voices behind him.

Casper had jumped a second after he did, and so had Kathryn. And aside from Andy Gilmore and Joey Caruso, there was no one on the face of God's green earth that George would have liked to strangle more than he would have relished the opportunity to slip his fingers around those two's necks.

Shrieking and wailing and whining—that had been the chorus to which he'd escaped *The White Rose*.

They'd quieted when they had to save their breath for swimming, but not completely. He still got the questions, "Where are we going?" and "What are we going to do?" and "Oh my God, why were they trying to kill us?"

He hadn't been able to outswim them either. Casper was a gangly, reedy critter, but he had good endurance. So did Kathryn. They kept pace with him as he went.

George had never been so glad to see the dark silhouette of land rising against the horizon. For a fleeting moment, he wondered if they'd reached the mainland. But, no. The coast was utterly dark. Which meant they must have returned to Carrington's Island, or some other little landmass in the area.

What that meant for their chances at rescue, he wasn't sure. He was too tired to think and too distracted by his companions. They lay on the shore, gasping and wheezing—and, to his dismay, talking.

But then another sound, the distant echo of voices on the water, reached his ears. "There's people coming," he said.

"Oh my God," Kathryn wailed, "they followed us."

"We need to get inland. It's dark. Hopefully they won't be able to find us."

"What if they have flashlights?" Casper countered.

"You think they had time to prepare a search party before the ship went down?" George demanded, as incredulous as he was annoyed. "I mean, if they did, I guess they'll find us and we'll die. But I'm sure as fuck not waiting around to make it easy on them."

"Me either," Kathryn agreed.

"Or me."

George wouldn't have minded if they did stay back. But they followed close at his heels, and he tried to pretend he had some idea of where they were going. There were three possible directions: inland, and to the right or left along the shore. The shore was exposed, and he felt the need to take cover. *Something about the sensation of bullets flying at your head will do that to a man.*

"This way," George said, picking a sandy path inland. It was dark, so he couldn't tell if this was a natural path or a man-made one. But the sand was white against the blacks and grays all around, so the way was easy to follow.

"You know," Casper said after a space, "the good news is, we're all alive."

"The others aren't," Kathryn pointed out.

"No. And that sucks. But it's survival of the fittest."

George rolled his eyes. Casper was about as fit as a toothpick. He'd just happened to jump at the right moment. If their escape had had anything to do with fitness, Matt would have been here, not Casper.

He would have preferred that. Matt had the good sense to shut up when George needed to think. And, anyway, the other man was a former soldier or marine. *Or something like that.* Whatever it was, he'd be able to handle himself a lot better than Casper. "Too bad," George said aloud. "Matt's military training might have been handy."

"Yes," Casper conceded. "But, you know, I took taekwondo in college. These hands..." George glanced up to see that the other man had raised his arms in some kind of fighting stance, although—mercifully—it was too dark to make out much more. "These hands are machines. I've broken one-inch boards with these bad boys. You compare the thickness of a board to the thickness of a skull? Easy by comparison. Those guys mess with us, they're going to regret it."

George rolled his eyes. Casper didn't catch the motion, but he wouldn't have cared anyway. The other man had jumped overboard, screaming like a baby, at the first opportunity. A "machine" he certainly was not.

They trudged on. The path changed from sand to gravel. The night got darker as foliage crowded in around them. A chill ran up and down George's spine, and his teeth chattered with every breeze. They were soaked through, but it was their circumstance that really chilled him.

The truth was, he didn't even know where he was, much less where he was going, or who might be around. All he knew was that there were killers behind them and uncertainty before them. Physical exhaustion and whatever alcohol lingered in his system left him utterly spent. Every muscle in his body ached and quivered. His lungs burned, and his ears ached from listening to Casper and Kathryn. And his heart felt heavier than his feet.

"Let's take a break," he decided.

"A break? What if they're still on our tails."

"You can keep going if you want," he said, a bit too hopefully. "But I'm taking a break."

"We shouldn't split up," Kathryn protested.

"No, we need to stay together. Where you go, I go, boss."

"Oh good."

They headed off the path, but not out of sight of it. The last thing he wanted was to get lost in the dark on a Caribbean Island. He wasn't sure what kind of predators lived here, but the way his night was going, he'd end up in some wild cat's stomach if he got lost.

Confirming that the ground was solid and safe, he plunked down. The other two followed.

"What now?" Casper asked.

"I'm going to close my eyes."

"Okay. What do we do after that?"

"I don't know. I need to think."

"Good idea."

"Your dad will send people after us, won't he?" Kathryn wondered. "As soon as he realizes we're missing?"

George sighed. "I don't know. Probably. But how long will that take? How long before anyone realizes anything's wrong?"

"What do we do if they don't?" Casper asked.

"What do we do if that guy who wanted to kill us sends people first?" Kathryn wondered.

"I don't know, dammit," George snapped. "I told you I need to think. And I can't think while you're going on like blithering idiots."

This, at least, silenced them. And for a while, he did try to think. But his mind was overwhelmed. The night had been too tiring, too depressing, too frightening to allow any kind of cogent thought.

So, before he knew it, George was asleep. His sleep was deep and dark and dreamless. And as abruptly as he'd fallen into it, he was drawn out, gasping with surprise.

He heard Casper shouting. "Hiya! You won't take Casper Caspersen a second time, you sons of bitches."

Anything else his subordinate might have said was lost to Kathryn's shrieking. And though she wasn't saying anything coherent, the fear in her cries was clear enough.

Fuck. They found us. George pushed to his feet and threw a desperate glance around him. He had half a mind to plunge into the overgrowth and make a run for it. But he had no idea where he was, or what horrors waited off the path.

He turned back to the fray. Dark forms grappled together amid shouting—though, thanks to Kathryn, he had no idea what was being said. If he had any chance at all, it was in helping Casper. Not that he had much faith on that score. But some hope was better than no hope. *And anyway, if I'm going to die, I'm going to break a few of these bastards' noses first.*

So, screaming with rage, he jumped into the mix. A burly man stood with his back to him, and George struck at his head. His target turned, and too late did he see that it was Kilbourne.

Matt raised a hand to block the blow, but it grazed his chin. "What the fuck?"

"Matt? It's you?" George glanced between the mountain of a man before him and the others. And, though he'd never have supposed these clowns could have brought him so much joy, a swell of pleasure rose in him at Angela, Heather, Conrad, and Bess standing beside Matt.

"What the fuck?" the latter repeated.

"Sorry. I thought…" Suddenly, he remembered Casper and wondered who the hell the other man had been hitting. Throwing another glance around, he found him, caught in some kind of elbow lock at Heather's feet.

George stared at him, twisted and contorted at such sharp angles he could almost feel the other man's pain. And he laughed out loud. *Such a machine.*

"What's going on?" Conrad demanded. "Why are you idiots attacking us?"

"Casper thought you were the bad guys. You should probably let him go, Heather. Or not. That works too."

"Bad guys?" Matt repeated. "How many are there? Do you know where they're at?"

"No idea. We haven't seen anyone but you."

"And we haven't seen anyone but *you*," Bess said.

"For the love of God, why is she screaming?" Conrad demanded, gesturing toward Kathryn.

George blinked. He'd almost forgotten about her shrieks. "I don't know. She does that. A lot."

"Hey," Angela said, taking the other woman's arm, "it's okay, Kathryn. It's just us."

"Stop yelling," Conrad added. "Or you're going to bring them all after us."

"We're okay," Angela added. "It's all okay."

George glanced at the ragtag band in front of him, and the dark night all around. And he scoffed.

★

It had taken a few minutes to quiet Kathryn. George hadn't been much help. He'd ranged between sarcasm and outright derision, suggesting after a space that they just leave her behind. He'd been joking.

At least, Angela was pretty sure he was joking.

Still, things hadn't gotten much better once she had stopped yelling. The recriminations started. Conrad led the way, jabbing a finger with an almost murderous intent into George's chest, demanding to know why he'd set them up.

Her boss protested that he hadn't, that he had no idea they were going to be attacked, and so on.

"But what the hell is going on?" Heather asked. "They were targeting you. They said we were going to die because of you."

Again, George protested his innocence. Conrad threatened to get the truth out of him "using any means necessary." Kathryn began to whimper again, and Casper protested that there was no call for such incivility.

"Who the fuck do you think you are?" George countered. "I'm George Sutherland. No one talks to me like that. You—" He shoved Conrad. "Get the fuck away from me. You two—" He jabbed a finger at Angela and Heather. "Shut her the fuck up." This was said with a gesture toward Kathryn. "And you—" This, finally, was directed at Matt, along with a jab to the chest. "Do something. Get us out of here."

Matt did something all right. He let loose a fist, hard and fast, at George's face.

The other man hit the ground with a groan, and lay there, blinking stupidly for a long moment. Then he said, "What the fuck?"

"I've been wanting to do that for a long time, for a lot of reasons. But let's start with this one. You ever put a finger on me again, and I will break your hand. You got it? One more jab of the finger, one more slap on the back... anything, and I break your fingers."

George blinked again.

"Now, you tell me what the fuck is going on. Because if you don't, we'll get back to breaking things."

Conrad grinned. "Spoken like a marine. I like it. And count me in."

George protested they had no business talking to him like that, and that he knew nothing.

Matt shook his head. "Bullshit. Your own father knows you're mixed up in something."

"What? How dare you bring my father into this!"

"Because he's paying me to watch you, you fucking idiot."

George's jaw dropped. So did Angela's, and Heather's, and Conrad's too.

"Wait, what? He's paying you?" Angela demanded.

"Yeah. To keep an eye on this piece of shit, and report anything suspicious. He thinks he's trading company secrets."

"Really?" Conrad laughed. "He's paying me too."

"I told you taking the job was a bad idea, darling," Bess sighed. "Too dangerous."

"You're telling me my father is paying you to spy on me?" George demanded. "Both of you?"

"Yes. Because he knows you're a corrupt little shit. He didn't count on you almost getting killed, I guess."

"He's paying us too," Heather added. "Well, he's actually *not* paying us."

"No," Angela agreed. "We're doing it for free."

"Which is its own level of bullshit. Why are they getting paid, but we're not?"

"Time out," Casper said. "Are you saying there's some kind of spy games going on? And I'm not involved?"

"Maybe if you did something other than watch porn all day, he would have asked you," Matt snapped.

The other man stammered out an angry denial, and Kathryn started to whimper again.

"So all of you are spying on me?" George demanded. He'd pushed to his feet, and his eyes flashed with anger.

The night, Angela realized, was fading. The first light of dawn was starting to break, the island a little grayer than black. She could make out his expressions now. And they were very ugly indeed.

"My own father has you spying on me?" George asked.

"It's not spying," Heather put in. "It's surveilling."

"At Mr. Sutherland's request," Matt agreed.

"Because you're a corrupt little shit," Conrad repeated. "And he knows it."

An ugly scene followed, and for a long time nothing but shouting came of it. In the end, George admitted he "might" have made a deal with someone "who I obviously shouldn't have trusted." No one believed his assertions that it was all "completely legal." No one particularly cared at the moment. The truth was, legal or not—and they were pretty sure it was not—there were armed men who wanted to kill them.

Whether they'd gotten into this mess because George was a buffoon or a criminal didn't particularly matter. They were here, and they needed to figure out a way to get out.

"First thing first, I think we need to rest," Matt decided, with a few significant glances at Kathryn.

It was true. The woman's nerves were barely holding. And Casper wasn't much better.

Hell, Angela felt like she might fall apart—physically if not mentally—if she didn't get some sleep. She'd been swimming or walking all night.

It didn't take much to convince the crew to nap. George protested, but that, Casper had pointed out, was only because he'd already slept.

Matt took the first watch and said he'd wake Conrad for the next.

Angela settled down to sleep, uncertain if she'd be able to. She was wet and cold and soggy, and terrified too. Heather wrapped an arm around her, and Angela nestled into her shoulder. Even if they couldn't sleep, rest would do her weary body good.

It seemed she'd only just closed her eyes when Matt was shaking her. "Come on, Angie. We have to move out."

She blinked into a gray morning. The sky overhead lay under a thick cloud cover, but the sun—a dim yellow glow behind the clouds—loomed high overhead. She must have been sleeping for hours. "What happened?" she said from behind a yawn.

"Those goons from *The White Rose*? Some of them made it here. They passed this way maybe half an hour ago."

She was wide awake now. "What?"

"It's okay. They didn't see us. We're all right. There were only two of them, the guy in the suit and someone else."

"Only two?" Casper gasped. "Why didn't you shoot them?"

"They were headed inland. We figure there's got to be some kind of compound here, or something. They'll lead us to it. But we have to get moving, so we can find them if they turn off trail. And if there is anyone else out here, they'll hear gunshots."

So, just like that, they were walking again. They'd had no breakfast because, of course, no one had food on them. Their clothes were still wet—or, more accurately, soggy. It didn't help that, despite the day being warm, it was very humid. Angela chafed with every step. Her bra was the worst. The underwire liner rubbed like sandpaper. The padded cups felt like sponges. Every movement ground and sloshed. *God, if I never see the ocean again, it'll be too soon.*

Of course, the ocean surrounded them. The island was, as Matt had guessed, only a few miles wide. While they were in the thick of the dense forest, the blues beyond were hidden from them. But when they ascended the heights, the endless ocean stretched in every direction, dark, ominous blue merging with an equally grim gray sky.

They walked for half an hour, perhaps. The going, in the full light of day, was much quicker than it had been in the dark. They didn't have to take every step cautiously, as if it might plunge them into quicksand. The day before, Carrington's Island had been beautiful, its green vibrant, its blues welcoming.

Today, it was hot and damp—the greens too dark, the breeze too infrequent, the air thick and choking. All the beauty and charm of the place seemed to have vanished. Now all that remained was humidity and the threat of death.

God, I wish I'd left Fenwood Bio when I said I was going to. But the idea of Heather being here alone, without her, sat wrong too. "I hope we get back," Angela said after a space.

"What?" Heather seemed to have been lost in her own thoughts.

"I hope we get back. I want to tell my parents I'm sorry about changing my mind so many times. I want to tell them I love them."

Heather nodded. "Me too. I haven't spent an afternoon with my folks in...well, too long. And I want to hug Ragnar."

Angela laughed. "Me too, actually. I miss that great furball."

George rolled his eyes. "Good to see you two have got your priorities straight."

"Fuck you, George." It felt good—damned good—to say it out loud, finally.

Conrad snorted. "I hope we get out of here just so I can see you end up in prison."

"Fuck you all. Bunch of ungrateful assholes."

This probably would have started another round of verbal sparring had not Matt intervened. "Quiet. The compound's just up there—look."

Angela followed the direction he was pointing to a set of roofs peaking above the palm trees, maybe half a mile down the road. "You think that's where they've gone?"

"I do."

"What's the plan?" Conrad asked. "Storm the place?"

"No. Not right away anyway. We don't know how many they've got."

"Good point. We spotted two, but others might have made their way here from elsewhere."

"And they could have permanent staff. If these bastards are in the business of disappearing people, it might be a year-round operation."

"Back up now," Casper said. "Did you say, 'storm the place'?"

"Yes. Once we get a head count, and an idea of perimeter security."

The younger man laughed nervously. "Storm...like, launch an attack kind of storm? Storm the beaches of Normandy kind of storm?"

"Yeah. That kind of storm," Conrad said. "You know, like you do in your video games?"

"Yeah," Casper returned. "But when I storm the beaches of Normandy in a game, I can respawn if I die. That's...not really an option here, is it?"

"Nope. That's the way real life works."

Casper hesitated in place. "I don't know, dude. This sounds awfully dangerous."

George laughed. "What happened to 'the machine'?"

"That was different." Casper licked his lips. "That was hand-to-hand combat."

"You got your ass handed to you in hand-to-hand combat," Angela reminded him. "Heather folded you up in about two seconds."

"Fuck you. I did not. But that's kind of my point. We'll die if we do anything crazy."

"And we'll die if they come looking for us and pick us off one by one. We'll die if they get reinforcements before we get the hell out of here." Matt shook his head. "Come on, man. You can do this. We're all going to have to come together if we want to get out of here."

"What he's saying is, it's time to sack up," Conrad added. "Stop being a little bitch." George laughed at that and earned the old man's death stare for his efforts. "Don't laugh too hard. You're going with us, dumbass."

"Me?" George said. "I can't go."

"What, you don't want to sack up, man?" Casper sneered.

"Fuck you. It's not that. It's—well, I mean, I'm the target. That'd be giving them exactly what they want." He shook his head. "No, it's much better for me to wait until you guys clear the place. Then I can join you."

Casper offered a protest that was more a wail than a sentence. Matt laughed out loud.

Conrad snorted and said, "It'd be better to use you as bait. But here we are. You'll do your part, or—if you get off this island—it'll be on a stretcher."

Chapter Forty

Conrad and Matt handled reconnaissance. They left the team under the cover of foliage some little ways from the walls of the compound. Then they disappeared. And despite craning her neck to catch a glimpse of them for the first fifteen minutes straight, and occasionally after that, Angela didn't see them until they materialized in their midst an hour later.

In their absence, the day had gotten darker, the clouds thicker and grayer. The air was still heavy with humidity, but the wind had kicked up in the interim. She was shivering and sweating at the same time.

Casper had taken to rocking back and forth in place and Kathryn to chewing her nails. Now and then, they'd swap—Kathryn would wring her hands or rock in place, and Casper would chew at the stubs that remained on his fingertips.

Bess alternated between praying and reassuring everyone. "Conrad is a veteran, you know. He knows what he's doing. And Mr. Kilbourne seems very competent. It will be all right."

Heather and Angela sat together, not talking much, but holding each other tightly. "You know," the former said after some time waiting, "when they get back, I don't know what their plan is. But there's a good possibility we won't get out of here alive."

"I know," Angela nodded. She tried to keep the fear out of her tone when she said it but didn't quite.

"I know, as far as settings go, this one sucks. But I don't know if I'll ever have the chance to tell you this otherwise." Heather glanced up, almost shyly, and caught her gaze. "I love you, Angie."

Despite the situation, and their likely imminent demise, Angela smiled. "I love you, too, babe."

"Oh for fuck's sake," George muttered. "I should have gone with them. What's the worst that would happen? I'd get shot, and not have to put up with this bullshit."

Heather ignored him. She continued, "I should have told you earlier. I just...it happened so quickly."

"I know," Angela nodded. "I should have told you. But I didn't, for the same reason."

Heather smiled, and the gray sky overhead reflected in her eyes made them seem almost a blue-gray. It was an odd thing to be struck by at such a moment. Maybe it was just Angela's heart talking. Even dirty, sweaty, and disheveled as they all were—Angela wasn't sure she'd ever met anyone as beautiful as Heather.

She leaned in and kissed her gently, sweetly. George sighed.

Bess said, "Now that's wonderful."

Casper kept crunching away at his nails, and Kathryn whimpered.

Aside from the odd complaint from their boss, or half-coherent complaint from Casper or Kathryn, they spent the remainder of the wait in silence. And, finally, the recon team returned.

"Well," Matt said, "looks like you'll get your wish, George. There's about two dozen guys there. No way we can storm the place. Not with three guns between us."

"We're all going to die," Casper declared resignedly. "We are all going to die."

Kathryn began to weep quietly.

"There's got to be something you can do," George said, aggravation seeping into his tone. "You're military, for God's sakes. Put some of that taxpayer funded training to use."

Matt scowled up at him. "We've got three guns between us. And me, Conrad, Angela, and Heather can't take a barracks full of guys."

"What about us?" Casper asked. "We could help?"

Conrad laughed, a quick, derisive laugh. "If we need anyone to puke on the bad guys, we'll let you know."

"In my defense, that was the distraction you needed—"

"Point is, we don't have enough people or weapons," Matt said.

"What do we do?" Casper asked.

Matt sank onto the ground. "I don't know. The place has a wall, but it's easy to scale. And the gate's open. They're clearly not worried about intruders. I think it's more to delineate the end of the clearing than anything.

"There are two guys on patrol, and they walk the perimeter. We saw Caruso in the house, and his guy with him. One of the guards came and went a few times. If there's more inside the house, we didn't spot them. And we got pretty close."

"Second-story balcony close," Conrad explained.

"But there's a barracks off the side of the house. Counted twenty-two guys inside. Some of them sleeping in the back, some of them playing video games."

"I'm surprised they're not out looking for us," Angela observed. "If that Caruso guy got back here, they've got to realize that we might have too."

Matt glanced up at the sky. "As near as I can tell, we're about to be clobbered. My guess is, they don't want to be out here in the thick of the storm. Once it's over, they'll probably scour the island until they do catch us."

Kathryn whimpered at the thought, and Casper groaned, and said, "God, I'm too young to die. I've got so much to do with my life."

"Yeah, all those computer games aren't going to play themselves," Conrad muttered.

If Casper caught the sarcasm in his tone, he didn't note it. Instead, he just nodded.

Angela shook her head. "There's got to be something we can do. I mean, they have to have some kind of comm equipment, right?"

"I'm sure they do. But I don't know where."

"Then..." She swallowed. "Why don't we go find it? It's got to beat waiting around to be hunted down, right?"

Matt considered for a long minute. "I don't know, Angie. It's an awfully big risk. I can't ask a civilian to do that."

"But we're dead either way," she persisted. "At least this way, we've got a fighting chance."

"She's right," Conrad put in. "And if we wait for the cover of the storm, we'll have an even better shot. They're going to be holed up in their barracks. If there are any guards left on patrol, they're going to be sticking to shelter."

"And visibility won't be great," Heather pointed out.

Angela offered a cautious nod. "And there'll be a lot of noise. So—hopefully—even if we're not all professionals, maybe we can make it out alive."

"Who would we call?" Heather asked.

"Anyone in the area. Send a distress signal."

"Call my dad," George said. "He'll know what to do."

He, however, was ignored. Matt threw a glance around the party. "If we did it...who would come?"

"I'll go," Angela volunteered.

"Me too," Heather agreed.

"Count me in," Conrad offered.

Matt nodded. "And me too, of course. That's four. Anyone else?"

Bess seemed to be considering. All at once, she said, "I'll go too. I don't know what good I can do. I'm not much of a fighter. But I'll go."

"Like hell, my Bessie. You stay here."

"If you're going, shouldn't I go too?"

The old man's expression softened, but he shook his head. "You stay here, so I know you're safe."

"But if what you say is right, none of us are safe. Not for long."

Conrad wrapped an arm around her waist. "No. But give me something to fight for, my love. Give me a reason to succeed—so I can know I'm keeping you safe."

The old woman smiled at him with a tender expression. "You better survive, Conrad Walters."

"For the love of God," George muttered.

"Okay," Matt said, "so no one else?"

The remaining three shifted under his scrutiny. Casper coughed. "I can't. My asthma...can't take this humidity. I'd give us away." He coughed again.

George shrugged. "I don't think I'd bring anything to the table. I'm no kung fu expert like Heather there. And anyway, I really am the primary target. I think for all of our sakes, I'd better stay behind. That way, if you guys fail and they get you, at least they haven't succeeded in their main mission, right?"

Kathryn blinked as the party's eyes fell on her. "I'm, uh, going to stay back here with Bess. To make sure she's okay."

Matt rolled his eyes. "Right. Very heroic of all of you."

Casper flushed to the roots of his hair, and Kathryn studied her shoes. Only George seemed unaffected by the rebuke.

Matt looked them over a final time, then nodded affirmatively. "All right, team, let's head out. We'll get in position and wait for the storm to start. The rest of you—you stay here and wait. If we're not back in a few hours...well, you're on your own."

Here, Kathryn perked up. "Wait. Before you go..." She reached into her traveler's purse. It was one of those small bags that slipped over one shoulder, across the chest, and under the opposite arm. Somehow, she still had it with her. "Here." She fished out a few granola bars. "Take these. For energy and whatnot."

Matt blinked at the proffered food. "I thought you said you didn't have any food?"

"Did I?" Kathryn laughed, a high, nervous laugh. "I don't think so."

"You did," Heather confirmed. "Everyone said they had no food. You included."

"Oh." The other woman shrugged. "I must have misheard the question."

"Where did these come from?" Angela frowned.

"Oh, I don't remember. I might have picked them up in the galley. Or one of the shops."

"You mean, stole them," Angela translated.

Kathryn's face flushed. "Of course not."

"Are there more?" Casper demanded.

She seized her purse, drawing it close as if to protect it from thieves. "No."

"Bullshit," George declared. "She's got more food in there."

"Give it here," Casper said. "I'm starving."

"We're in this together," George agreed. "We're a team. Share and share alike."

Kathryn took a step backward, declaring she had already sacrificed for their infiltration team, and anything she had left was hers. Casper wasn't dissuaded. He reached for the purse, and she took another quick step out of his way.

But her foot caught on a root. With one quick yelp, she went down, the purse went up, and the contents of said purse went every which way.

Angela saw granola bars and pens and crew name tags from *The White Rose*—and a strange, smallish orb.

Matt seemed to notice the latter at about the same time she did because he seized those standing nearest him and threw them all to the ground, covering them with his own body and screaming, "Grenade!"

Angela, Heather, and Conrad went down. So did George, swearing all the way. Branches slapped at Angela's face, and a root lodge painfully in her side. But she didn't hear the *boom* she'd expected at his warning.

She had no idea where a grenade might have come from, but she guessed Caruso's team had found them. They were going to die after all.

When, however, nothing happened, and the taut muscles of Matt's body relaxed against hers, she demanded, "What's going on?"

Matt scrambled to his feet a moment later, and they followed. He stared at the dull gray ball that had landed in the middle of their little clearing. "What the hell are you doing with that?"

Kathryn was on her hands and knees, scrambling to pick up her eclectic collection of pilfered goods. She'd just reached the ball, and Angela's heart leaped into her throat. *It's a grenade. What the hell?*

Casper yelped and George screamed as Kathryn reached for it. So did Matt, but his yell was more coherent.

"That's a grenade, dammit, Kathy. What are you doing?"

She blinked, her singular focus apparently broken. "What?"

"That grenade. What are you doing with it?"

"Grenade?" she repeated. Then, as if only now the word had sunk in, she screamed, chucked the explosive upward, and dove for cover. Everyone else dove for cover, too, and the seconds between the grenade going airborne and landing with a thud were some of the longest of Angela's entire life.

It rolled a few feet from the initial point of impact, and then stopped.

Matt sprang forward, presumably before she could touch it a second time, and grabbed the grenade. Examining it, he breathed a sigh of relief. "Safety pin is still there."

Now, all eyes turned to Kathryn. She was quaking, and as Matt approached shrieked, "Don't bring that thing over here."

"Kathryn, where did you get this?"

"I don't know," she said. "It isn't mine. Don't ask me."

"It came from your purse."

"No, it didn't."

"We all saw it," Angela said.

"I have no idea. Someone must have put it there. It wasn't me."

Angela shook her head. "Look, Kathryn, we don't have time for this. You're a klepto. Where'd you get it?"

"I'm not," she protested. "You're a liar. Nothing's ever been proved."

"For God's sakes, you've got name tags from the yacht's crew. And a grenade—a *grenade*. You expect us to believe you normally carry grenades?"

Kathryn stood there for a moment, her lip quivering.

Conrad, meanwhile, gasped. "Wait a minute...it was *you*, wasn't it? Not the janitor, but you—you stole my pictures."

"Not really important right now," Matt reminded him. "We need to know where you got this—and if there are more. You need to level with us now, Kathryn."

At this, the other woman burst into tears and started wringing her hands. "It's not my fault. It's a compulsion. I'm sorry, all right? I don't mean to do it."

Matt took her by the shoulders. "No one is mad at you, Kathryn."

"I am," Conrad snorted. "I'm pissed as hell, you fucking thief."

"No one," Matt repeated, emphasizing the words. "We need your help now. Where did you get this?"

"On the ship," she managed through sobs. "I snagged it from one of the crew's berths. I swear, I didn't know it was a grenade."

"Back on the ship, then?"

"Yes."

"Dammit."

"I didn't know, I swear," she protested. "I had no idea it was a grenade."

"Then what the hell did you think it was?" Conrad demanded, mouth agape.

"I didn't know. I just...took it."

★

This revelation shifted the situation. Angela didn't see how a single grenade could make that much difference. But as far as Matt and Conrad were concerned, even one explosive changed everything. They drew up a new plan. And this time, no one was allowed to sit it out.

"Conrad and I will take point," Matt told them. "Our first goal will be getting more guns. The two guards on patrol will be the target. Heather and Bess will get the first guns."

"Wait, what about me?" George demanded. "I should get one before Bess. She's old. I'm fit and young."

"She's not a coward," Conrad answered. "And she's not the reason we're in this mess."

It took Matt a few minutes to steer the conversation back on track, to quell the squabbling that broke out between George and the older man. Finally, he did. "Then we take the barracks. Again, Conrad and I take point. Heather and Angela, watch our sixes.

"Once that's done, we move on the house. There are at least two people in there—Joey Caruso and his henchman. We find them, and we neutralize them."

"Kill that fucking Joey," George said. "Show him no mercy."

Matt shook his head. "George, you're going to be looking for the equipment. Take Casper with you."

"What? Why am I stuck with Casper?"

"Because he's a techy. You may need his expertise."

"Whoa, hold on. That kind of comm equipment is way outside of my wheelhouse."

"What kind?" Matt asked.

"Well, anything we might find here. I mean, they could be using all kinds of tech I'm not familiar with."

"They could. Or it could be something you are familiar with. You won't know until we find it."

The wind had picked up to the point that they were almost shouting just to communicate.

"Come on," Matt called. "Let's get into position. We don't want to be trying to find our way through a hurricane."

"Remember the meetup," Conrad reminded them.

"The foyer," George repeated. "Not exactly tough to remember."

"Just make sure your dumb ass shows up." The older man shrugged. "Or don't. No one will miss you."

Angela and Heather held hands as they walked. They hadn't gotten very far when the rain started, in one-off droplets at first. But by time they got into position by the compound, it was coming down in driving sheets.

Angela couldn't see much in front of her. She had caught sight of the sprawling, sandstone-esque villa beyond the walls earlier in the day, and the handful of side buildings of similar composition and style. But now, the downpour obscured it all.

"Wait here," Matt shouted. "We'll be back." Then, with a gesture to Conrad to follow, the two men set out.

Angela tried to steady her breathing as she waited for them. Her heart was racing, and a steady, controlled intake and outtake of breath would help. But, dammit, it was hard.

Every time she got it under control, a flash of lightning or shriek of the wind or thump of branches or leaves beating against something would put her heart in her mouth all over again. She was soaked and shaking with cold and nerves.

God, how did it come to this? Never, in all of her life, had she imagined herself in a situation like this one. And yet, here she was...

Matt and Conrad returned a few minutes later with several handguns, magazine pouches, and rifles. These they distributed, with firm warnings to Casper, Kathryn, and George not to shoot until after they'd hit the barracks.

"The guards are down," Matt told them, screaming to be heard above the shriek of the wind. "The perimeter's clear. Stay on the alert though. Move out."

They went single file, staying close enough together to keep one another in sight. Matt took the lead, and they ducked into the open gates and past a few shrubberies and great leafy plants that were taking the weather even harder than the intruders.

Matt seemed to know where he was going, and Angela was glad of that—because she couldn't see a thing. Soon enough, though, lights appeared in the gloom, and then a midsized building.

They lined up single file along the wall, avoiding the windows. Conrad stood on one side of the door, with Matt on the other. At a signal, the older man opened the door, then Matt chucked the grenade inside.

A moment later, a deafening boom sounded. The windows shattered outward, sending shards of glass past them, and a flash of red came and went. Matt and Conrad stepped inside, firing as they went. Angela remained out-side, sweeping her pistol from one end of her limited vis-ible range to the next. Heather was on the other side of the door doing the same.

A minute later, the two men emerged. "All clear. Anything?"

"Not a thing."

"Move out, then."

They crossed the courtyard quickly, keeping low and out of the main path. The house emerged from the gloom, rising three stories tall against a gray sky and wrapping around out of view in the downpour. Matt was not leading them to the main door. Indeed, he wasn't leading them to *any* door.

Instead, they rounded to the back of the house and stopped by a window. They tried it, but it didn't budge. Conrad started counting, and Angela found herself at a loss to explain what was happening.

It was only when he smashed the butt of his rifle through the glass that she realized he'd been timing the strike to coincide with thunder. With the next boom, he cleared the remaining glass. Then, carefully, gingerly they made their way through the aperture.

The house was huge, and incredibly elegant. Angela's attention was mostly focused on getting around without bumping a knee or knocking a vase over though. The lights were out in this part of the house, and, of course, they didn't dare turn them on. Wherever Caruso and his man or men were, they certainly would have heard—and felt—the explosion. They didn't need to draw their attention.

They went as quietly and quickly as possible. They'd cleared a dozen or so rooms when they reached an office full of electronic equipment.

"This is it," George whispered. "Bet you anything."

"Right," Matt nodded. "All right, you and Casper stay here. Heather, I want you on that end of the hall. Shoot anyone who isn't us on sight. Angela, you're on that hall. Same to you. Kill anything that moves and isn't us."

"Got it."

"Get that message out as soon as you can," he continued.

"Will do," George said.

"Good. We're going to find Caruso. If you hear shooting and we don't get back, you'll have to retreat once you get that message out."

"Shouldn't I wait here with them?" Kathryn wondered. "You know, in case they need backup or something?"

Conrad rolled his eyes, but Matt nodded. "Sure. Just, don't shoot anyone. Leave that to Angela and Heather. Okay?"

She nodded eagerly and slipped into the comm room. Angela, meanwhile, took up her post. Matt, Conrad, and Bess headed off down the hall and vanished from sight.

The house was eerily silent, and Angela jumped at every clash of thunder or flash of lightning. In a few minutes, she heard voices from the comm room. That was a good sign. That meant whatever equipment they had was working. It meant rescue would be on the way, sooner rather than later.

Still, she hadn't heard any gunshots. And that meant Caruso was alive. The minutes ticked by. Now and then, she threw a glance at Heather, who would flash a nervous smile. She could only see it when the lightning flashed and, then, only for half a moment. Still, it was reassuring. She wished she could be with her, facing this side by side.

Hell, she wished they were back home now, going through the boring day-to-day of office life. She wished—

A sound, loud and terrible in the stillness, ripped her from her thoughts. *Gunshot.* No sooner than she'd come to that realization, it repeated, booming through the house three more times.

Screams and panicked shrieks came from the office. And, racing at breakneck speed, she arrived at the door at about the same time Heather did.

She expected to find Caruso or one of his minions there. She expected to find her friends dead or injured.

But there were no bad guys. And while Casper and Kathryn were cringing in corners, the only other person in the room was George.

"What the hell?" Angela demanded.

George smiled at her, a cool, condescending smile. "I reached my dad."

"What about the gunshots?"

"Oh, that? I was just making sure no one else could make any foolish calls."

"What?"

"I shot the SAT phone. And this gear." He gestured to a smoking server. "Just to be safe."

"Safe? What the fuck are you talking about?"

He shrugged. "I told you. I wanted to make sure no one did anything stupid. My dad's making sure help is on the way. We don't need to do something stupid like involving the United States government. Or worse, the Haitians."

Chapter Forty-One

He hadn't been lying. He'd destroyed the comm equipment, putting bullets through it all. And when the recon team returned, it was all Matt and Angela could do to stop Conrad from putting bullets in *George*.

They had returned with Bess and two prisoners: Joey Caruso and an olive-skinned man called Anthony. If Anthony had a last name, Angela didn't catch it.

"They surrendered when they realized they were alone," Matt explained.

Her party's explanations were a little more complicated. George, it seemed, had decided that his father needed to be the one to handle this situation. His assurance that help was on the way, and his condescending remarks about making "foolish calls" pissed just about everyone off.

Though they scoured the house from top to bottom looking for another SAT phone, they came up empty-handed. The best they could do was hope that George hadn't lost his mind.

"I swear to God, if any of Gilmore's guys get here first, I will personally cut your heart out," Conrad assured him.

But they didn't. The storm lasted a long, miserable day and a half. They slept in turns, keeping watch shifts during their waking hours and never straying too far from one another.

"Figures," Heather sighed. "I'm finally staying in a palace, and I'm basically a prisoner."

It was something of a palace too. Three stories tall and well over a hundred rooms, Angela couldn't believe the splendor. It seemed unreal to find such a luxurious home in the middle of the ocean. Yet, here it was; here *they* were.

Aside from shelter, a chance to dry their clothes, and food, they didn't dare enjoy the place too much. Matt and Conrad had cleared the men in the barracks, and the handful that remained in the house. But they didn't know who would show up, and when.

After two very long and painful days of waiting, someone did appear. Another yacht cruised into the harbor. They watched its approach on the big house's surveillance monitors, and then, clutching their guns, made their way to the shore. They waited in the greenery, just out of sight as the yacht docked and people began to pour out of it.

George laughed at them and strode boldly down to the shore. Seeing that he wasn't immediately gunned down, they followed.

George Sutherland Sr. had come after all. And rather than berate his son for destroying their comm equipment or concealing the whole sordid business from the authorities, he gently urged "reason."

"We all know Carrington's Island is disputed territory. I don't think any of us are keen to explain using military grade weapons—weapons of war—on foreign soil."

As far as the island's owner, they were assured that that would not be an issue. "He understands his people erred. He doesn't want trouble any more than we do."

And to his employees' assurance that they did, in fact, want trouble, George Sr. smiled patiently and reiterated the difficulties for those involved. "Lengthy investigations, multiple murders on international waters, sabotaging a vessel, maritime piracy...some of you might never see the light of day for a very long time. And you may say it's all in self-defense, but that comes down to who gets believed in court."

He wasn't blackmailing them, he assured them. "I have a stake in this; I won't lie. I don't want my name drawn into the story of the century. I don't want Sutherland enterprises ruined because of my son's actions.

"But my clout in this part of the world is limited. There are bigger players here than me, and they carry a lot more weight. I promise you; this won't end well for any of us. I have as much to lose as you."

It wasn't until he started talking about compensation that tempers cooled enough to listen. And the idea of fat settlement checks went a long way toward convincing his employees it wasn't worth a lengthy battle to prove that their self-defense had been justified.

The Sutherlands returned to the United States several million dollars poorer, but with critical NDAs signed. And their beleaguered employees returned with handsome checks, company stock and pension agreements.

Angela didn't like it. Neither did Heather. Gilmore and George Jr. belonged in prison for what they'd done. But George Sr. had his employees over a barrel, and he knew it. If they took a stand for justice, they could spend months or even years fighting protracted legal battles they couldn't begin to afford.

On the other hand, the money George Sr. offered was good, and the specter of Andy Gilmore's mysterious partners frightened them more than anything else. As far as Gilmore himself, George Sr. promised them that was being handled.

What that meant, and if they wanted to know, neither was sure. But they found out soon enough.

George Sr. called them into a meeting bright and early the Monday morning after their return. George Jr. was notably—and blessedly—absent.

He opened with a thanks that they could "come to an understanding that was so equitable to all parties involved." He reassured them that the drive containing the sensitive research "at the crux of recent events was rendered inoperable when the ship went down. It was completely waterlogged. But from an abundance of caution, we did recover and destroy it. There will be no further trouble where that is concerned."

Then he got to the meat of the matter. "I know you've been wondering about certain players in this fiasco.

"I am happy to announce that my son George has decided to take an early retirement from the family business."

"Retirement?" Conrad snorted. "He should retire to a prison cell."

Angela nodded, and Heather said, "He could have gotten people killed, Mr. Sutherland."

George Sr. continued, "My son has made mistakes. With the nondisclosures, we're all bound by how much I can say, but know that I hear you. And he understands his position. He believes the best way to make amends for what he's done is to devote his energies to philanthropic endeavors. We'll be announcing later today that he is heading the newly formed Sutherland Foundation, to give back to the communities in which we operate."

A few exchanged glances and harrumphs passed through the assembled employees. Angela wasn't surprised, exactly. Men like George Jr. were rarely held accountable, and his father's insistence on the NDA's had all but guaranteed he wouldn't be either. Still, it was disappointing.

But George Sr. seemed not to notice the misgivings among his employees. "In far more exciting news—and you are the first to hear it, outside of my lawyers—Sutherland Research is acquiring Gilmore Pharmaceuticals. This is, of course, a huge acquisition for us—and not least of all, since Mr. Gilmore was persuaded to sell his controlling share for a very reasonable rate."

"Jesus." Matt whistled. "You blackmailed his business away from him?"

George Sr. smiled. "Of course not. Like my son, young Andrew had a long, hard think about some of his choices, and where they might lead him if his actions were ever made public. And he felt it best to get out of the business that led him to make so many bad choices.

"If he sold for such a reasonable price due to some compunction of conscience, well, that is a testament, I suppose, to the fact that we're all capable of change in the end."

He spread his hands. "This, of course, is excellent news for all of you. As shareholders in Sutherland Research, our success is your success."

Chapter Forty-Two

"Are we completely insane?" Heather asked. They were sitting in Angela's living room after dinner, discussing the revelations of the day and the happenings of the past week and a half.

"I don't know. We could probably all wind up in jail if any of this came out. But how would we ever prove it if we didn't take the money?"

Heather rubbed her temples. "I don't know. I just hate the idea of George getting away with it all."

"Me too. And that son of a bitch Gilmore. He would have murdered us all."

"And whoever the hell he was working with. It sounds like he does this regularly. 'Takes care of problems' for rich clients."

"Yup. But, again, how do you prove any of that?"

They fell into silence for a moment. Angela shook her head. "I guess you don't. But, hell, I'm never taking another private cruise offer. Not as long as I live."

Heather laughed. "Me either."

"What do you think about the team? You think any of them are going to stay, now that we're all rich?"

Heather considered. "I don't know. I don't know what I'm going to do, to be honest. But as far as Conrad, I think he'll stay."

"Really? He'd be the first I'd think might retire."

"That'd mean spending more time with his grand-kids."

"Good point. That is the whole reason he took the job in the first place."

"But what about you? Are you thinking of leaving for real now?"

"I don't know. I guess..." Angela glanced up at Heather. "Well, I guess my plans are going to depend on yours. And what you want." The sixty-four-thousand-dollar question. She knew she would have to come clean with Heather about the sabotage-hiring business too. But later—one conversation at a time.

Heather smiled. "As far as work? I don't think I trust the place anymore. I might leave. But as far as us—as you—I don't plan on going anywhere, if that's what you mean."

Angela smiled too. "That's exactly what I meant."

"What about you? You planning on going anywhere?"

She shook her head. "Nope. Especially not after that 'vacation.' I might stay in Fenwood forever. But..." She reached out a hand and took Heather's. "I'll stay with you, wherever we go."

Smiling, Heather moved closer. "I love you, Angie."

"I love you, too, Heather." Angela leaned in, and cupping Heather's face in her hands, she kissed her.

"I've missed this," she sighed. "Kissing you, I mean, without wondering if we're going to be dumped overboard or murdered in the night."

Angela laughed. "Me too, actually. Hey, you know, we had some unfinished business from our last night on the cruise."

Heather grinned. "Yes, we did, as a matter of fact."

Smiling into a kiss, Angela asked, "Shall we, umm, take this upstairs?"

"I thought you'd never ask."

About Rachel Ford

Award-winning author Rachel Ford is a software engineer by day, and a writer most of the rest of the time. She is a Trekkie, a video gamer, and a dog parent, owned by a Great Pyrenees named Elim Garak and a mutt of many kinds named Fox (for the inspired reason that he looks like a fox).

Facebook
www.facebook.com/rachelfordauthor

Twitter
@rachelfordWI

Coming Soon from Rachel Ford

Ashes to Ashes

At twenty-five years old, the human body was a machine in its prime. Maybe, the perfect machine. According to the smart people of the world, the brain had fully matured by then. Or maybe it was at twenty-one or thirty. It depended on which study you read and which smart person you asked. But twenty-five was a nice number anyway, right in the middle of all the estimates. And it was the number they were working with. So Aubrey Blake went with it.

As far as the rest of a twenty-five-year old's body— Well, for most people, it would be in peak condition. The heart, the liver, and the lungs were the healthiest those organs would ever be. And barring some kind of high school or college sports injury, the knees and back hadn't started feeling the impact of age yet.

No, twenty-five was pretty much as good as it got. *It just goes downhill from there.*

So maybe, Aubrey figured, that was why a twenty-five-year-old kid in the prime of his life would eat a bullet. Maybe he'd sat in that darkened room, the shades drawn on a bright, sunny morning, and thought about the next seventy years of his life and how it would all be downhill from there. Maybe he'd thought about three or four decades of eight-to-five shifts. Maybe he'd thought about thirty years of mortgages and car payments and PTA meetings. Maybe he'd thought about a lifetime of diets and gym memberships and watching his cholesterol and counting how many beers he drank.

"Maybe," she said, "he was getting cold feet about the wedding."

"Bullshit, Aubrey. You know that's bullshit." Andy Jefferson drummed his fingers on the desk in an aggravated rhythm.

She shrugged. Andy had been her old partner, back when they were on patrol, and they'd risen through the ranks side by side. They'd made detective within a month of each other, so they had the kind of history to know when one or the other was full of shit. And he was right. It did sound like bullshit, and Aubrey knew it. But the truth was, she didn't much care. "Maybe. But if the medical examiner thinks it was suicide, I don't see what the problem is."

"'Consistent with.' She said the injuries are 'consistent with' a suicide. Not that it *was* a suicide."

"She would, though, wouldn't she?"

"Not the point. I'm saying, she didn't rule out anything else."

"What, you mean, murder most foul?"

Andy frowned at her flippancy. "I'm telling you, that kid was murdered. And Tim Callaghan did it. I know he did it. I can feel it."

Andy was an instincts guy. It used to piss her off because his instincts usually turned out to be dead-on. She sat back in a comfortable office chair and tapped a pen against her lower lip.

"Okay. But it seems to me there's one glaring problem with your theory. You have no evidence."

He didn't respond to her sarcasm though. "It's worse than that."

"Really? You got someone else who confessed to it?"

A flicker of annoyance crossed his face. "No, Sherlock. He's got an alibi. A good alibi."

Aubrey laughed. "Hell, Andy. This is one of those happy-ending cases. You've got a rapist who decided of his own accord to eat a bullet. Why are you looking for more?"

"Because he didn't do it. I know I don't have the evidence. But when I talked to the grandfather, I could tell he was guilty."

"Did he say anything?"

"No, of course not. I tried everything I know to catch him in a lie or a contradiction. He's sticking to his story. Damn guy's unflappable, I'll give him that. But I'm telling you, I could see it in his eyes. He knew why I was there before I said a word."

"Okay," she said again. "And so what?"

"So what? He killed someone. What do you mean, 'so what'?"

"Say he did kill Morehouse. Hannah Callaghan is dead because of Tyler Morehouse. Tyler Morehouse is dead because of Tim Callaghan." She shrugged again. "Seems like balance has been restored."

"Jesus, Aubrey, that's not the way this works."

"Maybe not. Maybe it should be."

He shook his head at her. "Look, I didn't come here to have this argument all over again. Are you going to help me or not?"

She considered for a long moment. Andy was a good guy. He really was. And he was smart, with killer instincts. If he thought Tim Callaghan had done it, chances were very good that Tim Callaghan did it.

But was she really going to help someone—even Andy—put a man in prison for killing the man who'd raped his granddaughter? Was she going to put an old guy in jail for killing the man who'd driven his granddaughter to suicide?

"Tell me more," she said in a minute.

"Then you'll help?"

"We'll see. Tell me about the alibi."

The alibi was about as perfect as an alibi could get. Tim Callaghan was a creature of habit. His neighbors could attest to that. The waitresses at the café where he had breakfast every morning at exactly ten fifteen could attest to that.

And his smart phone's fitness tracker could attest to that. Because as soon as the winter snows melted, he followed the same route. At exactly eight o'clock in the morning, Tim Callaghan left his home, walked half a block to the start of the town's nature trail, and for the next two hours, walked the four-mile trail around the lake. The same trail, every morning, rain or shine. He would rest for about five minutes on one of the trail benches and then walk the last ten minutes to the Homestyle Hearth Café.

Tyler Morehouse had killed himself a week prior to Andy Jefferson sitting in her office, around nine to nine thirty in the morning on a sunny Tuesday. Tim Callaghan had shown up at the Homestyle Hearth at exactly a quarter after ten, and his phone's GPS-powered fitness tracker confirmed he'd walked the same route he always did.

"And the app's maker confirmed he left right at eight, from his house," Andy said.

"That doesn't sound legal," she said. "Did you have a warrant to obtain that information, Detective Jefferson?"

He frowned at her. Her attempts at humor didn't seem to be hitting the mark. Or maybe they were. Maybe annoying him was the point. "I don't need a warrant. There's a clause, smarty pants, in the terms and agreements he signed when he installed it."

"Ah, ten pages, two hundred subsections deep, I assume?"

"Six pages. And I don't know how many subsections. Point is, he agreed that law enforcement could request the data without a warrant, and the developer was only too eager to comply. It's a startup, and apparently, they don't want trouble."

"Good thinking, to look for the app," she said.

"That's the thing though. I didn't think of it. He volunteered it."

For the first time so far, her ears perked up. "Really?"

"That's what I'm saying. It was like he had planned this whole thing out. He had his alibi all ready. And when I showed up asking where he was that morning, he knew exactly what to say. And had it documented. Incontrovertible proof."

Blake didn't work on instinct. Instinct, in her estimation, was a dangerous mix of bias and perception—and you never quite knew what blend you were working with at any one time.

Still, right now, her instincts told her Andy was onto something. But Callaghan was a seventy-something-year-old guy. It took him two hours to walk four miles. Tyler Morehouse was a twenty-five-year-old kid who'd played football less than a decade earlier. There was no way a guy like Callaghan could have overpowered a guy like Morehouse and made him put a gun in his mouth and pull the trigger.

A point that she made, and a point that Andy brushed aside, along with her suggestion that Callaghan had an accomplice. "He doesn't have the money to hire a hit. The rest of the family moved after the thing with Hannah. He lives alone. There's no one else to do it for him.

"And I didn't say he overpowered Morehouse. There's no signs of a struggle. More than likely, he threatened him."

"With what?"

"I don't know. Threatened to kill his fiancée, threatened to shoot his parents...who knows. Point is, he convinced that kid to pull the trigger. When I talked to him, you know what he said?"

"What?"

"He said, 'Maybe the weight of what he did to our Hannah finally caught up to him.'"

"Maybe it did," she said.

"Yeah, maybe. But I don't buy it. There was too much satisfaction in his eyes."

"I don't know. I'd be pretty satisfied, too, if the piece of shit who raped one of my family members blew his own brains out."

Andy drummed his fingers on the desk again. "Look, you know why I'm here."

"You need my help."

"Yes. Unfortunately. You could always spot the details I missed. And right now, I need that. Chief says if I don't bring him something by the end of the week, the coroner is going to come back with a ruling of self-inflicted death. So are you going to help or not?"

Blake nodded. "All right, I'll take a look. But it's a long shot, Andy. All you've got is an old man with a rock-solid alibi who is happy the guy who raped his grandkid is dead. That's shit for evidence."

"I know. And if you don't see anything, well, I guess I was wrong."

"You could be getting paranoid in your old age."

He snorted. "I'm a cop. I've always been paranoid. I've got the stuff on a memory card. When do you think you'll have a chance to look it over?"

She hemmed and hawed for a minute about the cases she was working on, as if it was more than a single cheating spouse surveillance gig. Then said, "I can probably get started later today."

"Good. And remember, this is all off the books. If the chief found out—"

She waved him away. She knew better than him about conduct unbefitting a police officer, didn't she? "Yeah, yeah. Not a word."

"Thanks. You're the best."

She snorted. "I know. And next time you bother me, you better at least bring me a coffee from Gecko's or something."

"You got it. Just like old times."

"God, I hope not. Just leave the card and go."

So he did, and she waited until he'd pulled out of her drive before loading it. She perused a folder full of documents and photographs—the kind of stuff that would get Andy fired in a heartbeat if anyone ever found out he'd passed it along. Much less to her.

She started with the report of the murder. Ashley Carter had been the one to make the call. She glanced through Andy's notes, and in a moment figured out where Carter fit in: twenty-four-year-old Caucasian female, engaged to and lived with the deceased.

Andy had a file of notes on her. She'd been at work the morning of Tyler's death. She was an RN at the St. Joseph's and Fredrick Morehouse Memorial Hospital in town, where she worked three twelve-hour shifts a week: Monday, Tuesday, and Wednesday, plus every third weekend.

Andy had confirmed that she did work her full shift. He'd spoken to her supervisor and coworkers. It had been a busy day, and even a temporary absence would have been noticed. That was what her boss had said, and that was what her coworkers had said. And, on top of all that, Andy had uniform go through the hospital's surveillance footage and document Carter's comings and goings. She had arrived fifteen minutes before seven, and she'd left ten minutes after.

That left one possible conclusion: Ashley Carter hadn't pulled the trigger.

Also from NineStar Press

You'll Be Fine by Jen Michalski

After her mother dies of an accidental overdose, Alex takes leave from her job as a writer for a Washington, DC, lifestyle magazine to return home to Maryland's Eastern Shore. There, she joins her brother Owen, a study in failure-to-launch, in sorting out their mother's whimsical and often self-destructive life.

Alex has proposed to her editor that while she is home she profile Juliette Sprigg, her former high school fling, owner of a wildly popular local restaurant, and celebrity chef in the making.

While working on the story and trying for a second chance with Juliette, Alex meets Carolyn Massey, editor of the town newspaper, and wonders if there's more to life than reheating leftovers.

Enter Alex and Owen's Aunt Johanna, who arrives from Seattle to help with arrangements. When Johanna reveals a family secret, Alex may have to accept her family for who they are rather than who she hoped they would be. And just maybe apply the same philosophy to her heart and herself.

You Know I'd Never by Kara Lowndes

Janey has been in the closet her entire life—even when she fell for her first girlfriend, Elise, back in high school. After Elise left their small hometown of Clitheroe to pursue her dreams of becoming a musician, Janey knew that the only thing she'd have to remember her by was the song that Elise had written about Janey.

But that love song soon turned into the biggest hit of the decade, and Elise and her band return to Clitheroe a few years later to pay tribute to their hometown. Janey, still stuck where she was five years ago when Elise left, knows that she can't let her ex slip through her fingers again.

But she's still in the closet, and has no intention or idea of coming out to her homophobic family. How can she make amends with the woman she loved when she can't even be honest with herself or the people closest to her?

Connect with NineStar Press

www.ninestarpress.com

www.facebook.com/ninestarpress

www.facebook.com/groups/NineStarNiche

www.twitter.com/ninestarpress

www.instagram.com/ninestarpress